BAIT F

The dread dragon Chaffinch spiraled lower, regarding the offered sacrifice. He had been without mortal flesh for a tedious time now. Landing his fifty-foot hulk, he lazily approached the still form. He extended his maw, opening his jaws wide, preparing for a leisurely and most-welcome repast.

Without warning, the cringing figure suddenly stood, veils flung aside while one brawny arm cocked back like a loaded catapult. Pomorski had pulled the pin from the white phosphorus grenade. Now he launched it with practiced accuracy. The small canister bulleted across the seven yards, landing true in the gaping jaws. Chaffinch recoiled, swallowing reflexively at the object wedged in his throat.

Then the grenade went off, creating 2500 degrees of blistering heat. The phlogiston-lime substance in the dragon's fiery reservoir exploded. His neck went ramrod stiff as his body shook with a cataclysmic spasm. A huge spear of malodorous flame gouted from his maw.

But dragons have bellies like boilers. And Chaffinch raised his head and roared dreadfully, looking around for the being who caused his pain . . .

The
Doomfarers of Coramonde

by Brian Daley

A Del Rey Book

BALLANTINE BOOKS • NEW YORK

Copyright © 1977 by Brian Daley

All rights reserved under International and Pan-American
Copyright Conventions. Published in the United States by
Ballantine Books, a division of Random House, Inc., New
York, and simultaneously in Canada by Random House of
Canada, Limited, Toronto, Canada.

Library of Congress Catalog Card Number: 76-30343

ISBN 0-345-30972-3

Manufactured in the United States of America

First Edition: March 1977
Fifth Printing: August 1982

First Canadian Printing: April 1977

Map by Robert C. Giordano
Cover art by Darrell K. Sweet

For
Fred, Jim, Judy—and
anyone else with the breadth of
spirit to embrace dreams

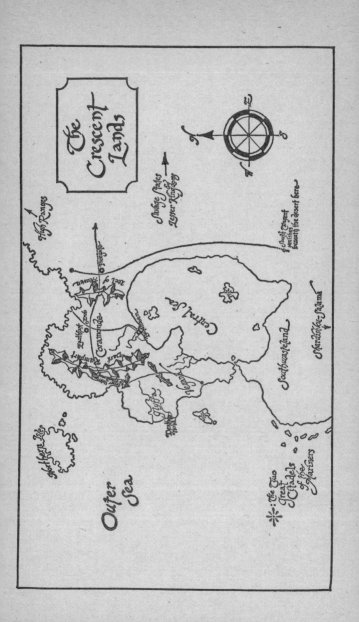

PART I

Of Deaths, Of Departure

Chapter One

*Man is soul and body, formed for deeds of high
resolve.*

Shelley,
Queen Mab, iv

"Earthfast," that place was called, aspiring skyward
from roots of caverned bedrock. There was nothing that
a palace demanded that it didn't boast, and no feature it
lacked that was required in a fortress. From it, the sov-
ereigns of Coramonde ruled.

Earthfast's formal gardens were extensive and elaborate, and so it took Queen Fania's personal guardsmen
some time to find Prince Springbuck as he brooded
near an orchid bower on an out-of-the-way path. He
passed his time resisting despair, for he now lived under
a death sentence of sorts.

Not particularly noteworthy to see, he was slightly
under average height; at nineteen, he hadn't yet come
into his full growth. He was an open-faced young man
with straight, dark hair, some of his late mother's
swarthiness of skin, and eyes a light brown like that of
his dead father Surehand. He kept his sparse facial hair
self-consciously clean shaven and had no scar or other
feature, as yet, to set him apart in a crowd.

Sollerets rang across marble and two soldiers, a captain and a ranker wearing gilt corselets of the Household, came to him there. The Prince resigned himself to
a mandate to appear in his stepmother's Court.

There was a modest bow and a barely concealed
command to accompany them. He did so with a sinking
feeling, and some true premonition told him that blood
would soon be let. That this was to happen was no fault
of the Prince's, though it stood as high probability that
the blood in question would be his own.

When Springbuck's father, Surehand, had died, he'd made no clear provision as to his chosen heir—who should, by custom, have been Springbuck. The old Suzerain's second wife meant to see *her* son on the throne and had garnered a good deal of support. There'd been dispute, argument and, in the end, a decision that the matter must be settled in combat.

Events had coalesced in such short order that Springbuck, a good-natured unaggressive young man, found himself under a tacit house arrest, slated to measure swords with his half brother Strongblade. It was disheartening enough that the ferocious Strongblade, at seventeen, was the bigger of the two and more accomplished in arms. But Springbuck was not so naive as to think that his stepmother and her adherents would leave this critical issue to chance. After all, the writ of the Protector Suzerain of Coramonde ran for the entire eastern half of the Crescent Lands, that tremendous sweep of lands which arcs around the Central Sea.

Even Springbuck's last-ditch offer to abjure his royal heritage without trial was rebuffed with a cold reminder that it was his duty to put the affair squarely in the laps of the gods.

Just as they'd said at Court, Springbuck was not the fighter his father had been. Surehand, a stubborn man with a quick temper, had been aware of his own shortcomings and had tried to school them out of his firstborn son. "Think first," he would tell worshipful Springbuck, "and don't let your hand be hasty to move. Have I not told you that haste is the thing that has caused me more regret than any other? Pause, reflect and weigh your options."

In the end, some impulse of self-preservation or awakening of the mettle of his ancestors had moved the Prince to plan escape to preserve his life. But he was unprepared for the events of this evening.

He attempted to maintain his dignity as he strode through the great doors—stalwart things of hard ebony bound up in iron and studded with thick rivets—and into the brightness of Court, so familiar in hours spent at his father's side, and now seemingly the camp of the enemy.

Lanterns cleverly wrought in brass and blown glass lit the spacious, tapestried room and filled it with their sweet scent. The windowless walls were hung with the banners of various legions and houses. Over the dais hung the royal standard, a snarling tiger, scarlet on black, and beneath it the personal ensigns of Springbuck, his stepmother Fania and his half brother Strongblade—a stag's head, dolphin and bear, respectively.

The throne was vacant; across its arms rested Flarecore, the greatsword reserved for the ruler of Coramonde—the *Ku-Mor-Mai*, as the Protector Suzerain was called in the Old Tongue. Springbuck's stepmother held Court seated in an ornate chair at the foot of the dais; she wanted no accusations that she was disrespectful of her late husband's memory or custom. She wore a robe of imperial white which contrasted well with her thick, raven's wing hair.

Because Earthfast was the best fortified place in Coramonde there were only eleven men-at-arms in the throne room itself. Eight archers watched, weapons at ready, from ledges above the milling courtiers, four at either side of the room. They wore brown leathers, had quivers of barbed arrows at their shoulders and were now sworn to Fania by secret oaths.

On the dais itself, behind the Queen, were three fighting slaves, family heirlooms after a fashion, yielded to Springbuck's grandfather by a conciliatory king after the epic battle at Skystem Crag. They were not members of the race of men, and many called them ogres. Bigger than humans, coarse and mighty as oaks, they were dressed cap-a-pie in plate armor thicker than any man might wear.

Springbuck heard muted laughter and murmurings from the throng as his entrance drew attention. The lush smells of their mingling perfumes and oils came to him, and the dainty scuffing of slippers and stirrings of extravagant clothing. The Court had, beforetimes, been composed of wise advisers, faithful deputies and stern fighting men. Under Fania it consisted of carpet knights and dissipaters; Surehand's old confidants didn't come often or stay for long.

He realized that, aside from the titterings, there was an unaccustomed silence in the chamber, then spied the figure—difficult to discern, since his vision was somewhat weak at a distance—of the famous and formidable Duke Rolph Hightower.

The Prince's entrance must have interrupted an exchange. With the note of one resuming a train of thought, the Queen said, "And here now is our stepson, come at his own good time from sulking alone in our gardens." Her voice was rich, vibrant, but always cold and closed to Springbuck, however much he'd tried to ingratiate himself to her. Still flanked by the two guardsmen, he forebore to reply; Fania was as expert at these skirmishes as his instructor in arms, Eliatim, was with the sword.

"He cringes from meeting Strongblade in combat," she persisted, "and would like to think up a way to avoid battle, but take the throne of the *Ku-Mor-Mai* nevertheless. But he will not! Not while my son and I live."

At this the Prince struggled to master his anger, refusing to be drawn into another contest of words with Fania. But the powerful voice of Duke Hightower rose then, with an edge to it to prove that he and the Queen had already had their differences that night.

"Who would not, facing a death under these circumstances?" he countered. "I'm very sure that Your Grace means what she says, that you mean for Strongblade to rule, but any man with sense in his head and a bit of spine might question the truth of your motives and the legality of this pending duel."

Springbuck studied the Duke, who stood defiant and alone in the exact center of the wide floor. Not Springbuck's friend particularly, he had still been a staunch ally and supporter of the Prince's father, though rarely a visitor to Court. He was even more conspicuous than usual in these surroundings, tall and broad-shouldered, contrasting the gleaming finery of the courtiers with plain, service-worn traveler's attire of gray. He bore an unadorned broadsword at his side and a cap held soldierly in the crook of his left arm. Greaved legs wide-spread, he set his right fist on his hip and glared at Fania without deference. The lantern jaw was set, the high forehead creased by beetling brows and beneath the flaring mustachios the Duke's mouth was drawn into something dangerously resembling a sneer of contempt, displaying large horse-teeth.

"Legality," Fania said, rolling the word off her tongue with a kind of languorous menace. "The Duke implies that I'm committing some crime? Hightower, who comes so seldom to our councils, would now countermand me? Too long has his insolence gone unchecked, I think."

The Duke's voice was brittle with rage. "Insolence? Insolence?" He slammed his chest with a battered, vein-mapped fist. "*I* am Coramonde's bastion in the East; from the shadows of Spearcrest to the foot of the Keel of Heaven I am the arm and eyes of Coramonde! How many times has my family defended our stone donjon with our lives at risk? Do you even know, you who were born in another country? I have paid my homage, aye, and paid again. Who questions Hightower's right to say his say at Earthfast?"

Fania couldn't speak to this, nonplussed in the face of truth so furiously set forth. But an inhumanly calm voice spoke next, one that had always sent fear shooting through every inch of Springbuck's being. He didn't have to turn or squint to know that it was Yardiff Bey—Yardiff Bey who was a figure of awe even among other sorcerers.

The Prince knew that he could never have emulated Hightower, who looked to where Bey stood, near the Queen, and met that mesmerizing stare without qualm. Bey's dark countenance was transformed into something unearthly by the eerie ocular of green malachite and silver that he wore in replacement of his left eye. All emotion was habitually hooded on his face, and it took an effort of will to speak with him and not somehow fall under his subtle influence. Springbuck had been moved to speak up a moment before as the words of Hightower had filled him, if not with courage, then at least with

some transient burst of outrage. But before Yardiff Bey
he held his peace.

"Hightower are you," the sorcerer agreed in that
voice so remote from the merely mortal, "who spurns
the decisions of the Court when he so chooses. Hightower who withholds levies, contending that he mounts
a more perilous watch than the rest of Coramonde.
Sanctimonious Hightower, poised and ready against imaginary foemen."

" 'Imaginary,' you say?" the Duke shot back. "Lies
are your nature as venom is a snake's, I say. Send any
doubters out with me to rural villages to see. Something
malignant is growing in Coramonde, and it wears many
faces. I have seen it, I have fought it. Still it grows. Last
month came a call to me from her people and I went, to
find the mistress of a great estate torturing children.
She'd been extracting their spleen and marrow for love
potions. She had once been a friend, but I knew her no
more and I slew her there myself." The Duke's palm
brushed once, uneasily, across the hilt of his sword.

Fania, recovered now that Bey had intervened,
soothed, "We are not unaware of these things. It has
become clear to us that such incidents come at the instigation of Freegate, the so-called independent city east
of the Keel of Heaven. Even now are leaders gathered
in Earthfast to discuss it, and legion musters will soon
follow, for a war of defense against Freegate. We ask
Hightower to look to his own array and prepare to see
the crimson tiger into battle." She waved her hand at
the royal standard and smiled a lovely, truthless smile,
finishing sweetly, "As he has done so bravely and so
well in the past."

But the Duke was having none of that, not from anyone fair or anyone fey. "These things I talked about are
not come from Freegate but from Coramonde herself.
Freegate has always been circumspect of us and everyone here knows it. To blame them is a lie."

A risky accusation to say the least, Springbuck reflected. Hightower was ever the brave warrior but never
the diffident diplomat. Speaking so to Fania was a far
different thing from saying the same to Yardiff Bey.

From the ranks of the courtiers—as if on cue

mark—stepped an elegant man in plum and amber, whom Springbuck recognized as Count Synfors.

"I would be honored to answer the Duke's insult," Synfors said. "If the coward will draw steel, I'll make my argument."

Hightower, head cocked to one side, was studying the urbane young Count with a hint of amusement. "How long," he asked, "have *you* been groomed for this occasion, little man? Never mind, never mind; shall we call the armigers, or shall I kill you without all that iron-mongery?"

The ends of the Count's lips curled for an instant and for answer he detached from his sash a case of swords, twin rapiers decorated *en suite,* hilts flattened on one side so that they fit together in one sheath. Synfors took the two hilts and, with an abrupt jerk, sent the sheath flying free and held a wicked-slim weapon ready in either hand.

Unarmed, Springbuck thought for a moment to intervene but checked himself. This was a personal contest, if unorthodox, and, it seemed to him, not to be meddled with since it had been fairly challenged and freely accepted.

Hightower tossed his cap aside, and the scrape of his sword coming clear of its scabbard was, to Springbuck's mind, a terse announcement of imminent death.

They closed upon one another with no further word, as quiet wagering began among the onlookers, who pressed inward a bit. Though Hightower was well seasoned, young Synfors was supple and generally known to be expert with his unusual blades.

They clashed for a moment, the hurried conversation of blades too quick to follow well, and were apart again. The Count had thrust with his right-hand rapier and replied to the Duke's instant parry with a second thrust from the left-hand one. Surprisingly, Hightower had managed to bring his big sword around in time to block that move too, but not in time to avoid sustaining a cut along his shoulder.

The conduct of the duel, as everyone there knew, was not according to form or custom. The inequity of weapons and the failure of the Queen to attempt mediation were improprieties of the first water. But in that entire room, no one thought that the Duke would live to register a complaint, whatever the outcome of the match itself. Springbuck was certain that all of this had been forseen and that the Duke's famous temper had triggered the spontaneous-seeming contest quite in accordance with some plan.

The Prince wondered vaguely where his stepbrother was and why Strongblade wasn't present. Perhaps Fania hadn't wanted her son to be involved, fearing even Strongblade's ability to cope with the fierce Hightower.

Synfors began his predatory glide again, nearing the Duke and initiating the same double-stroke attack, but suddenly found out to his brief dismay the difference between his own sportman's accomplishments and the battle skill of his opponent, the wage of a lifetime of war and drill.

Hightower took a double grip on the hand-and-a-half hilt of his sword and stepped deeply forward and to the left, windmilling the heavy bastard blade to the right. Such was the speed of the older man that Synfors missed his thrust as his point passed by his antagonist's shoulder, and such the force of the Duke's stroke that the beautiful guard of the Count's right-hand rapier was smashed, the hand beneath it broken and laid open to the bone.

Synfors screamed, dropping his right-hand sword and bringing the left up in futile gesture. Another time, Hightower might have let him live, but there was no restraint in him tonight. The second rapier was swept away, no more than thin procrastination, and the would-be executioner was himself dead a heartbeat later.

Fania was plainly shaken at this quick brutality, but she turned to Yardiff Bey. When she turned back to face the Court she seemed to have drawn strength and control from some quarter, and the Prince began to wonder, between Queen and sorcerer, who was subordinate to whom.

She rose to her feet, thowing back the white-furred splendor of her robe, and cried, "Murderer! This fight was not condoned; you had not my let to brawl, either one. The Count is beyond my retribution, but I shall visit my anger twofold upon you."

Springbuck expected to hear the order go out and see deadly shafts throw back the lamplight on their way to the Duke's heart.

But instead, Fania commanded, "Archog, slay me this man." At this Archog, the largest of the ogres and the captain of them, drew his huge broadsword from its scabbard at his back and shuffled forward.

Springbuck watched in horror. The match between Hightower and Synfors had been one thing, a bout between men by challenge given and taken. The assault of Archog was something else—a deliberate, merciless executioner about to do his work. The Prince's impulse was to go to the Duke's side and stand with him. Yet that impulse was drained, and the heir of the *Ku-Mor-Mai* immobilized at the ogre's terrifying aspect. His mouth had gone dune dry and he realized that to oppose Archog or, in his killing rage, even to impede him, would mean death. What would it profit to die?

But for a scant second, Hightower tore his gaze from the creature tramping to confront him and fixed the Prince with his eye. That look said nothing of expectation or resentment; there was no bitterness because Hightower had come to help him only to lose his own life. It was, Springbuck saw in that one instant, the Duke's way of ensuring that the Prince would see and understand. It simply said, "I am Hightower. This is how I live, and how I can die, if it comes to that."

And that stark message came through so well that the Prince lurched forward to join the Duke, and in the impact of the moment, none noticed the sob that escaped him. But he was seized from either side by the guardsmen and held fast in armored hands; in a moment the eight archers had leveled unswerving arrowheads at his breast. He stopped struggling to watch as the ogre closed with Hightower.

The Duke waited, perhaps bitter with himself for leaving his own liege men outside Earthfast; he exhibited none of the confidence he had shown with Synfors.

He shifted his grip on his sword and, uttering a piercing war cry, threw himself forward at his new enemy, swinging a savage blow.

But Archog met the Duke's weapon with his own with such terrific energy that the man's sword broke in two. Stunned, Hightower fell back on one knee, holding the useless quillons and stump of his blade before him as if his sword were still whole.

With a scream that had no message but animal anguish and loss, the Prince, beyond any care or caution for his own life, shook his captors loose and fumbled at the ranker's belt for his sword. The captain should have jumped back and let the archers do their work, which would have pleased his Queen well; but in the heat of the moment he instead brought down an iron-girt fist and dashed Springbuck into semiconsciousness.

Archog advanced and swung again, this time knocking aside the Duke's sword stump and beheading him.

The ogre stood over his victim's body, which streamed its hot life's blood across the floor, and his bone-chilling gaze lifted slowly to Fania, no trace of elation or rancor in it, awaiting further instruction.

Fania, whey-faced and glassy-eyed at the ghastly scene, tried to find her voice but couldn't. Again she turned to Yardiff Bey, and once more appeared to summon composure from that source.

"Take the . . . remains of the traitors away," Fania managed at last in a subdued tone.

Archog stooped and straightened, to move toward the portals, the Duke's body under one arm and the head cupped in the other gauntleted paw. Synfors' body was carried away, too. Finally the Prince was lifted by the two guardsmen.

In the whirling haze that had settled around him, Springbuck shrank back before the realization of his failure to aid Hightower as before the heat of a bonfire.

Chapter Two

This before all else: be armed.

MACHIAVELLI

NERVOUS, whispered conversations sprang up among the courtiers. Fania glanced about her in sudden, imperious anger.

"Where are my stepson's mentors, Eliatim and Faurbuhl?" she demanded.

The majordomo, resplendent in filigreed cloak and bright sash, carrying his staff of office, stepped forward and bowed. "Your Majesty," he intoned, "Eliatim accompanies guests of state home to their embassy houses and the philosopher Faurbuhl seems nowhere to be found."

"In that case, have the Prince taken to his rooms and left in the care of the Lady Duskwind."

Springbuck was hoisted and carted away as she turned to the Court.

"Have the servants rinse clean the floors. Fetch drink and chargers of food and let the musicians strike up."

As the Prince's bearers exited the Court, he groggily heard the crowd call tentatively for an air wherewith to dance. In quick fashion the arena was changed back to a ballroom; delicate feet would soon mince where the blood of men had been but a short time before.

Springbuck ascended slowly from his bodiless fog, jounced along, slung over an armored shoulder for a trip that seemed endless. Then there was the sound of a discreet knocking, the officer's respectful voice: "My Lady Duskwind?"

"Yes?"

"It's Captain Brodur, and we have the Prince with us, my Lady."

What odd inflection was that in Captain Brodur's

13

voice? Springbuck wondered dazedly. Was it urgent, almost nervous? His wits were beginning to return and he felt a growing desire to vomit.

"He is somewhat, umm, incapacitated," Brodur continued, "and the Queen instr—"

"Oh! Bring him in and leave him on the bed. I shall attend to him. Only wait a moment when I unbolt the door, then you may enter."

The enlisted man made a rude, whispered jest at the Lady's expense and was rebuked by his officer as the two brought their burden into the room and dropped him onto the brocatelle spread of his wide bed. He bounced once on the soft mattress and lay in a sprawl, holding down bile.

The instant Springbuck heard the door close, he vaulted clumsily from the bed to stand and take his bearings, bracing himself both literally and figuratively. With Eliatim, his instructor-in-arms and warfare, away, he wouldn't be under the close scrutiny he'd endured lately. Had the captain left for good, thinking he'd be unconscious for a while? The certainty was suddenly in him that his chance to escape had come on this least likely occasion.

He couldn't see Duskwind and so assumed that she was in the bath chamber. Crossing to one of his wardrobe chests, he extracted three broad, silken headbands, then leaped back to stand beside the door leading to the bath. Watching it carefully, he groaned as realistically as he could.

"Coming, my love," Duskwind called from the next room. "You drank overmuch, perhaps? I'll ease your sufferings; we'll see what steam and massage can do to help it."

So saying, she opened the door and walked into the bedroom. She must have been preparing to bathe when the guardsmen had knocked, he reflected in the brief moment in which she stood with her back to him, puzzled by his absence. She was naked, her honey-streaked hair unbound and the big knuckle-shield rings missing from her slim hands.

He pounced on her from behind, snatching her wrists from her sides and drawing them together at the small of her back. She gasped in surprise but couldn't turn around, as he confined her hands with two deft loops of a headband.

"Springbuck, is that you? Stop it! This is no time for drunken games, you idiot!" There was a strange, sharp note in her voice that he'd never heard there before. She squirmed and struggled in his grip and he couldn't have answered her if he'd wanted, because he held the remaining two headbands in clenched teeth.

Tightening the second loop, he whirled her around, tripped her and lowered her to the thick carpet on her stomach, straddling her.

Alarmed now, she shrilled, "You mustn't do this! Listen to me—"

He'd used the second headband as a gag. The third he fastened around her vigorously kicking legs, fettering her at the ankles. Lifting her as carefully as he could manage under the circumstances, he carried the wildly protesting Duskwind to the bed. Even then he found himself marveling at the warmth of her smooth, brown-gold skin and the fragrance of her, as he threw her across the covers. As a precaution to her thrashing efforts to free herself, he added extra bindings and, out of modesty, pulled the covers over her, leaving only her head and graceful feet exposed.

He bent to peer into her gray eyes. "I'm sorry," he told his lover, "but I'm leaving and I've decided that there's no place for a highborn and gentle Lady on the journey I mean to make." At this her eyes went wide and she began to shake her head violently, attempting to speak through the gag.

He nodded sadly. "Yes, I must go and I cannot take you, though life will be desolate without you." This last was rather an exaggeration; he looked forward to going forth a free agent. But he was fond of her, had been happy with her. She had even consoled him against his pending combat with the vague reassurance that something would happen to prevent it.

Well, now something would.

Duskwind shut her eyes tightly in exasperation, then stared imploringly skyward. Perplexed, he nevertheless decided that he had spent enough time with her. He went to another chest, dug under some robes of state and drew forth the things he had assembled for flight. He unlaced his buskins and threw them to one side, took off his tunic and removed his copper bracelets and bandeau. These he kicked into a corner, done with them for all time. Turning then to his preparations, he was arrested by a glimpse of himself in the cheval glass which stood against the wall. He moved closer and regarded himself, an open-faced young man in his nineteenth year.

Smiling experimentally at the mirror Springbuck was rewarded with a totally unremarkable smile. He was positive that he would attract no attention or recognition as the Prince. He felt stirrings of confidence that his escape would be successful.

He abruptly remembered the door and whirled on it in apprehension. It was closed but unlatched. Thankful that Duskwind's one outcry had elicited no inquiries, he darted to the door and shot the bolt to, congratulating himself on his luck and, at the same time, feeling a growing knot in his stomach, fear reaction from the events in the throne room and an ache to be away.

He knew brief regret that Faurbuhl was not to be found. He had considered taking the old philosopher with him, though he had revealed nothing of his plans to his teacher. Indeed, the idea had come full-blown a week before, in the strange period between waking and sleeping when the mind was most flexible and receptive. A whisper of a suggestion was enough, and he knew that he must escape, and in that same moment was glavanized to search out the magician Andre de-Courteney and the madman Van Duyn.

Forcing himself to matters at hand, and putting Faurbuhl out of his thoughts, he looked to his equipment. He had decided upon and surreptitiously collected the costume of a bravo of Alebowrene, subdominion of Coramonde. Though he knew there would be several of such men in Earthfast during the High Durbar preceding the death duel for the throne, the clothing of a servant or merchant would have been less conspicuous, so that Springbuck approached his adventure with perhaps more romantic notions than he admitted to himself.

He donned the brief cincture, comfortably supple and, in his opinion, overwhelmingly preferable to stiff, heavy robes of state. He then strapped to each forearm the leather demisleeves which guarded against wounds from wrist to elbow. It was difficult work manipulating the numerous buckles on each leather with one hand, hampered in fastening the second by the hand-cupping cuff on the first. Still, these were an infighter's defense he'd used before and he knew their value well. He pulled on high cavalryman's boots and picked up his sword, his newfound sword.

A curious weapon. He'd come across it poking around in the older, ignored rooms of the armories at Earthfast. Basket-hilted, it was much like a cavalry saber except that the blade was only slightly curved and a bit lighter than that, made of some unfamiliar, pewter-looking metal. On the pommel was struck a single complex glyphic which the Prince with his sketchy knowledge of such things, found undecipherable. On either side of the blade, just above the narrow fullers, was written the name *Bar*, an odd-seeming name for a sword, evocative of defense rather than offense. It's most puzzling aspect, however, was that even after obvious long neglect Bar was bright, and its edge sharper than any he'd ever thumbed. Convinced he'd found a weapon of some special property, he'd kept his discovery to himself. Its scabbard had been unserviceable with age, and so with some difficulty he'd procured another to accommodate it, of black, polished fish skin with bindings and fittings of white brass, and a belt to bear it.

He buckled the belt about his hips and fastened the tie-down around his leg. Then he slipped his parrying dagger into the sheath stitched inside the top of his left boot. Its hooked pommel rode just high enough to protrude from the boot top below his sword, ready to be seized at need in his left hand.

He'd thought of wearing a helmet and his fine chain mail, but discarded the idea of several accounts. For one thing, both of his suits of mail were known in and around Earthfast. The risk of recognition would be increased, even if he were well cloaked and hooded. For another, he didn't care for its weight, since he wished to travel as lightly as possible. And lastly, he'd never grown to like the burden of armor as had his half brother Strongblade. Though trained as most young nobles were in riding, running, jumping trenches, climbing and fighting encased in mail or plate, he had always hated its hindrance. He much preferred to be free of its encumbrance like the Alebowrenian or the Horse-blooded of the High Ranges.

Almost ready to leave his ancestral home, he thought that his renowned forebear Sharplance might have felt just so, fleeing the distant East in the dim past. He went to fetch the cache of coins secreted behind a carven ivory panel in the bathing chamber, stopping first to check the bonds of the still-furious Duskwind. He strode into the next room, anxious to be away, but stopped in midstride at the sight which greeted him there.

The large pool contained no water, but rather the body of Faurbuhl the philosopher. His face was blackened, eyes swollen and darkened tongue bulging from his mouth, hands still clawing in death at the garrote yet inbedded in his neck. Springbuck experienced momentary dizziness and a refusal to absorb the death of his would-be companion, who stared sightlessly at the decorative water apertures above his head.

A moment only, and the Prince realized that the Lady Duskwind had been in this room when the guardsmen entered but had made no outcry and thus must be implicated in—perhaps had committed—the gentle old man's murder. Springbuck's lips drew back in a soundless snarl.

He prized loose the panel and retrieved his wallet; then he took out his sword and, gripping it so tightly that his hand shook, returned to the bedroom. Through hot tears forming, he saw a bundle lying behind the door and opened it with a vicious kick to survey its contents, Duskwind's traveling clothes and accouterments. He moved to the bedside, glaring down at the bound girl, his face fell to look upon, until she consigned her soul to the gods of her house.

But they had been lovers; she had meant a great deal

to him in that time, and he could not bring himself to kill her. Shame at events in the throne room and his growing impulse to be away, coupled with grief for Faurbuhl, numbed him and drained his thirst for revenge; he'd shown no merit himself in the night's tragedies. He searched her imploring eyes.

"What reward did they offer you?" he wondered aloud. "What wages to slay my friend and then flee? Was it to be blamed on me? Is that why Captain Brodur left me here so handily? Be still! I'll not kill you, though I ought to; I give you your life and leave you to your own devices. But I vow, the next moment that I see you will be your last."

And because he wouldn't have her see a Prince of Coramonde weep he sheathed his sword with a clash and took up the brightly lacquered war mask he'd obtained, with its colorful crest of plumes. He set it on his head, covering all of his face save mouth and brimming eyes. Tying the wallet to his sword belt, he fetched his long cloak and swirled it around him. Concealed from throat to heels, plumes bobbing behind, he drew back the bolt and let himself into the corridor. There were no guards in that part of Earthfast, nor were any needed since Fania's own picked men manned the gates with orders not to permit him egress, and they were under the impression that he was in custody and under guard.

But of this he cared little; he simply wanted to leave Earthfast forever.

Chapter Three

*They all hold swords, being expert in war; every
man hath his sword upon his thigh because of fear
in the night.*

THE SONG OF SONGS,
Which Is Solomon's

HE'D readied a story against being stopped by the portglaves, of being confused and lost in looking to rejoin
his "master," the envoy from Alebowrene, the sort of
thing that happened often in Earthfast with so many
visitors and their retinues quartered there. Crossing the
open exercise areas he came to the stables, filled with
the ceaseless sounds and thick smells of horses of all
sorts: brave coursers and glum-faced palfreys, massive
destriers, well-formed jumpers and the enormous draft
animals that pulled the war drays of the entourage from
Matloo.

Springbuck had planned to take his own horse, Fireheel, but found the big gray gone from his stall and was
afraid to inquire after it with a groom for fear of recognition. Instead, he selected a light reconnaissance cavalryman's saddle and began to ready a swift-looking roncin bearing the markings of the High Ranges on its
flanks and Earthfast's croppings on its ear. The horse
proved balky though, shying from him and whinnying
softly. His warmask, light as it was, yet made things
more troublesome, and so he removed it and set it
aside. He finished quickly and turned to reopen the stall
door, to find himself faced with a figure from his past.

The light was poor but he still knew his old playmate
Micko, stableboy now, but close companion back in the
days when rank meant less and larking was the order of
the day. Micko was at one with animals, just as his father was, though he hadn't inherited his sire's affinity

for forest and field, and was most at home in kennel, aerie or barn. But even Micko, never one for insight or subtlety, knew the drift of things at Court and must know it was his obligation to raise the alarm on pain of a traitor's fate. Springbuck could only wait and taste bitterness. But Micko, a sorrowful expression on his grimy face, said only, "Do not let him take his head, as he likes to; he will wear himself out early in the ride."

Springbuck's cheeks burned. He wanted to explain why he was flying by night like a criminal, how his enemies had an infinite number of ways to ensure that he wouldn't survive a duel for the throne, but he couldn't think of any words which did not strike him as self-serving.

So, he brushed brusquely past Micko and, mounting and masking, guided his horse through the stable and out across the main bailey, clopping over smooth paving lit by fluttering torches and toward the portcullis, raised in this time of moribund festivity. He fell in with a group of riders, laughing celebrants who'd just mounted nearer the palace proper. The gate warder did not try to delay them, obvious guests of the Queen. As they all rode down the rampway from Earthfast, Springbuck gradually fell behind his temporary escorts.

Once down the long slope, he stopped and turned in his saddle for one last look at the ancient keep with its bright lights and whipping flags and battle pennons, as the faint sounds of gaiety drifted out over the night. With a sigh, he faced back to the way before him. He knew he must make good distance before dawn, and started down the broad boulevard which led from the palace-fortress through the city spread at its feet. He'd thought to perhaps hide in the city for a while until it was feasible to travel overland, but had dismissed the idea. Kee-Amaine would be torn brace from beam in the search for him and the rewards offered would guarantee betrayal from anyone else who identified him— unless Micko had already changed his mind.

He cantered slowly down the way, not wishing to attract attention by moving any faster.

Kee-Amaine, the City of the Protector, surrounded Earthfast as a gaudy collar does a desperado's neck, being here fine and colorful and there frayed and badly used. The street saw little traffic at this hour and the lanterns that lined it flickered fitfully in the night wind.

He passed a detachment of the civic watch making its rounds, but they didn't bother to hail him or ask his business, seeing him come from the palace-fortress, since things had seemed quiet this night. It was getting colder, and they were anxious to finish their tour and return to lay down their heavy pikes for the warmth of their barracks berths.

Before Springbuck's grandfather had imported the twin innovations of night patrols and streetlighting, life in Kee-Amaine had been confined after dark, since none but the well-armed or foolish ventured out into the threatening blackness to risk robbery or murder.

Two riders approached from the other direction, that of the Brass Lion Gate, which gave access to the Western Tangent. Their course would bring them right past him, but Springbuck thought that conspicuously avoiding them would be poor strategy, and so rode along.

He was soon sorry he did; as they neared him, he recognized them for Novanwyn, a Legion-Marshal and favorite of Fania's, and his senior captain, Desenge. They stopped and stared at him curiously just as he drew even with them, and Desenge called out, "What does an Alebowrenian do here, sitting a horse which I myself saw in the royal stables only this afternoon?"

The Prince stopped, like it or not. To ignore them would demand pursuit and ruinous inquiry. Besides, Desenge carried in its saddle rest his long spear, Finder, heavy and black and said by some to be unable to miss its mark when it flew from its owner's hand, with many ill deeds to its name.

The Prince attempted to disguise his voice, hoping that the war mask would help, as he faced them and answered, "I have just made obeisance for my liege, Knight-Commander to the Warchief of Alebowrene, at the feet of your Queen. My horse was lamed and I was given this one to take Her Grace's regard to my lord."

Novanwyn inclined his head politely. "Please excuse my aide's curiosity." He smiled blandly. "And let us keep you tarrying no longer. Oh, and if you would be so kind—Legion-Marshal Novanwyn's respects to your liege?"

Springbuck grunted noncommittally and continued on his way, shaken. Passing long walls and hedgerows bordering the way in this area, he rode for a time, then paused in a side street and squinted back along the way to see if he were being followed. To no avail; either he wasn't pursued or his nearsightedness made it impossible to see those behind him.

He decided, though, to take a circuitous route, swinging past the marketplace and coming round to the southern wall and the Brass Lion Gate by back streets. He hoped that, in tomorrow's turmoil at his escape, no one would link a renegade Prince to a lone Alebowrenian. Then it occurred to him that it was a foolish hope; Duskwind had seen his attire.

Memories of Hightower's death began to intrude again and he spent the ride in painful examination of his conscience. Alternate outcomes spun in his head; if he'd moved sooner, faster, fought harder, could he have saved the Duke? Should he have stayed in Earthfast and fought the duel? At best, he would eventually have had to meet Strongblade in arms, Strongblade who was wont to toy with two lesser opponents at a time and who'd often bested their instructor, Eliatim.

Springbuck's stealthy leave-taking and the deaths of Hightower and Faurbuhl began in him a desire for some act of violence and retribution, with a vague idea that he could expiate his shame and redeem his self-respect.

Perhaps there would come an opportunity in the promised war between Coramonde and Freegate, if things actually went that far. No major war had been fought in or by Coramonde in nearly a generation, but Fania—and Yardiff Bey—seemed set on starting one. There were many and diverse substates under Coramonde; to greater or lesser extent internal friction was a constant. It wasn't beyond conceiving that Springbuck could find support for an attempt at wresting back the Crown.

But there came to him the lines from the Old Tongue, impressed upon him with admonishments by his father, regarding civil war:

He should pause and search his heart well
Who thinks to go Doomfaring
In the War that is war between brothers.

A single house bleeds with
Every internecine fall of the sword
And the abattoiral axe.

Could such wounds to Coramonde be justified? The
Prince was unsure.

Still, if armies were waging war on the far side of the
Keel of Heaven, the situation could come full ripe for
the dislodging of Fania and Strongblade.

And Yardiff Bey.

Springbuck thought again of the look that had passed
between the Queen and the sorcerer in the throne room,
that of vassal to Lord.

Bey in command?

How much, after all, did anyone know about him?
The archives had it that he'd first appeared in Earthfast
over half a century earlier. Since then he'd been away
often, for as long as ten years at a time. He'd come
back from one such sojourn, twenty years earlier, with
the bizarre ocular in place of his left eye, object of cautious speculation.

Rumors about him were inexhaustible: that his sword
Dirge dealt wounds which couldn't be healed, that he
had an enchanted flying vessel concealed in the mountains of the Dark Rampart, that some of his hidden conspiracies and secret liaisons led ultimately to the distant
south, to Shardishku-Salamá, where oldest magic still
worked against men.

But little was known of Bey for sure, and few dared
pry.

The Prince called to mind the one time that he'd seen
Yardiff Bey betray emotion. On that occasion, six
months earlier, the wizard Andre deCourteney had
come to an audience with Surehand, bringing with him
the madman Van Duyn, who claimed to be from another
universe, or some such.

Bey had scorned Van Duyn as demented, but appeared to regard Andre deCourteney as a threat, not so

much to his position as councillor extraordinary to the *Ku-Mor-Mai* as to his very well-being.

But, with Van Duyn making his outrageous claims and propounding his scandalous ideas for a government by plebiscite, Surehand had hardly needed Bey's urgent prompting to banish the two from Earthfast, provoked as he was by their heresy.

As far as Springbuck could determine, Van Duyn and deCourteney had gone to the little village of Erub, to the northeast, to establish an unorthodox school of their own. The Prince hoped that it was so, and meant to seek them out. He had questions to ask them, particularly about Yardiff Bey.

As he rode along mulling all of this, the scenery had gradually changed from the walls of the gentry who lived near Earthfast to common residences, shop and tavern, and finally the empty market plaza. He cut across the wide square past the Temple of the Bright Lady and quickly made his way up winding byways to the Brass Lion Gate. The guard commander there had just come on watch and was uninclined to pester himself over an Alebowrenian, all of whom were known for their truculence, especially since the gate would soon be opened anyway for the predawn influx of farmers with their produce and other goods for vending, and so accommodated Springbuck's exit.

The gate yawned behind him as the Prince rode across the hard-trodden earth to where the Western Tangent shone gray and straight in the light of the watchtower. Storm clouds had gathered and a sparse rain began to fall as he spurred his mount away eastward toward Erub. Eastward where, perhaps, Andre deCourteney would have answers and the Prince's confusion and misgivings would be thrown open to the light of wise counsel solicited from one of the best-known wizards of the day.

He let the roncin out to a gallop, heedless of Micko's warning, diverting tension and venting frustration in a wild ride down the broad, seamless Tangent. The rain misted in a dew on his cloak and the sleek, rolling hide of the horse beneath him, and he removed his war mask to feel the moisture on his face.

He rode expertly, crouched low over the roncin's neck, letting the tearing wind snatch the events of the night from his brain. Lightning was flashing intermittently when he came upon a horse incongruously leg-hobbled alone at the roadside. With a start, he saw that it was his own, Fireheel, and came to a halt.

"I *thought* that your own horse would give you pause," said a familiar voice, and the Prince's heart clenched with dread. It was a voice he associated with long hours of exhausting training during which he was exhorted to match its owner—endless, impossible effort—one of the most capable warriors alive.

Though the rain was heavier now, and the night dark, Springbuck had no difficulty identifying the man with bow in hand who stepped from behind a nearby tree and up onto the raised surface of the Tangent, arrow nocked, deadly confident.

The lightning flashes showed him Eliatim.

Chapter Four

The secret of happiness is freedom, and the secret of freedom is courage.

THUCYDIDES,
the funeral speech for Pericles

HE could see his former martial instructor only dimly in the broken light until the other brought forth a small lantern which had been covered, unshrouded its glow and turned up the wick. He set it down near Fireheel, who dug with a nervous hoof at the impervious Tangent; then he trained the drawn war arrow, barbs glittering coldly, on Springbuck.

The Prince considered his options. His mount was tired and Fireheel looked well rested, so that Eliatim would have no trouble in overtaking him should he bolt. Besides, the man was an uncanny marksman when mounted and an incredible one from stance; Springbuck wouldn't get two lengths before he was spitted. He gnawed his lip and watched the rain splatter down, and a hope began to grow in him. If he could occupy the other's attention for some little while, perhaps the master-of-arms' bowstring would become moist enough in the downpour to make it slack and give him a chance at escape. In any case, he must make some sally or be shot down here and now, on the instant.

Thinking all of this, he answered, "You needn't threaten me. As you can see, I'm leaving Coramonde for all time, going far and for good, I swear."

Gone now were thoughts of retribution. He wanted only to live, and that urge would supplant any other but the strongest. The biting memory of his earlier failure of Hightower tore at him, but immediate danger preempted any bold or defiant words and his survival instinct prodded him to dissemble and say anything, anything to live.

Eliatim cut him short, words curdling with contempt. "You know better than that, boy. We can't afford to have you wander off, even if you mean what you say; it wouldn't be long before you were located and exploited by some troublemaker or other. One of the Southern Warlords, or that heretic deCourteney, possibly? Now, look how easy it was for me, Your Grace. When I returned and found you gone, I had little problem surmising what had happened. Is it of any interest to you that the stableboy is dead? I thought so. I had to interrogate him in some haste. And we'll hoist that damned slacker Brodur, too, when we find him.

"You must have taken a roundabout way to the Brass Lion Gate, but I had the guards pass me through and I knew that we would meet here one last time."

Later, Springbuck promised himself, he would think about poor Micko, how they'd played and joked together, later remember how Micko could sleep between the legs of the most spirited horse in its stall, since he was that close to animals, and how he could never lie well, it being foreign to him to twist things or dress his words up. The Prince must grieve later because now he was poised for the one chance he might get to elude death.

The appalling idea struck him that Eliatim was reading his every thought and intention when the other said, "Come down off your high horse, and I will explain some facts which, I confess, have been kept from you."

Springbuck groped in vain for some reply that would permit him to stay mounted, but complied.

The master-of-arms' eyes were glazed with strong drink or drug. While his tone was almost amiable, the arrow leveled at the Prince's heart was not. Springbuck stood near the roncin and watched the bowstring as if hypnotized, but Eliatim showed no doubt about his weapon's effectiveness. The older man's body was limber and relaxed, hand steady, and the string seemed taut.

As Springback shuffled his booted feet on the hard, tractive surface of the Western Tangent, Eliatim smiled through his stiffly waxed mustache and suddenly lowered the bow, easing tension on the string. "How is it,"

he asked huskily, "that you never sensed how I anticipated this moment? Long and long I've waited to put
you to death, and send my star into the ascendant."

At this the Prince's stomach knotted with fear and
the fist with which he held his reins balled even more
tightly. His fleeting impulse to leap back onto his horse
was cut short at Eliatim's next statement.

"If you try to run I can cut you down before you
have both feet in the stirrups. But I do thank you for
saving me a long and tiring chase on horseback, for I
fear that my bow cord became rather wet as I waited
for you. I'm grateful that you follow instructions so well
and that you quailed at the sight of my arrow. Now, you
see, we can test whether the years I've spent teaching
you the policies of combat were wasted. Let us now
weigh your prowess with the sword."

So saying, he hurled the bow and arrow aside and
took from its scabbard his long, heavy cavalry rapier.
Springbuck tried to moisten his lips with a dry tongue.
A vault to the saddle was out of the question. He let fall
his reins and took his cloak from his shoulders and
draped it over his horse's croup. He reluctantly unsheathed Bar, whose grip did not feel slick despite the
rain and his clammy palm. Eliatim's eyes narrowed at
Bar's bright aspect.

"That hanger is unknown to me," he said. "From
whence does it come? Ah, let it pass. I shall have a
chance to inspect it at my leisure, presently."

He grinned wickedly. "And while I think to tell you,
your ill treatment of the Lady Duskwind was unwarranted. She was no part of our alliance against you.
How you found out that Faurbuhl was with us though, I
cannot imagine. Serves him justly, the old dough-pate,
that you garroted him; he was so damnable certain that
you trusted him."

Springbuck's mind whirled as he juggled this new information. Faurbuhl a traitor and Duskwind loyal? He
played a gambit to learn more.

"How high do you stand in this, Eliatim? How many
are arrayed against me?"

The other threw his head back and gave a short crow of
laughter. "How many? Oh you fool! All, or almost all!

Duskwind proved difficult to subvert, but we had little need of her. She's probably been attended to already. The Court's been weeded carefully, with some stubborn holdouts like Legion-Marshal Bonesteel exiled to duty on far marches and some, like Hightower, killed." He sighed, then giggled, and shook his graying head regretfully. "I'm sorry I missed the end of the great Hightower, but I have business of my own tonight.

"I must say, though, that you were quite clever to kill Faurbuhl and depart while I was gone. Since he had no opportunity to signal your escape, no one suspected it at first. But when Novanwyn and Desenge described their encounter with a peculiar Alebowrenian whom they thought resembled you, I went to your room to investigate."

With this he brought his blade into line and moved forward on the Prince, who retreated a step, still hoping for the chance to break away and avoid a duel. To delay further, he said, "You and Fania and Bey forget one thing: Strongblade is still my father's son. It may be that he won't bend to your plans as readily as you think."

That brought the blademaster up short, but his face was filled with glee, not doubt. "Idiot child," he scoffed, "your 'stepbrother' is not Surehand's son, he is Yardiff Bey's! D'you think that's a hard thing for the greatest mage in the world to accomplish? It was no more difficult than slaying your mother by his arts; and those stupid Court physicians, how easily they were misled. He'd groomed Fania almost since birth for the one task of marrying your father and—hi!—how it vexed him that just as he was about to introduce her at Court, Surehand married another. Well, all's remedied and things are on their proper course. Your father was well taken with Fania, even in his mourning, but on their wedding eve it was Yardiff Bey's seed in her belly; Strongblade is no part of your lineage. Bey's victory over the Crescent Lands will rest on three children of his body, the first a girl-child, the second male and the third both and neither."

Eliatim told the tale with huge relish, enjoying its effect on Springbuck, venting long-checked hatred. "He purchased my soul, yes, but I'm satisfied with the bargain. We two closed a pact long and long ago on the High Ranges when the Horseblooded had cast me out, and he brought me to Earthfast when you were a week old. I've served him well and waited out this hour. When you're dead—few questions will be raised about your disappearance, I think—I go on to better things and vengeance of my own."

He giggled again, a thing seldom heard from grim Eliatim. "But I keep digressing. Let us tally what you've learned from my lessons, for in one wise I've been honorable; I was engaged to teach you the arts of war and I have done it as best I could. Mayhap if you've paid sufficient attention you'll yet keep your life."

And he advanced, all jocularity gone in the application of his trade. The Prince circled warily, knowing that at his best he was not likely to match the other, who was himself something of a magician in matters of bared blades.

Then, unlooked for, came a violent gust of wind, so strong and cold that it might have come from the straining lungs of an intervening deity, to blow out the little lantern and hurl a leafy branch into the face of shocked Eliatim. He gave a startled curse and brought his free hand up involuntarily. Springbuck knew that his chance had miraculously come. He had only to mount Fireheel and wheel into the nearby wood to escape under mantle of night and storm. He'd already gathered the gray's reins in hand when he stopped, for he was no longer alone with his foe in the darkness. Rather, he saw those of whom the blademaster had spoken, his mother—or, more accurately, as he had no recollection of her, the pale death mask on her coffin—Micko and Duskwind. And over all was the death of Hightower, merciless officiation of Archog.

And all at once he felt the desire to sneak away, to escape like some hunted animal and leave more unavenged deaths behind him, driven out before another emotion, as one incoming wave is broken and scattered by the next. Shame drained his fright; fury made him contemptuous of his own helplessness.

Springbuck stood like a stone statue while the other

struck flint to rekindle the lantern. When it was done, Eliatim was astounded to see the son of Surehand waiting, an unfamiliar light in his eye, but the martial instructor quit his mocking, relieved laughter only when the Prince brought Bar slowly to guard.

As he was accustomed, Eliatim took the fencing distance that gave him maximum advantage: close enough for him to hit, far enough to render many of the shorter Springbuck's moves overextensions. The Prince felt a despair coming over him, born of countless humbling experiences at Eliatim's hands. Tension began to rob him of his natural fluidity.

Swords crossed tentatively in the wavering light, the master-of-arms waiting his pupil out. At length, Springbuck began an attack-in-advance, feinting a disengage and hoping to turn a final disengage into a lunge, but harbored little confidence of success; sure enough, Eliatim's blade was elusive lightning. Another thrust from the Prince was met with a quick croise, and the son of Surehand was lucky to escape with a slash along his upper arm which would have been serious, had he not been wearing leathers. Springbuck changed lines of engagement several times, and Eliatim, all cool control, followed suit almost indifferently.

Springbuck made a feint and was met with a flickering extension, but this was no news; Eliatim's defense was as strong as his offense, and the stop-thrust was his heart's delight. The Prince felt that Eliatim indeed foresaw his every thought, and decided that a second-intent attack launched from a false one would be foolish.

Springbuck's heart was pounding, sweat slick on his face. He could think of no feasible maneuver of the blade that he had not tried on Eliatim a hundred times in vain. But this time, he thought as Eliatim gave his blade a ringing beat, a faulty try would be met with deadliest rebuke.

Eliatim deceived the parry with which Springbuck replied to his beat, dropping his point just low enough for the nervous parry to pass over it in derobement, then deliberately forfeited his chance to attack in return, laughing at the Prince's hasty retreat.

Now Eliatim brought forth his virtuosity. His casual

changes of tempo had Springbuck flinching in anticipation. The threat of his bind and the menace of his false attacks made the younger man feel humiliatingly inadequate. But the new determination flared in Springbuck again; how he wanted to see laughing Eliatim die!

He thought of the parrying dagger in his left boot top, and it occurred to him that if he could bring it into play unexpectedly, the main-gauche might give him an advantage for one critical exchange; but again, possibly not, since Eliatim fought in the new profiled style, forcing Springbuck to do the same.

Determined not to be drawn out, but rather to wait out his chance, the Prince tried to put aside his preoccupations and fence from the subcortical. In that combat, as in lovemaking and music, immediate past, present and immediate future took on a peculiar fusion. Neither man made much use of his edge, and their weapons joined in whirling motion, springing apart again to punctuation of steel vibrating, chiming in notes almost too high to be heard.

In his surrender to reflexes, coming as it did in close pursuit of his decision to fight it out with Eliatim, Springbuck found that a new and radical thought had blossomed in his mind: all his life, Eliatim had been coaching him to lose this particular match.

The Prince had been taught patience, counseled prudence—and infused with hesitation. Certainly he'd become a superior swordsman, but he'd been ingrained with responses that made him prey to Eliatim.

And on the heels of this thought—his mind insulated now from the exertions of hand and eye to keep him alive—came insight. He must depart utterly from his conservative style of swordplay, or die.

He could think of only one tactic to meet the need, though he considered and discarded a desperate flèche. He'd seen it only once, brought back from southern parts by Lord Roguespur and called—what was it?— the "ballestra."

Inspiration became motion. He poised his body and released it like a gyrfalcon from the gauntlet. With barely adequate stance, he pushed off with his left foot, right preceding him in search of purchase.

He skimmed forward, fleet and lethal as the Angel of Death, the untried move coming to him with surreal ease, into an immediate lunge. The actions came as one, executed virtually as the idea occurred to him.

Eliatim's defense was there, but calculated to stop another feint or convictionless attack. Bar slid by and found his throat, and the blademaster's point shot past the Prince's ear. Abruptly, Springbuck stood very close indeed to the great Eliatim as crimson gushed into Bar's blood channels and across its basket hilt. He barely retained the presence of mind to pull his sword free, and gaped in wide-eyed amazement. His adversary sank to the unheeding surface of the Western Tangent, corpse-face covered with steaming blood and disbelief.

The Prince slowly wiped Bar clean on Eliatim's sleeve and returned it to its scabbard.

"I shall go Doomfaring now, in earnest," he whispered through persistent rain, "and what final lessons you have taught me tonight, I shall never forget!"

And his sudden laughter rang above the wind.

I galloped out of Earthfast, with running in my head,
And putting leagues behind before the Queen's guard
*   knew I'd fled*
I killed a man in darkness, to live until the day,
And whether that were wrong or not, I can't, unbiased,
*   say.*
But he was dead and I alive, and you may take from me
That as I fought, I knew that's how I wanted things
*   to be.*

From *The Antechamber Ballads,*
personal compositions attributed to
Springbuck

Chapter Five

So many gay swordes,
so many altered wordes,
and so few covered boardes,
  saw I never
So many empty purses,
so few good horses,
and so many curses,
  saw I never.

JOHN SKELTON,
"The Manner of the World Nowadays"

HE cast Eliatim's body back into the trees from which it had emerged. The horses presented a knottier problem.

Determined to take his own gray favorite now that fate had given him the chance, he took the heavy, over-gilt saddle from Fireheel and hid it, too, among the pines. He gave brief thought to taking along Eliatim's bow and quiver, but since his poor vision rendered him an inferior archer, he decided to forego the trouble.

He then transferred the reconnaissance saddle to the powerful, long-legged Fireheel, blew out the little lantern and hurled it in the general direction of its owner. Picking up his dampened cloak and resuming it with a slight shiver, he mounted and took the reins of the riderless horse in his right hand. His way lit by occasional bolts from above, he trotted off eastward.

Thoughts buzzed around each other, vying for his attention. He knew that he'd been lucky in his duel with his late instructor. Still, he perceived that there was more substance to the encounter than that. He'd thought for himself, taken a gamble when the situation demanded, won on the resources of eye and hand and brain alone. It was possible, he thought, that he'd been undersold to himself all along.

35

Eliatim's other words came back to him, particularly those that made reference to his mother. Had Bey, as Eliatim had implied, caused the death of that Lady, to clear the path for Fania?

The Tangent, raised above the surrounding ground and gently pitched to either side, drained itself of water quickly as the rain abated. Some traffic moved there already: farmers on foot or with carts bringing goods to market, a troop of traveling players bearing torches, forming a swirl of color and motion and song, an officious dispatch rider hastening past them all, various merchants.

Springbuck, relieved at the lack of troops on the Tangent, was the only one bound eastward and so, the way being wide, went quickly. The solution to the problem of his extra horse came to him at dawn, when he encountered a band of tinkers camped at the roadside.

Rather than being bound toward Kee-Amaine, they were about to swing southward. There was brief haggling, and the Prince rode on with a considerable sum of money and some provisions, comfortably sure that the roncin's brands and cropping would be promptly obliterated.

He loosened his cloak as the sun warmed him. Elation over his victory against Eliatim swept into him again. He reappraised himself in light of his own simple and profound decision to stand and fight. He was exhilarated but steady, confident but unimpulsive.

Fireheel happily increased their distance eastward, and a new Springbuck rode into the day, of a far different mettle than he with whom Fania's forces had been so sure they could cope.

It was two days later, and well along in the afternoon, when he reined in magnificent Fireheel on the summit of a low hill to gaze upon Erub.

His hunger had been growing for hours, his provisions gone since breakfast. He would have preferred to spend his nights in some inn or tavern on the way, if only to sleep on a bench by the hearth, but had avoided the Tangent since that first dawn for fear of apprehension skirting the odd farm or crofter's hut he'd spied.

Seeing the end of the narrow, rutted road was good compensation for this, though. The little town was in a valley spread below, and on a rise beyond stood an undersized castle of antiquated design. He knew from his own research at Earthfast that the castle was untenanted.

A silence hung over Erub as he rode past the crude daub-and-wattle hut that was its outermost limit. He saw no one living, but came upon the dead and all-but-dead in numbers. There were villagers scattered here and there, war arrows in them or the bitter, evident tales of sword and lance wounds.

He rode with hand close to hilt and, coming closer to the square at the center of town, encountered a remarkable thing: soldiers of Coramonde, light cavalrymen, lay slain near an improvised barricado. Of these, many bore injuries from scythe or pitchfork or were pierced with hunting shafts. Many others, though, had odd wounds through their vests of ring mail, small, rounded holes; one had such an opening fairly between his eyes and a huge and hideous gap torn in the back side of his skull. An eldritch smell, unlike anything the Prince had ever scented before, hung in the air.

He decided to continue on to the castle, wondering if the lancers had been sent to find him or to interfere with the school that Andre deCourteney had set up. He knew that word of his escape could have outraced him via dispatch riders on the Tangent, if those in Earthfast knew where to look.

He passed through the town without seeing anyone who might have given him information, but on the track leading up to the little castle he came up to an elderly couple urging a recalcitrant donkey to pull a cart loaded with their personal possessions, bedding and household goods of questionable value. The donkey remained stubbornly seated.

The old man, seeing him, snatched a short bow from the cart and fumbled for an arrow. Springbuck laid a hand to Bar and said, "I carry no quarrel to you, yet do not nock that shaft or you force me to show you my sword. What's come to pass in Erub?"

The old man was a shrunken specimen without an

excess ounce of flesh on life-weary bones. He laid aside
his bow after a moment and removed his shapeless hat
from years of habit in talking to a mounted warrior, but
there was a spirited glint in his eye.

He swallowed once, and admitted, "This noon a detachment of lancers came to make arrest of our teach-
ers, Andre deCourteney and Van Duyn. We didn't want
their new teaching to end, and so there was fighting.
But now more soldiers are coming and we must go. The
only safety lies in the keep with Van Duyn and de-
Courteney."

"What?" exploded the Prince, baffled. "Are you so
enamored of these teachings that you'll leave your
homes and defy the regulars?"

The toothless mouth became, for a moment, firm and
set. The grizzled chin came up, and the man's reply was
slow and emphatic.

"I have lived my whole life within a day's walk of
this town," he began. "I've worked hard every day that
I can remember for my overlord. I go forth in the darkness each morning to follow his oxen in the furrows, my
lot scarcely better than theirs. I have watched my wife
grow old and crooked with endless toil, she who was
once so fair and gay. Two sons have I lost to plague,
two to war, one daughter to famine and another at her
birth. There is small enough difference between me and
the beasts in harness, so constant is my labor and so
seldom have I given any thought to my own life and its
meaning. I just tendered my tithes and worried about
the crop.

"Then there came two who made me pause and wonder about the wherefores of life, who told me about the
world beyond my furrows. They quoted the words of
learned men, glorious thinkers and doers of whom we
had never heard, and when they asked what we thought
of this and I spoke, they listened. All this, though I am
only an old man, stooped with the years.

"And it was as if I had been shut up in darkness all
my life and only now let out. So now, the Queen at
Earthfast has decided to put an end to the practice of
teaching here, to make of us again what we were. But
when the cavalrymen came we fought them. Fought

them! Few of them left alive, and Van Duyn brought down many with his weapon that reaches out to kill at distances.

"Do we love this new learning, you ask? Well enough, I say, to leave this fief forever if we must, rather than submit again to our overlord."

Springbuck was silent, calculating what their hard life had cost these old souls. Their children gone, life must now be spent in constant labor, since the sons and daughters who would have cared for them in the winter of their days would never return. It was, perhaps, the end of the man's name forever when he died, with no one to keep his memory alive or light incense for him at the altar of his gods.

In this light, the war that Springbuck had contemplated against Fania and Strongblade was not so brave or glittering a thing to entertain.

While he'd been angry at such disrespect shown for a liege, he was fascinated with what energies had been evoked in this aged breast. The peasants were yanking at the donkey's harness again. And critical choices can be made as quickly and as simply as this: the Prince unsheathed Bar and, leaning down, struck the beast loudly across its rump with the flat of his blade. It bucked to its feet, kicking the cart behind it, and the couple tugged it into motion once more.

The heir to the *Ku-Mor-Mai* trailed behind.

The moat outside the castle was long dry and choked with high weeds. One of the double doors beyond the drawbridge had been left ajar, doubtless for such late-comers as they. The gates, like the drawbridge, were of old wood but looked sound. The keep's walls were worn but substantial, though rather low by modern standards.

Springbuck brought up the rear into a courtyard where plants had pushed up insistently through defeated cobblestones. There was much debris in sight—broken tools, a useless wagon wheel, forgotten benches—and after three nights in the open, he was sourly willing to wager that the roof of the place leaked.

The little courtyard was filled with villagers dashing to and fro. Standing atop a wagon at the center of it all, giving commands to bring them to some semblance of

order, was the man known as Van Duyn, whom Springbuck recognized from his one previous visit to Earthfast. He was a tall, lean man with gray-white hair and a
dour look about him that had made the Prince wonder
if anything ever quite satisfied him. His face was
creased with worry, and a strange metal framework secured a circle of glass before each of his eyes. Springbuck had once reflected on a possible connection between this and Yardiff Bey's single ocular, but it was
said that Van Duyn's lenses simply helped him see more
clearly. A small part of the Prince wondered now if he
might be able to acquire such a device for himself.

Springbuck began to understand the discomfort of his
father, the Protector Suzerain, at hearing the thoughts
of Van Duyn; the man could well bring disaster and
chaos to Coramonde. What caused usually docile com-
moners to respond to him so readily, to jump with a will
to his every order and stand by him so staunchly?

"See that you use the barbed arrows first," the outlander was saying, just as the Prince caught his eye.
"Are you a Queen's man, sir?" Van Duyn snapped
curtly. "With some new mandamus of arrest?"

Thankful that his war mask hid his features, the son of
Surehand responded, "I was unaware of your predicament
when I came to hear your new teachings."

The outlander laughed, scant humor in it. "My 'predicament' grows rapidly worse," he shot back. "Of these
good people, one in three sees fit to offer his help. And
you? A week ago I would have welcomed you as a new
student, but now you'll have to run or fight before you
can learn." He seemed to think his own words over for
a moment. "Perhaps you'll prize the knowledge more
for all of that. What do you say?"

The Prince considered this. He had nowhere else to
go. But to stay here was to court capture or death. *They
were both the same for him,* he realized.

"I say," he replied at last, "that your people had better not use their barbed arrows. Use the narrowest
points first; they'll punch through armor more readily.
How will so few resist troops of the Crown?"

"I'm at a loss to tell you. But you seem familiar with

this sort of thing. Come, hold conference with us, and we'll decide."

Springbuck dismounted and lead Fireheel toward the wagon as the locals gave way before him. Van Duyn jumped down from his place and two others detached themselves from the scurrying peasants to join him.

The first with the scholar was a man far shorter and bulkier than he, and the Prince knew him as Andre de-Courteney. The famous wizard was squat and plump, with a promise of underlying muscle, and dressed, as was Van Duyn, in commoner's clothing, but had his sleeves rolled up and tunic open to reveal thick-matted hair in dark rings on arms and chest. Although he was clean-shaven, his chin and flopping jowls retained deep blue shadows. His head, however, was mostly bald. In his eyes the Prince could see only a friendly look to second the smile he wore.

The other one was even more easily identified, if only from reputation. She was an intimidating beauty of no certain age, with astoundingly red hair. Her brows were high-arched over sea-green eyes, prominent cheek-bones and a wide, sultry mouth, contrary to the pouty vogue current at Court. Her skin held the whiteness of milk and, unlike those around her, she dressed self-indulgently. Gracefully wrapped in a long robe of glossy green-black silk that left much pale throat and bosom exposed, she wore a girdle of red leather sewn with pearls caught tightly around her waist, and her fingers blazed with rings. She met the Prince's gaze squarely, looking him up and down, smiling a cryptic smile, and he knew that this could be no one but Andre's sister, the celebrated sorceress Gabrielle deCourteney, though she'd never been to his father's Court.

Van Duyn *ahemm*ed, and Springbuck realized that he'd been staring.

"You have no doubt heard of my esteemed colleague, Andre deCourteney and, of course, his sister, Gabrielle," Van Duyn introduced them. But his hand reached out to squeeze the woman's gently and received answering pressure, eloquent that she was far more to the scholar than merely his associate's sister. He finished, "And I am Van Duyn. You are—?"

"How far away are the troops?" Springbuck asked, ignoring the invitation to introduce himself. For now, he preferred the anonymity of his mask.

Andre deCourteney shrugged. "We have the word of—informants—that they will be here momentarily."

"I would not much care to defend this relic against regular soldiery," said the Prince.

"Nor do we," Andre confessed, "but we hope that it will not come to that. The truth of the matter is that we must come at bay for a little time; we have weightier problems than a few soldiers." His speech was cultured and well modulated, in contrast to his unpolished appearance.

"Few!" snorted the Prince, "What if they send more than a few? What if they use their heads and send infantry, cavalry, knights and archers and siege artificers to pull this stone artifact down around your ears? And if you're really ill-fortuned and they have magicians of their own with them, Yardiff Bey's underlings? They'd make very short work of you indeed, is what would happen."

"That would seem to be the promised scenario," Andre conceded mildly.

A shout broke their conversation. They went to the open gate and saw a long column of mounted men wending their way from the edge of the forest into Erub. A smaller contingent had broken off and was steering for the castle.

"Time to close up shop," said Van Duyn. Springbuck, standing near, put his shoulder to the gate and heaved, but couldn't budge it. Then portly Andre was next to him, and the balky gate moved smartly at the wizard's push. Springbuck noted to himself that there must be muscle to spare under all that avoirdupois.

"What about the portcullis and drawbridge?" the Prince asked as two men lifted a thick beam of wood braced with iron across the gates.

"Rusted into place," replied Van Duyn, "but for now I suggest that we repair to the rampart. Heralds are due, I think."

Springbuck followed the outlander and the deCourteneys up the stone steps, arriving just as a truce-flag bearer and a herald rode up before the castle to parley. Another group sat their horses in the meadow out of bowshot.

"Fetch me my rifle," Van Duyn instructed a youngster who had been on watch there, and Springbuck puzzled over just what thing that might be.

The two soldiers wore long mail hauberks and steel caps and had triangular shields slung beside them. The truce flag was a white rectangle of cloth on a lance decked with heron feathers.

"Now heed us, the castle," roared the herald. "For crimes both treasonous and seditious, all who are within merit the death penalty. Clemency will be shown only to those who quit these premises and surrender to the duly authorized representatives of His Grace, Strongblade, by right of ascension imminent the Protector Suzerain of this place."

"Strongblade," the Prince repeated to himself, hand hard and resolute on Bar. Bey hadn't lost any time having his puppet proclaimed rightful Heir.

Now Gabrielle had passed her brother a scabbarded sword of ancient design and Van Duyn held the exotic implement he'd sent for, a "rifle." It was a curious club-like affair of wood and metal, longer than a man's arm.

The scholar leaned out over the merlin's lip and spoke back. His teeth were showing, but it was no smile. "Tell your commander and your counterfeit *Ku-Mor-Mai* that we don't surrender ourselves to usurpers or their ass-kissing messengers."

"I wonder what's happened in Earthfast?" Andre was saying, one cogitative finger at his thick lips.

"—and if you've seen what I did to your friends in Erub," Van Duyn continued, apparently with huge enjoyment, "you'll know enough to stay well away from our walls. Or would you like a taste of this?"

He brought his rifle to his shoulder, sighting down it, Springbuck thought, rather as one would squint down an arrow to gauge its trueness. There came an explosion.

A spit of flame and smoke shot from the armament's end and a clot of dirt leaped between the feet of the herald's horse. The air was filled with the same smell that the Prince had noticed lingering in the air in Erub, and the horses threatened to go mad, eyes rolling white and ears flattening to their skulls in terror as they screamed in fear.

Springbuck staggered back with a yell of alarm at this, ears ringing from the blast. The outlander was calmly lowering his weapon, watching herald and standard-bearer withdraw in disarray.

A small capsule of metal had been flung from some hidden opening in the rifle and now lay smoking at his feet. Springbuck picked it up, juggling it to keep from burning his fingers, and found that it exuded that peculiar odor. He thought about the tongue of flame and about the curious wound-holes in the dead cavalrymen in Erub.

"Who were the two who remained at a distance with the other troops, those in bright clothing?" Van Duyn was asking.

The sorceress answered, perfect brow wrinkled for an instant in thought. "Creatures of Yardiff Bey. He in the golden full-helmet is Ibn-al-Yed, Bey's right arm. The other, I believe, is Neezolo Peeno, known as a premier druid. It would seem that, while he cannot do us the honor of attending our demise in person, Bey sends his closest vassals to do so." Amazingly, she chuckled. Seeing Andre's face afflicted with doubt and concern, she stopped her low laugh and asked, "Why so glum, brother dear?"

"What about the soldiers?" Springbuck interrupted.

She turned her mocking gaze to him. "What about them? Here you are, dressed and plumed for war and wearing a sword. Have *you* no suggestions?"

She slipped her arm possessively through Van Duyn's and waited.

Springbuck's ire rose. Spotting the youngster who'd fetched Van Duyn's rifle, he said, "Find yourself four more men and begin making forked poles to push scaling ladders away from the walls. Make them at least fifteen feet long."

The boy looked from the Prince to Van Duyn and the deCourteneys. At length Andre cleared his throat and said, "Do as he tells you, Byree. His idea makes sense."

Byree dashed off as the wizard turned to Springbuck. "What else can we do?"

Springbuck showed no sign of hesitance, knowing how important confidence was in a leader. Other, more vital abilities would come only with painful experience.

"Start some of the others assembling makeshift mantlets and have them brought up here. And set out buckets of water and earth or sand in case they loft fire arrows at us. We'll need anything we can get as polearms: scythes, flails, pitchforks, anything."

"Have you no orders for me?" Gabrielle asked with heavy sarcasm.

"Yes," returned the Prince, "you could gather some help and pull the birds' nests from the chimneys."

The patchwork command took shape quickly. A room was prepared for any wounded they might suffer. Springbuck walked among the men of Erub and divided them into subgroups, selecting those he deemed most alert and aggressive-looking for leaders.

By this time it was deep dusk and the cooking fires were burning in the two hearths of the main hall. Noticing that some of the Erubites appeared to resent his new authority, Springbuck commanded each subleader to pick two men for sentinel duty, and announced that he and Andre deCourteney would take first watch. This struck the peasants as fair—the Prince wondered what his father would have said about placating farmers—and the wizard raised no objection.

The two began to pace their circuits of the walls in opposite directions, and though the Prince would have liked to ask Andre a number of questions, he decided to keep his own counsel for the time being. Van Duyn was sure that the soldiers would come no closer to the castle, fearing his rifle and the deCourteneys, and so far he'd been right. Springbuck hoped that he would continue so; if there were a major assault now, they'd all be slain unless the outlander's weapon could kill many men all at once.

During the watch he felt the fatigue of the day overtake him. He considered the chain of events that had begun with Hightower's death, and pondered his new allies and their strange self-assurance.

At the end of the tour he and Andre awakened their relief, for the balance of the band had toppled into sleep after the exhausting day. He made a final check of Fireheel's accommodations and groped around by a dying fire until he came across an unfinished bit of sausage and biscuit.

Propped against a wall, he huddled in his cloak as it became chillier, and heard Andre snoring loudly nearby. He removed his war mask and gobbled the cold meal quickly, licking his fingers afterward and wishing that there were more.

Divesting himself of boots, demisleeves and sword belt, he went to sleep with his head pillowed on his saddle pad, not considering first that, without his mask, he would be recognized by those who saw him in the morning light.

Chapter Six

On what wings dare he aspire?
What the hand dare seize the fire?

WILLIAM BLAKE,
"The Tyger"

"BREAKFAST, O *Ku-Mor-Mai*," said a female voice. But why did it use his father's title?

He burst to his feet, cloak flung aside in alarm. He found himself facing Gabrielle, who offered him a bowl of thick stew, no longer warm, and a succinct nod, even colder, for the day's beginning. He knew instantly what had happened and told himself with some chagrin that it would have happened anyway.

"You sleep like a dead man," the sorceress was saying, "long after others are up. But Edward said to leave it so."

Rather then extend the bowl in common hospitality she set it on the ground and turned to leave.

"Wait," he called after her. When she turned back he found himself with nothing to say.

"Ahh, who is Edward?"

"Edward is Van Duyn. Do they have to teach you everything fresh each day?"

She left as he mumbled, "I didn't know." He wolfed the stew, watching his new compatriots bustle around the courtyard, carrying trash and rubble from the interior of the buildings and bearing arms to the ramparts. His meal downed, he buckled on demisleeves and pulled on his boots. Taking up mask and sword belt, he searched out Van Duyn and Andre, who were studying the countryside from the ramparts.

Andre greeted him with a friendly clap on the shoulder. "In truth," he declared, "I knew you as soon as ever I saw you yesterday, though you've changed. But

47

what brings the royal Heir to join us? I'm afraid we must ask."

The three sat on a make-do bench under the climbing sun while Springbuck told them the tale of his escape from Earthfast. He found himself irritated by Van Duyn, who was skeptical throughout, but discovered the wizard to be an amiable fellow and a cordial listener. Both showed keen interest in the portion of his story dealing with Eliatim's remarks. They asked questions, going back over the conversation almost word by word. By then the sun had grown warm and the Prince was glad to accept a gourd of water at the conclusion of his narrative. The two listeners were comparing thoughts on their new information when Gabrielle arrived.

"What preparations we can make have been made," she said. "I'd like to speak to you, Edward." The two left, arm in arm once more.

"Does your sister find in me some offense?" the Prince asked Andre. "She seems hostile to me."

"Perhaps," was the answer. "Or again, perhaps her motives are quite the opposite. Of all the things beyond my power, reading my sister's thoughts is foremost."

He took Springbuck on a tour of the castle's defenses. These were none too reassuring, though one could scarcely hope for better under the circumstances. They discovered a number of the men drilling awkwardly in the courtyard, and the Prince was so disgusted by their ineptitude that he took charge and corrected their more obvious lapses.

Others joined, and soon he was putting a sizable body of tyros through their paces in such fashion that one might almost have thought that they knew what they were doing.

With a flash of inspiration he drew rude diagrams on the wall with a charred stick and showed them where armor of various types was most vulnerable to arrow, pike or sword. Andre slipped away as he began to explain the technique of pushing scaling ladders away from a rampart, undaunted by the fact that he himself had never done it.

When reliefs were changed at the walls, those who came off duty were eager to try their hand, and the practice continued. There was no sign of any activity from the troops occupying Erub, except that a company of light horse kept watch on the castle from a nearby rise.

The Prince began thinking of ways for the lot of them to escape under cover of night. He stopped his impromptu lessons when the afternoon grew too hot for them, and once more sought Andre de Courteney, who was thoughtfully gnawing a bit of jerked meat, sitting on a crenel.

"We cannot leave tonight," the wizard said in answer to Springbuck's ideas. "We can't afford to be caught in the open come dawn."

The son of Surehand leaned against another crenel and waited.

"Van Duyn, Gabrielle and I can deal with those soldiers out there if the necessity arrives. For that matter, the two magicians with them don't worry us overly."

"But there's Yardiff Bey," the Prince ventured.

"But there's Bey," Andre agreed. "He can't touch us directly with spells, because of this."

From his shirt he drew forth a chain of some black metal from which depended a shimmering, chatoyant gem the size of a large grape, set in a simple retainer of silver. The Prince sensed that he was in the presence of an object of tremendous consequence.

"Calundronius," Andre explained. "Because of it, my sister and I are alive. Because of it, no one can spend a spell against us directly, or against anyone close to us whom we choose to protect. But Bey intends to destroy us himself, nevertheless. Tomorrow, just at dawn, we have learned, he'll summon a being of the half-world: Chaffinch, a winged fire-dragon who is proof, like this gemstone, against enchantments."

Springbuck couldn't frame any remark, and so gulped air and listened.

Andre felt of his rough face with the back of his hand as he returned Calundronius to its shaggy resting place. "Well, we think Van Duyn may have the solution here. Bey will summon Chaffinch in Earthfast or some other place far from here and send him against us. Van Duyn's idea is to conjure up a defense.

"Edward, you see—or, will see—comes from another reality than ours. 'It's simple, Andre,' he told me once, 'I just hail from different probabilities than you.' Don't let that sour look fool you; he must have his little jests, that one.

"At any pass, Edward's learned a good portion of sorcery from Gabrielle and me since he came here and contacted us. He has a peculiar, sideways aptitude for it. He says that there are, in the world he left behind, machines of war that could slay even Chaffinch. One such is a thing all of metal in which men ride, driven by some internal motive arrangement, mounting weapons like Van Duyn's but far larger. What he proposes is to conjure one of these machines here—and gods know, the spell will be nearly as dangerous as the jeopardy in which we find ourselves now. Yes, but it's either that or die under Chaffinch's flaming breath."

Andre got up, wiping fingers on thighs. He checked the sun's declination and said, "Come with me; it's nigh time."

They set off together, entering the once-respectable main hall to climb a winding, spiderwebbed staircase and walk down a dusty corridor. They came to a musty suite of rooms uppermost in the castle. There, a hasty sanctum had been set up.

Van Duyn and Gabrielle were already there, and when the other two entered, they both looked strangely at the Prince, and Springbuck had the impression that they'd been arguing.

He perched on a stool while Andre drew obscure diagrams on the floor over a pentagrammic inscription and Gabrielle read in an inflectionless tongue from a codex of unguessable origin.

Van Duyn was charging the braziers which were placed in each corner of the room; seeing the Prince, he asked, "Well, boy, do you want to stay on with us? I intend to see Yardiff Bey thrown down. I owe him that."

Springbuck answered haughtily, not liking Van Duyn or his tone of address. "I will—accept your aid in regaining my throne, if that is what you're offering."

Gabrielle laughed again, but this time the outlander was the butt of it and he colored with fury.

"Stupid brat! The days of throne and crowns are over here! D'you think we're toppling your brainless brother just to replace him with you, you spineless coward?"

Springbuck restrained himself no longer. He lurched forward and grabbed a fistful of the scholar's shirt with his left hand, preparatory to striking him; but before he could, the man seized his left wrist with surprising strength and in some clever, rapid manner twisted it so that Surehand's son was forced to his knees, wrist painfully doubled over and in real danger of breaking. The Prince cried aloud in shock.

The deCourteneys were both watching now. "You must be quiet," Andre reproved. "We dare weighty things here; we must concentrate to the fullest. Edward, please take your place."

The outlander unwillingly released the Prince, who locked eyes with him in mutual agreement that the issue wasn't settled and resisted the impulse to cut him down on the spot. The scholar and the deCourteneys stepped to various prearranged locations among the occult designs on the floor.

Springbuck held his throbbing wrist to his chest and flushed with shame. He was sure that he had lost face among them irredeemably, and regretted most that Gabrielle had seen it. Then his gaze met with hers, and he read a rare message there, a soft and feminine one of sorrow that he had been hurt and worsted. He tried to fit this with what he knew of her already and made his first dim start at understanding the enigma that was Gabrielle deCourteney.

"Your Grace," she said softly, "please stand there—yes, there in that circle of protection, that any powers liberated here work no harm upon you."

He stepped into it, a small circle picked out in dust that looked like crushed emerald. Flexing his fingers, he decided that his wrist had not been badly sprained. Van Duyn, white-faced, set the braziers to burning.

Springbuck noticed with curiosity the contrast be-

tween Andre and his sister: he with broad torso, bowed
legs and fat, jiggling belly and buttocks and she mysti-
cally lovely. She posed unconsciously, weight on one
firm leg, the firelight sending ruby combers breaking
across her hair. Springbuck felt a desire rising in him,
one he'd not wished to acknowledge.

Old Van Duyn, now, was an angular sort of fellow
whose muscles had begun to show the slack of age, but
with considerable sinew about him, as the Prince now
knew to his discomfort, and moved with the ease of fit-
ness.

As the unusual trio—unusual foursome, he amended,
for surely he was as oddly met as they—moved to their
tasks, Andre took the lavaliere from his neck and took
his sword from its scabbard. Unscrewing the pommel
knob, he dropped the chain and Calundronius into the
hollow there, then replaced the cap.

"Within this container Calundronius is itself nullified
for a time," he explained, laying the sword in a corner.

He took his place again and he, Gabrielle and Van
Duyn began a unified chanting in some monotonous
language, unlike that of the codex and somehow much
more disquieting.

The windows were curtained, but some daylight had
penetrated prior to the incantation. Now, though, it was
as if all light was forced from the room save the glow in
the braziers and a single candle in the center of the pentacle. They were in darkest night and a bone chill had
taken over. Springbuck couldn't supress the conviction
that they had somehow left the room and arrived elsewhere, in a place where it was beyond his ability to ori-
ent himself or apprehend reality.

Gabrielle threw her hands over her head and her entire body began to glow with a blue light that pulsed
and flickered.

An amorphous shadow rose amid the runes, expand-
ing from the floor in a manner which struck the Prince
as unwilling. He had the distinct impression that it was
listening to the chanting, that it scrutinized him briefly
and then ignored him, and that it received instructions
with a hateful resentment.

Gabrielle and the scholar were silent now, though the

woman still radiated the eerie aura and gave the appearance of being in a trance. Andre changed his tone from a chant to a steady, placid mode of speech. Springbuck thought that he assumed the attitude of a schoolmaster assigning a complex task to a defiant and not-terribly-bright student.

Without warning the darkness rolling within the pentacle was throwing itself from one side of its invisible confinement to the other, straining to break free and destroy the mortals in the room. Andre spoke a syllable of duress in a voice fearsome and completely unlike anything Springbuck had heard from him before. The thing within the pentacle was instantly quiet.

Andre issued a last instruction and, with an almost vocal snarl, the being was gone. Light and warmth returned to the chamber.

Andre stepped from his spot to recover Calundronius and Springbuck noticed that he was bathed in sweat and that his pudgy hands trembled badly.

"Well," asked the Prince as Gabrielle began to reorder the room, "where is our defender? Where is this fabulous metal war machine?"

Van Duyn, extinguishing a brazier, replied, "Our . . . unwilling benefactor has gone to arrange for its transportation here. It wouldn't do to have the contraption materialize in this room, so Andre specified that it be brought to the meadow outside the castle. If it's moving when it arrives here, it could do damage within the confines of a room or the bailey."

The scholar and the wizard hurried off together to watch for the fruit of their handiwork, chattering importantly in the way of experimenters everywhere. Springbuck shifted his attention to Gabrielle as she bound up her hair with rawhide throngs.

She came to him where he stood nursing his wrist and there was much, much in the glances they exchanged.

"I—I knew that you and Edward would come to conflict, knew it in my heart when I first saw you," she told him, her eyes still holding his. She took his injured wrist between cool, elegant hands.

"Not hurt seriously," she decided after exploring it gently with her fingertips. "The pain will leave it soon."

They stood quite motionless so, for a moment.

His gaze was first to fall away.

"I suppose we should be on the ramparts with the others," he murmured.

Her hands left his and he was immediately sorry he had spoken. He would have continued, for there were more words that he wished to say to her, but he was forestalled by a staccato blast from the distant meadow.

PART II

APC

Chapter Seven

We will ride 'em, we'll collide 'em,
And we'd drive 'em straight through hell.
We're the Chosen Few who ride the APC's.
                    From "APC's," *an unofficial song*
                    of the 11th Armored Cavalry Regt.,
                    U.S. Army

THE metal monster forged along to the squeaking and clanking of full-track treads, the reddish dust of the anhydrous dry season spuming behind it, doing maybe forty-per on the flat, straight road from Phu Loi.

If we were in a convoy, thought Gil MacDonald to himself as he stood in the track commander's cupola, *I'd be digging that shit out of my teeth right now. But I'd feel better.*

The vehicle he rode was known by assorted names: "Armored Calvary Assault Vehicle," "track," or "Armored Personnel Carrier," but was most often referred to as an "APC." He shifted his weight at the hips with automatic ease to compensate for the rigorous swaying and tossing of the journey; the rhythms of his mechanical environment had long since become part of the substance of life, like the rolling which fosters sea legs.

Silly idea of the Old Man's, he reflected, to have the crew come into base camp to pick him up instead of waiting for a chopper to ferry him out to the forward area. Still, it pleased the twenty-one-year-old sergeant in a personal way to know that Captain Cronkite wanted him back on the job immediately after his return from R and R. The run forward wasn't such a long one, but enemy activity was on the upswing in the wake of Operation Big Sur.

He resettled his headset under his helmet liner and steel pot, not as comfortable an arrangement as a crew helmet, but crew helmets don't stop shrapnel too well either, and so, just as they endured hot, heavy, fiberglass flak jackets, he and his men opted for safety. He squinted around him through the searing heat that floated in waves from the baked road.

At least, he knew, Alpha-Nine, his APC, was topped off with fuel and stocked with ammo. He ran his eye over the .50-caliber machine gun on its mount before him, satisfied that it had been well maintained in his five-day absence. He knew, too, that Handelman, Olivier and Pomorski were sitting on the open cargo hatch behind him, scanning the terrain as he was. Sometimes he found himself thinking of them in simple terms of rates and fields of fire, the first two as M-60 machine guns and the latter an M-79 grenade launcher. They were his friends, but they were part of the APC, just as he was, the parts that guided it and reached out from it to kill. *Spend enough time in one of these things,* he mused, *and maybe you'd become integrated altogether, stop thinking of yourself as a human being.*

The big V-8 engine pulled them briskly, equal to operating conditions even in Southeast Asia. He blinked sweat from his eyes and made a mental note to grab a salt tablet the first time they stopped. A sudden hissing from the radio brought him back from a brief reminiscence of his stay in Bangkok.

"Steel Probe one niner, Steel Probe one niner, this is Steel Probe six, Steel Probe six, over."

A cultured voice, it carried the faintest hint of the Southern Black drawl. Wondering why Captain Cronkite would want him right now, Gil flipped the transmit switch on his headset.

"Steel Probe six, this is Steel Probe one niner, over."

"Steel Probe one niner, this is Steel Probe six. Halt and remain at your present location. Ahh, Steel Probe one zero will rendezvous with you there in approximately one five mikes. Do you roger? Over."

"Steel Probe six, this is Steel Probe one niner, roger your last transmission, over."

"This is Steel Probe six, out."

Gil flipped his microphone over to intercom and told Al Woods to pull the APC over to one side of the road for the fifteen-minute wait. He didn't like the stretch they'd stopped in; the grass grew high and there were dense stands of rubber trees nearby, abandoned to undergrowth. He forgot all about his salt tablet. But the rendezvous wasn't too far off, and he didn't know from which direction the other APC would come. Steel Probe ten would be Bronco Jackson and *Gunfighter,* Alpha-Seven, maybe the second-best track and crew in the 32d Armored Calvary Regiment.

Of course, Gil MacDonald and his squadmates, known collectively as the Nine-Mob, knew past all question that no better track flattened turf than *Lobo,* their own Alpha-Nine.

Still keeping watch as Woods killed the engine, he said conversationally, "News reports about Operation Big Sur had me worried about you clowns."

"So," answered Pomorski from behind, "whip some current events to us. We been beatin' the boonies for a week; haven't seen a *Stars & Stripes,* even."

Gil dug a late copy of the American serviceman's newspaper out of the pouch pocket of his jungle fatigues. He opened and began to read it, glancing over the top of the page to check out the landscape with nervous caution.

Getting shaky, he chided himself, *letting the Shortimer Syndrome get to you.*

He read: "An ancient tactic in the timeless business of war was employed this week by commanders of the U.S. Army's Second Field Forces as a part of the ongoing effort to maintain the safety of the Saigon Capital Military District.

"In simplest terms, the maneuver was a well-coordinated trap, tempting bait with crushing jaws poised around it. The bait in this case was from the 32d Armored Cavalry Regiment.

"Counterintelligence sources permitted the compromise of information concerning a convoy route and schedule. The convoy, to be made up of thin-skin cargo vehicles, rolled on time, but was actually composed of the 32d's durable 1st Squadron.

"As hoped, Charlie showed up to make his kill on easy pickings promised by the bogus rumor, but received a rude shock upon springing his ambush. With lethal precision, assembled APCs and tanks turned their firepower on the Communist infantry, repelling them and killing many while close air strikes were called in to F-4 Phantom fighter-bombers already in the air.

"Airmobile troops were flown in by helicopter immediately after the last strikes to support mop-up operations. In all, over forty-three enemy dead were confirmed by body count.

"1st Squadron Commander Colonel J. B. Woolmun—"

Gil stopped reading and looked up. "Hey, anybody want to hear a quote from Wooly?" The mildest reply he received was to the effect that the colonel had Oedipal tendencies.

"What journalism washout wrote that?" Pomorski wanted to know. "And how can a timeless business have ancient tactics?"

Gil folded the paper and stared across the quiet countryside before him, gnawing his lower lip, nerves still on edge. Then they got to him, and he thumbed the transmit switch.

"Steel Probe six, Steel Probe six, this is Steel Probe one niner, Steel Probe one niner, over."

He repeated the call twice, drawing no response whatever, with the same results when he tried to raise Bronco Jackson. Stuffing the newspaper back into his pocket, he snapped, "Light it up, Al. Everybody look sharp, we're haulin' balls out of here. I got the boss five-by on his last call and now I can't raise him or the boys on *Gunfighter*. I never asked the CO to authenticate his message because I thought I recognized his voice, but it doesn't sound like him to stick us out here and wander out of radio contact."

They were all alert now, suspicious as wild animals. *Sure, they can tell something's wrong, just like me. You show up at a convoy point and there're no kids or mama-sans around or at night on the perimeter you hear the cans you've tied to the hurricane wire start clanking. Or something like this happens. Ice on your backbone and knots in your belly.*

Woods' hands were firm and quick on the laterals, the

braking levers, but moisture covered his brown face. While the three machine gunners searched anxiously around them, Pomorski, nosing his grenade launcher apprehensively this way and that, played what he called "tailgate trombone," eyes-behind on the rear hatch.

They'd reached a stand of particularly high grass when the ambush came. Later, Gil was thankful that Charles Cong hadn't come up with a land mine for the occasion; the radiotelephone deception implied that someone had been planning it for a while. The enemy op's imitation of Captain Cronkite's voice had been extremely adept. Probably the ambush of *Lobo* was a trial, a tryout preparatory for a more ambitious trick.

He never knew why the first RPG-4 rocket missed. At that range *Lobo* was a sure hit unless the man handling the launcher was awfully unsteady, the only explanation he could think of.

The rocket sizzled a foot or so in front of the APC and exploded to the left and rear, sending shrapnel *spang*ing off the cupola and splash shields.

The clout of an AK-47 opened up to the right. Gil brought the .50 around and he and Handelman, who manned the right-side M-60, opened up on the deep grass in blind reply, the slower base boom of the sergeant's piece coupled with the rapid tattoo of Handelman's weapon. The man who'd fired the RPG-4 was cut to bits, but they couldn't spot the covering man with the AK.

A gut conviction gripped Gil. As Woods sent the APC shooting forward, he traversed his gun to the left and watched for a backup man. He missed the parting of the grasses caused by the extension of the second launcher, and so did Olivier, for all their intense surveillance. Gil caught the movement out of the corner of his eye only in the last, irrevocable moment. The man had waited until they were slightly past him and he had no worry about hitting his comrades. The Vietnamese stood up and took quick, competent aim on *Lobo*'s broad side. Even as he wrenched at the .50 Gil knew with dismal certainty that neither his gun nor Olivier's could come to bear on the track killer in the half second available to them before the rocket was sped on its way, small and invisibly swift and incredibly destructive. There was only time to know mournfully that the next instant would see the missile punch its way through Alpha-Nine and destroy them all, men and machine.

All at once the small brown man who was about to dispatch their deaths from the tube on his shoulder was flung sideways, bent double. Another cover man with an AK-47 stood up in surprise, looking to *Lobo*'s rear, then collapsed in a paroxysm of pain, leg flying from under him at the sudden insistent pounding of a .50 machine gun. Gil swiveled his head in the direction of the fire, his rear.

Over Pomorski's shoulder he could see, perhaps ten yards behind *Lobo*, another APC. It was layered with mud and dust, sides gouged and apparently scorched by flame, its wooden trim vane crushed and splintered. Bronco Jackson? Impossible; the transmissions about Jackson had been a hoax.

The track commander in the following APC raised a clenched fist to Gil, who returned it gratefully. He couldn't read any unit markings on the newcomer because of its battered condition, nor had he heard it or been aware of its approach until its main gun had opened up.

He turned back to the grips of his own .50, moving to cover the opposite field of fire, when an intense chill passed over him. *Lobo*'s surroundings were blotted out by a world of gray, 360 degrees without content, gone almost the instant it appeared. Alpha-Nine, 32d ACR, U.S. Army Vietnam, was plunging over a green sweep of lush meadow, VC and Asian road nowhere to be seen.

Woods brought the track to a halt in surprise. Pomorski scanned to the rear as the remaining three peeked up over their splash shields, all searching for enemies who'd threatened them and the friendlies who'd rescued them moments before. They craned their heads around, taking in the view with their mouths hanging open.

They saw an unusual building rather like a small castle on a nearby rise, some copses of trees and a primitive village farther back down the meadow.

"Cut the engine," Gil ordered. He needed to hear himself think.

Slowly, Pomorski said, "MacDonald, what . . . what's happened? MacDonald?"

"What is this, *Jeopardy?*" the sergeant roared back. "Am I buzzing my answer buzzer? *Am I?*"

A large body of curiously dressed men on horses had appeared at the edge of the trees and were regarding the Nine-Mob with a good deal of interest. Gil looked at them and tried hard to remember if either side was using cavalry in Vietnam. *Horse type, that is*, he thought.

Four of the mounted men detached themselves from the rest and moved liesurely toward the APC. The Nine-Mob was still hunting with growing urgency for the disappeared VC and related familiar landmarks, but they were not, as individuals or a group, slow to recover or react. The four riders reined in front of *Lobo* and Gil spoke softly into his intercom.

"I am now open for hints."

"Pass," said Pomorski, and that was the only help the sergeant got.

"Right," he said after another moment. "Pomorski takes the fifty and the rest of you hang loose. I'm gonna talk to these bananas."

His brain wasn't sluggish. He knew from gross physical evidence that he was no longer in the situation in which he'd been only a few seconds before. There was absolutely no sign of ambush, ambushers or, for that matter, Southeast Asia.

Pomorski put down his grenade launcher as Gil took off his helmet and headset and leaned down into the APC and plucked up his submachine gun and a bandolier of ammunition. He climbed up over the cupola as the grenadier came up from underneath and replaced him at the machine gun.

The sergeant slung the bandolier over his head, checked the safety on Shorty, an abbreviated M-16, and jumped to the ground. Once down, he flicked the safety over to autofire and walked unhurriedly to the waiting men, chopper cradled comfortingly against him.

All four sat horses decked out in splendid harness. The two to the rear wore long outfits made from metal

rings, covering them to the wrists and falling like shirts
to their knees, and steel caps with nasal guards. Moreover, they bore triangular shields and wore long swords.

*Armor? Swords? Had they wandered into some kind
of pageant?*

Of the two in front, one wore a caftan with a hood
which hid his face in shadow. The other was in gaudy
robes, sashed pantaloons, pointy-toed shoes and a fur
busby, and was decorated with a good deal of jewelry.

*Hallucinations? Had somebody been putting some-
thing in the Lister bags?*

The one with the hood threw it back suddenly and
stared out—although Gil couldn't actually see his eyes—
from a golden mask which enclosed his entire head. The
mask featured red, jutting fangs and a distinctly hateful
expression with graven scowl and *V*-shaped brows done
in black. But where the eyes and mouth should have
been there were only dark apertures.

Golden Mask spoke, voice echoing eerily from within
the headpiece. "Who are you, who appear in the fields
of Erub for no possible reason save that you are in
league with the renegades?"

The sergeant didn't waste time with meaningless
sounds of shock and disavowal. It was his experience
that people with submachine guns didn't have to.

Until today.

"Uh, MacDonald, Gilbert A., sergeant, U.S. Army,"
he said from habit and by way of introduction. "I don't
think I know where I am right now. Who are *you*, Jack,
and where are we?" He watched the faces of the other
three for reactions, since Golden Mask was unreadable,
but they gave him none.

Golden Mask turned to his fellows. "They are confused, at a loss for their Reality. They obviously don't
belong to this place-and-time, they are an invocation.
Let us eliminate them now, before those in the castle can
offer interference."

Gil, who hadn't missed "eliminate," was about to
shove his way back into the conversation when the two
armored men drew their mounts back cautiously.
Golden Mask kept his place while his colorfully-turned-
out companion urged his steed a few steps closer to the

sergeant. Without taking his gaze from the men in front of him, Gil called, "Pomorski! Cover the two in back; it anything goes down, you ace 'em."

"Roger-dodger."

Fancy Pants stopped a few feet from where Gil stood. He extended his bangled and braceleted arms toward *Lobo* and the Nine-Mob. His fingers clawed grotesquely as he began to chant loudly, nothing the American could comprehend.

The same instinct that had prompted him to look for a backup RPG made Gil's hackles rise and sent a signal of fear down his spine. There'd been only the slightest of breezes a moment before but now a stiff, driving wind began to swirl around him. It tore at his fatigues, threatened to throw him headlong, yet didn't seem to affect Fancy Pants or any of those behind him.

Gil risked a glance behind him, to start in horror at the murky funnel of air forming around *Lobo* and, impossibly, rocking the giant weight of the APC. The wind raged around and around in that small circuit, grew in intensity on its confined course. The cantor continued, in a voice grown loud beyond belief, deafening even over the tornado howl. The Nine-Mobsters were hanging on for life, their helmets blown off and their clothes tearing from their bodies.

The sergeant was obliged to drop to his knees to avoid being blown off his feet. Insane as it seemed, this gaudy character must be the one responsible for the wind. In a live-or-die fix, with a conclusion based on the way things must be—no matter how crazy—that was enough for Gil MacDonald. He brought the chopper up and fired from the hip, quick-kill style. It was almost impossible to hold even a stationary target in the malevolent wind, and so he emptied the entire eighteen rounds in his magazine at Fancy Pants to be sure. Man and horse collapsed in a spray of blood; M-16 slugs tended to wobble when they hit and eight hits were more than enough to make a mess.

As quickly as it had begun, the were-wind died. Gold Mask and the others stared at the form of their dead companion for a moment as they tried to control their maddened horses, and Gil slammed home a new maga-

zine from his bandolier and covered them. They backed
their horses away and the American wasn't sure if he
ought to stop them or be glad they were leaving. Considering all the buckaroos they had to back them up, he
decided that further exchanges would be ill advised.
The entire mounted body moved off, stopping at the
tree line several hundred yards away, in the opposite
direction from the castle.

Gil backpedaled to the APC and scrambled up as the
Nine-Mob pulled themselves together. Pomorski relin-
quished the .50 and they were all silent for a minute.

Then Gil said, "The guy and his horse are both dead;
each took a couple in the head. Guess I was shooting
high."

"A shame to stop him just when he was getting going
good," said Pomorski, as the green began to leave his
complexion, "but conservatively speaking, all isn't well
here and the obvious question, as I pointed out earlier,
is—where are we at?"

"We're someplace without VC or dry seasons, okay?
Where people dress for Halloween and have their own
cyclones on call, ride horses and live in castles." Gil
waved his hand at the countryside and said, "Look
around you. Everything's different—climate, plants, terrain, the works. Everything's utterly not-the-same as before we cruised through that gray fog. So Pomorski,
carefully now, I want you to apply all sixty-eight of
your Famous College Credits and tell *me* where we
are."

"How about this?" Woods asked. "How'd we get
here?"

"Damned if I know, Sportin' Life," the sergeant
sighed. "This kind of action usually happens to girls and
little dogs after Kansas twisters." Thoughts of The Outer
Limits bobbed in his brain.

Olivier, thin face even more pallid than usual behind
thick glasses, yelled and pointed toward the castle. Galloping full tilt in their direction, plainly come from the
now-open castle gate, was a single horseman. He wore a
brightly painted mask with a rooster tail of tall white
plumes and sat a big, long-legged gray—seventeen

hands high, Pomorski thought to himself, if he was an inch—whose neck was thrust forward in exertion. The rider fairly flew across the meadow, bringing his horse to a stop near them in a shower of turf as they looked to their weapons against another attack; if they'd been less disciplined they might have dropped him on the spot without questions.

The rest of the fellow's dress matched his war mask. He wore high rider's boots, leather guards covering his forearms, loinband and a sword belted to his hip.

"Welcome!" he cried, "And hurrah for a fine deed in slaying Neezolo Peeno. Andre deCourteney could not extend the protection of Calundronius to the meadow but Van Duyn said that the men with—guns, are they called?—would be able to defend themselves admirably and so you have. But we must hasten now, back to the Keep, before the soldiers decide to make a sally or Ibn-al-Yed cooks up some wizardish attack to our sorrow."

The five soldiers had been mute throughout Springbuck's speech. Now Gil rubbed the back of his sunburned neck with his hand as if it would help. Woods said, "Simply astonishing."

"All right," said the sergeant, "take us to the fella who knows about guns. Maybe we can get a little info. I guess we might as well leave the Dearly Departed over there for his friends and loved ones."

Fireheel became skittish as Woods fired up the track's big Chrysler with a roar, and Springbuck was careful to trot him a goodly distance in front of this thing, this machine, which the Prince found delightfully loud and menacing. Gil noticed that none of the other riders, the ones who had confronted them before, moved to stop or follow them. In a place where firearms seemed at least a rarity, from their guide's remarks, Gil's response to the were-wind must have been most impressive.

Shades of the Connecticut Yankee!

Springbuck led them to the very drawbridge of the castle, then galloped across. Gil studied the wooden span and the dozen or so faces staring round-eyed at them from the ramparts above. That some of them were

women, and one in particular an absolute red-haired
fox, did not escape the American's notice even in these
disconcerting circumstances.

"Hell," said Gil at last, "we're better off stepping on
in than sitting out here to rot. I'll ground-guide."

Pomorski took the .50 again and Gil walked ahead of
the track as Woods followed his hand signals, easing
Lobo over the drawbridge. Shorty was at the sergeant's
side again. Woods nursed the ponderous APC along as
if he were treading eggs, but the timbers held firmly
enough and they found themselves in a large, cobble-
stoned courtyard filled with weeds, refuse of one kind
and another and some very curious people. These last
were dressed in attire as peculiar—from the Nine-
Mob's point of view—as any other they'd seen in the
past fifteen minutes; mostly woolen clothes, baggy shirts
and pantaloons and shapeless dresses. All were staring
in total fascination at *Lobo*, but were definitely afraid
to approach or touch it. Gil wanted to pinch himself.

He wondered if the Veterans Administration had a
nice, comfortable nuthouse anywheres close to home?

Chapter Eight

The soldiers are the cleverest,
their wisdom they display there,
They know that miracles like this
don't happen every day there.
                    HEINRICH HEINE,
                    "I Dreamt I Was the Dear Lord God"

THEIR guide had dismounted and pushed his way through the crowd, mask now in hand. He was quite young, with an open face bearing an exuberant smile. The imposing saber he wore notwithstanding, he appeared friendly enough.

Springbuck, for his part, saw five bewildered faces studying him and the Keep's other temporary inhabitants. The leader of these foreigners, the one who'd made the decision to come along with him to the castle, was fairly young, perhaps the youngest of the five who rode this nonesuch machine. He had brown hair cropped short, fair skin burned by the sun and premature age lines bracketing his mouth. Of the others, one was a big husky fellow with a lantern jaw and a curling mustache, another a frail-looking and pallid sort of individual who wore the same sort of little lenses as Van Duyn—glasses. This one was addressed as Olivier while the fourth, a rather short, heavily built, acned man, was called Handelman. But most amazing of all was the one who pulled himself up to sit on an open hatch at the front of the vehicle—the Prince hadn't caught his name in their conversation—for he was completely brown. Or at least, his hands, neck and face were, and his black hair curled tightly to his head.

Springbuck was phrasing a hundred questions in his mind when the deCourteneys and Van Duyn reached his side. The Americans didn't miss the holstered pistol at Van Duyn's belt as he asked preemptorily, "Which of you is in charge here?"

"I am. MacDonald, sergeant, U.S. Army. Mind if I ask your name, pal?"

"Edward Van Duyn. I imagine that you and your friends are confused as to your present situation. I'll try to explain your circumstances to you in terms you can comprehend and allay your misgivings, since your dilemma is, no doubt, quite beyond your, er, grasp."

Gil stood, arms akimbo, and replied airily, "Uh-uh, not so. Fact is, you're all under my guns and I'm going to start knocking this rock outhouse down around your ears unless I get a whole lot of answers in a big hurry."

Van Duyn was plainly annoyed by this, but didn't pursue the topic. "If you'd care to step inside, Sergeant, I shall be happy to clarify matters for you."

Gil hesitated, then decided that there was little he could do until he found out what in the world had happened to them, how the Nine-Mob had gotten here and where here was.

"Okay," he conceded, "wait a sec while I tell the crew what's going on." He clambered back aboard *Lobo* and had Woods take the .50 caliber, then squatted in conference with the burly grenadier and second-in-command.

"So, loan me your hog, Ski, and keep an eye on things till I get back. If I don't show, say, in thirty minutes, do whatever strikes you as best, although I can't imagine what the hell that would be. We just can't do anything until we dope out what's happened to us."

He took the other's .45 automatic and slipped it into his belt under his jungle fatigue jacket. Pomorski watched dubiously. "Pardon my candor," he said, "but this quixotic foray of yours is not particularly bright. Just load up on hardware and charge out all dewy-eyed and shooting, that's your style, MacDonald."

Gil felt the heat of his own face as anger sent his blood racing. Friction with the gregarious Pomorski was a frequent problem. With two years of college, light-hearted Pomorski was better educated. He was also a former football player and dangerous with bare hands and feet; neither of them was certain who would win if they fought. They'd drifted into a sort of rivalry as dominant personalities in the crew.

"Dewy-eyed, my aching, dying ass," Gil whispered fiercely. "If you've got any alternatives, any at all, let's hear them."

Pomorski stared at him for a moment, looked conspicuously at Gil's three stripes and his own spec-four patch, and shrugged. "Gunboat diplomacy," he grumbled, and climbed back up through the cargo hatch.

Gil removed his flak jacket, followed him up and jumped to the ground. He faced Van Duyn, though his eye rested for an instant on the breathtaking woman at the man's side. "After you," he said. "I'm all ears, to put it very moderately."

They set off across the courtyard and up the broad steps which led to the double doors of the castle's main hall. This was being used as a sort of communal cooking-living area, and Gil didn't miss hints that it was a temporary camp. There were cobwebs in the roof beams and the dust of long disuse was almost everywhere. Aromatically, it reminded him of a barn. Meat was being broiled over flames in an enormous fireplace, the only source of heat and light in the room aside from slits of windows set high in the walls. Other culinary preparations were being made by four or five young women and one dowdy specimen.

The curious and ill-smelling crowd—*he probably was not too fragrant his own self*—had fallen away as they had entered the hall, and now Van Duyn preceded him to a staircase leading to the upper levels of the building. With them went the woman, the rider who'd met *Lobo* and a short, fat, thuggish-looking man who reminded Gil of a dockworker.

The staircase and the corridor at its top were surprisingly narrow and built, like the rest of the structure, of brownish stone. Mold smeared across the ceiling, walls and floor. They entered a modestly spacious room furnished with a large table, several panlike things on tripods, live coals still glowing in them, a few odd stools and rotting tapestries. Complicated designs and polygons were drawn on the floor. There was a small fireplace, now dark and empty. Van Duyn showed Gil to a stool and took another for himself, while the young rider perched one buttock on the table and swung his leg idly and the girl and dockworker sat together on a window bench.

Van Duyn smiled heartily, unconvincingly, and rubbed his hands together.

"Firstly," he began, "I will introduce my illustrious companions. That bravo there at the table is Prince Springbuck, and these are Gabrielle and Andre deCourteney. I believe I have already introduced myself."

The soldier nodded as Springbuck studied him, this alien who commanded the metal war-machine. Sergeant MacDonald if that was his true rank and naming, was attired all in olive green, pants and jackets of some thin material. He'd been wearing a heavier vest of some sort, but had left that in his machine. He had many large pockets about his clothes and wore boots of faded green canvas and black leather, with corrugated soles. He'd plainly passed much time on strange roads and there was red dust upon him and his clothes. On his upper arm he wore three chevrons and at his right shoulder was a small emblem, a cavalry saber, point uppermost, picked out in black against an olive background. Springbuck wondered if the man were an accomplished swordsman to bear such a symbol, not knowing that it was simply the 32d's regimental crest.

"Well, from the look of you men," said Van Duyn, maintaining his false joviality, "I'd say we plucked you out of that Asian mess."

"I'm in no position to know what you mean by *plucked*, but we were on duty near Phu Loi about half an hour ago, or so it seems to me," Gil replied. "Now what I want to know is, how were we brought here? And if it was you that did it, I want you to send us back."

Van Duyn, with a condescending air that the sergeant found extremely abrasive, continued, "My dear boy, you and your, er, comrades and your armored car have been brought here by a process which I need not explain, even if you had the faculties to absorb it, which you don't. Events taking place here concern you not in the least but for this one fact: in order to be returned to your former place and time in the scheme of things, you will do one small job for me tomorrow morning. In the evening we'll send you back to that foolish war. In fact, it will be as if you were never interrupted."

The prince and the deCourteneys winced, sensing that Van Duyn was taking the wrong tack altogether. Andre shifted uneasily on his window seat and seemed about to speak.

But the soldier was on his feet, the stool kicked backward. "You highhanded old bastard," he said levelly. "If you can send us back, you're going to do it now, or I swear I'll grease you right here." He grabbed a double handful of Van Duyn's shirt, yanking the older man to his feet. The scholar's hands darted up to seize the sergeant's, and work one of those cunning, disabling tricks. The other three there, expecting to see Van Duyn restrain or injure Gil, were startled at what followed. The sergeant avoided the grasping hands with two short, vicious chops, the sides of his hands hacking away his opponent's wrists. He snapped his fisted left hand, knuckles cocked outward, up into Van Duyn's face just underneath the nose—but controlled what could as easily have been a death stroke—and drove a stiff-fingered right into the solar plexus, finishing with a hammer blow to the exposed neck as the other went down in a heap.

The Prince and the deCourteneys were on their feet, and Springbuck swept Bar from its sheath. Stepping forward to separate the soldier from his antagonist, he was unprepared to see Gil jump back, nearly tripping on his overturned stool, and claw the .45 from his belt.

The two faced each other in frozen tableau, the Prince with the gleaming length of cold edge poised close, near enough for a lethal flourish, and the sergeant with his pistol leveled at Springbuck's heart. They held their positions so for some seconds, neither truly sure of what the other would prove capable. The son of Surehand recognized the gun as being, like Van Duyn's, a fearsome weapon. Gil, on the other hand, knew that the gleaming sword was a fraction of a second from his throat. Van Duyn began to wheeze and attempted to sit up.

"I didn't hit him as hard as I could have," Gil said, stepping backward a pace and bringing his back up against the wall. Gabrielle broke the frieze as she rushed to see to Van Duyn. Gil swung the muzzle of his pistol to cover her, but his eyes didn't leave the Prince.

"Stay back. He'll be okay in a minute, but if you give me any grief I'll have to hurt him and maybe you, too. Someone could get zapped."

She hissed at him and the sergeant knew he'd made a deadly enemy. Andre took her hand and restrained her from calling the bluff. Springbuck wavered, uncertain whether to attack or sheathe his blade. Finally, he withdrew a pace or so and lowered his point. Gil relieved Van Duyn of his Browning as the other sat rubbing his neck where the hammer blow had caught him.

Gil, trying to sound calm, said, "Now you—I told you that I want some answers. It could be you'd mind your manners and chat more if we play this game over at my house."

He uncocked the .45 and, without losing track of what the others were doing, deftly took Van Duyn's left hand and wrist in a harsh come-along hold. Battered and subdued as he was, the older man came to his feet at the irresistible pressure.

Gil turned to the others. "Okay, he and I are going for a parley in *Lobo*. Don't try to stop us and keep clear of the track once we're in it. I don't know if any of you have been told, but my friends and I could kill everyone in this gravel heap just like I blew away that joker in the meadow."

"Let them go," Andre advised his sister and Springbuck. "We have no hope anyway unless Edward can convince them to help us."

This last puzzled Gil, but he took quick advantage of the wizard's attitude to hustle Van Duyn out and down the stairway, being on guard against any attempt the other might have been inclined to make at tripping him or otherwise trying to escape or resist.

The women were the only ones remaining in the hall, and they made no move to stop him, but stood gawping in amazement at the sergeant and his prisoner. One of the main doors was still ajar, but when the two reached the courtyard, they found that many of the locals were gathered there around the APC, some of them holding or wearing swords or other weapons, primitive but deadly. Woods was leaning over the .50 cupola chatting amiably with two young girls who were giggling shyly and blushing.

The sergeant barked his name and Woods' gaze came to him. The driver assessed the situation and reacted instantly. Traversing and depressing the machine gun, he brought it to bear on the crowd to Gil's left, calling to Olivier as he did. Olivier, already behind his gun, covered the group to the track commander's right. Pomorski popped his head up through the cargo hatch, cursed and ducked back down to open the rear hatch.

"Tell your friends," Gil grated to his captive, "to stay away from *Lobo*. We're going in."

Van Duyn did so, and the twenty or so Erubites moved away from the track and permitted Gil to drag his unwilling guest to it. The rear of the boxlike APC was designed to be lowered by winch cable to serve as a ramp. There was a smaller hatch set into it, and it was this that Pomorski unlatched. Gil thrust Van Duyn through headfirst and the grenadier caught the dazed man up effortlessly and slammed him into one of the two interior benches set along the walls, covering him casually with the submachine gun.

Gil confronted the crowd outside, pistol in hand. "We're not going to hurt him," he said. "We just want him to tell us a few things."

The people looked at one another doubtfully. At last a man stepped forward and said, "You may rest assured that if you give hurt to our teacher, we will try as best we can to kill you, and in any case you'll have the wrath of the sorceress Gabrielle deCourteney and her brother to contend with."

Sorceress?

Rather than bandy words, Gil backed to the rear hatch and slid through it. Pomorski was sitting in the bench opposite Van Duyn, very relaxed. When it hit the fan, the sergeant reflected, the spec-four never balked or asked dumb questions. Demands of violence pushed aside all rivalry and debate.

"What's the problem?" Pomorski asked mildly.

Gil sat down, trading off the .45 for Shorty. "This dude and the redheaded babe and one or two others are the ones who got us here, I think—I don't know how yet—with the idea of making us do something or other for them. Your man here got nasty about explaining details and got kind of, you know, high-strung, so I invited him over for some Nine-Mob hospitality. I don't think the adoring public outside will give us any trouble for the time being, as long as this one's not messed up too much." He thought for a moment. "Al?"

"Yeah, Mac?" answered Woods from the cupola.

"Are the gates locked? If so, d'you think we could bust out of this brick barn?"

"The gates are barred, Mac. We might be able to crash through, but it seems to me we'd come down hard on that old bridge; might go right through it into the ditch outside. I don't know that we could climb out again."

The sergeant bit his lip. Van Duyn was sitting up, watching them and listening to the interplay. Gil glared at him for a second, ready to speak, but Van Duyn began first.

"MacDonald, I appear to have misjudged you seriously, at least as far as temper and tractability go. Rather than lose all chance of your cooperation, I'm prepared to try to explain to you all that I can. I warn you though; it won't be easy to accept or, for that matter, to express."

Pomorski snorted, and said, "A while ago a Dink with a rocket launcher was going to smoke us, had us dead to rights. Then we roll through a gray fog bank and we're in Fantasyland. I'll be real surprised if the explanation is anything *but* loony."

Van Duyn considered this. "Quite so," he decided. "Very well, I'll ask you not to interrupt until I've finished, and kindly to suspend your doubts for the duration of my story. If you find yourselves outraged from a commonsense standpoint, I suggest that you examine your surroundings; that should make you receptive."

Gil nodded. "You three stay at the guns," he told Woods, Handelman and Olivier, "and let us know if you can't hear what's being said. Mr. Van Duyn, the floor is yours."

Chapter Nine

What is now proved was once only imagin'd.
WILLIAM BLAKE

DESPITE his request, his story was subject to frequent interruptions for questions and comments. But as his quiet, composed voice continued, the Nine-Mob listened with grudging, growing credulity:

My name is Edward Van Duyn. I hold degrees in a number of fields, some earned and some honorary, but they are of little importance to me now, here, as they are part of a life I no longer wish to live. They are of no further use or interest to me.

You see, I come from the same Reality as you gentlemen do. But I had long since grown bored and frustrated with my existence before leaving there. I had fallen prey to ennui; never saw it coming or felt it arrive, but one day there it was.

I had essayed to do some teaching, but one must sort through so much gravel for the gems. And then what is their attitude? "Teach me; it's my right." I tell you, there is a surfeit of left-handed monkey wrenches in the world compared to the supply of worthwhile students.

So, I restricted my activities to pure research. It was for this reason that I accepted a position with the think-tank center called the Grossen Institute. I don't suppose you've heard of it? A foundation supported by sizable governmental and industrial endowments for abstract projects of scientific inquiry. I was not specializing in any one field. I was responsible, like several others, for "synthesizing," exploring correlations and interfaces between various areas of research.

About two years ago, I became interested in three studies being done at the Grossen. One was a rigorous

mathematical investigation of the theories of a plurality
of universes, another a new attack on the problem of
the relationship between perception, reality and the effect of altered expectations on perceptual reality. The
third was an attempt to establish new data on the basic
nature of matter-energy systems. I began to acquaint
myself with each of these endeavors and even began to
do a little independent study on my own. I began to see
parallels and correspondences in the three projects. I
conferred in detail with each team but didn't reveal the
dovetails I'd spotted, for as time went on I became
more and more certain that I'd come upon a major
breakthrough, perhaps unequaled in history.

Because of the rather relaxed administrative regime
at the Grossen, I wasn't interrupted. It's not unheard of
for Senior Consulting Fellows of the Institute to work
for years before presenting their findings with only
sketchy progress reports in the interim. In fact, that's
the only situation some of the better researchers will
stand for. Too, as a synthesist and a Senior Consultant,
I had unrestricted access to computer time and privacy.
I was even permitted to recruit a former student of
mine, no questions asked, to assist me. Actually the boy
was the only one I thought I could trust.

Things became unbelievably complex, forever evading us with one more unexpected factor. How many
times we hit dead ends I do not even remember, but it
never seemed to matter. We always knew that somehow
we would find an answer. And a disturbing thing happened in those days; I felt myself coming alive again for
the first time in years. It can be a bit traumatic, I assure
you, to feel your *vallum* of *tædium vitæ* slipping.

I am the scarred veteran of two divorces. I had become bored with the company of my colleagues and in-
tolerant of everyone else's. I found most of life's pleasures either empty or juvenile. Yet now there was this
desire awakening in me to make this project work, a
desire in no way connected with scientific kudos.

Making practical application of the findings I had
developed was more difficult than I can tell you; you'll
pardon me, I'm sure, but you simply don't have the vo-
cabulary. I built a device to permit access to the per-

haps infinite universes which coexist with our own—if, indeed, you and I are from precisely the same one. To put it another way, I had—hmm, let me see if I can put this in terms you can follow—yes, isolated a technique for translating the Reality of one cosmos into a form perceptible in another. Call it a kind of transportation if you will, or the creation of a contiguity between universes. That's no more or less accurate than calling it a translation.

The first model was rudimentary, a sort of framework which served as the contiguous point. I searched through a number of different universes, once with almost disastrous results, and never seeing any that looked at all inviting, until at last on a Friday evening I looked out at this one, at an empty field in Coramonde, this place where we are now. I don't remember actually stepping through the contiguity. All at once I was standing on the other side, my hands in my pockets and my cigar still in my teeth. The breeze that came up was . . . intoxicating. I felt full and at peace for the first time in years. In the distance I could see a small village, lit by torches and candlelight. The air was clean, with no hint of city or machine. In a way I cannot explain, it was as if I'd come home.

When I returned, my assistant, nearly hysterical, was plucking up the courage to come through after me, although he'd been able to watch me the entire time through the contiguity. He did not share my enthusiasm for exploration, for personal involvement in research.

But the few minutes I'd spent in Coramonde had changed me irrevocably. I had been given a last-minute reprieve from the barren life that I'd accumulated around myself. I had no one to consider; my ex-wives were well off and my children—a daughter by each marriage—thought even less of me than I did of them.

I monitored the contiguity for days, watched the shape and pace of life in Coramonde, and decided that it was for me—though it wasn't until later that I ran afoul of its rather exotic natural laws.

Of course, it was impossible to sneak the entire machine out of the Grossen, which was my first impulse; I didn't intend to enter another world and another life only to be followed in time by the people I'd come to despise. My world weariness had become a sort of spiritual impotence, yet here was the extraordinary chance to change my entire life, an out, and I didn't want to risk having it spoiled through the interference of others. So I compromised by removing two essential components from the contiguity apparatus and smuggling them out in my briefcase. I then destroyed all my notes and tapes, erased my computer runs from the banks and in general concealed my research as well as I could. I left the components I'd taken in the keeping of my assistant, who agreed to keep silence of a sort. In the meantime I was preparing a second contiguity generator at home; it is not as hard when you've conquered the basic problem of what it is you're building. The second-generation model was a platform which would transport itself along with its cargo. I equipped myself with a rifle and some gear and, four months after my first trip to Coramonde, left that world for good. I'd used up all the cash and credit I could lay my hands on in building the second apparatus, but what did I care? I've no intention of returning. If Coramonde begins to pall, well, I've universes waiting.

My preliminary experiences in this cosmos are not important at this time, but I met Andre and Gabrielle. Unfortunately, I took the contiguity generator to Earthfast—that is, when I met the local ruler and proposed some political revisions—and it was impounded when we were forced to take hurried departure. I believe Yardiff Bey—an agent of our enemy—has it now.

I know that all this seems like circumlocution, but I want you to see the full string of events that lead to your being here. Let me explain some things about reality here, to help you understand the situation. You're now in a place where phenomena that you might call magic are operational, and *usually* controllable. Laws of nature in this universe permit outrageous things like that air elemental that nearly toppled this APC. This is a world of conflict, and the beings who influence movements of—call it good and evil—are often active participants in the struggle.

How shall I tell you about our enemy? I'm afraid it'll

be a bit simplistic-sounding. We're menaced by a, a *force*, if you will, directing uncounted servants and driven by a monomaniacal urge to dominate everything, *everything* in creation. Hard to accept? Oh, yes, quite. Well, gentlemen, here's one that's harder, albeit closer to home: tomorrow at dawn our enemy is sending a dragon to destroy us here in this castle."

The Nine-Mob's declarations of disbelief tumbled over each other, but Gil was thinking about a miniature tornado that had almost turned their thirteen-ton APC over on command. Van Duyn continued.

"My friends and I invoked a being from the spiritual plane to open a way between worlds and bring you to us. We've no adequate way to defend ourselves, but yours should prove effective enough."

Pomorski leaned forward, eyes narrowing. "Even if what you say is true—and I don't concede it by a long shot!—why shouldn't we *make* you send us back right now?"

Van Duyn's eyebrows arched.

"So homesick already, even if only to return to a war, Mr. Pomorski? As to your question: transitions, summonings, invocations and things like your being brought here and sent back again are governed by, among other things, astrological configurations. Just as the dragon cannot come before tomorrow, we can't send you back before tomorrow evening. If we're still alive, that is.

"This means that, help us or no, you'll be here with us when he comes. And if he destroys this castle, I doubt very seriously if you'll find anyone in this world both willing and able to send you home. But if you'll use your weapons to fend off Chaffinch or kill him, we'll return you to the selfsame point in space and time from which we summoned you."

Gil slouched back, stiff from sitting hunched over on the low bench. Even with the cargo hatch open, the APC was uncomfortably warm.

"We've got no reason to get our tails mangled for you," he said, "and none of this has anything to do with us."

"Nonetheless, you're here."

The sergeant bridled but checked his anger, and took

a ballot by eye; Olivier and Handelman nodded, Pomorski and Woods shrugged.

A tie.

"All right," Gil told Van Duyn, casting the deciding vote himself. "If there *is* a dragon, we'll grease it for you; but I'm goddamned if I know how I'm going to explain this later."

Van Duyn pretended to think for a moment, though he already knew what he would say to them.

"Since you will be returned to the point from which you were taken, may I suggest that you simply say nothing? You won't be believed anyway."

Pomorski nodded. "Good thinking there. The best we'd get if we opened our mouths is a two-oh-eight discharge for the Jungle Jitters and maybe a stay in the upholstered ward."

Gil, who'd shifted from decision-making to practical details of the problem at hand, said, "Look, exactly what is this dragon—Chaffinch, you called it? What's it like, anyway?"

It was only afterward that the Nine-Mob realized how easily they'd gone from incredulity and suspicion to the problem-solving attitude. Pomorski and Gil, speculating later, thought that the nature of the spell that had drawn them there for that one purpose had perhaps predisposed them to accept their mission with minimal objections.

But they were never quite sure. Hadn't their actions been logical, rational under the circumstances? What, if anything else, could they have done at the time?

Van Duyn peered through thick glasses, down his long nose, in a manner that had intimidated even seasoned graduate students.

"Chaffinch he is indeed called, after the little red-breasted songbird. But it's a grim sort of joke, because his breast is the red of scaly, almost metallic armor, and his song's a song of flame. Andre's given me a, ah, 'ball-park guess,' I think you would call it, that Chaffinch is on the order of fifty feet long, nose to tail.

"And he's winged, flies quite well I understand, against all aerodynamic laws. But the most dangerous thing about him is that he's a fire breather. In fact, I had something a little more formidable than this armored personnel carrier in mind when we began our invocation. I was, perhaps, a bit hazy in my phraseology when I described my desire to Andre, or again it may be that the entity we summoned was unable to make distinctions. I'd wanted a tank or large piece of self-propelled artillery."

Lobo's crew went hostile, and Van Duyn perceived that he'd made some sort of subtle gaffe.

"So we're not a goddamned tank," Handelman allowed, "but we go like a japed ape, and three machine guns and the grenade launcher are pretty heavy clout."

"Of course, Mr. Handelman" Van Duyn soothed quickly. Were these kids that sensitive about this rattle-trap? "It's probably just that I don't know enough about, er, *Lobo* to appreciate her."

They invited him to poke his head through the big cargo hatch and take a look. Gil had Woods traverse the cupola and pass the end of the .50 ammunition belt to Van Duyn. The older man had seen .50-caliber ball ammo in World War II, but forgotten its size and weight.

"Couple hundred rounds per minute," said Gil MacDonald, "at three thousand feet per second. We're more than enough to bump noses with anything alive, be it a dragon, reluctant or otherwise."

He passed the end of the belt back. "But this is screwy. I mean, what else do you know about this lizard?"

Van Duyn thought for a moment.

"To begin with, he seems to store a reservoir of whatever heat source he uses, because it occurs to me that Andre said he's been known to exhaust it from a time after prolonged use. Could be it's something like the mythical phlogiston, I suppose. I'd imagine he distills it within himself. Also, he's been placated at times with the offer of a sacrifice, usually a young woman. This time, though, he'll not be put off by such an offering, even if we were so vile as to make it, which we most assuredly aren't."

Gil hitched himself up on the cargo hatch and sat,

chin on fist and elbow on thigh, swinging his feet ab-
sentmindedly like a kid on a sofa.

*Okay, suppose this beastie shows up; allow yourself
that much for the sake of argument. How do we fight
it? Like it was a plane, maybe? Like it was a flame-
thrower? Or, with all that fiery stuff inside him, maybe
he's a bit more like a fuel depot. If we can just cancel
that torch, it'll be a simple matter of target practice
and we'll have the world's biggest snakeskin hatband.
But—whoops! Ah, yep.*

"Got an idea" he said, and the Nine-Mob drew
closer.

After Van Duyn had been taken into the metal war
carriage that was crouched in the courtyard, Springbuck
and the deCourteneys retired to the ramparts to keep
watch on both *Lobo* and the encircling countryside.

The majority of the little group, save the women at
the cooking fires and the men at the bartizan, had
ringed in the APC at a distance.

Springbuck and Andre speculated on this and that aspect of the APC and its crew. Gabrielle, on the other
hand, was distracted and ill at ease, peering for long
moments in the direction of Erub.

She suddenly cried out, a cry that was half a sob. The
other two turned at this unaccustomed and unexpected
show of emotion and saw that parts of the village were
in flames.

Gabrielle whirled and pushed past her brother and
the Prince, striding off in the direction of the main hall.
As they watched her go, Springbuck observed to Andre
that there were many differences between the thaumaturge and his sister.

"My half sister," Andre corrected him, "for her father was not mine, though both of us use his name, one
that traces back to the time of the Great Blow, when the
whole world was in upheaval.

"Hasn't it occurred to you how odd my surname
sounds? Its origins go outside of this cosmos, and the
first man in my family to bear it came into this plane if
tradition is to be believed, back during that time of rifts

in the fabric of the universe and rents in the cloth of reality."

He looked at the young nobleman, pondering whether there was call for further speech. And, knowing his sister as well as anyone could, he concluded that there was, and went on.

"My mother—our mother—is a sorceress and an aristocrat of Glyffa, an enchantress of surpassing power. Her husband, my father, was a lesser mage, and, though there were strong ties of love between them, he was always conscious of the fact that of the two he was the minor magician and she the sorceress paramount.

"He became resigned to this in later years, but in the beginning of their marriage he sought in many ways to increase his power in order to become his wife's equal at sorcery, or perhaps her superior.

"How is it thus so often between men and women otherwise in love? I cannot speak to this beyond the observation that it simply is. Wife or husband resents the spouse's fame, knowledge, authority or beauty, reputation or might. Love waxes cancerous with jealousy and often malignant with ambition. My father grew bitter at length that his skill and acclaim were only a fragment of hers.

"I know only the bare details, how after a particularly heated argument he committed himself to an infernal compact, promising in the flush of anger to pay any price for his own aggrandizement. But any supernatural contract is suspect, my friend, and since his did not specify permanance, my father's prepotency lasted for the space of a night and a day only. But he had to concede that the contract had been fulfilled. The payment demanded was the opportunity to . . . to beget in my mother a child. Though she wept unconsolably, that great lady submitted, against the forfeiture of her husband's soul. Ha, does your lip curl with contempt, young Pretender, for such a man as would yield to that? Save your opinion until, as I have, you look upon Hell and see with what choice he was faced.

"But the union, if such it may be termed, proved fertile. It became evident thereafter that my mother had conceived. The fruition of it was my sister, born of enchantress and incubus. I was born years later, child of a normal union between my parents.

"Gabrielle and I have become parts of a greater whole. She is a repository of sheer elemental force, occult energy, but her control is erratic and she has a savage, yes and vicious, side which she must hold constantly in check. I am the stable one; I find that I am talented in the delicate ordination of our arts.

"My sister never harbored partisanship one way or the other in the struggle in which we have fought for so many years; she adhered to the side of Right, I think, more because it was the side I chose than for any reasons altruistic. I am the one dependable thing in her life. There was only one other human being to whom she was ever truly attached outside of our parents, a knight-errant, a proud, penniless member of the high lineage which produced Balagon of the Brotherhood of the Bright Lady. This knight was everything Gabrielle was not, a trifle naive, idealistic, patient, without guile and of an even temperament. She was attracted to him but fought, oh, wildly against her own emotions. In the end she adored him, practically worshiped him, and he her.

"They were wed and she bore him a child, a daughter, perhaps two years before the second coagmentation was essayed. That was the only time, I think, when she was truly happy, but it was all too brief. Her husband was killed and an attempt made on the child's life, by Yardiff Bey's agents, I'm sure. And that was strange; though Bey and I have contrived against one another for years, that is the only onset he has ever made at Gabrielle. Indeed, the one most dedicated to her undoing is Bey's chief rival for infernal favor, the ice witch Mara.

"But with the death of her husband, Gabrielle's become the Infernality's most implacable enemy. No mercy or compassion does she show, and she never curbs her hatred of Bey and his works. Yet he has always avoided a confrontation with her and I think that, in some way which is not clear, he is vulnerable to her. The reason I have told you all of this, my Prince—ah, you wondered?—is because I see my sister becoming attracted to you, and you to her. Yes, yes, deny it not. But it is important that you know what sort of person Gabrielle is. She is subject to cruel whims, she is often selfish and aloof. She is also a vessel of power, the greatest sorceress of the age, and those in her presence are well advised to be careful; her anger can shake the earth itself. I was happy when she became interested in Edward Van Duyn, with his experience and maturity to draw upon. But now her fancy has wandered to you, and yet am I unsurprised; I doubt if she will ever again restrict herself to one man. If your association with her prove emotional, I beg you, be circumspect. You are dealing with a woman unlike any other in the world."

They stood looking out upon the fires drifting up from Erub as the sounds of argument and disputation reached them from *Lobo*.

"You know," said the Prince, "I think that this is the first time that a town has been put to the torch in Coramonde in fifty years and more. Why is Gabrielle so upset about it, though?"

Andre pursed his lips for a moment before answering. "As I told you, there was an issue from her marriage, a girl-child. In order to ward off any further attempts on the girl's life, Gabrielle sent her away. It was with her that my sister stayed during the battle in town yesterday, for my niece is now a healer in that place and has been for many years. And it is for her daughter's safety that my sister is distressed. So far, they have only burned a few houses, but Gabrielle is afraid the villagers will be put to the sword, though we did not think that the troops would bother with Erub once we had left. It was to keep the girl safe that Gabrielle forbade her to join us in the castle."

They turned their conversation away from these things to talk of Chaffinch and of the strangers and their machine. Dusk came on and Erub began to glow before they saw Van Duyn emerge from the rear hatch of the APC. The two went down from the bartizan to meet him, and Springbuck considered, as he walked on, the peculiarity of the fact that he felt so much more familiar and at ease with Andre deCourteney, whose abilities and skills were intimidating, than he was with

Van Duyn, who was by comparison not that many years older than the Prince, and a common mortal.

"They will help us," Van Duyn said when they'd joined him. "They are still a bit dubious but they understand that we are in trouble and need their help, and that they can't get home without us, and that's enough for them. That sergeant is an unusual chap. Oh, and I told them we'd send out some food and something to drink. I guess they're pretty tired of canned rations. Where's Gabrielle?"

But they couldn't find her, not in her small room nor anywhere inside the castle walls. Andre and Van Duyn looked one at the other.

"Erub. She's gone to fetch back Foraingay," said the magician.

"Foraingay?" Springbuck asked.

"Her daughter. She must have decided to try to bring her to the castle. If my sister chooses to slip away, there are few who could detect her going and none who could stop her if they did."

"But, is she in danger?" the Prince persisted anxiously, and Van Duyn's mouth grew rigid at the tone that was in his voice. "I mean, she is the most competent of sorceresses, is she not?"

"Yes, she is expert," Andre answered. "But a spell is not something that you can carry ready in your hand like a bow or spear. In time that is consumed in calling down a helpful spell, some rustic can stick a pitchfork or a hatchet into you. That is part of the reason I carry this." He slapped the big sword at his side.

His agitation growing, Van Duyn interrupted. "We've got to go and get her. There's no way of knowing what may have happened to her already. I'll get our horses. We'd better make it a small band, Andre. You and I." He looked at the Prince and said as if against his better judgment, "And Springbuck."

Surprisingly, deCourteney said, "No, Edward. I don't think that you have reasoned out the best way of doing this thing. If we must go into the middle of an enemy force, why not do it in our guests' machine and improve our chances of coming back?"

Van Duyn looked at *Lobo,* just as Gil was changing

places behind the .50 with Woods. "Very well then."
the scholar decided. "I'll try to get them to agree to it.
I'll explain that we can't send them back unless we can
return with Gabrielle."

"Speak with them," answered Andre, "but do not tell
them that. We don't know what they might do if they
knew their true peril. And I cannot go with you; if I
leave, Ibn-al-Yed is sure to use the occasion to devas-
tate the castle with some spell or other. Springbuck, you
and Edward must get my sister back without my help."

The Prince could see that Andre's impulses were
bringing terrific pressure to bear on the man, conflict-
ing leverages to safeguard those who depended on him
and rescue his sister. Springbuck hesitated only an instant before answering with a heartiness he did not feel.
"Don't worry, Andre; we'll clank down there and be
back with her in minutes."

The wizard gave him an unconvincing smile and, not
knowing what else to say, Springbuck dashed off to
Lobo.

Chapter Ten

War is delightful to those who have no experience in it.

DESIDERIUS ERASMUS

WHEN Springbuck reached the APC a very angry Sergeant MacDonald was confronting a red-faced Van Duyn.

"Okay, okay," said the soldier. "We'll go look for her but we aren't taking you with us. Thing is, I run *Lobo* and I don't like people who try to tell me how to do it, and you're just a leetle bit too inclined in that direction, so you stay here. We'll take the kid there." He gestured to the Prince. "And we'll park outside the village. Then whatsisname and I, Springbuck, will do one, repeat, one fast dismounted scout. If we don't find the woman, tough rocks; we're not sticking around."

Van Duyn opened his mouth to protest but closed it again at the set expression on the soldier's face. "Agreed," he said, though there was that in his features which conveyed his fury well enough.

Springbuck was hustled into the track, his sword hilt catching on the narrow rear hatch. The other crew members, already at their stations, gave him one cursory glance before turning their attention to their trade. He studied the sinister-looking black M-60 machine guns with interest and started when the big engine howled to life. A rapid, persistent vibration made the entire APC quiver. The two side gunners were nervously checking belts of linked ammunition in feeder trays as Pomorski leaned closer and shouted into his ear to be heard over the engine. "Stand up front there and hang on with both hands. Just stay out of our way."

The gates were thrown open and the Prince thrilled

91

as the APC lurched ahead. He shouted to Pomorski, "Where is Sergeant MacDonald?"

"He's ground-guiding us across the bridge, since we're still in friendly territory. I think."

Once they'd passed slowly and carefully over the drawbridge, Gil came swarming up over the front of the track and lowered himself behind the .50 caliber. *Lobo* accelerated and Springbuck found himself bouncing along through the gathering darkness, fighting to keep his balance in the swaying machine. Too late, he remembered his war mask, still back at the castle. He shrugged, thinking that it would have been a bother in these cramped quarters anyway, and concentrated on appreciating this singular ride.

The early evening moon was quite bright as they hurtled down the meadow, and the Prince wondered if the noise of their approach wouldn't alert the enemy in Erub. *Lobo* slowed until it merely crawled along. The vibrations coming through his boot soles made Springbuck's feet itch, but he quickly forgot about it. When the track had come to a stop and its engine fell quiet, he could hear, in the new silence, cries, shouts, screams and curses. Evidently, the Erubites had decided in their desperation to fight back at the ravaging troops.

"With all the racket, I don't think they've noticed us," Gil said. "We're still over half a mile out and we came in without even blackout lights. Springbuck and I will go in and look around. You guys stay put in this gully unless you hear shooting, in which case I would be deeply grateful if you'd come and inquire after our health."

"Why don't we just take the track in?" Handelman wanted to know.

Gil, removing his headset and helmet, shook his head. "I don't like the way that town looks—narrow streets and more likely than not all twists and turns. I don't want to chance getting *Lobo* stuck or lost. Besides, don't you think we'd attract attention?"

He slung Shorty over his shoulder. The son of Surehand followed him over the side of the APC and jumped down next to him in the sand of the gully. They set off toward Erub, the open terrain making the sergeant ill at ease, a swipe of memory from his days in Recon.

"Where do you think she'll go?" he asked Springbuck.

"It would be the healer's house, in the very center of town," was the considered reply.

"Swell-oh."

They went on for a time and, when they were closer to the edge of Erub, stopped behind a tree to study it. Gil took a strip of camouflage cloth out of his pocket and tied it around his forehead to keep hair and perspiration out of his eyes and cut any telltale gleam in the darkness. Then he remembered that his companion wore gleaming leathers and had large areas of light, exposed skin and shiny metal. Too late to rectify that now.

The fighting seemed to be concentrated in the other end of the village. The two entered the fringes of town undetected, shadowed against walls by the fires that had been set there. They occasionally saw bodies lying dead or injured in the streets, most of them civilians showing sword cuts or lance wounds. Women bore signs of abuse and at least one child had been ferociously mistreated. Gil said nothing, but his face was filled with revulsion and anger, and the Prince's was not good to look upon in its loathing.

They moved cautiously toward the center of the village. Weaving in and out of doorways, ducking into alleys, they encountered no other living thing until they stood at the brink of the plaza. Springbuck found it hard to believe that the battle which seemed to him now to be so long past had transpired here only the preceding afternoon.

Gil, for his part, reflected on the impossibility of the scene and his predicament. But, as in his encounter with Neezolo Peeno, the order of precedence drilled into him took over—first, survival; watch your tail and do the job, son; introspection later; one thing at a time, or you'll never live long enough to get anything done.

"There," said his companion, pointing to a two-story house bordering the square. Two horses were hitched in front of it. "That is the house of Gabrielle's daughter, as

Andre described it to me. It is almost certain that there are soldiers in it. Whether or not she will be, I cannot say."

They were at the walls of the house in one dash; Gil could see no reason to make their approach by the numbers since the other could not provide cover fire for him. Perhaps he should have brought Pomorski, but he hadn't wanted to leave the track any more under-manned than was absolutely necessary.

He leaned up and peered over the sill of a low, opened window. He could see no one within and drew back down to think for a moment.

"Now we go in. I'll take the downstairs and you check upstairs. If anything happens I yell and you move out—and you do it right away, read me? Good. Your redhead is probably on the second floor if she's here at all, so look it over tight, but don't take all night doing it."

The Prince nodded, irritated by all this ordering, but a curious little spark of pleasure ran through him with the words "your redhead."

The American settled his belt and shifted on his haunches. He said, "Right." Then he was up and on his way. Springbuck followed once again wondering if the single word had been a mere signal or the other's war cry.

Gil swung the door open and covered the empty room, a large kitchen-living-dining space. The Prince went up the rickety wooden stairs three at a time as Gil started to search the rest of the house. The sergeant was about to go into a room at the back of the building when he nearly ran into a cavalryman coming the oppo-site way.

It may have been that the man had heard him coming and was waiting for him; he jumped out and almost caught Gil on his spear. The American dodged back-wards desperately, the quarters too close to get off a shot, but the spearblade slid along his side, slicing open his flak jacket. Somehow, it hooked in the submachine gun sling; as the man brought his weapon up sharply, the chopper was torn from Gil's grasp and sailed across the room.

The cavalryman yelled a warning to some unseen companion but did not take his eyes from the business at hand, which was Gil.

The business at hand dropped into a defensive crouch. He didn't realize it at the time, but he was lucky; his opponent hadn't carried his sword when he'd dismounted. When the next thrust came, Gil did the only thing he could think of; he took it on with tactics dictated by the manual on combatives against a rifle bayonet: block with the forearm—he got sliced doing it; a deep, oblique step with both hands on the foeman's weapon, turn and twist—and he was honestly surprised when his antagonist went flying past him. The other was no slouch, however, as Gil found out. He was on his feet with a bounce, a long dirk in his hand.

The sergeant shifted his grip on the spear and jumped in close, swinging at the man as if he held a baseball bat. The other ducked as the spear whistled over his head and cracked against the wall beside him and retaliated with a vicious slash. Again the American barely avoided the disembowling stroke. The spear's head and a full third of its shaft had broken off. Gil threw the stump at his foe and reached around with his right hand, snatching out his survival knife from the back of his belt, and went on guard. He would have tried for the chopper but doubted that he could get to it before he was stabbed; the other might not know what the submachine gun was, but he wouldn't let such an opening go unexploited.

The man's armor and helmet gave him a tremendous advantage in the fight, even allowing for Gil's flak jacket. Too, knife-fighting is an ignored art in the U.S. Army. But one of Gil's training cadremen had been a Ranger who, loathing the flashy, impractical street styles, insisted his men learn the proper handling of edged steel.

Gil attacked his opponent in a forward crouch, sidling and crow-hopping, knife held close to his side in a fencing grip, left hand extended to block and parry, knees bent and stomach clenched back, left foot foremost. It discomforted him when his enemy took approximately the same position—a knowledgeable antagonist.

Gil closed watchfully, alert for an opening and keeping in mind the twin objectives of speed and aggressiveness. The two circled, making feints and hand cuts, each careful that he wasn't backed into a corner. Gil was beginning to wonder if an opening would present itself, if he would be able to deal with this horse trooper, when a thumping ruckus reached his ears and he realized that it had been going on for some time. He let his eyes stray to the stairs, for the commotion was coming from the second floor, and in that instant the other made his move.

It was dangerous, expert; a swift, upward thrust, a snapping try for the soft abdomen; and the American didn't know if his fiberglass flak jacket would have stopped it or not. He blocked instinctively with the outward edge of his left hand and forearm, twisting to the right and using a poised left leg karate-style as a backup. The hand block missed—the gash he'd caught from the spear was bleeding badly now, slowing his left-hand moves; but the forearm connected with the other's wrist and arrested the thrust. Gil delivered a simultaneous knife chop to the cavalryman's left wrist, opening it to the bone and rendering it useless. Though the wound was far from lethal, the pain and shock put the man off balance. The American followed up instantly by driving the heel of his left hand up hard beneath his enemy's nose, a deathblow. It was only later that he learned that many helmets featured nasal guards which would have made his move ineffective.

As the armored man reeled backward with a moan, Gil pursued him with a slash to the stomach to make sure; the only dead enemy was one you could stomp your foot on. But hauberk turned the knife and the sergeant stood over the body, wondering if it were dead and for what reason he'd had to kill.

A wailing horn brought him out of his unaccustomedly careless inattention. He spun to confront another dragoon. There was no question of being able to say alive with a knife any longer. Gil backed to the wall where the submachine gun lay. He dropped his blade and had Shorty in his hands before the knife hit the floor. The first burst caught the dragoon in the midsection and folded him up like a cot.

Gil sprang to the foot of the stairs and called, "Springbuck! God's sake, let's go!"

While the outlander engaged the guard on the first floor, the Prince dashed up the stairs, grabbing for the hilt of his sword. He reached the landing with Bar and his parrying dagger ready. A commander of cavalry, a full-ranked rittmaster, had been standing guard, waiting with a broad-bladed rapier in hand.

Springbuck engaged him and the rittmaster proved to be a marvelous swordsman, lithe as an otter and strong of wrist. Their blades wove and danced, contested for right-of-way and warded each other in a dialogue of light and ringing metal. The Prince remembered little of the match, worried as he was about Gabrielle. Overturned furniture, shouts and curses mixed with an appallingly fast interplay of points which left Springbuck's left leg bleeding; all these things were confused. But the rittmaster bore only his rapier, and so, inevitably, Springbuck blocked with his parrying dagger and found clear way for Bar. Once again the strange blade bit flesh with a preternatural keenness, cleaving muscle and tissue as if they were custard.

He seized a handful of the dying man's tabard and pulled his face close. "Where is Gabrielle deCourteney?" he demanded.

"Gone with Ibn-al-Yed, who left me here to do you murder, my Prince, and I have failed. Well fought, sir, though if you'd been without your main-gauche this day, I wonder—" And the rittmaster died.

The victor was suddenly aware that a female corpse reposed on the bed. The dead woman was perhaps thirty, with graying temples and a peaceful face which held lines of laughter and kindness. Her throat had been slit. He stared down at her for a moment, knowing that this must be Gabrielle's daughter Foraingay, and was brought anew to awareness of the enchantress's age. Then there was a burst of gunfire, and he heard Gil's yell. "Springbuck! God's sake, let's go!"

He wasn't sure which god the other was calling upon, but complied at once.

Gil met him at the bottom of the stairs, his knife returned to its sheath and weapon cradled nervously. He looked at the Prince, who was grim-faced, with his sword covered with blood, and whistled softly. "Find her?" Springbuck shook his head. "Me either," Gil admitted. "C'mon."

They plunged into the street and were off the square when the dragoons, drawn by the horn and the submachine gun blast, charged into it from the opposite side. They ran furiously toward the corner nearest them, from which the sergeant sprayed the remainder of his magazine and fought a fresh one into the weapon while he ran. A roaring came to his ears but he lacked the time to identify it. They raced around another corner, screaming cavalrymen closing on them rapidly despite the gunfire. Springbuck knocked Gil to one side as an arrow zipped into the rutted dirt street. Gil spotted the archer on a nearby rooftop and stopped long enough to shoot him.

"Listen!" shouted the Prince. Without giving the sergeant a chance to, Springbuck dragged him off at right angles to their previous course. They skidded to a stop as they beheld *Lobo* bearing down on them, source of the roaring. Woods pulled APC to a stop as Pomorski leaned over the .50 cupola and deadpanned, "Want a good time, sailor boy?"

"Run!" Gil bellowed, shoving Springbuck forward. He then spun and bracketed the fast-approaching cavalry in his sight blades and emptied the full magazine, pitching men and mounts to the ground in agony, and jumped for the track. He got a helping hand from Olivier as Woods slewed *Lobo* broadside in the cramped street and Pomorski and Handelman opened fire. Gil spotted the grenade launcher on the floor of the APC, grabbed it and let fly a round at the massed riders. He missed; the flip sights had been set for much longer range.

After seconds of withering fire the terrified dragoons withdrew in a rout. They'd had the APC explained to them by Ibn-al-Yed as a mere machine, but this was nothing that they could cope with. Gil and Pomorski tried to talk coherently as Woods headed the track back toward the castle. They'd barely left Erub when Olivier barked, "Here they come again."

Gil could never figure out how anyone could convince those men to face *Lobo* again, but evidently someone had done so. In fact, there were over a hundred men coming breakneck after them. Without instructions, Woods veered Alpha-Nine to the right.

"Where's he going?" Gil shouted.

"Don't squawk," Pomorski cut in. "When you left, we set up a surprise, then came in after you. We can shake those cowboys and then head back to the castle."

Gil decided to shut his mouth and let the Nine-Mob run things. They dipped into the gully with a bone-wrenching jar and came to a stop in a spray of sand. There was a large oak tree growing by the village side of the gully, and Pomorski jumped down and ran to crouch behind it. "Everybody down," he called, and they all pulled their heads back inside the APC. Seconds later there was a deafening explosion and Gil knew that his men had set up a claymore mine. The detonation had sent seven hundred steel balls screaming through a sixty-degree arc. None of the pursuers had been within the fifty meters or so wherein they would have been cut to shreds, but many, both of the men and beasts, were wounded and possibly dead. Gil thought about the destruction back in Erub and could feel pity only for the horses. Those of the dragoons still able to do so fled.

Pomorski returned. As Gil and Springbuck put dressing on their wounds, there was a good deal of *whew*ing and quiet chatter. "You even managed to bring Junior back with you," Handelman laughed, but the sergeant reached over and partially drew Bar from its sheath. It was still covered nearly to the hilt with the rittmaster's lifeblood, and they were all silent when they saw it.

"He does pretty good by himself," was the only comment Gil made. They looked at Surehand's son with new respect, and he in turn felt closer to them, initiated to their peculiar brotherhood by violence, thinking that this Nine-Mob was close as people are only in war, joined by necessity or force through laughter, tears, death.

They went on, rocking and swaying as the APC climbed back up in the meadow. They did not bother to ground-guide. Before Woods had even cut the engine, Van Duyn was at the rear hatch. He and Andre did not have to look within, though, for the expression on Springbuck's face as he emerged told them that Gabrielle had not been found.

In halting words the Prince told what had happened. The dumpy Andre looked close to crying and Van Duyn's mouth became a straight, bloodless gash in his face.

"I will consult the auguries," the magician said tiredly at last, "to see if I can perceive whither they have taken her."

The Prince sat on the cobblestones, brief laughter forgotten, head buried against his knees, despairing at his failure. The scholar just stared angrily into the night sky. The Nine-Mob looked from one to the other.

"You're all very welcome," said Gil MacDonald.

Chapter Eleven

The civilized man is a more experienced and wiser savage.

HENRY THOREAU,
Walden

DAWN came chilly and clear with Gil checking the ammo belt in its tray and trying to ignore Pomorski.

"Explain it again, MacDonald," the grenadier persisted. "Why am *I* the Lucky Pierre who gets to bell the cat?"

Gil, exasperated, said, "Look, if you don't think you can do it, don't. You're the fastest sprinter in the Nine-Mob and I'm the best fifty gunner, but I'll change off with you if you want."

"Do it?" snapped Pomorski, his nonvolunteer image saved here by chance for indignation. "Do it? I could do this number with my boot in a bedpan and my butt in a cane chair, even supposing this thingie shows. You just make sure you hit what you're aiming at, MacDonald, and nothing else."

"I'm betting this dragon or whatever doesn't come," Woods commented. "Nobody's even seen it. Primitive superstition."

Springbuck, seated on an interior bench studying *Lobo* and doing his best to stay out of their way, said, "I think there will be a dragon, since Andre says there will be. I only wish I could go with you; it's a man's place to fight his foes, not watch others do it."

Gil shook his head. "Thanks for the offer, pal, but you'd be in our way." He waved his arm around the cramped track. "You see how limited we are for guest rooms. I mean, we'd take you if you could drive or shoot or something, but from what you told us about

101

your stepmother and what-all, you'll have plenty of hassling left to do after we finish this little job and leave."

"Hey, riddle me this," Olivier said. "How come we can speak to you people and you can understand us? Why do you speak our lingo?"

Gil would have echoed the question, but found that he couldn't quite frame the word for his native language, as if it wouldn't come into focus in his mind.

The Prince shrugged and answered, "Van Duyn says it's the translational effect; when you were brought here, an adaptational shift occurred. That's all he'll say."

"Bet he doesn't know, either."

"Mayhap not, but you and he speak the common tongue of Coramonde as well as I—with your own, um, personal nuances, that is."

Van Duyn's voice came from outside. "Sergeant, it's time." He stuck his head in the rear hatch. "Chaffinch will have been conjured by now, beyond our means to interfere, and he's on his way."

"Let me ground-guide," Springbuck offered. "I can at least do that."

Gil nodded. The grass smelled fresh and sharp as *Lobo*'s foot-wide treads crushed endless paths through the dew and Gil craned his head to watch the castle gates swing to. They picked their spot near a stand of silver birch trees and took up watch. Their antagonist wasn't long in coming, with a slow, distant gale of enormous wings. He came from the west, where Yardiff Bey had conjured him, and they could see him well, high in the morning sun.

He was fully the fifty feet promised and more. Gil couldn't see how Chaffinch, even with his impressive wingspan, could stay aloft. The dragon's powerful claws were curled up close to his belly and his head swung this way and that in search, some enigmatic instinct of predation dictating his course. His armored hide shone with many colors, green predominant, with a broad splotch of brightest crimson along the underbelly.

"Let's get at it." It was Pomorski who had spoken. His words roused them all from a paralysis, and *Lobo* was off again, rolling forward a short distance. Woods

reached back and up with his right hand and worked
the lever to lower the rear ramp. Chaffinch noticed the
movement and banked ominously toward the track to
see what strange thing it might be, though he was unworried that it might be dangerous to him. Was he not
Chaffinch?

At that moment a figure all in white was flung out of
the rear of the APC. Gauzy veils and robes swirled as it
hit the ground and lay stunned in a quivering heap.
Lobo was instantly in motion, describing a tight circle
around the body in white, then drawing back to a position closer to the trees. Chaffinch's baleful eye swung to
the lone form in the center of the circles left in the dew
by the track's treads.

"Let's hope," breathed Gil, "the big mother doesn't
gulp his meals without sizing them up." His thumb hovered nervously over the butterfly trigger of the machine
gun.

The dragon spiraled lower, regarding with reptilian
glee the foolish offered sacrifice. He didn't particularly
care whether she was a virgin or not; he had been without mortal flesh for a tedious time now. First, he
thought greedily, a bite to eat, then the razing and ravaging of the other contemptibles in that ridiculous with-
ered husk of a castle.

He landed, poised almost delicately on short, immensely strong legs and lazily approached the still form,
eyes glowing like green cinders and head weaving back
and forth hypnotically. He expanded his maw, opening
his jaws wide, preparing for a leisurely bite of his prey.

Then, instantly, the cringing figure was standing, Gabrielle's best robes and veils flung aside with one
brawny arm while the other cocked back like a loaded
catapult. Pomorski had pulled the pin from the white
phosphorus grenade he held when the monster had circled in. He'd released the spoon, the grip safety, as he
jumped to his feet. Now he let his trained body launch
the grenade with practiced accuracy, using all the seasoned muscle of his arm and shoulder. He regretted that
it couldn't be fired from the launcher like a fragmentation grenade, regretted it a great deal.

The small canister of the WP bulleted across the

seven yards separating man and dragon, landing true between the still-gaping jaws. Chaffinch recoiled in surprise, swallowing reflexively at the object wedged so uncomfortably in his throat. Pomorski, though, was not watching. The instant he'd released, he'd spun on his heel and dashed to the right, headed for *Lobo*, feet pistoning the ground and strides adrenalin-wide. His backup WP grenades slapped at his belt as he ran.

The monster had negotiated the bothersome thing in his craw before Pomorski had taken eight steps. What happened next depended on the big soldier's timing and aim, which were accurate, and the WP grenade, which went off. Detonating, it created 2500 degrees F. of blistering heat. The phlogiston-like substance in Chaffinch's fiery reservoir ignited, exploded. His neck went ramrod-stiff as his body shook with a cataclysmic spasm. A huge spear of malodorous flame gouted from his maw, licking out for a hundred feet. It was with this in mind that Pomorski had cut off at right angles to the creature's path, to avoid being fried. It was fortunate that he was already several yards away; he felt the heat scorch his back through his jungle fatigues but it only served to spur his now-frenzied speed. He zigzagged, giving Gil what he hoped fervently was a clear field of fire at the dragon in case the WP hadn't worked.

Which it hadn't, not completely. Gil had hoped to see the monster blown to bits or knocked out, but dragons have bellies like boilers, though the thing was dazed and almost certainly injured. Chaffinch raised his head and roared dreadfully, looking for the author of his hurt. He spied Pomorski's pounding figure. Chaffinch reared up, spreading his great wings and preparing to swoop after the soldier just as the man was far enough out of the way for Gil and Handelman to open fire. They aimed for the juncture of wing and body, bent on keeping the creature from getting into the air. Gil watched his tracers, corrected his elevation and was rewarded with sustained hits on the thing's right wing. Figuring one round of every six on the belt was a tracer, he estimated that at least eight of the heavy rounds had slammed on target there, piercing the gristle of the wing joint.

Then the monster began to thrash, his other wing

moving too fast to hit, his awesome bulk coming partway off the ground. Gil and Handelman were concentrating on the wounded pinion and shooting at the weaving head when Pomorski dove headlong through the still-open rear ramp, just over twelve seconds after standing up to confront Chaffinch. Woods hit the winch lever and the cable began to haul the one-ton ramp back into position.

The dragon was back on all four feet, his wings folded as far back as possible against his body. In a life even longer that that of most of his kind, he had never experienced such pain by the impudence and treachery of humans. He vowed to cook them alive but was prevented by the damaged condition of his throat and stomach. The bullets were still punching at his tender wing and bouncing from his armored body as he threw himself in a rush at the metal thing menacing him. With crocodilian speed he scuttled forward, head darting madly, an impossible target at the end of the sinuous neck.

Woods slammed *Lobo* into gear and the APC tore chunks from the ground as they jerked into motion, guns still hammering at the thing closing on them. Streams of hot brass empties and bits of linking flew from the machine-gun breeches. In a few seconds they were among the trees, dodging in an attempt to evade Chaffinch's first rush, pouring more fire at him. Pomorski was shoving round after round into the launcher and firing grenades as rapidly as he could. They continued to make hits, painful ones to the wings and ineffectual ones to the body. The .50 was the only weapon with sufficient force and weight to penetrate the thick scaly hide, and even it was not able to reach any vital organs. Chaffinch's head continued to elude their aim while the soft underside never presented itself.

When he reached the tree line Chaffinch barely slowed down. He was weakening but still a rampaging horror. He drove through the trees, simply shoving them aside, bending or breaking them, or crunching them under his claws. The trees farther in, though, were stouter, and his anger increased as he bulldozed his way with greater effort, occasionally snagging his injured wing painfully. The ground shook and the leaves trembled to the reverberations of his rage.

Lobo burst through the opposite side of the little wood seconds ahead of the pursuing dragon. All gun barrels were growing hot with the constant firing, and the Nine-Mob's best efforts had done little more than antagonize the ponderous monster behind them. *Might as well face him here,* Gil thought to himself, and ordered Woods to bring the APC around.

Lobo completed its turn just as Chaffinch broke through the last line of luckless trees. *My God, I never dreamed that he would be anything like this. So strong, so fast and big. We didn't know; we just couldn't have guessed.*

They were in motion, arcing away to the creature's right. Chaffinch turned his head and let fly a single lance of foul-smelling flame, weak and cool by his normal standards, but it licked at the right tread and washed across that side of the APC. Handelman howled in pain, flinging his arm to his face and falling to the deck. Pomorski leaped to the vacant machinegun, knowing that if he stopped to check Handelman none of them might survive. The monster's head reared like a cobra as he crossed in front of the track and struck at it just as Woods threw it into reverse. Chaffinch's head connected with the wooden trim vane, splintering it, the venom of his fangs etching the wood and peeling paint from the metal. He shook his ugly head, punished by an impact that had rocked *Lobo*. The trim vane, backed by armor, was a painful target even for him.

Woods yanked the transmission lever. Chaffinch crouched in front of them, head stationary for the first time in the bizarre battle. Gil fired a burst at the top of the cold, plated skull. Blood and hide and chips of bone flew as the dragon pulled his head down to get it out of the murderous torrent of bullets, until it nearly touched the ground.

"Keep going—run it down!"

As the APC shot forward, Woods deftly steered it into line with the thing's head. It happened so quickly that before they knew it they were lumbering unevenly, right tread elevated, as a grisly crunching sound, mixed with reptilian hisses, came from underneath the treads. Chaffinch's huge body convulsed, nearly upsetting *Lobo*, but they were off a split second later, continuing until they were out of range. While Pomorski looked after Handelman, Gil emptied dozens of rounds into the spasm-racked body. Then they sat and watched the death throes of a dragon, a being far older than any of them could imagine.

Chaffinch's tail was still twitching when Gil looked at his Seiko. Five minutes or so! Five minutes that had shattered his confidence in sanity and reason, myth and fact. A short episode that could make a permanant place for itself in his nightmares.

Then for the first time he considered what this creature would have done to the people in the castle.

As they rode back they spotted two men watching from a distant hill, a column of troops off to one side. Gil thought he recognized them as the ones from the preceding afternoon, the leaders of the cavalry and, in all probability, the bulk of their surviving force. As he watched, the two rejoined their men and the column moved off westward. The sergeant noticed that Erub was still smoking, and stuck his hand out to the withdrawing dragoons in the Sailor's Farewell.

The castle's inhabitants all waited at the gates. Van Duyn was unsmiling and contained, Andre somber and Springbuck was jumping high as he could and whirling his sword over his head and laughing. The thirty or so others were weeping, standing silently, rejoicing or offering prayer for this miracle, according to inclination. Many were aware that, without Gabrielle, these aliens were stranded.

It occurred to Gil that from a distance it might have looked easy; boom, pow, clank, crunch and a dying, twitching Chaffinch. But when they were inside the walls again they found that the Erubites could scarcely express their gratitude.

"Nothing really," Pomorski grinned to a girl who handed him a flower with timid grace. "Well within the talents of any archangel or running back." They all felt good, their relief and laughter growing as fear retreated.

While Andre looked after Handelman's burns, which weren't as serious as they'd first thought, they ate breakfast. Evidently the splash shield on which Handelman's M-60 was mounted had protected him from most of the flame, and his eyes weren't damaged. Andre applied several balms and salves.

"We saw the troops pulling out," Van Duyn said. "Ibn-al-Yed has long since departed. Thus the way is clear for escape eastward." Andre looked up from his ministrations. "So," the scholar continued, voice strangely tired, "no matter what happens, you men can flee with us to friendlier lands."

"Whoa-up right there," Gil broke in. "The arrangement, if you recall, was for you to send us back where we came from, which in itself isn't a peachy deal. What's this escape crap?"

Springbuck saw that Van Duyn intended to hedge around the subject and it struck him that these men deserved better.

"They cannot send you back without Gabrielle de-Courteney," he said. They all turned to face him. "If it should happen that you can never be returned, I shall make every effort to make amends to you," the Prince went on. "You shall be as Lords Paramount in my realm. But you are caught up in a struggle that is none of your doing and there is little that I can do for you now."

Gil ignored him. He was close to Van Duyn now, fists cocked, his face marred with hatred. "I don't care what's wrong," he snarled, and the scholar should have been observant enough to interpret the danger in his quavering voice, "but you're sending us back."

But the older man seemed distracted, unaware of the peril before him. "Back?" he replied as though in a dream. "Sorry, no. Not without her. Not without Gabrielle."

Gil cuffed him on the side of the head and got a cruel arm-bar on him, forcing him to his knees. Van Duyn cried out in pain and surprise as Andre and Springbuck looked on in bewilderment. Pomorski had his .45 out and Olivier snatched up Gil's submachine gun from where it rested against the wall next to him. The sergeant shifted the arm bar and took the automatic from Pomorski, placing its blunt muzzle up against his captive's temple.

The Prince and the magician moved to the defense of their friend. Both knew the deadliness of the outlanders' weapons but neither could watch Van Duyn come to harm and do nothing. A small part of Springbuck reflected on his change in attitude since he'd watched Hightower die at Earthfast. It was now better to risk death than live with the memory of cowardice and the knowledge that another had died through his failure.

Gil saw that the two wouldn't be stopped by the threat of guns. Andre was sweeping free his sword, almost involuntarily, while Pomorski blocked Springbuck's way. Gil thumbed back the hammer of the pistol and grated, "If you two move just one more step, I'll blow his brains all over the floor. I swear, boys. I've got nothing, absolutely nothing to lose."

Woods and Handelman were moving to cover the doors; both had their M-16s with them. Van Duyn was gasping in pain, wild-eyed with the .45 at his temple.

Deciding, Springbuck returned his sword to its scabbard with a clash. "Gil MacDonald," he said, "what he says is true. You cannot be sent back without Gabrielle's help. Oh, you might persuade Yardiff Bey to help you or steal Van Duyn's contiguity device back in Earthfast, but I doubt it. Your best chance is to help us recover Andre's sister."

The sergeant considered this. The panic that had prompted him to act was passing. He rather doubted his own ability to kill in cold blood anyway. He released Van Duyn and the older man fell away, nursing his arm just as Springbuck had eased his wrist when the scholar had humbled him the day before.

"Damn," said Gil, "sorry about that. All right, we need her; how do we find her? How do we get her back?"

The Prince responded, "There is a tie between Andre and Gabrielle, of magic and of blood. We know where she is even now."

"So? Spill it. She can't be too far away. We can go get her for you."

Andre's plump, unshaven face was a study in agony as he replied, "She's been taken to the place of Yardiff Bey's liege Lord, Amon."

Gil could only look puzzled.

"My sister has been taken to the Inferno, Gil Mac-Donald, to Hell, and from there we must free her if you are to return to your place and time."

"I want a cheap lawyer," Pomorski said.

The moment of confrontation was gone as quickly as it had come. They were now bound up by events to attempt the rescue of the enchantress. They didn't even bother to vote; they were without alternatives.

Chapter Twelve

Lo! Death has reared himself a throne
In a strange city lying alone
Far down within the dim West.

EDGAR ALLAN POE,
"The City in the Sea"

"HELL," sighed Springbuck, "what chance do we have to rescue her from the fires of the Pit?" They stood now in a circle around Andre.

The wizard's voice shook but there was conviction in it. "There are . . . defenses. Just as spirits of the Inferno may be injured or warded against here, they have vulnerabilities in their own sphere. We have Calundronius. We have Gil MacDonald and his men and their weapons. And there is *Lobo*."

"Only, how do you get to Hell?" the sergeant interrupted. "Short of dying, that is. I have no intention of getting scragged so we can visit among the shades. And while we're chewing it over, how do you know we can play Orpheus for your sister?"

"For the last question," Andre said, "I maintain, as I have said, a connection with my sister. She is not yet dead or I would know; nor will she be soon, I think. Dead, she is simply another wraith, but alive she is a well of ethereal force. I do not believe that Yardiff Bey or his Lord will claim her life, but they may well enslave her, unless we can get her away from them as soon as possible. This is the first time that Bey has struck at Gabrielle directly; he must be confident that she will be unable to give him fair battle while she's in his hands.

"What we will do is draw upon her enormous stores of power. I will harness her energy, make her call us to her. In tearing her from me, snatching her away bodily

111

to Hell, Bey has created an imbalance between the Terrestrial and Infernal planes. He will not be able to seal her away from me. He probably does not think that we would dare try to beard him in his master's den. She is yet whole; I can feel that she still possesses her full vitality. There is nothing holding her there aside from the physical restraints and sequestering spells engendered by Yardiff Bey. They haven't her soul yet."

He turned to Gil, whose jaw had been open for some time. "Do you have any more of those burning sunlets, the like of which good Pomorski threw down Chaffinch's throat?"

"White phosphorus grenades? Yeah, we have more."

Andre clapped his hands. "Good! When that one detonated, I perceived that the terrific heat and the particular energies it exuded were of a special sort. They resemble solar light and would probably be excruciatingly painful to our opposition."

Van Duyn stepped forward. "Then we'll go now. According to the altazimuth readings the stars will not be more favorable to this thing for days. I propose that we should leave on the moment."

Andred nodded. "We shall indeed go, Edward, but you will have to stay here. You will be our anchor, our guide and mainstay against a quick return from the Infernal realm."

The scholar incensed, stabbing his forefinger at the magician's paunch. "No, by God, Andre, I won't be shoved aside again. Dammit, I want to go to her."

"Who else," the soft question came, "can accomplish the task I have set you? I must go with them on this sortie to protect you and guide them insofar as I may. Of us all I am the only one who has made the trip before."

Van Duyn blew his breath out with a *whooosh*, his frown slackening, and turned from them to stand staring into the hearth.

Andre looked to the others. "Springbuck, you will come with us, for I think that somehow you have begun to play your part in the march of events. You must begin to assert yourself in the battle for ascendancy, particularly since much of it will revolve around the throne of the *Ku-Mor-Mai*. Sergeant, please look to your equipment; I shall begin inscribing a pentacle and the other requisite insignia around your vehicle. When I close them, we shall be on our way."

Andre deCourteney was no longer an amiable, comfortable man. All present, from the GI's used to command to the intractable Van Duyn, obeyed his orders without objection or hesitation. They adjourned to the courtyard with some of Andre's magical paraphernalia. He removed Calundronius from his neck and again placed it within the pommel of his sword, confining his mighty talisman but thus keeping it close to hand for need.

They evacuated all the other residents of the castle to the main hall, instructing them to bar the door; then Van Duyn was installed in a space traced around with colored dusts and powders. There he stood reading from an ancient tract as the Nine-Mob and Springbuck boarded *Lobo* and Andre began to delineate a far more intricate design around the APC. Time passed as he completed it with many an enchantment and much strange speech in unfamiliar tongues.

He turned and jumped through the rear hatch, light as a cat, and stood in the very center of the deck, stooped forward with his eyes shut. He continued to chant and the Nine-Mob watched agape as a blue glow began to emanate from his body. Springbuck knew that it was the magic of Gabrielle deCourteney reaching out to enfold her brother and draw him to her.

Gil took his position, staring in amazement out over the splash shield of the .50 as their surroundings went to gray, just as they had on the road near Phu Loi. It became mortally cold and he could not but hope that by some mistake they'd find themselves back in Vietnam—not that he was fond of the place, but at least he'd know his way home.

A split second later he was looking out over a vast, barren plain, a place of cracked, dry earth, radiating heat. He wasn't sure if it was dark there or if his mind had difficulty interpreting the data of that gruesome world; his senses seemed to be operating aberrantly. In the distance, a reddish glow lit the horizon as if some

huge city were there. More than anything else, he noticed in that first instant an oppressive sense of the alien,
of a distorted atmosphere threatening to fill him and
smother with dread beyond mention. It was, he supposed, the very essentially human part of him recoiling
in primeval alarm, repulsion in the core of his being,
product of his total incompatability with this place. His
soul in rebellion.

The air was filled with menacing smells and un-
speakable odors. Unintelligible sounds reached his
ears, suggestive of distant howls of pain and torment
and blasphemous laughter. He twisted around as the
others pulled themselves up for a better look.

Between *Lobo* and the limitless plain in the distance
was a river a half mile or more in breadth. It was filled
with a glowing lava-like fluid, yet there were eddies and
ripples in its surface as if there were swimmers within.
On *Lobo*'s side of the river the ground was of black
sand, drifted in low hills and valleys. After his arrival in
Coramonde, Gil half expected the misshapen building
that stood nearby. It loomed to their rear, lit with eerie
auras and leaping flames and its design was grotesque
and disturbing, grating on human sensibilities.

Between it and the APC was a high, gleaming-black
wall which paralleled the river and ran in both directions as far as the eye could see. The only visible access
was a tall double gate close by, shut and forbidding.

"The river," said Andre calmly, "is a little device the
residents use to keep the Confined from escaping. Just
beyond the horizon, where the sky glows, begins the infinite continent of Hell proper, where punishment is dis-
pensed and the mustering of the Hosts conducted. Behind us, beyond the wall, is the palace of Amon, Yardiff
Bey's Lord and sponsor demon. He is an ancient being,
chief of forty legions. Tonight there will be high cele-
bration in his house. To get there we shall have to
breach yonder gates. I know of no incident in time
when such a mass of metal as *Lobo* was transported to
the Infernal plane. I think that cold metal will have the
requisite properties to deal with the gates."

Gil glanced upward. He thought he saw, against the
sky, darker figures soaring and gliding threateningly

through the air. Here and there on the sands around them black, obscure shapes hulked or scuttled.

"What about watchdogs?" he said.

"I don't think that the lesser guardians of the Pit will bother us, who are men of flesh and substance and ride in a thing of metal. They despise true life and fear iron greatly."

"Except that our armor's mostly aluminum," Pomorski said. "But, hey, won't the . . . owner be warned?"

"Possibly," Andre conceded, "but we will have to hope that the entertainment will occupy the attentions of the dwellers in that place."

The Nine-Mob divvied up the WP grenades among them. Springbuck and Andre both refused the offer of firearms; they were afraid that their lack of familiarity would lead to some misfortune, and Gil had to agree.

"I wonder," said Pomorski, "if there isn't something produced by burning white phosphorus that they've filtered out of their light sources here?"

Andre replied, "I am almost certain that in order to protect themselves from your grenades those within the manse will have to take on substantiality in forms our weapons can bite."

Ready now, mastering his spiritual vertigo, Gil settled his hands on the .50's familiar grips. He experienced a pulse of confidence, not of triumph or even of survival, but simply the feeling that he was no easy quarry for man or devil, and that any being who came against him would find the confrontation costly. He gave Woods the go-ahead.

The engine caught and they plunged at the gates as he braced himself and repressed the urge to call out to Woods to stop. Their objective looked as if it could withstand an antitank round. Yet when the prow of the APC struck the doors, he thought they moaned, and they shrank and buckled from contact with *Lobo*, whithering from their hinges.

The APC sped toward the manse and Gil gave the order to slow until speed and engine noise were as low as was feasible. They drove up to the very doors of the building, towering two-story-high panels, and stopped. The bedlam coming from within was amazing; cries, mad laughter, wailing and shrieks mingled with music which set mortal teeth on edge and made their hackles rise in alarm. Andre spoke into Gil's ear. "You and I shall look around while the others wait. Tell Al Woods to take the machine off to one side of the doors."

Pomoroski took the .50 as Gil took off his helmet and headset once again and grabbed Shorty. Andre drew his sword from its sheath and they stepped out of the rear hatch and watched the APC move away to the right of the entrance.

Then they circled to the left, bent low, running close to the wall. They paused after thirty yards with a wide, balconied window above them.

"We'll climb up the cavern giltwork and take a look," Andre said. Gil slipped the submachine gun over his shoulder and they began the ascent. The carvings, horrid faces and tortured human figures, man-woman-animal shapes and things less describable, provided ample grip and footing. The material of which the building was fashioned was coarse and abrasive to their hands and unpleasantly warm to the touch. They pulled themselves onto the balcony in the perpetual half-light and stepped to the doorway, keeping low and to one side.

The manse itself was more immense than Gil had realized when they'd approached it. The room into which they gazed was enormous. He spotted the twin doors, dwarfed in relation to the titanic chamber; the ceiling was lost to sight. The walls and the center of the place teemed with groups and individuals, people and things which were not human. There were appalling combinations of animal and mankind and other celebrants bearing no relation to either. But all had about them an aspect of malice and evil. Fangs, shaggy flanks, horns, gleaming torsos, barbed and scaly tails, clawed and webbed feet, restless talons, all of these there were. Old, young, beautiful and hideous were spinning and capering in a primitive, hysterical dance to music of insanity and hatred and abandon which came from no source that the American could see. In that moment there flashed into his mind the works of Hieronymus Bosch, inadequate and mild when held now in comparison with the real thing.

At both sides of the room were rows of tables laden with food and drink and set with black candles shaped like tumescent phalli, which guttered with flames of various colors but were not consumed. On a raised dais was a statue of the Goat. Gil stared at it and terror rose in him again, for the red eyes seemed alive and directed toward him alone. Then Andre placed a hand on his shoulder and he regained some of his control.

A steady stream of dancers was leaving their writhings momentarily to run to the statue and kiss its hairy rump, then anoint themselves with salve. On the dais one figure towered above the rest, an apparition with a wolf's head, a bare, manlike torso rearing on lion's hind legs and having a thick serpent tail which twitched behind it. Before it, on two bread slabs of obsidian were the forms of Gabrielle and what appeared to be a baby, the latter wrapped in a coverlet. Andre's hand tightened on Gil's shoulder in a grip which threatened to pulp it until the magician became aware of his excess and relaxed it.

"My sister," he said anxiously, "there, in front of the Wolf. He is Amon, Bey's liege and Lord of this place. There's Bey, standing next to Gabrielle's slab."

Indeed the sorcerer stood near her, but offered her no harm and only saw to it that no one approached her too closely. His face was closed to scrutiny and his exotic ocular threw back light from its moon-cold silver and verdant malachite. He watched coldly as the revelers anointed themselves with the sabbat ointment compounded of poppy, hellebore, hashish and human flesh, rubbing it behind knees, ears and arms, and on neck, armpit and chest. Here and there on the cyclopean floor flame leaped from pits and troughs, fitting illumination for the scene.

Gil asked Andre the reason for the infant's presence. "A sacrifice, in all probability. Yes, the blood of an innocent."

All color left the soldier's face, though it was not an expression of dismay he wore, but rather one of anger beyond anger. Andre watched the interplay of the sergeant's features and nodded to himself, satisfied.

They were distracted a moment later by the arrival of

a new guest. The crowd cheered and threw their hands up as a woman, a big, imposing blonde, rode out of the shadows at the end of the dais and stopped before Amon. Her steed was a naked man upon whose shoulders a sort of saddle had been fastened.

"That is Mara, the ice witch," said Andre, "Bey's rival for Amon's favor and often at odds with him."

"Who's her . . . her mount?"

"Perchance some poor soul she— Ah, gods, no!" Andre leaned forward, staring intently at the dismounted Mara, whose bearer kneeled docilely. "What madness is this? That is none other but Thom, the Land's Friend. Oh, my poor, poor comrade, how have you come to this? Come, we must get my sister out of here."

They clambered back down, then sprinted to the track. Back behind the .50, Gil took over the assault. He told the Nine-Mob what to expect but didn't get graphic about it; they'd soon see for themselves. And as he spoke the sergeant felt a tide of emotion building in him, a yearning to bring some terrible retribution upon those within the manse as though he, *Lobo*, all of them were instruments of some higher justice.

They drew up closer to the doors but with enough distance yet to gather momentum, as the insane music from within crowded over the track's rumble. Woods raced the engine and they all braced themselves; then he slapped the APC into gear and they tore across the black sand. *Lobo* hit the stairs before the doors and shot up them in a single bounce, crashing against the high portals. Unlike the gates at the outside wall these did not crumple. A shock ran through the track's occupants and jolted the vehicle, then the doors shattered to either side. There was a reeling impression of stunned, demented faces drawing back in sudden consternation as Alpha-Nine thundered down the center of the cavernous hall.

No attack came, only a general drawing back by those assembled, as Amon and his two lieutenants stepped to the front of the dais. It took an eternity to get there, and Gil's palms were wet at the .50's grips. Woods braked to a halt next to the two slabs. There was an ancient crone hovering nearby, an enormous spike-studded aclys held light as a feather in her decaying hands. Gil spoke into the intercom. "Olivier, cover the old gal with the club. Al, kill the engine."

Andre climbed up through the cargo hatch and stood next to Gil's cupola, noticing the sergeant's shaking hands as he did.

"Well, my Lord the Wolf," he said to the silent Amon, "I have brought another wolf to visit you, hight *Lobo*."

The demon answered in a deep voice, harsh with hatred and frightening in volume. "The wizardling Andre deCourteney, come to join his sister with his new friends and bringing the snot-nosed Springbuck, if I smell aright. I knew you were sniffing at my windows, but I also knew that you'd come to me presently. Ha, so predictable are you of the Terrestrial plane. Can I entice you to light repast?"

"Thank you, no," Andre answered. "Carrion and putrefacation do not attract me."

"Then, why invade my hall? In hastening the inevitable—for I would have had you here eventually—you've upset my guests. Still, I suppose I should expect such behavior from bothersome little spell-workers. Do you know that I am the final word here? Come down from that clanking kettle, deCourteney, and we'll let your sister take a final look at you."

"I thank Mighty Amon," was the retort. "But first, be pleased to accept these small gifts from us." And with that, he tapped Gil's shoulder. The American, nearly paralyzed until that moment, lobbed the WP he'd had waiting in his hand and it landed fair at the feet of the demon, who looked at it curiously. A second later the canister went off with a hiss, and a flare which grew into a burning nimbus.

Amon staggered back from it, shaggy arm thrown across his eyes, and howled. The other members of the Nine-Mob tossed their WPs in all directions as Olivier, poised at his gun and taking the most careful aim he ever had, cut down the crone without compunction.

Yardiff Bey, who had been racing toward the two slabs, skidded to a stop at the first sound of gunfire. He bit his lip in indecision as his resolve wavered. Andre drew his sword and jumped to face Bey while Springbuck threw open the rear hatch and ran to Gabrielle's side. Bar severed the bonds holding her as if they were rotten cordage. He swept her up in his left arm and dashed for *Lobo*.

The hall had become a scene of unimaginable chaos. Those creatures of the depths who had been closest to the buring WPs were lying stricken on the floor, among these Amon himself. Many more were shifting their shapes to afford protection against the torturous light. Human adherents, in a turmoil, were beseeching their Lord for help and Bey himself had drawn Dirge to meet the advance of Andre deCourteney. But the Nine-Mob had cut loose with all guns and the pandemonium became a slaughter. Gil had elevated his barrel and was quartering the air, bringing down the flying creatures— huge bats, bloated birds, nightmare fliers—which some of the celebrants had become.

Bey cursed, turned and fled before Andre could reach him, no doubt moved to do so by the gunfire but perhaps unwilling to face the portly magician in a physical contest. Mara had resumed her mount and was fleeing, too. Andre cried out to his old friend to stop, but to no avail. Springbuck and Gabrielle were back aboard the APC and Gil called out to the wizard to follow. A swollen thing of gorilla body and pig-snouted face made to slaughter Andre with scythelike claws before he could regain the track, but Handelman saw, and cut its legs out from under it, continuing to fire after the magician skirted the convulsing body and raced on. Andre reached the APC and dogged the hatch behind him, turning instantly to his sister.

She was sitting up, apparently well and unharmed. She shrugged their helping hands away. "The infant," she insisted, seizing the Prince's arm. "Get the child; we cannot abandon it to them." Springbuck exchanged glances with Andre, who nodded. The Heir of the *Ku-Mor-Mai* sprang up through the cargo hatch.

The Nine-Mob were men possessed, lashing out with all their strength at the things gathering for attack. They swiveled smoking weapons here and there as swarms of bullets found this or that target, paused to decimate it, and moved on. Torrents of slugs reached out implacably for the creations of the Infernality whether they groveled, fled or gave battle, as if some cleansing holocaust sped through the hall. They steered their barrels back and forth as if the outpouring of death and devastation would never end. They had no thought but to walk the paths of tracers from one annihilated enemy to the next. The racket of machine guns and the popping of the grenade launcher overwhelmed even the screams of fury and wrath ringing through the room.

Gil was destroying an elephantine atrocity that had been bearing down on them, its features those of a lovely woman. It staggered and collapsed under the hail of automatic fire. Bar in hand, Springbuck pounded Gil's shoulder and pointed out the baby wailing alone in the midst of the carnage. The American was growing sated and wanted only to leave; Woods had started the engine and they could go at any time. It made no difference; he knew that they couldn't desert the child there. He traversed his gun to cover.

The Prince launched himself through space, landing by the slab. The infant was not bound and he reached to take it up. A burst went over his head and he ducked, peering around for the sergeant's target. An obscene bird-thing lay convulsed and dying, brought down in midstoop. He turned, the baby cradled in his left arm, only to find that a more frightening phantasm had come up behind him, a grinning, decaying corpse swinging a khopesh.

Gil had fired the last of his ammo belt and was locking and loading another, unable to help. The corpse closed with the Prince, its blade whistling savagely. Hampered by his burden, he parried and cut back. Bar flashed eagerly and severed the grinning head from the spine bone, but slowed his opponent not at all. Horrified, he fought on, concentrating on the khopesh and the bleached arm which held it, and these alone. The baby was making it difficult to fight; he had to keep his torso turned awkwardly to shield it from the dead body's attack.

Then he heard Gil's voice. "Get down, Springbuck,

down!" He whirled and threw himself headlong, losing Bar but protecting the infant by landing on his right side and arm. He saw the corpse above him, khopesh raised in triumph for the final stroke, but it dissolved in a shower of bone fragments, rotting meat and dust as Olivier and Gil scored concurrent hits on it.

The Prince regained his feet, tottered to the side of the APC and handed his small burden up to Olivier's open arms. He then remembered Bar, still lying where he had dropped it, and ran back to recover it. When he had it in hand, he looked around for Yardiff Bey, thinking to settle accounts with him. His eyes fell upon the still-squirming form of Amon. Ignoring the pleas of those in the track, he ran to where the demon lay. The intense heat and brilliance hurt his eyes as he bent next of the huge Lord of that place. The wolf head had ceased howling and now regarded him with red-slitted gaze.

"Mighty Amon," said the Prince, "if you will but answer me one question we will leave your halls. If you will not, I'll place another of these burning sunlets upon your breast and let it eat its way through. I know now that Strongblade is Yardiff Bey's son. Who, then, is his daughter, his firstborn, and how may we find her?"

The demon, even in his great suffering, barked one short laugh and answered. Springbuck backed away from him, bewildered, and walked back to *Lobo,* leaving the Lord of forty legions in such agony as he had not felt since that first battle against his eternal opponents. So distracted was the Prince that he did not even notice the minions of Amon, now summoning their courage and arming themselves, as the WPs were beginning to burn low. A threatening ring was slowly closing on Alpha-Nine.

Pomorski jumped out and threw him bodily through the rear hatch, pulling it shut as the screaming slaves of Amon rushed toward them from all sides. The Nine-Mob lobbed fragmentation grenades among them and ducked. The explosions were tremendous. Metal bits flew in all directions, bouncing harmlessly off *Lobo*'s armor but doing fearful damage to the attackers. Smoke billowed through the chamber as broken figures crawled or expired among those already sped.

Woods got the APC into gear, describing a tight circle, and drove at top speed, crushing anonymous obstacles beneath them as they made their way back to the black sands outside. Andre and Gabrielle joined hands and the girl went into a mystical seizure, the blue glow of power coming from her as from the filament of some strange, pulsing strobe. Of this the others saw little; the Nine-Mobsters were busy looking for pursuit and the Prince was pondering the words of Amon.

Cold broke around them like a wave and the black sands disappeared beneath, replaced by weed-assailed cobblestones. Woods had to brake very hard indeed to keep from plowing into a wall of the castle near Erub.

Chapter Thirteen

If you wish to know what a man is, place him in authority.

ANONYMOUS PROVERB

THE baby, a beautiful little girl, was the immediate center of attention. Stories were demanded, told in confused style and received with wonder and acclaim.

The Nine-Mob regarded *Lobo* ruefully: scorched, dented, gore-streaked and littered with brass casings and bits of metal linking from disintegrated ammo belts.

They all adjourned to the main hall for a meal amid the shouts and laughter of the Erubites. Springbuck was sitting to one side, lost in thought, when Gabrielle came to him. She knelt before him, face level with his, and took his hands in hers. He guarded his expression as, smiling ever so faintly, she brought her mouth to his. Van Duyn, standing near the hearth with Andre, watched without comment and at length returned to his conversation, animation gone from him but with no other indication of the hurt he felt.

Andre spoke to his sister for a moment as she hovered yet near the Prince, then went to where the Nine-Mob sprawled, relaxed and mellow on the floor.

"We will be able to return you shortly before dusk," he said.

"What'll you do then?" Pomorski asked.

Andre seated himself somberly as Van Duyn joined them. The wizard said, "I have talked this over with Edward. Since the slaying of Chaffinch, many of the Erubites have come to the castle, along with a number of stray horses they recovered. We are going to take the nucleus of our school eastward over the mountains to Freegate, where the King is an acquaintance of mine

124

and has already said that we may establish ourselves there."

"School?" Gil demanded, "But what about Cora-monde? You gonna just leave it to Yardiff Bey? After what his men did to Erub last night and the kind of backing he had from—back there; you know—I can't believe you're dealing yourselves out and moving on."

Andre fiddled with Calundronius, now back around his neck. "The situation has changed since my last com-munication with the King of Freegate. Now we are cer-tain that Yardiff Bey plans to make war on him and indeed on all the lands within his reach, one by one. But we have the Prince with us now, a viable approach to unseating Strongblade and turning out Yardiff Bey, if we can evade capture and win the factions of Cora-monde to our side."

Gil considered this. "But what about the people you'll be leaving behind? With a little teaching, they could start a working resistance movement. There's all kinds of things they could do—propaganda, intelli-gence, sabotage and like that. Guerrilla warfare."

"Oh, well," Pomorski cut in, "too bad we never got to shoot Yardiff Bey. We'd have saved Coramonde a lot of trouble."

"It would have been a great service," Andre agreed. "Bey is the engineer of our present troubles. But he has his counterparts in other places; rest assured that there are replacements waiting in the wings if we eventually pull him down. We can only do, each of us, what we may.

"But I feel that there is much that you might do, Gil MacDonald. You speak of ways of using our people here in Erub, things with which we are not conversant. Edward assures me that, though he does not agree with the war you were fighting, you have many skills and techniques which we do not know."

The sergeant yawned and stretched, looking to Van Duyn. He took a tug from a beer bucket as the older man spoke carefully. "I won't argue a tired and sore point with you, MacDonald—"

"Oh, God, no, please don't," Pomorski said quickly. "You'll start him quoting the SEATO codicil again."

"—but," Van Duyn plodded on, "let me ask you this: what are you going to do with that military head of yours when you get out? There isn't any room in civilian life for you as you are now. You'll have to do things their way or starve. And perhaps, if you feel strongly as you say, you wouldn't find this war so very different from yours."

Gil rolled to his feet. "I'm going to check out the track," he said. "I'll be waiting for word on exactly when we can leave."

As they watched him go, Van Duyn took his lower lip between his teeth thoughtfully. "What kind of soldier is MacDonald?" he asked the Nine-Mob.

Typically, it was Pomorski who answered for them. "You meet his sort more and more now in the army, a good troop who hates soldiering. He's got it chalked up as his duty and he doesn't kick, but he hates to take orders and I think he hates giving them, too. They lost a good candidate when he didn't push for OCS."

He twisted his villainous mustache. "Take my handlebar, for instance. It's against regs to wear it this long, but I like it this way. Mac knows it but he doesn't care about things like that; minutiae and housework don't interest him. He ignores it as long as he can, until our new platoon leader, a wet-eared West Point sonofabitch, calls him down about it. One thing leads to another and eventually Mac's in front of the Old man, but he never once suggests that I cut off my broom. As far as he's concerned, it's mine and it isn't hurting anyone.

"So he ends up with his heels locked in front of Cap'n Cronkite, who's just taken over as CO of Alpha Troop. And do you know what he says, even with this newly minted looie standing there right beside him? He says, 'Well, sir, Pomorski's a helluva good grenadier and ammo humper and a pretty sharp gunner. The 'stache keeps him happy and doesn't cost the government a red cent. I always figured that it's more important that what a soldier shoots at get killed than what his tonsorial preferences are.'

"So it turns out that the skipper, Captain Cronkite, feels the same way and the matter is dropped. But none of us forget it and just after that the looie refers to us as 'that raggedy-assed Alpha-Niner mob' and the name stuck—the Nine-Mob.

"Anyway, MacDonald's terribly conscientious about his job. He feels that as long as he has people under him—us—and he's supposed to be a noncom, he should give it his best shot. He's always trying to pick up something new, getting people to teach him what they know. He reads a lot, a bit of everything but heavy into military subjects. He never once volunteered us for anything, never tried to suck up to Command, but he's never shirked anything either. When they give him a job he does it right down the line.

"Oh, he's a strange one, all right. Likes to try his hand at new things, even writes poetry occasionally; but it stinks, especially his haiku. Pretty good with the hands, too, but I gather that you've already found that out."

They talked a bit more, then Van Duyn went out to speak to Gil, who was checking oil levels in the road wheels of Alpha-Nine, digging dirt from the little glass circle at the center of each wheel with his thumbnail and frowning in concentration.

Without preamble the older man said, "Sergeant MacDonald, I'd like you to come back to Coramonde when your time in the army is finished, or simply stay here when we send your friends back. You could be of inestimable value to our cause."

Gil straightened. "Look, I've got nothing against Springbuck. In fact, I'm certain he'd be a good King or whatever, but—"

"You don't understand. Springbuck's job as Pretender and true Heir to the throne is to back our plan to institute a more equitable government in Coramonde. We are going to seek the help of other nations and factions within this realm."

"Van Duyn, do you know what the hell you're talking about? Have you ever seen civil war? I'm not saying it isn't justified here, but I hope for your sake that you realize what price innocent people will have to pay. Are you ready to provoke something like that?"

"If my companions and I do not," the other answered steadily, "the scenes you saw in Erub and at Amon's mansion—oh, yes! Andre has told me!—will be repeated throughout this part of the world. Even now it will be a difficult thing to prevent."

"Why look at me? Why don't you come back with us and appeal to the government for help?"

"No, for several reasons. I cannot leave at this critical juncture, for one thing. Besides, think for a moment what would happen, even if I took time and managed to convince the right people of our situation here. The chances are that they'd either slap a security cover on the whole issue or they'd throw it up to the UN. If the latter, there'd be a land rush to get guaranteed economic and political spheres. Who's to say Yardiff Bey wouldn't win support for Strongblade as incumbent? Then there'd be study missions with the results digested through every committee on Capitol Hill. And in the meantime don't you think the Vatican would be outraged to find no vestige of the Christian mythos here? That would prompt an ecumenical council to end them all. No, I have no intention of involving my old world in the problems of my new one; the contiguity effect will stay a secret if I can help it. It may be duplicated elsewhere—indeed, if the number of cosmos is infinite or near infinite, it is constantly being discovered—but I shall do all that lies in my power to keep it from the poeple and nations whom I quit when I developed it."

Gill shifted tactics. "How would I get back? Because I can't just stay here. You snatched up *Lobo* more or less by chance, and your machine was kept in Earthfast."

"Yes, but the first apparatus is still at the Grossen Institute, as far as I know. And that is another worry. If anyone at the Institute should ever deduce its purpose and operation, I suppose that a gifted man or team could reconstruct my breakthrough and devise new activation components to replace the ones I removed. But you could come back by using it; I'll give you the address of the man with whom I left the missing parts and a note of introduction."

Gil exploded. "You've got a lot of hide on you, Van Duyn. Get myself mixed up in this crazy business again, maybe on a one-way ride this time, and bring your gizmo along as a bonus? You're insane, is what; strictly out-of-your-tree."

Springbuck, who had come up to listen, stepped between the two. He was more authoritative, more martially erect than he had been when Van Duyn had first met him. The past day or two had left a profound mark on him. He faced the sergeant. "I am asking you to return to help us," he said. "And I offer you as reward anything which might lie within my suzerainty. But I do not think that, if you returned, you would do it for payment. We will understand if you don't fare again to Coramonde, but your aid would be of immense value to me and those who will stand with me."

Gil blew out his breath between pursed lips, long and loud. "Van Duyn," he said at last, "get me your address book. We'll figure out a target date for me to come back through." To the Prince he said, "You know, it's been said that the first guy to be King was a lucky soldier. Okay, you've been getting lucky lately; let's see what happens."

They had all washed sketchily and eaten lightly. A change of clothes would have been nice, but they were used to being grubby.

"Don't change the settings on the programming input," Van Duyn was saying for the fifth time. "I already know just where you'll come through and I'm fairly sure that the time relation is on a one-to-one order, so there'll be someone waiting to meet you." He held in his hands a sheaf of papers covered with shorthand scratchings, product of several hours of rambling dictation by Gil with assists from the rest of the Nine-Mob on the topic of warfare with particular attention to guerrilla fighting. In a pouch at the scholar's side were the few hand grenades they'd had left, to be kept against the sergeant's return. Gil had vetoed the suggestion that they leave behind a few small arms, since they couldn't foresee how badly they would need them in the war to which they were returning.

The sergeant was nodding his acknowledgment,

shrugging on his flak jacket with its rip from the cavalryman's spear, and looked to his squadmates. "How about it? Any of you guys coming back with me?" All four answers were negative. *No surprise. Olivier and Handelman are married, Pomorski's engaged and Woods is dying to start college. They all think I'm nuts and who's to say they're wrong? It's not all that unlikely that I'll never get out of here again, once I come back. Stupid ass.*

He gave a wave to Andre and Gabrielle deCourteney. "You can do it, right? Send us to a few seconds before you grabbed us and a couple of yards farther back?"

Andre waved back and nodded with a smile, but his sister merely studied the APC coolly.

Van Duyn left the track's side, closing the geometrical designs and lines of its runed pentacle behind him. Then they stood, Springbuck, the deCourteneys and the scholar in a circle around *Lobo*. Gil had an impulse to shout out, to tell them that he could not come back and not to expect him. But he was cut short as Gabrielle's marvelous form, arms upraised, became the center of the now-familiar blue pulsations.

Cold grayness broke around the APC again, then they were sitting in the midst of a dusty road as waves of heat rose in the searing dry season. Ahead of them another track was rumbling along as a movement stirred in the grass to the right. Then *Lobo* was in motion again, sent, as Andre had promised it would be, to a point several yards behind and seconds before the ambush, overlapped with itself in time.

Gil watched the first rocket go off, saw his own crew responding out ahead of him. Woods goosed the track as he searched for the second RPG-4 man, and spotted him. The Gil MacDonald in the lead APC did not see the man in time, but his older counterpart to the rear had already been through this ambush once and was waiting when the man stood. He cut the small figure down with his first burst and killed the backup man with the AK-47. The track commander in the cupola of the other *Lobo* turned in confusion. Gil, knowing what a blackened, battered sight they were, raised a fist to Gil MacDonald, who returned it with a grateful grin.

Just then the lead *Lobo* faded from sight and the second rolled forward to mop up what was left of the confused ambushers.

PART III

❧

Freegate, Beyond,
and Elsewhere

Chapter Fourteen

I wish all men to be free,
As much from mobs as men—
From you as me.

LORD BYRON

TAKING into account the scavenged horses plus those belonging to Springbuck and the deCourteneys—they didn't want to use any of the draft animals as saddle horses—they settled on a party of fifteen for what Van Duyn termed their hejira to Freegate.

Besides basic provisions, the thaumaturgical apparatus and the few books and scrolls, they took only a minimum of personal belongings and their weapons. All had intended to take part in the journey, and those not chosen to go were disappointed and were mollified only when Van Duyn took them aside to explain the commission of war with which they were to be invested as guerrillas. The others saw to what little packing was needful.

Gabrielle found several occasions to brush against Springbuck or let her hand touch his, and each time his skin tingled and his face burned red. He was not unaccustomed to female companionship and had taken his first lover years before; but he felt gawky and sheepish in her presence and suspected that she liked things that way and was contriving through outwardly innocent acts to keep it so.

When Van Duyn returned, the scholar was not pleased; his wretchedness as Gabrielle's favor drifted from him wouldn't permit any such uplifting emotion. But he was satisfied. "I put Treehigh in deputation over them," he said. "He's self-reliant and physically competent. I think that he's the sort of man we'll need here, though he is petulant at not being able to go with us."

The Prince recognized the name, its owner being a big, bearded lumberman, quiet and intense.

"All of these people should be able to return to their homès, once we're gone," the scholar added. "Yardiff Bey'll have bigger fish to fry than Erub."

It was decided that they'd rest a bit longer, then depart under cover of darkness. Springbuck's sleep was fitful, filled with slow-motion excerpts of the battle in Amon's mansion and passing glimpses of Gabrielle. When Andre shook him awake by torchlight, he was bathed in sweat. He dashed himself with water from the trough, then resumed boots, sword and other gear and saddled Fireheel. The gray snuffled his master, scenting strange places upon him, but was eager to be away. The war-horse had stood too long in a stall's confinement with tamer beasts. The dressing on the Prince's wounded right leg, just above the boot top, began to fret him and he removed it. The cut wasn't nearly healed but looked as if it would remain closed, and he wanted to let the air get at it.

There was plenty of room on the reconnaissance cavalryman's saddle for the meager share he was to carry. He was up and mounted in a moment and Fireheel pranced and curvetted happily. Van Duyn was ahorse with his rifle and was followed by the deCourteneys, with Gabrielle in boyish hose and jerkin, and the other eleven, mostly young, with two women among them. The baby was carried papoose-style on one rider's back. One of the women, whose husband and infant son had been slaughtered in Erub, had volunteered to care for the child and was plainly happy for the consolation.

Waving final good-byes to those few still in the castle, they turned and filed out across the drawbridge. One of the locals, a slight fellow with kinky brown hair and a freckled face, led the way with the deCourteneys and the other Erubites strung behind. Springbuck and Van Duyn, at the outlander's suggestion, fell back to the end of the column.

It required full attention to guide their horses at first, but soon they were on a broad trail and could see somewhat better. The Prince wondered for a moment what would happen to the vast carcass of Chaffinch, lifeless on the fields they left behind them.

Van Duyn said, "I haven't had much time these few hours we've known each other to tell you about my country, about the ideas and ideals from which I draw my philosophy. I thought that, since we'll be passing some time travelling, you might care to hear a little of them."

Springbuck agreed guardedly, partly because he felt guilty about the older man's anguish over Gabrielle's change of fancy, wanting to show that he bore no ill feeling. Van Duyn spoke at length, fascinating the Prince, about his home and the great documents and statements of his Reality and his nation. The Heir of Kings was oddly moved by passages from compacts, speeches and laws. He considered much of what he heard blatant heresy, held it seditious and immoral. But it was compelling withal, a vivid narrative of the struggle of imperfect Man, through battle and the intricacies of law, toward human enfranchisement.

The monologue came to an end "I've explained this," Van Duyn finished, "because I must ask something of you. When we've gained control of Coramonde, I'd expect you, as *Ku-Mor-Mai,* to abdicate and create representative government in the suzerainty."

Springbuck was speechless for long moments. Just when he'd begun to dream of taking his father's place with such allies as the deCourteneys and Gil MacDonald!

Receiving no answer, Van Duyn pressed him harder. "After all, you'd already forfeited the throne, more or less, when you came to us."

The Prince chewed his lip and slapped his reins against his thigh. Fireheel pranced nervously, chaffing at being held to a walk.

"This, then," said the son of Surehand, "when I depose Strongblade, we'll hold a plebiscite and let the people of Coramonde decide."

Van Duyn nodded. "Fair enough. In return for this, though, your commitment to our cause is unstinting?"

Springbuck concurred, and they rode on together in silence.

Andre left his sister's side and fell in with them. The deCourteneys, of course, could have gone on to Freegate at far faster pace by means open only to them. But Andre had reckoned that the others might well need guidance and perhaps other, special help as well, and so the two went by prosaic paths.

"One thing you've not yet told us, young Pretender," Andre said. "When you ran back to speak to Amon in his hall, what words passed between you and the demon?"

His mind yanked back from thoughts of the carven throne in Earthfast to the unpleasant problem he'd been wrestling with since their return from the Infernal plane. The Prince hesitated, but he judged that the others had a right to hear.

"I told him that I knew that Strongblade is Yardiff Bey's son, and I asked who Bey's daughter is. He laughed even then at the humor of our not knowing and said that . . . that Bey's firstborn, his daughter, is Gabrielle."

Van Duyn went white. "A lie!" he whispered.

Andre said nothing.

"No, I think not," Springbuck said. "And I have tussled with this thought for some time. Rumor has always had it that Bey can wear many disguises.

"Put aside your prejudices, then, and think. Why could it not have been him, Bey, who tempted Andre's father and won for himself the default to beget a child of Andre's mother. Look you: why has Bey been at odds with Andre for years untold but never with Gabrielle? He has never offered her hurt, never struck at his daughter once except in killing the husband who had won and held her unswerving affections.

"And who has been Gabrielle's enemy? Mara, who is Bey's rival before their mutual patron, Amon. When Bey had Gabrielle at his mercy in Amon's hall he did her no harm; knowing that Mara would be there, he posted the old woman with the aclys whom Olivier killed as a guard over both his daughter and the baby we rescued."

"I resist this thought," Andre said, "but I find it well

reasoned and convincing. It is supportive of . . . things I've suspected."

"Why then would Bey try to capture her?" asked Van Duyn. "Can he possibly hope for some sort of reconciliation with her?"

Springbuck replied; "Andre's sister has told us that she knew that the baby is extremely important to Yardiff Bey, but I think that it is no offspring of Bey himself. Now consider this: one of his two children, Strongblade, has given Bey access to tremendous worldly power, the armed might and political influence of Coramonde, while the other child, Gabrielle, is the greatest source of pure sorcerous force, a potent tool in his second sphere. I think he meant to win Gabrielle over somehow by using the child."

But Andre was shaking his head. "No. The omens, the stars, every divination my sister and I could carry out over the babe point to this, that she is of critical importance in some facet of the battle being waged against Shardishku-Salamá. But I doubt her use as a lever for my sister."

Springbuck was about to speculate again when a cry came to them from ahead. Their eyes pursued the direction of an arm raised to the sky and saw there, high above them, a silvery object riding the night, uncertain of shape and poised on columns of red flame.

"Bey's flying ship," Andre said, and they halted to gape at the sinister visitation. They were exposed on a grassy, rock-studded slope in the moonlight, but the aircraft came no lower nor did it linger, but sped unheedingly eastward.

Gabrielle galloped back to them excitedly. "Yardiff Bey! He's scum, of course," she said, her breathing quickened, "but, oh! What a thing to accomplish. To get the Gnomes and the Deep-Rock Dwarves to labor together for twelve years and forge a metal beyond metal and imprison a fire elemental within."

The three looked at her worriedly, searching for any approval or enthusiasm for her father beyond his works. Andre said, "Springbuck and Edward were about to take the head of the column for a while. Why don't you ride here with me? I will speak with you for a bit."

She glanced from face to face to mask in the moonlight, perplexed; but as the group began to move again, she brought her roan lightly around until her knee brushed her brother's. As Van Duyn and the Prince trotted to the head of the band, the older man unslung his rifle from his shoulder. "We'll have to accelerate the pace a bit," he said. "Yardiff Bey was no doubt scouting for us. I don't think he's seen us or has many loyal troops in this region yet. The slaying of Chaffinch and the raid on Amon's hall gave him reason for pause, but he'll come after us eventually and we have a long way to ride before we can breathe easily." Nevertheless they held a slow pace while Andre and Gabrielle rode speaking at the rear of the file. They glanced back occasionally and saw after a time that the magician and his sister had stopped and it seemed in the dimness that she burrowed her head at her brother's shoulder as if weeping. They both wanted to go to her. They both restrained themselves.

Soon the deCourteneys were apart and moving along again. By mutual agreement, the American and the Prince started the company moving at a fast trot. Conversation ended as they all concentrated on guiding their horses across the rough ground, the trail being rutted. By cutting overland they might have saved distance, but Springbuck felt that they'd lose time. Since they might have been sighted by Yardiff Bey, they elected to take the route affording the greatest speed, albeit more perilous.

The Western Tangent was deserted except for the fugitives. The Prince wondered that Bey had not raced to alert some outpost of their coming; then it occurred to him that the wizard, if he had seen them, would still have difficulty in locating a friendly garrison at night, for there were a number of family Keeps in the area that would show him scant hospitality.

Old and broad as it was, built before the Great Blow fell, the Tangent rose, dipped and turned but little, striking through the countryside like a bowshot. Their progress was rapid; when they passed an occasional waypost along the road, they found each unmanned, relieving them of the necessity of bluffing or forcing their way past the Constabulary of the Road. Twice they spied approaching groups of travelers, the first mounted and the second afoot. But in each case the others left the Tangent to avoid them. Springbuck speculated that these were highwaymen grown bold with the absence of the Constabulary, but Andre said that it might just as well have been honest folk thinking *they* were brigands. As for the missing Constabulary, the wizard felt that they could have departed for fear of Bulf Hightower, brother to the slain Rolph, who would no doubt swear death to any man of Strongblade's or Fania's whom he encountered, for the land they approached was under his seigniory.

The country changed from relative openness to more densely wooded stretches. At one point the soil under the Tangent had been etched away by a river which had not been there when the Tangent was built. They rode an unsupported span of the Western Tangent for a stretch of thirty yards or more while angry waters roiled beneath, yet the Tangent was as steady and unyielding at this point as at any other.

The sky was brightening with the rising sun when they went some distance into the wood at the side of the road and encamped in a small glade by a watershed pond amid lush grass, strange scarlet moss and clusters of peculiar purple blossoms. At one end of the glade were sections of ruined wall, some remnant of times before the Great Blow. Beyond was an interesting antiquity, a crystalline cube with sides the length of a tall man and, within it, like a fly in amber, a delicate and lovely black fern arched, ancient and unidentifiable.

They picketed their horses and one of the Erubites volunteered to stand the first watch. The two women, who had enthusiastically followed Gabrielle's notion of dressing in male clothes, insisted on being assigned a turn at guard, too, as full participants in the company. Springbuck was surprised, but could think of no reason not to accommodate them. He and the rest slept immediately, too fatigued to eat or sleep.

He stood his hour of guard about noonday, half-drowsing in the heat. He finally arose and paced about the small encampment in order to stay fully awake. He dashed water in his face and rubbed Fireheel down with handfuls of grass, feeding him a bit from a small store of oats he'd brought from Erub. He then cut a green twig with his parrying dagger and stripped the bark, crushing one end to separate the fibers, and cleaned his teeth with it, a practice the late Faurbuhl had enjoined him to follow daily. Once or twice the baby stirred and complained and her nurse saw to her sleepily.

At length the shadow of the makeshift time-pole indicated the end of his watch and he awakened his replacement and sank back gratefully to slumber.

When he awoke, the sun was sloping toward the horizon once again and he and his companions made a quick meal of cold meat and bread, washing it down with swigs of water from a skin filled at the pond. As they saddled their horses he thought to ask Van Duyn, "Will Gil MacDonald bring back more guns with him?"

"No. He told me he knew where he could get many, and that he'd be able to bring other weapons back with him; but I told him that before we introduce more fire-arms, if eventually we must, I'd like to see if we can rectify matters here without them. I did, however, give him a list of books and other source materials we need."

Perhaps this was sensible, but the Prince thought of the Legions of Coramonde under Strongblade, and would have liked to have had one of those amazing guns.

Gabrielle looked less distraught than she had last night and even managed an enticing smile for him. She'd slept the night at her brother's side and appeared to be coping well with the shattering disclosure of her parentage.

The Prince ordered their column and they were all in the saddle and away. At first, the Tangent was as vacant as it had been the night before. They passed a number of small villages along the way, which looked to be deserted, but they didn't stop to see. The gates of the inns were boarded up, too. When they'd been riding for some hours in the darkness, the man whom Springbuck had set out at point returned, telling of the approach of a large body of riders. He had his companions dismount and move with their horses into the canopied blackness of the trees at the side of the road. Together they stood, each holding his horse's bridle, as a full squadron of heavy cavalry clattered past. Those troops rode quickly, not as those who search for outlaws or renegades, but as if on a long and urgent journey. The baby began to cry and the woman holding her was forced to clasp a hand over its mouth.

The fugitives regained the road and moved on, traveling as quietly as possible through the ranks of the brooding forest. Now the point man rode with muffled hooves. Twice more during the night they were forced to avoid oncoming bodies of soldiery, a small group of armored knights and, close to dawn, a battalion of foot.

At their last unscheduled pause Van Duyn whispered, "Odd, all these men on the road at night."

Springbuck sighed. "Strongblade and Fania call their supporters to them at speed," he said softly over the dwindling sound of marching buskins. "But they'll have few enough from the east, where we're going. News of Hightower's death must have stirred up those parts already. If there's to be an uprising, its kindling spark will come from the eastern provinces. Mayhap we ought to take our stand there."

Andre said, "Save the extreme East, no other region in Coramonde will take arms against the throne for the time being, until we've primed them for it. And there are those in the southwest and northwest who would rejoice to plunder the rich lands near the Keel of Heaven. We must leave this country and organize puissant aid if we're to be of any use to your people, young Heir. We mustn't let haste make our hand go astray or spend itself too soon."

Springbuck nodded, the gesture lost in the darkness. They were on their way again then, toward a ripening dawn. As they moved off the road for their second encampment, the Prince asked Andre, "What can you apprise me of the King of Freegate—called Reacher, is he not? I know little of him, though I've met some of his emissaries. Yet we hope to ally with him and you have his acquaintance. Tell me of him."

To this the wizard agreed, and so they took the first two watches together, the better to carry on their conversation and conserve sleep time.

Andre began. "His name, in the Old Tongue, was given as *Toa-wa-Day*, Lord of the Just and Sudden Reach. But early on he was nicknamed Reacher, and is called the Wolf-Brother by some. He's the descendant of a line of mighty men, but in his generation a thing unwonted came to pass. Reacher's father was presented with a daughter as firstborn. To complicate matters, Reacher was unusually small at birth, rather than a doughty specimen like his father and grandsires. He was to serve as proof of the ways in which appearances deceive us.

"Many advisers and seers counseled the then King to allow Reacher's older sister Katya to reign rather than her diminutive brother. Traditionalists opposed any coparcenary solution and refused to see a woman sit the throne. The case was not altogether unlike that between you and your . . . Strongblade, except that in this case there was a wise King of will and conviction to deal with it; would that Coramonde had been so lucky!

"He kept tight rein on his advisers and subordinates and carefully guided the development of his two children after the death of his wife.

"Reacher, though his size remained less than average, began to boast remarkable strength and agility, much more than his birthright, even from formidable ancestors. More than one lusty warrior-in-training was knocked atumbling by the boy, and the bigger they were, to paraphrase the shaggy adage, the farther they tumbled.

"When the lad was still twelve, his father dispatched him to live and learn for a time with the Howlebeau, the Steppes Runners. Though a small tribe, they're the proudest and hardiest folk on the High Ranges. They disdain horses, but are hunters by nature and travel on foot, capable of great feats of stamina and speed. They, along with most of the other peoples of the steppes, had compacted peace and bonds of friendliness with Freegate, and were pleased to take Reacher with them on endless roamings.

"The boy's special gifts flourished under the tutelage of the Howlebeau. He learned to use their traditional weapons of clawed glove and cestus. He lived among them for six years and became a legend on the High Ranges, and the greatest hunter and fighter of all by the time he was fifteen, brother to wolves and winner of many single contests and combats.

"While her brother roved the steppes with his adopted clan, Katya was nurtured by her father, her education carefully ordained. As Reacher ran with the Howlebeau and their furry kin, she was kept close to her father's side to watch the subtle arts of statecraft, and she didn't fail to acquire them. The boy became a champion warrior in a land of warriors; I, who have seen many places, tell you that I've never seen better. The sister grew wise beyond her years in the clash of politics.

"The boy was called back six years ago, at the age of eighteen, to begin a new phase of study. With the help of his father, counselors and sister, he's absorbed much knowledge of regnancy and integrated it with the honest, equitable attitudes of the Howlebeau. He is intimate with the techniques of moving men and women to his will, but does it without the impulse to control; his highest mission is the well-being of his people.

"His father fell in a skirmish with desert raiders from the eastern wastes. Reacher ascended the throne with his sister as first minister and virtual coruler. He is, I believe, much by way of a paragon of what a man and king should be, and he and his sister, devoted to their subjects and well thought of by them, are still much feared by enemies.

"You know of course of the free city's radius of purview; when we're at the base of the Keel of Heaven we'll see one of the merestones which mark its circumference. Within that boundary, no one may war or transgress without danger from the vengeance of Reacher and his army. From the High Ranges to the wastelands, they've tracked their enemies and wrought hard justice. No army has ever prevailed against Freegate, my friend, but several have perished attempting it."

"Why is the city so impervious, then?"

"You'll see when we arrive. It was thought of and constructed even before the Tangents; the four major Ways emanate from it as spokes from a wheel. I don't know that the army exists to violate its gates."

"I hope that we won't need to find out," the Prince responded. "The endless legions of Coramonde assembled would be force enough to break any city, be it ever so strong and stout a garrison. Kee-Amaine, with Earthfast to bolster it, could never hope to stand against all Coramonde's banners."

The wizard didn't chose to rebut this, but moved to another topic.

"In Reacher's service, it may interest you to know, are the last of the reptile men still in the world. If any natural beings I've seen are the equal of your Earthfast ogre guards, they are the reptile men of Freegate."

They spoke of assorted things for a time. Springbuck had removed his mask on making camp, but now his sword began to irk him, encumbering him as he sat. He removed it, and as he did so Andre eyed it attentively and asked that he might examine it.

"BAR," he read, thumbing the characters near the blood channels. "A curious name and not without meaning, I'm sure. What was it meant to bar, I wonder, and from what? Hmm, I perceive that though this glyph was struck upon the pommel at the time of the blade's forging, the lettering was mechanic'd into it later. The whole is of an age of generations; the glyph is of great efficacy and appears to have something to do with permanence, though I cannot make out what property or conditions it preserves. How intriguing, and I seem to half-remember—"

Springbuck told Andre of Bar's uncanny keenness and how he'd come on it, neglected in the armories at Earthfast. The plump sorcerer scanned his memory.

"That's it, then," he said. "A glyph to keep the blade eternally sharp and imperishably honed. This is the sword Never Blunted, first carried by your great-great-grandfather. His elder son carried it for years until he won the sword Flarecore in Veganá and gave Never Blunted to his younger brother. This brother carried it during the first campaign against the Meerionites and it served him bravely when he and a small detachment defended against a flanking sally. They held high ground while your great-grandfather carried the day—"

"Unaware that he'd come close to disaster," Springbuck finished, the tale coming back to him now. "And later the sword went to its owner's son, Pon. And when Grandfather was assaulted by an armed host as he bivouacked at a river tower near Daggerdraw, he and a few sword carls held the door of that small donjon."

"—and his cousin Pon fought a lone battle in its cellar, holding at a sally port for an hour against dozens of attackers before his war cries were heard over the hubbub of battle, after help had arrived." Andre nodded. "As I've said, young Heir, your heritage is proud. Court chroniclers recognized the deeds of the sword and the men who have borne it. Because it had ever been the defense at the back of the *Ku-Mor-Mai,* in the teeth of things, as it were, it was renamed Bar."

"And Pon became Pon of the Iron Arm," Springbuck said, having heard the story before, but without the redesignation of Never Blunted as Bar. He pulled the gleaming weapon from its scabbard of polished fish skin and white brass and cut the air with it. "Almost would I rather bear it than Flarecore, the sword of tradition."

"There was more honor in Bar, forged for the Protector Suzerain, than in Flarecore, which is stolen and is not with its proper owner," Andre said.

The Prince was indignant at this and retorted angrily, "Won by Springbuck's great-grandsire in Veganá, you mean. Would you deny spoils of just battle? Return a dangerous weapon to criminals?"

Andre shook his head.

"The sword belonged to one in Veganá who fought for Right with vigor as great as the *Ku-Mor-Mai.* Yardiff Bey met your ancestor on that journey with lies and distortions, hatching friction and feud between those who should have been friends and allies. When the Protector Suzerain returned to Earthfast, he took with him that which should have remained as a bulwark and symbol of resistance against harrying invaders.

"Even now Flarecore's spiritual legatee is an need of it to contend with the foes of Veganá."

"Andre, you're sure, you're certain, that Flarecore is the selfsame brand? The one that the *Ku-Mor-Mai* have used cannot be another?"

"Even so. As it was described to me, a cut-and-thrust greatsword, the blade green-blue and lustrous, damacened with silver and with many runes and sigils laid upon it. And the potency of the runes is that for whoever knows the proper incantation the blade breaks into flame which devastates whatsoever it touches. Even the arming girdle on which it's borne was described to me precisely, ornate and backed by mail and formed of oblong plaques, on each a raised crest that is the Leopard of Veganá. Is this not accurate?"

"To any detail," Springbuck confirmed. "And from whom comes this exacting inventory?"

"The sword's given name is Blazetongue, and I have its description from its true steward. You know, your great-great-grandfather had the knack of calling forth flames from it, but the trick was not passed on and the process is thought lost. Yet, I fear that Yardiff Bey may have the ability and give it to Strongblade to reinforce his claim to weapon and throne. It's not for nothing that Bey is named by his masters *al naiir Shardishku-Salamá hotan*; the Hand of Shardishku-Salamá in the Crescent Lands."

Yardiff Bey! The Prince flushed with anger at the name. The man had woven a web across the face of the world and his plots were without number, all meeting at this point in time. Even in his rage, the son of Surehand could see that the sorcerer had labored with absolute genius for long years and in many quarters and that his schemes were well thought on and far-looking.

"I suppose," he said to Andre, "that when I gain the throne you'll want me to return Flarecore—Blazetongue, I mean—to Veganá?"

"Justice dictates it, honor demands it. Veganá has always been a mainstay against invaders from the southwest, protecting the entire seaward end of the Crescent Lands, though at such a distance from Coramonde that your people have all but forgotten it. But that nation will fall soon unless some sort of aid arrives. Moreover, you already have one sword of high renown and weighty deeds; what would you need with two?"

Springbuck laughed, despite himself.

"And how is it, Sir Wizard, that you know so very much about my family and our affairs?"

"Hum, I, er, must confess, I became interested only when I understood that Yardiff Bey was. It behooved me to find out all I could about the lineage of the *Ku-Mor-Mai,* to unearth what I could of Bey's dealings with them over the years."

Springbuck nodded and shrugged, wishing to leave the subject, and cast an eye to the hour pole.

They'd spoken beyond the end of their watch, and so roused their relief and were both soon asleep.

They eluded several more contingents of fighting men during the nights thereafter, the soldiers always moving westward, hard. But on the third night, and from then on, the Western Tangent was empty and they encountered no one.

Prowling wolves and lions didn't care to molest so many men together, and they went their way untroubled. The landscape changed as trees once again grew in stingy copses and grassland was the rule. Terrain became less even, and the Tangent frequently notched through small hills, exposing naked rock walls to either side. With the moon waning, their going was slower than formerly, but they pushed their mounts to make all distance possible in darkness, and hid as best they could by day.

Still, Springbuck found time to be with Gabrielle. He was shy at first, clumsy with his conversation and self-conscious. Her cold reserve had softened to him, and she coaxed him along discreetly, holding back derision.

Van Duyn knew jealousy at this peculiar courtship, but hardened himself to it and resolved not to let it occupy his thoughts.

On the ninth night, or more correctly the dawn ending it, they came up through low foothills and saw a great obelisk twice the height of a man and hewn by much moil from the stone of that region. The merestone, marking the purview of Freegate, had engraved on its surface facing them a raised fist bearing a shattered chain. On the far side, Springbuck turned in passing and saw that the reverse face held the snarling tiger of Coramonde.

They tracèd the Tangent up into the cold mountains, and though it was seldom used, it was still in excellent condition. Once the way began to wind even higher in the peaks, however, they came to places where it was tilted by shifts in the very roots of the earth, convulsions from the times of the Great Blow.

Here the lordly eagle soared, companion to the wind, stately monarch of an empire of sheer canyons and star-challenging crags. They crossed spans of bridging, long stretches resting on fragile-appearing arches. Genteel plants had fallen away, leaving hardy scrub. The Tangent reached the highest summit by means of a long, winding uphill climb through a valley with several draws branching off—to dead ends, Andre said—to the right and left. They came to a stop at the apex, a narrow saddle of barren ground bordered by rocky swells at whose feet loose rubble lay. Then they pushed on, in daylight now, cold and tired. The road dipped into a smaller valley ringed with balanced boulders, then pushed its irresistible way down toward Freegate.

They stopped at a rain pool to water the horses, and Van Duyn considered how hard up they'd have been to traverse the Keel of Heaven had the Tangent not pierced the mountains for them. He wondered how, if the Tangent antedated the Great Blow which was rumored to have, among other things, created the range they traveled, the road seemed to have been built over the mountains. He made a mental note to inquire as he examined the rock walls at the side of the way. The stone gave the impression of having been molded aside, compacted somehow.

They camped just below the tree line at nightfall. Animal noises in the dark, disturbing even in the more familiar countryside of Coramonde, echoed and ululated through the mountains to grate on the nerves and conjure primeval fears. Andre caused their fire to burn high and brightly, for they had few apprehensions of pursuit now, but were wary of whatever solitary, malicious things there might be skulking through the Keel of Heaven. Springbuck rolled up in his thick, fleece-lined cloak with his back to the fire and didn't turn or voice surprise when he felt someone move up close to him, lying with back against him and face turned contemplatively to the fire. He knew that the revelations of the past days were working on Gabrielle's control, and was gratified that she sought solace in his nearness.

Van Duyn slept with his back to a boulder, his big rifle across his knees. Presumably, Andre deCourteney slept, though it might have been his choice to leave his material body, to contest against ill wishes and nightmare thoughts directed at his friends by spiteful inhabitants of the mountains, to send them flying before his undeflectable wrath.

At any rate, no harm came to any of the renegades from Coramonde there.

Shepherds hadn't been in evidence on the western side of the range, having fled rumors of war, but the eastern side was something else again. As they rode down the next morning, they encountered many flocks of rank-smelling sheep and goats and traffic of various sorts. The people seemed a fairly amiable lot, though they watched the riders with care.

Before long, a body of horsemen bearing lances showed up to block their path and ask their business. They were well armed, dressed in shirts of gambeson under mail, with plaid woolen pantaloons and colorfully enameled helmets. Their leader, wearing a winged casque, identified himself as a captain of the border guard of Freegate.

Andre came forward and said his name, adding, "These are my friends and allies, here to caucus with your King and at his behest."

The captain was plainly impressed but dutifully skeptical, and instructed his second-in-command to proceed on patrol with half the complement, positioning the remaining men before and behind the newcomers to serve as both honor escort and guard detail.

They went at a rapid pace toward Freegate proper; one soldier plucked a horn from where it hung at his side and blew loudly when the party approached any town or obstruction in the road. People and livestock alike scuttled from their path and the riders' travel was unimpeded.

By midafternoon they were down out of the foothills and passing through shallow valleys and occasional stretches of wood. Springbuck saw none of the remnants of times before the Great Blow which one encountered in Coramonde.

Finally, just beyond a last wide band of forest, the sun splashed from the white, lofty spires of Freegate. When they left the shadows of the timber, those who hadn't theretofore seen the free city gasped; Springbuck understood why it was one of the foremost strongholds of the world, a place where men walked with heads up proudly and eyes bright. Andre knew of only one place as imposing, the sea citadel of the Prince of the Waves.

And when the company of tired fugitives looked upon Freegate the Enduring, much of their weariness was forgotten and hope lifted their hearts once more.

Chapter Fifteen

With a host of furious fancies,
  Whereof I am commander,
With a burning spear and a horse of air,
  Into the wilderness I wander.

TOM O'BEDLAM'S SONG

FREEGATE stood upon a plateau in the valley. But perhaps it would be more accurate to say that the city and the table of land on which it was built were separated from the rest of that country by a gulf some half mile or more wide; while the plateau was level with the rest of the region, the chasm around it dropped nearly a thousand feet to a moat of extremely dense jungle—the only visible means of entrance to and egress from the city. The Western Tangent met the other three Ways at an awesome roundabout a mile or so beyond Freegate, connected by an approach artery to the stone bridgeway.

Perched on their side of the jungled gap, an imposing barbican defended the entrance. Through it passed a steady flow of people and animals, for the stone avenue was broad enough for a passage of men, vehicles and beasts in both directions. Sentries occasionally stopped this or that one, but most who went through the barbican to Freegate did so unmolested.

Nor were the newcomers to be discommoded by stoppage or search; at the blast of the patrolman's horn, the sentries cleared the passage and traffic stood to either side of the road to make way for King's business.

The view of the chasm far below, with its carpet of jungle, was a dizzying sight for most of them. The gates of the city proper, enormous valves of metal set in gleaming walls, stood open as evidence of Freegate's peaceful posture. Within them, an officer of the metro-

153

politan Watch sat horse, behind him two score of mounted men with coats of plates and pennoned lances carried butt-in-rest.

"What transpires?" he bellowed at the procession, which drew here to a halt.

"King's business," responded the captain of patrollers, and the Prince saw that this was formulaed challenge-and-answer.

"Specifically?"

"The thaumaturge Andre deCourteney, whom I recognize from his previous visit here, and his entourage for audience with the King."

"Return to your duties, if you please; I shall conduct them to His Highness."

The patroller rendered a salute, a raising of his flattened right hand, and was saluted in return. He then wheeled his horse and set off to the west, with his men behind him.

The watch officer addressed Andre. "My lord deCourteney, the King is at the hunt, but his sister, the Princess, will certainly wish to receive you at the palace."

Springbuck thought to intrude but decided not to; Andre must have reasons for not acknowledging his presence.

They resumed their way again with metropolitan Watchmen taking up the positions vacated by the border troops and brazen cymbals replacing the blaring horn to clear their path. They clattered through well-kept streets on wide cobblestones, passing shops, inns, countinghouses, temples, vendors' booths and homes. The palace, seat of the Freegate Kings, stood a short ride from the gates. Encompassed by a dazzling wall, it wasn't nearly as extensive as Earthfast. Storerooms, armories and a capacious cistern were located beneath it, and relatively few troops were quartered there. They reined in near the broad, chalk-white steps leading to the main doors of the palace. A groom stood nearby holding the ornate bridle of a graceful dun mare, the majordomo personally seeing to the arrangement of its riding tack. The officer explained his mission to that worthy, who came before Andre and addressed him with much deference and dignity.

"Eminent sir, the King is at the hunt, whither her Radiance the Princess Katya plans to go straightway to join him."

"We will wait here then," said Andre, "and I shall speak with her when she arrives." Again, the Prince wondered that the wizard did not demand an audience in the throne room with more formality. But Andre disliked the obligatory graces of royalty with their circuitous language and formal dithering, and the outdoors suited his taste well enough.

The majordomo hurried away as Van Duyn craned his neck to study the royal palace. It was a graceful structure and, like the wall surrounding it and most of the rest of the city, light and fair. There were many windows, balconies and terraces to it; scarcely architecture conceived with thought of war. The monarchs of Freegate must have implicit trust in the might of their outer fortifications and fighting men, he thought. At the top of the building was a large windmill. Van Duyn had noticed a number of them since coming to the city and wondered about their use.

The American's gaze, by some coincidence, went to the double doors just as a young woman appeared at the threshold; she was plainly the Princess Katya, for the majordomo bustled in her wake. Van Duyn sucked in his breath as she stepped into the light, stricken as so many had been by their first look at her.

She was tall, extremely so, with long, show-girl legs, full hips and a slim, supple waist. Her shoulders were limber and athletic, and her white-gold hair was caught up in a single hawser-like queue, bound with thongs. Her features were finely molded—a sensitive coral mouth, long nose and flaring dark eyebrows over violet eyes. She was in hunt clothes of glossy leather, britches with attached boots and a halter to contain full breasts. Low at her hips, a belt supported a brace of knives strapped down to either thigh. She was eating the last fragments of meat from a brochette. As she paused to toss it to the majordomo, Van Duyn studied the arresting profile.

She faced back to speak to them and he found her
voice quite pleasant and orotund. "Welcome, Andre."
She smiled, and it was as though the day had become
brighter and warmer. "You have come with a considerably larger retinue this time, if in obvious haste. It's always enjoyable to have you visit us with your—" She
hesitated for an instant, and when she continued, her
voice was tinged with amusement. "—your darling little
sister."

Gabrielle's carriage stiffened, and she scorned even
the curtest of acknowledgments. *Meeoowww!* thought
Van Duyn.

"I have other companions of no small prestige,"
Andre was saying. "This gentleman is Edward Van
Duyn, who comes from far away and even farther. And
here is our leader, His Highness, Springbuck, of Coramonde *Ku-Mor-Mai.*"

Katya betrayed no surprise as the Prince doffed his
plumed war mask and bowed politely in the saddle, returning his courtesy with an inclination of her head and
a wider smile. Springbuck was gratified with Andre's
reference to him as leader and Protector Suzerain. His
vision was sufficient to permit him to study the Princess
fairly well at this distance. The wizard had told him
that, on seeing her for the first time, some of Reacher's
blood brothers from the Howlebeau had instantly
named her *Sleethaná,* after the beautifully dangerous albino snow leopardess of the steppes. Springbuck understood their reference immediately. She had an elemental
appeal, conveying wild, free, supreme self-reliance.

"Ah, yesss," she said, and he saw the feline eyes inspect him and felt his heart beat speed up. "The
Prince—no, His Highness, you said? The *Ku-Mor-Mai*-in-exile is your title then?"

He shifted in his saddle and responded as casually as
he could. "Madam, I am Surehand's heir and have been
in exile since I passed the merestone on the border of
our two lands."

She laughed. "Exile? On the run, you mean, but
more of that later. My brother will want to hear. It took
you all long enough to get here, though. We shall go;

you, Van Duyn and the deCourteneys and I to join Reacher at the hunt. That is, unless any of you feel too fatigued to come?" She spoke her last sentence gazing guilelessly into Gabrielle's eyes. The sorceress returned the look with hauteur and Springbuck hoped that she was not about to unleash some horrible spell in a fit of pique.

Instructing her servants to see to the other members of the party, Katya leaped lithely into the saddle, spurred her mount and was away, the others trailing behind in varying amounts of proficiency. Without escort or entourage, they galloped through the streets; and though the people didn't bend knee or otherwise abase themselves at her passing, many called gay greetings with obvious affection for their spectacular Princess. Van Duyn had the thought that the Snow Leopardess probably never received any overly familiar or rude halloos; she struck him as being quite capable of defending her dignity against all comers. He speculated as to whether her brother would turn out to be a self-conscious twerp dominated by a bossy older sister. It would fit the pattern in a case like this, with an elder, female Tarzan sort of sister.

They raced through the city and the gate at the opposite side of town from the stone bridgeway, then past areas of open drill field and military exercise lots. On uncluttered ground, Springbuck gave Fireheel his head. The long-legged gray, with the grace and speed of small desert breeds and the size and endurance of northern bloodlines, surged forward; after a short but fierce contest for passage, Fireheel gained the lead from the Snow Leopardess, who was urging her mount determinedly. Her single braid stood out behind her in the wind as she shouted and laughed for the pure joy of competition, while they tore past cultivated fields and farmers stopped to straighten from their toil and watch. The others' horses were not up to this race, being fatigued, and the exclusive duel was resolved when Springbuck got a sufficient lead to bring Fireheel to a complete stop and turn before she could draw even with him.

She, too, drew rein. "Why did you stop?" she demanded. "I was about to cajole my girl into another try at that gray brute; it hurts her to see anyone's hooves in her face."

The Prince again removed his mask. "I merely stopped to give you and the rest a chance to catch up. After all, I don't know the land around here and I didn't want to get so far ahead as to become lost all alone."

She laughed at his gibe, no discreet titter but a full-blown roar, her head thrown back. "Aye, the plateau lands are big enough to get lost in; twelve miles long and nigh eight wide."

Springbuck spied the others coming up behind. "It could not be a natural formation then, I suppose."

"In part, but it was altered back before the Great Blow fell. The stone bridgeway was narrowed some, I guess, and the jungle in the chasm is part natural, part man-made. And of course, the jungle itself was fostered and stocked."

"Stocked?"

"Surely. No one goes down there, and there are numerous stories about what lives there, but when the dragons of the waste waged war on the city over one hundred years ago and were repulsed with runic bolts whose art is lost now, some that were wounded fell to the treetops below to be dragged down into them by something which men never saw or identified." They were riding stirrup and stirrup now, like old friends, as the other three caught up and fell in behind. Springbuck was thinking of her story, remembering Chaffinch, a *small* dragon. What could possibly prey on such as that?

"Interesting," he said. "I'd never heard that yarn."

"No? What sort of Prince doesn't trouble to inform himself on the doings of neighbor-states?"

He glanced over his shoulder for help. Andre and Van Duyn were looking on with some amusement, but Gabrielle stared poisoned daggers at him. "Actually," he replied lamely, "I had to spend a good deal of time studying the affairs and history of Coramonde, so diverse and complex are they."

Van Duyn moved up even with them. "Your Radiance," he said smoothly, "please tell me more about your country, since I, too, am in ignorance. I'm particularly interested in your free trade system."

The Snow Leopardess' attention was effectively diverted. While the American feasted on the sight and sound of her, the Prince fell back and rode next to Gabrielle, who was busily ignoring the existence of everyone on the road. Andre moved up to the spot vacated by the Prince, the better to hear Katya. The son of Surehand leaned close to the red-haired enchantress and whispered, "It was only a horserace. I just didn't want her to have the satisfaction of beating us all."

Her eyes stayed fixed coldly ahead but, without turning, she reached out and grasped his wrist in one white hand with a grip of surprising strength.

"You're a puppy and a fool, who chases tomgirls," she hissed softly, but the pressure of her hand was not that of anger.

"Your knives," the scholar was saying, exhibiting more charm to the Princess than Springbuck had seen him employ in all the time he'd known him. "They are unusual weapons for a woman to use. I notice that you've a long and a short one on each side. Why is this?"

"Ha! The bigger ones, that are canted backward so that I may take them quickly, these are combat knives, infighting knives. The smaller ones are throwing daggers, and I wear them so that I may have either type of blade in either hand if I will. But here, what is this strange thing you have across your saddle bow?"

Van Duyn hefted the M-1. "It's a rifle, a weapon of my people, unlike anything you have here."

They rode through some patches of undergrowth into a series of thickets and glades. To her companions the Snow Leopardess said, "A farmer hereabouts brought in a brace of wild swine, hoping to domesticate them, the idiot. They savaged him and broke free early today and it is them we hunt."

A man arrayed in green livery approached them on foot, a hunting bow held with arrow nocked.

"What word, huntmaster?" called Katya.

"His Highness even now closes on the beasts," came

the reply. "And as always he will not use spear or bow
but wears his steppeman's gear and courses with the
very hounds, leaping along among them. He picked up
the swine spoor before they did and now drives his prey
this way. I think I may have a shot at them before too
long."

With a crow of delight the Snow Leopardess jumped
to the ground. "No, huntmaster," she said. "I have had
to attend to matters of state while my brother hunted.
Fairness says that I should get the kill and not he. Stand
by our guests." And so saying, she reached to her saddle and drew forth a boar-spear-bladed sword, one with
a straight blade which was circular in cross section for
most of its length. It widened at the end into a broad,
heavy spearhead with a bar to fend off impaled prey. It
was, the Prince reflected, a weapon to be used only by
the most daring and capable of hunters; any falter or
miscalculation would mean maiming or death. Just as
he was considering violating etiquette by suggesting that
the Princess allow the bowman out front, Van Duyn
dismounted and, taking his rifle in hand, walked over to
stand near her.

"If you miss, perhaps I'll get a chance to show you
how this thing works," he said, holding up the Garand.

She smiled savagely but with an air of camaraderie,
and told him, "I don't miss."

The baying of the dogs came nearer, accompanied by
the shouts of their trainers. The group waited in various
states of tension for long minutes. When Gabrielle
would have dismounted, the Prince instructed her to
stay ahorse. She looked at him in a way he could not
interpret, but complied.

A crashing in the undergrowth brought them around.
The boar, a five-hundred-pounder, broke from cover
across the clearing from them. To Van Duyn it resembled nothing so much as a porcine locomotive. It
ground to a halt when its tiny, insane red eyes fell upon
them. It lingered for a moment, razor-sharp hooves
tearing up the turf, then gathered itself to charge as the
Snow Leopardess braced herself.

The American threw his rifle to his shoulder. His
first look at this terrifying animal, with its long, froth-

covered tusks ripping the air in search of a yielding target, decided him; there was no question of going after such a hydrophobic monster with a sword. But as he made to bring it into his sights, another figure sprang from the brush with an ear-shattering battle cry.

Van Duyn had only a fleeting glance at the man who threw himself at the rampaging boar. He was short, a fair-haired, deeply tanned fellow who was well muscled and yet moved easily as he eluded a murderous rip of the foam-flecked tusks. He was barefoot and wore gauntlets and a loin clout, and had no weapon that the American could see.

Van Duyn raised his M-1 again, certain that the man, whom he took to be Reacher, would meet a painful death if he didn't act. He found, however, that as the monarch feinted and dodged to avoid the boar's rushes, Katya showed no sign of concern for her brother's safety, but waved her sword and bawled encouragement.

The baying, grown steadily louder, reached a crescendo as two sleek hounds burst on the scene. The boar found itself in the midst of three enemies now, all nipping or feigning at him as he spun and slashed. Then he made a fatal move; facing the man, he felt a tug at his rear as one of the dogs took a fierce bite at his rump. He swung his head viciously, mad from incessant baitings. In that instant, the King darted in, lifting his left hand and bringing it down in a terrific blow to the weighty collar of gristle protecting the wild swine's neck.

As its front legs buckled, the beast dropped to its knees, stunned as if by the slam of a sledgehammer. Then it surged wildly in an effort to regain its feet. The King's hand moved again, more swiftly than the onlookers could see or fully appreciate, gripping the boar's snout and pulling up and back, drawing the throat taut. The hunter's right hand, fingers clawed and flashing, swept in a blindingly fast rake across the exposed target, and blood fountained. He jumped clear of the death throes.

With the exception of the Princess, all were speechless at the speed and power of the triumphant King of

Freegate. Van Duyn, standing on the extreme left of the company as Katya clapped her hands and cheered, was first to catch a glimpse of a brown blur breaking from the foliage on his left. It was the second wild hog, bearing down on the King, who was apparently unaware of its approach behind him. The American took no time to yell a warning or check to see if the huntsman could get in a shot with his bow; he brought up the Garand and fired in one programmed motion. His hours of painstaking practice served him well, and he never again regretted the inconvenience and sore shoulder that range time had cost him prior to his second departure from his home cosmos. The boar stopped as if it had hit a wall. The heavy slug, moving at 2800 feet per second, caught it just behind its head, pitching it sideways.

The rifle's effect on the people of Freegate was nearly as drastic. Reacher, who had pivoted and dropped into guard to face the second swine just before Van Duyn had fired, gazed from the dead quarry to its slayer in calm curiosity, head tilted inquisitively. The huntmaster had dropped his bow and, screwing his eyes shut, clapped his hands to his ears with a scream of fear. The Snow Leopardess whirled and brought her sword up with a hiss of surprise which dissipated almost immediately. Like her brother, she glanced from carcass to scholar and smoking weapon.

"Remarkable," she breathed after a moment. "How far away will it kill?"

He didn't answer, since Reacher joined them at that juncture. Save Katya and Springbuck, all bowed in courtesy. Without touching it, Reacher examined the M-1 with much interest. Close up, his diminutive size was more obvious. At age twenty-four, he was no more than five feet four or so, but muscled like a panther, his legs long and shoulders wide for his height, and they'd already been shown his astounding quickness and brawn. He'd destroyed the boar in sport, without qualm.

"You should know," Katya said almost huffily to Van Duyn, "that my brother was aware of the second beast's proximity; his senses are the equal of his prowess."

Springbuck was studying his royal host, now that the man was close enough for the Prince to make him out without difficulty. He knew from the first moment that he'd never be able to match this King in sheer fighting ability and predatory keenness.

The King's skin was weathered and his eyes, slightly darker versions of his sister's, crinkled at their corners. His gloves were of two types; the left a heavy cestus covering the hand from just behind the wrist to just beyond the middle knuckles, tough leather bound up tight and banded about with metal to form impact surfaces. The right glove was longer, laced almost to the elbow, and where his fingers ended within the fingertips of the glove, long claws glittered wickedly, artfully affixed artificial talons.

"Your Highness," said Andre, "may I present His Highness, Prince Springbuck, lawful Pretender to the throne of the *Ku-Mor-Mai?*"

The Prince doffed his mask as the monarch turned to him, returning the scrutiny the son of Surehand had exercised on him moments before. Both inclined their heads slightly at the same time, satisfying protocol. Springbuck found the Lord of the Just and Sudden Reach's presence not uncomfortable, though the small ruler spoke not at all.

Katya turned a haughty eye to the huntmaster, who was attempting to pull himself back together. "My brother will use your horse to return to the city. Fetch it; the King shouldn't run beside mounted folk. Oh, and see to the kills and distribute their meat at the beggars' plaza. Slain as they were, their meat will be bloody and unfit for daintier palates."

Then other huntsmen came to the scene, drawn by barking dogs and the single shot. They were set to dressing the quarry after bringing up the huntmaster's horse, while Van Duyn and Andre complimented Reacher on his success. He made no comment in return, but didn't seem aloof or impolite; he merely listened and studied the newcomers silently.

Then they were all mounted and away, back to the city proper in the thinning light.

"I see all the land, nearly, put to use for cultivation

and grazing, Your Radiance," Van Duyn said to the Princess. "But I see no villas or manses in this pleasant place. Why so?"

"In case of siege," she said. "Every inch of land on the plateau must work for us and our stock. If fat merchants or idle nobles want to build pleasure houses outside the city, they may do so, but only on the other side of the bridgeway. We don't permit them to occupy an important defense asset with drafty dust traps and rambling, artsy sculpture gardens. And you would do me a favor in foregoing that Radiance nonsense among us, comrade."

She then turned the talk to his rifle, intrigued with it in a good-naturedly bloodthirsty way. He was evasive, and glad when a troop of household cavalry, in tall plumes and armor of varnished cuir-bouilli shaped to their bodies, met them to escort them back to the palace.

They left their horses and entered the building via the broad front steps, though it was said that Reacher and his sister had other, less conspicuous ways of entering and leaving their home. Springbuck had noticed that Reacher seemed to miss little; on the ride back he'd been interested in the condition of the citizens they'd passed, had inconspicuously inspected the troops and been always attentive to the wind and the sounds and smells he read from it. Now, the Prince saw him notice each small detail of the palace's maintenance. It also occurred to Springbuck that it had been coincidental that the King had made his kill in the precise place where the rest could see it, and he wondered if Reacher hadn't arranged matters somehow, perhaps by driving the animals there, to display his competence.

The King and his sister conducted their guests to the first of their home's unusual conveniences, an elevator which, Katya explained to Van Duyn, worked from the same source which impelled water throughout the building, the windmill he'd seen, regulated by an intricate system of weights and pulleys and capable of storing its energy against windless days by lifting great ballasts, to be gradually lowered later. The device seemed slow to Van Duyn, reminding him of those damnable machines he'd encountered in France.

The elevator, barely big enough for the six of them, ground to a halt. Its doors opened on a wide lawn, the blue sky serene around them and Freegate spread below. They were at the pinnacle of the palace, high above any other structure in the city. The roof was covered with turf and small trees, flowers and foliage. A multitude of birds of all sorts nested and perched at all parts of the garden, making full-throated song. At the center of it was a luxuriously appointed belvedere housing Reacher's private chambers.

"And in case of siege, will this become a cabbage patch?" asked Van Duyn of the Snow Leopardess.

"That and carrots, I should think," she replied.

They were ushered into the belvedere, which offered thick fur carpeting, silken drapings and furnishings of highly polished, fragrant wood and black-veined marble that were upholstered in velvet, silk and the hides of rare beasts. There were also sculptures, mosaics and paintings of the hunt, warfare and sybaritic subjects. Springbuck sensed that Reacher hadn't done the decorating here and decided that it probably reflected his sister's taste.

King and Princess disappeared for a few minutes, leaving the visitors to the ample hospitality of deferential servants. Soon they were all together again, four guests and two hosts, weapons and equipment put aside, sunken in comfortable furniture and eating and drinking from trays of refreshments. The servants were dismissed and the wayfarers fell to with gusto.

"There'll be time later for display of paraments and formal speaking," said the Snow Leopardess, "and I think perhaps that the easiest way to state our respective positions is for you to say on, and tell how you come to be here."

"I will tell the tale then," the Prince said, and Katya looked to her brother, who bobbed his head once.

"Agreed," she said, and they all knew beyond a doubt then that, though he spoke seldom, Reacher had the final word on all matters within that realm.

Springbuck told the story completely, including some of Van Duyn's history, with but the deletion of the matter of Gabrielle's parentage. If she wished it known, he thought, she could bring it out herself.

The King and Princess listened to the unfolding account of the conspiracies of Yardiff Bey and his warmaking plans for their nation. When Springbuck had finished, the room was hushed for a moment. Then the Snow Leopardess spoke.

"You had a difficult time of your escape, Highness—I'll call you Springbuck, with your let—but you would have reached here with greater dispatch if you'd not made one fundamental mistake."

So saying, she rose and strode to a curtained doorway, drawing aside the hangings.

The Prince's astonishment knew no bounds as the Lady Duskwind stepped forth. Taken off balance, he could do no more than gape at her dumbly.

"The Lady Duskwind is our cousin," Katya said. "She has been our agent in your father's court for these past two years, and a capable operative even before she was sent there. She was about to spirit you away here, and had slain the traitor Faurbuhl to prevent him from raising the hue and cry, when you were returned to your room that last evening at Earthfast and misapprehended all. Before she could explain, it seems, you trussed her up like a naming-day gift."

The Prince wasn't shocked by the revelation that Freegate kept spies in the Court of the *Ku-Mor-Mai;* this was standard procedure and Coramonde had occasionally returned the courtesy. He experienced a stab of bitterness, though, that one of them should have been Duskwind; he'd been under the impression that she was from a place other than Freegate. But it was quickly replaced by a wave of relief that she hadn't been harmed and gratitude that she'd been prepared to act in his interests at the risk of her life. The painful details of the incident, including Hightower's death, threatened to intrude again, and so he turned his attention to the loveliness of Duskwind.

She was, as ever, marvelous to look upon. Her honey-streak hair was bound tightly at the nape of her

neck in a simple twist, her demure gown covered neck
and wrists; as always, her slender, elegant fingers blazed
with rings, while anklets clinked and jingled softly at
her barefoot steps. She smiled faintly at him. As she
turned to seat herself in one of the plush chairs, he saw
that, modest as her attire was in front, it dipped shame-
lessly low in back.

Arousing as the sight of her was, however, he found
his thoughts and gaze drifting back to Gabrielle. Travel-
worn and weary though she was, the sorceress drove
Duskwind from his mind. She met his eye now with an
expression more eloquent than words, her languorous
smile and the humor in a lifted eyebrow saying, "Content yourself with looking at this girl of your youth. I
am Gabrielle deCourteney; you are with me now, and
know it." Some jolt or thrill ran through him then, but
of ecstasy or of dread, he didn't know.

"Needless to tell," the Snow Leopardess was continuing, "she was hard put to escape and find Captain Brodur, whom she'd enlisted in her plans—you have a rude
way with a girl, Springbuck! But my cousin is a re-
sourceful female. She was successful at relaying news of
your flight to those who remain loyal to you, and in
persuading them to play a waiting game. She's still possessed of enough blackmailing information to assure us
a flow of news."

Van Duyn was fascinated by all this. Duskwind
couldn't be more than a ripe eighteen, yet for two years
she'd been calmly, patiently spying and contriving, con-
cealing her actions in her role as courtier and later as
consort to the Prince. When the crisis had come, she'd
kept her head and done what she had to, accomplishing
what she could before fleeing for her life. His admiration was very, very high.

The scholar glanced around the room, deciding that
the three women there were the most striking collection
of femininity he'd ever seen in one place. The Juno-
esque, pallid Snow Leopardess, the fiery Gabrielle de-
Courteney and now the doe-eyed Duskwind vied for attention to the delightful point that he no longer knew
where to look next. His spirits were on the decided upswing. During the trip from Erub he'd tried to eradicate

all feelings for the enchantress from his heart, aided by her obvious affection for Springbuck.

After hearing from Andre of her ill-fated love and marriage, he'd identified the nature of her hurt and its effect on her behavior and had resisted the impulse to become deeply involved, recognizing that eventually she'd leave him. But at his age, an affair with such an extraordinary woman had led him to give more of himself than he'd intended. Objectively, he had to admit that Gabrielle held her own against the other two women. His musing turned to Katya; he began to consider ways in which he might become more intimate with her. Contrary to his usual habits he drifted into a daydream. He was healing.

"His interests are not limited to war against Freegate," Springbuck was saying. "Bey intends to use Strongblade to dominate the High Ranges. Then his reach will turn westward until his fist encloses all of the Crescent Lands."

Katya asked, "With what plan do you come to us, outlaws? The strength of Freegate cannot go forth against the numberless armies of Coramonde. Even now Legion-Marshal Novanwyn is assembling the forces of the southwest. Evidently the murder of Hightower has evoked much unrest in his family and friends. Bey is taking no chance on using eastern troops, whose loyalty is in doubt. So you see, there is little refuge for you here; we will shortly look to the safety of our own halls. What do you offer us?"

Before Andre or Van Duyn could muster an answer, Springbuck seized the initiative. "We come with the same idea which must have been in your mind when you tasked Duskwind to aid in my escape. You cannot win in unqualified warfare, but you might be able to delay the reach of my enemies, distract them sufficiently for me to fan popular support in Coramonde and launch a revolution to take back the throne at Earthfast. We will work on these two fronts and woo the help of Glyffa and other western states that we may topple Bey's puppets. The question which occurs to me first is whether Freegate can hold her own for the requisite time."

The Snow Leopardess leaned forward. "We do not plan to stand alone. We shall enlist the aid of our allies, the steppes dwellers. And the question which occurs to *me,* my young cock-a-hoop, is whether you have any hope of swaying the support of the substates of Coramonde."

The Prince's head was erect, his posture rigid with pride and his face was fell to see. "They will rally to me. I am their Protector Suzerain." And those in the room were aware of a new imperiousness, a fixed and firm confidence, and there was approval now in the expression of Gabrielle.

"On the way to Freegate we formulated plans for the implementation of an underground movement," he continued, "and it is even now being germinated by a kernel group we left behind in Coramonde." He went into the details of the guerrilla campaign as outlined by Gil MacDonald, its directions, tactics, organization and priorities. He considered mentioning Van Duyn's intention of changing Coramonde's government, but rejected the idea; these royal siblings might see it as a threat to their own monarchy.

"This MacDonald sounds as if he knows his business," murmured Katya. "You say you expect him to return from wherever it is that he went?"

"Just so. We agreed on a time and place for his reappearance. His help may be critical in this campaign."

The consultations continued, and soon all were contributing suggestions and criticisms to the materializing plans; even the unspoken hostility between Gabrielle and the Snow Leopardess was eased. All spoke, that is, save Reacher. The King sat his chair, smallest member of the group, as if he were enthroned—not with pomp and posturing, but wearing an invisible mantle of authority. If it had not been for his hunting call in the glade earlier, the Prince would have thought him mute. Somehow, without offending them, he managed to make all those around him feel like subordinates. Springbuck studied and learned.

But it was Reacher who brought the conference to an end when, late that evening, he interrupted his sister in midsentence by rising to his feet. She faced him at once, speech forgotten, attention exclusively for her brother.

"I must confess that I shall need time to let my slow wits absorb all these things," he said, though Springbuck knew that this wasn't true; the King had made his analysis and conclusions already. "Tomorrow I will leave for the High Ranges to confirm the aid of our allies the Horseblooded. Prince Springbuck, if he feels sufficiently rested, is invited to accompany me, as befits a cobelligerent. I thank you all most sincerely for your excogitations, welcome you as comrades-in-arms and bid you make yourselves comfortable in this place. It is as much yours as mine now."

And this was proof positive to the son of Surehand that the King of Freegate lacked nothing in the way of diplomatic graces, however much he pretended otherwise.

Chapter Sixteen

By a knight of ghosts and shadows,
  I summoned am to tourney,
Ten leagues beyond the wide world's end.
  Methinks it is no journey!

TOM O'BEDLAM'S SONG

EACH of the four was shown to a comfortable suite of rooms not far below the belvedere. The Prince would have liked to return to Gabrielle's rooms to tarry, but as leader he felt compelled to find, with the help of a household portglave, the quarters of the Erubites and inquire after their well-being. Satisfied that they were provided for and well situated, he returned to his own rooms.

He permitted the domestics, two women, to bathe and groom him and to take away his weapons and attire for servicing. He thanked them sleepily as they led him to his bed; as they tiptoed out, he settled himself snugly in puffy pillows and heavy covers, dropping into the deepest sleep he'd enjoyed since leaving Earthfast.

When he arose late the next morning, he performed his ablutions without aid. When the servitors entered, he requested that they have a selection of clothing and armor brought. He'd broken his fast and was evaluating various suits of mail, mesh and plate when Reacher knocked and entered.

"We may yet make much distance today," said the King, who was dressed as for the hunt, cestus and clawed glove on his hands. "I don't suggest you wear armor. Steppes people are not unlike your Alebowrenians and consider such things effete. Your traveling outfit, the bravo's gear, is more fitting, but I warn you not to wear spurs. The Wild Riders don't use them. I go appareled as you see me, and will await you in the courtyard and see to our mounts."

Springbuck, uncertain up to this point that he even wanted to accompany the King on this mission, had little option.

The servants hadn't needed to see to Bar's perpetually keen brightness, but they'd scoured all blemishes from his main-gauche, honed it, put all tarnish from the metal parts of his trappings and cleaned his leathers, coating them with a light dubbing of oil and drying them. As in Earthfast, he judged that he didn't want to be burdened with armor.

Booted, armed and bearing his war mask in the crook of his left arm, the Prince was guided to the courtyard. Fireheel had been well cared for and was standing ready, provisions strapped to the reconnaissance saddle with his cloak. Reacher was astride a small bay.

The Coramondian Pretender heard a piercing whistle and looked upward for its author. Leaning out over a balcony was Gabrielle, wrapped in a fur robe. She laughed and waved, showing much white skin, but the Prince, about serious business, was unwilling to do more than incline his head perfunctorily.

"I see no mounted men," he said to the King. "Are we to be slowed by footmen?"

The majordomo at his liege's side answered for him. "Your Grace, your faring will be slowed by no one. His Majesty prefers no retinue, since your trip is one of urgency, and feels no need of armed companions. Who could hope to prevail against the King and *Ku-Mor-Mai,* all in their strength?"

The Prince made no response to this shrewd question, but mounted Fireheel. Donning war mask, he was away at the King's side, wondering how many more times he'd sleep huddled in his cloak before he encountered a bed as soft as the one he'd vacated. It wasn't long before he began wishing that the trip had been delayed, or at the very least that he'd fought off his fatigue the preceding night and visited Gabrielle.

And he thought, too, of the issues of life and death which murked the future for all of them.

Van Duyn awoke to the racket of hooves and looked out of his balcony doors just in time to see Reacher and Springbuck ride through the palace gates. For some time he followed their progress from his vantage point as they moved down the city's streets.

He summoned servants, bathed and shaved, then dined as he selected a new outfit from those shown him; soft sandals, loose trousers and short, wraparound jacket with a sort of cummerbund. He left the Garand and its bandolier behind the curtains where he'd hidden it the night before, but tucked the Browning inside his waistband.

Since no one had informed him of any schedule of activities, the American decided to explore the palace. He passed unhindered through beautiful galleries, elegant reception halls, huge storerooms and glittering armories. What sentries and domestics he met bowed to their ruler's guest and treated him with all respect. He came to pass a door near the main armory and heard a quick *wwhhht-chunk,* repeated a second later. Curious, he opened the door and stepped inside to find the Snow Leopardess engaged in practice with her knives.

She stood twelve paces from a swinging target dummy, a case of blades on a stand next to her. She turned at his entry. The sight of her made his day.

"Good morning, Van Duyn. No, don't go; wait until I throw a final brace and we'll talk."

He didn't need to be invited twice, and she returned her attention to her exercise. He had difficulty seeing the motion as she released her left-hand knife with an upward snap, letting fly with the right one overhand. The blades drove home side by side at the bull's-eye.

"Superb," Van Duyn said.

She accepted his praise as her due. "I try not to throw more than fifteen paces in combat, but I'm always accurate under that. I don't recall the last time I missed, in fact."

"Combat? Surely Your Rad—you don't actually go into battle?"

She grimaced. "Reacher usually doesn't let me, but once or twice I got away for a go at bandits and border raiders. In fact, I tried like hell to go to the High Ranges with him, but he said no, and that was that."

Like her brother, she wore hunt clothes. Van Duyn was to discover that the two preferred them whenever possible. She reached into a cabinet and drew out her knife belt, buckling it at her hips and settling the weapons precisely, then strapping the tie-downs at each thigh. She offered to show him around a bit more and he accepted at once.

As they walked, they spoke of this and that, though her interests lay primarily in politics and war. He found her less aloof and more open than at their first meeting, not quite so guarded. The American saw that she shared some measure of her brother's physical aptitudes and disliked the fripperies of Court, as Reacher did.

As they came to the bottom of a sweeping flight of stairs bordered by a walnut banister studded with silver nails, they rounded a corner and Van Duyn received one of the great shocks of his life. He cried aloud and threw himself backward, groping at his pistol, eyes goggling in horror at the monstrous creature blocking their path.

The Snow Leopardess laughed. "Don't be alarmed at the sight of Kisst-Haa. Hideous as he is, the old dear, he's a brave and faithful guardian, and leader of our reptile-men."

The being scrutinized the American for a moment, then made a deep bow, rumbling softly. The man stared back in slack-jawed amazement. Tall as she was, Katya was dwarfed by the reptile-man, who stood close to seven feet and seemed to resemble a sort of simian tyrannosaurus. His face, if that's what one would call it, held strange intelligence in yellow beacon-eyes, offsetting the enormous fangs jutting from his jaws. His shoulders were wide to facilitate movements of arms and handlike claws. His movements were brisk. His body was covered with a thick, green-scaled hide, and while he wore no clothing—nor needed any—his great tail was encased in articulated caudal armor from which spikes and razor flanges projected. At Kisst-Haa's back was slung an immense broadsword nearly as tall as he. So colossal was it that the pommel knob set to balance the weight of its ponderous blade was the size of a cannonball. Considering the titanic girth of the reptileman's wrists and arms, Van Duyn was willing to bet that he'd have no difficulty working the greatsword like a hickory switch. All things being equal, Van Duyn agreed with Andre: the reptile was the match of the brutal ogre-guards in the Court at Earthfast.

Katya led him closer; her touch was light, but he felt a shock, as if a spark had crackled between them. Kisst-Haa demonstrated his familiarity with the human custom of shaking hands. The American's large hand was lost in the other's grasp. Kisst-Haa carefully exerted only infinitesimal pressure, but the man knew that he could have crushed puny flesh and bone to paste, effortlessly.

When amenities were finished, the scholar stepped back as Katya slipped her elbow through Kisst-Haa's tree-bough arm and laid her fair head against him. "He is my confidant and one true friend since childhood."

She disengaged herself and Kisst-Haa bowed to her, boomed briefly in his own sibilant tongue, bowed to Van Duyn and set off again on his nameless errand.

The Princess and the American took up their interrupted tour once more, and after some time Van Duyn said, "Surely a Princess must have more friends than one. Are you truly so desolate for acquaintances?"

"Not for acquaintances, certainly, but for friends. I dislike the sort who come to Court in greatest numbers; they tend to be idlers and fops, and those toward whom I feel admiration, the officers and warriors of the Realm, hold Reacher too much in awe to do anything but bow and stammer in place of conversation. For truth, the coming of your fellowship—even that scarlet-haired spell spinner—is welcome surcease from my bland life."

He presumed that she was exaggerating, but didn't say as much. "Katya, I can't lay claim to courtly manners, but I'd consider it an honor to do what I may to alleviate your, er, tedium."

"Splendid! But if I hadn't seen you use that flashroar weapon of yours I'd fear that I'd another amorous coxcomb on my hands. Very well—Edward, is it not?—

Edward then, you'll sit at my side at dinner and while those ninnies prattle about the proper length of tippets, you can regale me with details of military practices and state intrigues in your land."

Van Duyn shrugged mentally. It was a beginning.

The north country sloped gradually up through fertile river valleys into rising hills. Springbuck had expected at least to guest at inns or local officials' Keeps until they were at the steppes, but Reacher asked almost shyly if he would mind camping outdoors, explaining that this was something he rarely got to do at Freegate. The Prince acquiesced and spent chilly nights bunched in his cloak by a fire listening to howling predators. Yet Reacher curled up without cover and slept blissfully.

Riding swiftly and, as far as Springbuck could tell, without being recognized by the few people they saw, they breasted a low mountain range within four days of their departure from the palace. Spread before them, limitless and somehow inviting, were the grassy steppes, the High Ranges, subcontinent in their own right. To their left they could see a small outpost ringed by a palisade of thick logs laboriously brought up from the south. The last permanent concentration of humanity on their trip, a trading station, was where Reacher left his mount in the care of the local justiciary. This was the perimeter of Freegate's purview; a merestone stood by the outpost's north gate. On the side facing Freegate was carved a galloping horse, to let the traveler know he was entering the ranges of the Horseblooded.

"But why not ride the whole way?" the Prince asked. "You rode in Freegate to preserve dignity, rather than walk alongside us afoot. And aren't the Wild Riders going to think less of you?"

The King made an unusually long answer. "I ride in the low country; that's a matter of Face. In the high country I am Howlebeau; none of us would rely on an animal for transport."

"But you said you'll take part in some sort of contest or match when we arrive at the meeting grounds. Why tire yourself trying to keep up with Fireheel?"

Reacher grinned. "Fireheel's a fine horse. I think we'll run well together, he and I."

Springbuck's wonder increased when they set out, the justiciary and his deputies seeing them off at the mere-stone, because the King fell into a steady lope, matching that of the gray. The horse, though visibly irked at the man-creature pacing him, was in high spirits at his first excursion on the High Ranges. He tossed his head, petitioning for a gallop through the ocean of grass.

They moved along all through the long day and for two days thereafter, seeing no other human beings on the treeless steppes. They frequently spied tremendous grazing herds of horses, antelope and bison blanketing the land for miles, and saw packs of wild dogs and outsized wolves. All avoided them. Their campfires were pungent, since they had to use dried animal droppings for fuel. Springbuck suspected that the King permitted the fires only out of courtesy and would rather have done without. He couldn't see how Reacher navigated on the featureless plain, whether by sun and stars or some instinct, and didn't ask.

Reacher would occasionally dash away from their course to return with some type of small game for their meal. The rest of the time he forged along mutely, heels never touching the ground, nose high to test the wind, to all appearances as happy as he could be. The two generally held quiet conversation for a short time at night before retiring. Yet the Prince began to feel closer to Reacher as the steppes began to expand in his mind, their boundlessness stretching to fill the world and crowd more populated countries into insignificance. He found this feeling untroublesome, his companionship with Reacher unlabored.

At midmorning of the fourth day on the steppes they came on a sprawling tent camp, a temporary city, with miles of scattered clusters around clan banners. As they entered the camp they instantly collected a trail of small children and dogs, who in turn were joined by their elders, who raised an even greater commotion than the youngsters. Reacher was plainly a favorite here. Springbuck was never sure how he'd found this bivouac, whether by prearrangement, smell or some hidden signs.

On their way down systematically aligned streets, they passed practice fields, animal pens—the whole camp reeked of them—communal water barrels, trading areas and cooking fires.

Of course, there were many mounted men, some sitting horses close in size to Fireheel, but most on small shaggy mounts bred of the fierce tarpans roaming the steppes. Fireheel filled the air with high whistles of challenge until Springbuck curbed him sharply.

The Horseblooded, as they called themselves after their close attachment to their animals, were for the most part a ruddy, stocky sort with straight, strawlike blond or red hair, usually caught up in the back like a tail to emulate their beloved horses. There was an air of formidability about them, yet they were friendly and open, delighting in Reacher's arrival as that of some special hero. The men wore fleece vests, breeches of wool or silk and many bracelets and armlets. Most wore some form of riding boots or pants bound tightly with thongs, and all carried a variety of weapons. Springbuck noticed one in particular, a big fellow on a white gelding fully of a size with Fireheel. He wore sword and dagger at one hip and a mace of flanges thrust through his belt at the other. Three long darts and an atlatl were tucked into one high boot and a horsehair quirt hung from his wrist, which surprised the Prince, since he'd been told by Reacher that the Horseblooded eschewed quirts or spurs. The man's saddle supported a bow and quiver of arrows, a gaily decorated shield and a braided rope, and he carried two javelins in his right hand. He didn't laugh or applaud Reacher, but watched him carefully with no liking in his expression.

At what was approximately the center of camp, they came to the largest tent of all, nearly big enough for a traveling circus. Their rate of progress was hampered by the exulting, spontaneous parade of honor to the point where it was impossible for even Reacher to obtain entrance to the tent. He was now pressed up against the nervous Fireheel by the throng, exchanging continuous handclasps.

A roll of drums and winding of horns smote their

ears and the crowd fell back, as children and dogs alike were hushed to silence.

"The Hetman comes," Reacher said.

The curtains of the Hetman's tent were drawn aside by well-armed guards in cloaks of fur-bordered silk. He came out, a man of authoritative bulk with a thick, flowing beard like many of the men there, but darker than most. He was aging, but little gray had touched him yet and he had an enormous belly which, with his imposing height, made him seem to grow as he approached. His cloak and vest were of fine white furs and he was ornamented with many trinkets and pieces of jewelry, including a necklace of coins. But he wore a weighty scimitar in a back sheath, its grip at his left shoulder; tucked through his wide girdle were a hatchet, garrote and a large poniard. In one legging was a brace of throwing knives.

He and the King of Freegate faced one another for a silent moment, then lunged at each other like angry bears, with mighty hugs. Reacher was whisked from his feet and whirled around as if weightless. Springbuck, who'd been fingering his sword hilt nervously, now clapped his hand to it and went for his parrying dagger, convinced that the combat vaguely mentioned by the King had been joined and certain that he, too, was about to be assaulted.

Then he realized that the King was laughing, as were the Hetman and those on the sidelines. Again he was grateful that his war mask hid his expression.

The two separated, each with hands on the other's shoulders. "Welcome, Wolf-Brother, Champion of the Howlebeau," said the steppesman. "Welcome to the fires and fellowship of the Horseblooded. As usual, the Howlebeau do not attend the High Contest, but send greetings."

"I thank Su-Suru for the grace of his fire and his corral," replied Reacher.

Ceremony over, they were conducted into Su-Suru's tent, sumptuous with thick, colorful carpets and plump cushions. Several others were seated there, dressed as finely as the Hetman. They rose as one to clasp hands with the King. Springbuck, impatient at the lack of introductions, cleared his throat and appraising eyes went to him at once.

Reacher said, "Springbuck, Prince and rightful *Ku-Mor-Mai* of Coramonde, I give you Su-Suru, overchieftain of five of the tribes of the Horseblooded. These others are the chieftains of the various tribes, Lords Paramount of their respective ranges."

There was general bowing and trading of courtesies, after which the five lesser chieftains took their leave as if on cue. The remaining three reclined among soft cushions and Su-Suru clapped his hands peremptorily.

Women appeared, the first that the Prince had had an opportunity to observe closely. They didn't give the impression of servility, but went about their hospitable chores expansively, as much hostesses in Su-Suru's home as he was host; they were in fact his several wives and daughters. They bore no weapons, but each had a highly individualized costume of fanciful design and wore a good deal of jewelry and cosmetics, even the youngest, a girl of fourteen or so, and one had a bird tattooed on her forehead.

As they were offering food and drink, another woman entered, knelt on a cushion in the corner and began to play softly on a cheng. She was slender and almond-eyed, with gracefully erect carriage and blue-black hair piled in a complex coiffure. She wore a flowing robe covered with elaborate embroidery and her earrings, necklace and rings had much jade in them.

The men listened to the restful strains for a time. When she paused between one air and the next, Su-Suru turned to Reacher and asked, "Is it to be a challenge?"

"Not my choosing. You've heard of developments in Coramonde?"

"All rumors drift in time to the High Ranges. The East will soon be in revolt, we hear, and Strongblade's already called Usurper when the soldiers aren't listening. Is it your wish, then, to lead my people into war?"

Springbuck interjected, "It's either that or wait for the legions of Coramonde to come for you, once Yardiff Bey's puppets overcome the Crescent Lands."

"But can you hope to win, Prince Springbuck? The

Horseblooded can spread across the ranges like wind-blown dust and avoid an enemy forever. But then, of course, our ranges would no longer be truly our own."

"We plan to fight for time," the son of Surehand answered. "To ignite insurrection from within."

Su-Suru considered this as he toyed with the silver mamelière on his furred vest. "You'll need to fight our current Champion then, Wolf-Brother, just as you thought. Ferrian doesn't believe in foreign adventuring. You challenge as Champion of the Howlebeau, so no one can dispute your right to do so. A pity; Ferrian's been quirt bearer and war chieftain for only two days."

"A war chieftain who councils against war?" asked the Prince.

"Aye, stouthearted fighter, hunter and horseman, but with no love of killing, and I was glad when he won the quirt. Ah, well, necessities of state, as you Lowlanders say. Do you wish to rest, Wolf-Brother, or will an hour from now do?"

"Let this regrettable thing be by all means done quickly."

Su-Suru sent a sentry with instructions. "Ferrian is probably girding himself even now." He sighed, then brightened. "But let me show you, in the meantime, something I acquired in a little horse-trading deal."

He brought a small golden bell from his wide girdle and shook it. It summoned two more girls, one with a drum and one with a stringed instrument like a harp; but unlike the first musician, these were Horseblooded. The tempo of the music accelerated. Six dancing girls filed ito the room and began a sinuous performance. They were comely, well-formed with coppery complexions and hair the same shade, wearing shifts of fine black fabric which suited them well. They moved alluringly and the Prince thought them to be from one of the lesser city-states near the Outer Sea. Immensely interested, he didn't turn his head as he asked Su-Suru, "Why is the Hetman not Champion, or the Champion not Hetman?"

Reacher answered for him, morosely ignoring the dancers as he played idly with his wine cup, tracing its design with one falciform finger. "The Hetman's chosen for wisdom and honesty by vote of the tribe members. The Champion is selected by a series of tests and trial combats. Neither process could be used to accomplish what the other does, so warrior is subordinate to Hetman."

The dancers had just completed their performances to Su-Suru's enjoyment and Springbuck's enthusiastic applause, when the sentry returned and whispered in the Hetman's ear. The leader of the Horseblooded rose majestically to his feet. "Ferrian has anticipated your requisition, Reacher. He's awaiting you at the contest area even now. Oh, and I'm told that some friends of yours are in camp."

Flanked by guards, the three left Su-Suru's tent and walked toward the appointed spot across hard-packed earth streets that were trampled firm by many feet, hooves and paws. Then the crowd, and indeed the sentries, drew aside as three enormous wolves trotted into view. Reacher went to one knee to embrace their chief, a pure albino with a wicked look in his old eye, wrestling with him and growling gently. The wolf, tail wagging, pawed the small monarch, biting softly at his nose. In return and with obvious affection, Reacher nipped the beast's muzzle, and Springbuck recalled hearing that this was a lupine custom of greeting; Su-Suru's use of the King's nickname occurred to him—Wolf-Brother. But what wolves! Big as lions, these monsters and their packs must rule the steppes. No wonder the Horseblooded valued the friendship of the Howlebeau and the resultant treaty with their brother-allies, the wolves.

Reacher exchanged salutations with the other two wolves and the procession was resumed, the beasts trotting at his side, until they came to an open square among the tents, measuring fifty paces on a side. A ring of people had already formed there. With no further word the King went to stand waiting in the center, leaving the Prince, Su-Suru and his furry brothers at its edge.

There came a blast of trumpets and the cry: "Ferrian! Champion-at-arms Ferrian! 'Way, all!"

Pressing through the crowd opposite Springbuck were

six husky men, bearing on their bulging shoulders a platform of wood, atop which stood Ferrian, who turned out to be the grim man whom the Prince had noticed when first entering camp. He stood, feet spread and arms at his sides, fists clenched and features composed in that same cryptic stare, not deigning to notice those beneath the level of his gaze.

He rode easily, as if the platform were not moving at all. When his perch had been carefully lowered at the rim of the crowd, he stepped forward, now looking directly at Reacher.

"Who challenges?" he demanded.

"The Lord of the Just and Sudden Reach, Champion of the Howlebeau."

Ferrian extended his hand behind him and his shield and a long spear were passed to him.

"Won't Ferrian lose face?" asked the Prince. "Going fully armed against one who bears no sword or shield?"

"You evaluate from ignorance," Su-Suru replied. "All here know that, as Champion of the Howlebeau, Reacher will be nearly impossible to defeat, however well armed Ferrian is. Yet our Champion goes fully prepared to make his best effort. All here know the truth of the circumstances, and Ferrian's determination to do his best will be to his credit, win or lose the match."

He thought for a moment. "He won the ceremonial quirt after some of the hardest striving I've ever seen at High Contest. With it he gained his choice of willing women—many with husbands who'd cherish the child of a Champion—and horses, the rarest of honors and plaudits; barring a miracle, all of that will be taken from him now.

"It's all a greater pity for this—they were both, Ferrian and Reacher, great friends at one time."

The two were circling now, the Horseblooded moving easily for a big man. They spiraled slowly closer, the King in a feline, crouching guard and the steppesman poised behind his shield, spear at ready. When they were close enough, Ferrian began to feint as Reacher backstepped, parrying with his cestussed left hand.

Then Ferrian shoved forward with his shield, attempting to drive his smaller opponent off balance, and making as if to skewer him with the spear at the same time.

But Reacher dug in his heel and stopped the shield with one hand, brushing the spearhead aside with the other, as he tried to slip around the edge of the shield to strike at Ferrian's unprotected left. The Champion of the Horseblooded in turn quickly crouched and pivoted on his left foot, the pivot matching Reacher's move and neutralizing it. Both drew apart then and came at one another again. Fast as thought itself, Ferrian made a long thrust with his spear, which Springbuck thought to see rip through the King's abdomen. The Wolf-Brother, though, spun to the right; as the spear passed close in truth to his body, he brought his left hand down in a fearsome stroke, thrusting his right knee up at the same time. The spear shaft broke in two, as the wild boar's neck had given way before the murderous cestus.

Ferrian hurled the useless stump of his spear aside with an oath and ripped his broadsword from its sheath. Reacher's fighting attitude, now that he no longer had the spear to contend with, was more erect. He didn't attempt to meet the vicious cuts, but evaded them, backing nimbly around the circle. Ducking one particularly strong slash, the King took advantage of his opponent's momentary lack of balance and leaped in, unleashing a fast and powerful stroke with his clawed left hand. More by happenstance than design, Ferrian managed to protect himself with his shield. The taloned glove ripped through the first three plies of the shield, though it struck glancing. Because he was a tried Champion, who could fight by blind instinct when he must, Ferrian somehow managed to launch a backhand blow with his sword, forcing Reacher back while he regained his footing.

Abruptly, the King stooped down to snatch the head of Ferrian's broken spear, which still had a foot of shaft affixed to it. Just as Ferrian understood what he intended, he drew back and whipped the improvised missile with all his strength. It was fortunate for Ferrian that he'd begun to drop to one knee in face of this new tactic; the flashing spearhead struck the upper part of his shield and stuck there, penetrating all seven plies and throwing it against its bearer's shoulder.

Now Ferrian came back on guard. Angry at Reacher's ploy, he advanced with a strong attack of cuts and slashes. The King again backed, evading all blows. But as Ferrian brought his sword down in an arc aimed to cleave the Wolf-Brother's head, the King revealed his full speed and strength, deflecting the descending blade with one blow of his cestus and with another striking the broadsword from Ferrian's grasp with such force that the sword loop around the Champion's wrist snapped and the weapon flew free. There was a gasp from the gathered Horseblooded as Ferrian stood disarmed by impacts which had come so close together as to be practically one, dazed by this sudden turn of events.

Ferrian would have shaken off his shock and fought on with a knife from his belt or bare hands if he must, but the King gave him no chance. Reacher seized the Horseblooded's shield with both hands and twisted, snaking around behind him as he did so. Ferrian's arm, trapped by his shield's enarmes and Reacher's strength, was twisted in back of him. With a single chop of his left hand, the King rendered Ferrian unconscious. Calmly taking the symbolic horsehair quirt from the belt of his prostrate foe, Reacher slipped its thong onto his own wrist.

"I'm glad that he wasn't forced to kill the fellow," Su-Suru said.

That evening there was feasting, revelry and the sharing of Faith Cups in Su-Suru's tent, though the celebratory atmosphere was due more to the time of tribal assemblage than Reacher's victory.

When told of Yardiff Bey's intentions toward the High Ranges and Freegate's decision to fight, the sub-chieftains had voted unanimously to make common cause against Bey. The complots of Shardishku-Salamá were hated even at the farthest corners of the steppes.

At the Wolf-Brother's insistence, Ferrian sat at his side during dinner as both were attended to by the six dancing girls from the afternoon's entertainment.

Though the deposed Champion made a virtuous show of forgotten enmity and good sportsmanship in approved Horseblooded manner, he became silent and made to leave the fete early. But before he left Reacher stood and said to the crowd, "This man whom I fought today is as strong of arm, wise in thought and gentle and brave in spirit as any I could wish for a comrade. For this reason, as I must depart soon, I designate him Champion once more in my absence. Let any who dispute him be prepared to meet me in the most earnest combat."

This won approval and clapping from the crowd, and was declared a thing worthy of a Horseblooded.

Typically, the party became louder as time wore one. The three wolves sat near, consuming large amounts of raw meat and glancing about with burning, slitted eyes.

Springbuck, now the object of attention of the girls deserted by Ferrian, grew unsteady in his cups. Some streak of ill humor, complicated by Ferrian's obvious depression, made him turn bleary-eyed to Reacher and slur, "Well, pig-killing's easier than throwing hands with this local lad, eh? Almost halved you, crown to pizzle, didn't he?"

The King, sober despite diligent drinking, turned a face of stone to the Prince and answered in a voice that none but those two could hear. "I could have killed or humbled him when first we rushed together. But now he'll be able to say, 'I lost to Reacher, but as anyone will tell you, it was a near thing.'"

He stood and said to Su-Suru, "I go to rest now." Facing about on his heel, he strode out, followed dutifully by four of the copper-skinned, copper-haired dancing girls.

The Hetman sighed as he left, a minor hurricane. "Ahh, I have lost the spirit of the festivities with my mullings and the wine no longer fills my head. I'm away to bed, young Prince. Your bed is through there; Kishna and Fahna will show you the way."

The two remaining members of the troupe giggled.

Springbuck smiled, sheepish at his lapse of the moment before. "What's this? Four girls for the King of a small city-state and only two for the *Ku-Mor-Mai?*"

Su-Suru yawned. "No, four for the Champion-at-arms of the Horseblooded and two for his friend, a deposed princeling. Be happy at the implication that you're half the man he is."

Springbuck thought about this, and was.

At last he let his new companions lead him off, though he leaned rather heavily on them, in search of repose, among other things.

Chapter Seventeen

*One can stand still in a flowing stream, but not in
the world of men.*
ANONYMOUS JAPANESE PROVERB

EDWARD Van Duyn sat busily recopying his shorthand
into script for duplication by scribes of Freegate's War
Ministry. These were the notes he had taken during the
long afternoon he'd spent listening to Gil MacDonald
ramble at length on what he knew of warfare. The sergeant had displayed exhaustive knowledge of tactics,
intelligence gathering, organization, theory and practice.
He had spoken of the principles behind guerrilla fighting as he'd distilled them from many sources, among
them standard Armed Forces texts, and this was to
serve as the basis of a manual for the irregular army
now being raised in Coramonde. For his own purposes
Van Duyn saw in this popular movement a tool to be
used toward the political revision of the suzerainty,
though he knew that this would have to come later.

He sighed contentedly, took another small sip of the
excellent brandy with which he'd been supplied and
turned to the next topic, the incorporation of guerrillas
as auxiliaries for regular troops.

The tax collector fingered his medallion of office
nervously despite his cavalry escort. The young officer
who rode at his side in the quiet woods was blithely
confident that no peasant would dare challenge armed,
armored men on horseback.

But the tax collector was not so certain. When his
predecessor had quit in disgust at the severe new policies instituted by Strongblade he, a former clerk, had
moved up to fulfill those duties with a certain relish of
power and prerogative. Putting illiterate, base-born yo-

kels in their place and making them toe a stricter line
was the sort of work for which he considered himself
singularly suited. He had always felt that they were permitted to retain far too much of their income, anyway;
now, with new campaigning in the east being planned,
more money was needed.

He reached back nervously to pat the bulging satchels on his horse's croup as he thought of how efficiently
he was helping in the collection of that money—with an
unofficial honorarium for himself, of course. But there
were disquieting rumors, tales of other tax agents being
set upon, robbed and killed in a particularly unpleasant
fashion. And at that, not being accosted by outlaws or
wildmen but some new element which killed with cold
precision. . . .

These were his final thoughts as a white arrow, fired
by an unseen hand, sprouted without warning from his
throat. He stared down at it stupidly as the snowy
fletchings so close to his eyes were covered by spurts of
his life's blood. Then he toppled from his saddle.

The cavalry officer yelled in surprise and reached for
his sword, reining up. Before he could organize his
thoughts or his men, however, he was slain by an arrow
twin to the first, driven into his chest by a heavy bow at
close range.

There was a minute of pure pandemonium as most of
those soldiers who tried to flee were cut down. All of
those who tried to stand and fight an enemy they could
not see met a like fate as the woods suddenly produced
a blizzard of white shafts. Then calm returned to the
forest once again, while hard-eyed men dressed in dark
brown or green slipped from their careful concealment,
bows in hand, to approach their victims.

Their leader, a tall, gaunt, scar-faced man, weighed
the money satchels so recently in the custody of the collector, and smiled to himself. He said to his waiting
men, "You know what to do. Two measures of three go
back to the people who paid it, and the third stays with
us." His voice was soft, and he had never been known
to speak loudly.

His second-in-command began retrieving the taxing
rolls from the collector's sanguine robes. "They'll be

more careful next time; there will be more dragoons in escort and they'll soon begin to try to force people to tell who we are."

The gaunt man—who had once had a son named Micko, the boy tortured and murdered by Eliatim on the night of Springbuck's escape—was at once happier and grimmer at his lieutenant's remark.

"Let them," he said. "The more they abuse people, the sooner they'll be hated by one and all. You can see our ranks swelling as quickly as Strongblade can send in fresh troops. Let them grieve to learn how we trap them, elude them, torment them, stalk them and remain yet unseen! And it must always be this way; the tax collectors die first of all, with the white arrow in their throats."

They stripped the soldiers' bodies of their weapons and departed noiselessly, to hide their scavenged swords and liberated funds along with the quivers of white arrows.

The next day another tax agent heard of the incident. Blanching in indignation and fear, he immediately drafted a request for additional protection and called for reprisals against the population of that area.

DEPARTMENT OF THE ARMY
Headquarters, 32d Armored Cavalry Regiment
APO 96766
SPECIAL ORDERS: 099-6921
MACDONALD, GILBERT A./ US 12732836
SGT/E5: Individual will proceed via transport as directed in subsequent amending orders to Oakland Army Terminal for separation from active duty IAW pertinent regulations.

Yardiff Bey, the Hand of Shardishku-Salamá, sat black-robed in the monolithic carven onyx chair in his sanctorum at Earthfast's central donjon, looking out through the dusk over Kee-Amaine, pondering. This room had once been the retiring place of the *Ku-Mor-Mai*, but as the sorcerer's influence in Court had waxed over generations, he had requested and received its use for his own purposes. Now it suited him to sit in his seat where the *Ku-Mor-Mai* had taken their leisure, anticipating the day when he would sit on the throne itself.

In the center of the chamber, a giant pentacle was engraved on the stone floor. It had taken him, what with constant interruptions and travels on one mission or another, over twenty years to complete the pentacle, so intricate and efficacious were the runes he forged into it. But this and many other things he had done, always piloting his course through resistance, interference and distractions, gradually putting circumstances into the order in which he wished them. He had used much of his long life conspiring toward the events now culminating; yet the unforeseen had occurred, and for the first time he perceived discrepancies.

An energetic, swarthy man whose handsome face was marred only by the eerie metallic ocular fastened where his left eye had been, he watched the sun set over the city. The deviations suffered to his plans were traceable to the appearance of Van Duyn, the foreigner whom Yardiff Bey, to his own astonishment, could not quite fathom fully. Then there was the Prince's escape on the night Hightower had been disposed of and the subsequent besting of Chaffinch by those irritating outlanders and their machine and weapons, summoned from somewhere by Van Duyn and the hated deCourteney. The invasion of the Infernal plane had come as the rudest shock of all, and now this bothersome banditry, forcing his hand to acts of repression before he was ready to introduce them.

He had brought all his perception and cold reason to bear on the tidings he'd received and was now convinced that the entire carefully contrived structure of his conspiracies against the Crescent Lands was in jeopardy if he could not mend it quickly.

Still, there was time and there were ways. He had already directed Strongblade to call for more troop levies and soon there would be manpower enough to swamp Freegate and punish the insurrectionists.

But for their leaders, ahh, that would be more difficult. There were the deCourteneys—Gabrielle, of course, being his own daughter—to contend with. Neither might stand against him alone; but in concert they could

prove troublesome. Springbuck, disturbingly, was showing more potential than the sorcerer had thought him to
possess. And most recently, Legion-Marshal Bonesteel
had mutinied to go over to the Prince's side, taking his
legion command with him.

But all these Yardiff Bey knew he could overcome,
bring to their knees with a single word when the time
was ripe. It was the aliens who worried him. Van Duyn
and the men he had conjured were an unknown,
unlooked-for quantity in the great equation of his plan.
Their presence from another cosmos might upset natural balances, set all his prophecies and calculations
awry.

Yeessss. His hand toyed with the catch of his ocular—though even *he* would only dare open it at dire
need—as he came to a decision. He must eradicate this
Van Duyn, as he should have done earlier, and with
him any fellow interlopers. Bey's eye went to a pigeon-
hole in the wall where rested a melon-sized crystal of
complex cut which he had used for the imprisonment of
a mighty demon after long struggling. He considered
calling it forth and dispatching it to slay Van Duyn, but
he knew he could only demand one service of it, it
would be foolish—and dangerous—to use the demon
unnecessarily. Besides, there were other ways open to
his hand and mind.

His attention was broken as a rapping came at the
heavy, bronze-bound cedar door. He spoke a syllable of
Command. The massive valve swung inward by some
silent agency to reveal Fania and his bastard son
Strongblade, ostensible *Ku-Mor-Mai*.

Fania still boasted much of the beauty that was close
to being her only asset, regal bearing being an effective
disguise for the fact that, while clever in some ways—
and most capable of treachery—the now Queen Mother
was far from bright. There were pearls secured among
the locks of her hair, which she kept the color of jet.
The robe she wore emphasized length of leg, whiteness
of throat and the yet-youthful tautness in her waist.

He felt a momentary flash of hunger for her but dismissed it immediately. He disliked yielding to grosser
appetites, preferring to go his own fastidious way,

avoiding contact with mere mortals as much as was feasible.

Strongblade was wearing fine mail armor of black iron and red gold; he carried at his side the enchanted greatsword Flarecore, and his face held a stubborn aspect. It was none too intelligent a face, and in centuries of life Yardiff Bey had seen its type often, had frequently been forced to break and discipline the people he'd chosen as tools. He was completely confident in his own supremacy.

As always in the absence of onlookers, the two bowed before him, but not so low as they had been taught and, in contravention of form, Strongblade spoke without receiving the wizard's let to do so. "The new levies are near ready to depart. I'm told I'm not to be their commander." His face flushed red. "Am I not *Ku-Mor-Mai*? It is my right to lead my liegemen."

Fania interrupted, never one to stay long out of a conversation. "He is your son! *He* should be the one to destroy Springbuck and bring back the coward's head on a lance." She drew herself up dramatically, puffed with pride. "Then he can sit the throne with the respect of his people."

Bey leaned forward, elbow on knee; when he turned his eye on her, what she saw there made her tremble and turn from his face. In his intimidatingly controlled voice, he said, "Do you think Yardiff Bey would play his pawn as if it were a knight? I had Strongblade trained at arms so that when the time came he could kill Springbuck, then sit the throne and obey me—and nothing more. What is his smattering of military lore to the likes of Bonesteel, who marches now to throw in with them?"

He turned the frightening gaze from the Queen to his son. "I shall warn you this one time not to presume on our kinship again—ever! Ours is a relationship of convenience alone, *my* convenience. Take the place I grant you and show gratitude; do not think you could any more lead and rule than you could use that sword you're wearing as it's meant to be used. Or can you? Come, show me."

Teeth bared furiously, Strongblade took Flarecore

from its ornate scabbard. The green-blue blade was filled with minuscule writings and runes. Holding the weapon in both hands, he thrust it toward his father. "I can't work its damned enchantment," he grated, "but I can use it to effect, if that occasion should come to pass."

Yardiff Bey stood, face cold and awful to see. He said, "I see that you have both forgotten your places." He made a quick pass with his hand and the room was dark and chill, and Fania and Strongblade felt a sudden terror clutching their hearts. The sorcerer stepped forward and calmly pulled Flarecore from his son's weak, quivering grasp. He moved back and whirled the big blade one-handed over his head as if it were a feather. With the other hand, he formed a Sign of potency which left a glowing red trail suspended in the air behind it. Thunders filled the room and he called out in an unnatural language and was answered as from afar by howlings and shrieks. Flarecore's blade began to glow, then abruptly went white-hot, throwing off flame and spark.

Fania screamed and buried her face in her hands. Strongblade had gone dead-pale with fear. The wizard came close to them again. "Down!" he roared in a voice terrible to hear. "Down before your Master for the peril of your lives and souls!"

They instantly threw themselves down at his feet as Strongblade began to froth with madness and plead while Fania wept and kissed the hem of his robe, begging incoherently for mercy. He let them go on so for some moments more, until he saw that they might be permanently impaired if he continued their punishment. Then he spoke a Dismissal, whereat the room was light once again and the thunder and other sounds died away, as did the light along Flarecore's blade.

When they were able, the two staggered to their feet and helped one another to the door, sobbing and leaning on each other, and were permitted to leave.

Bey was left holding Flarecore, satisfied that they would give him no more inconvenience for some time to come. Still, it had been rather sharp of Fania—uncharacteristically so—to scheme thus. With Strongblade gone warring, she would naturally reassume the authority she had been forced to yield at his coronation. Perhaps he'd better ease the *Ku-Mor-Mai*'s dependency on his mother to inhibit further plottings. It might even be a good idea to teach his son the spell which caused Flarecore to burn. That would look impressive, add some legitimacy to his reign and infuse him with a measure of independence from Fania.

The little hunting party wound its way up the easy slope leading away north from Boldhaven Bay and the city of Seaguard, Coramonde's primary trading outlet on the Central Sea. The city harbor falling behind was divided by a long, fortified promontory, effectively separating the small fishing craft and common commerce ships from the luxury barges and military vessels.

Seaguard itself was protected from land by a high, thick, well-fortified wall along which watchtowers were spaced, each virtually an independent fortress. To the east were the salt marshes.

The party was small but illustrious, and so had taken precautions to make an inconspicuous departure. It included five members; a tracker-guide, two military men of high ability and rank who wore no insignia of command and two of even higher station. These were the emissaries of the Prince of the Waves, Lord Paramount of the Mariners, and the King of Seaguard, whose title in the salutations of Coramonde was Seashield, though in truth he was more inclined to sharp bargaining and profit than war on the deeps.

They wended their way through the low foothills of greenery and bright flowers, giving no attention at all to tracking other than to see if any other riders had preceded them, for they were not hunting the beasts of the forests; they hunted coconspirators. Two days they spent riding, though it pleased the emissary of the Prince of the Waves little, for he was more used to the roll of a deck under his feet in a following wind, not liking having to ride this uncertain-tempered creature with its disturbing gait. Still, he forebore to complain, since he was there at the direction of his liege, He who Sails Forever.

He had been selected for this mission of conspiracy

because he possessed in good measure the ability in suave dissembling and courteous haggling so prized by landsmen, although he was known on his own ship as a martinet. For this reason, too, he did not bewail sleeping on the ground or hearing the howls of wolves and the roars of lions in the night; he controlled himself when, once, they were menaced by a giant bear whom they had surprised on the narrow track they traveled.

On the night of the third day they found—thanks to the guide's almost magical sense of direction—a small lodge built into the side of a hill at the foot of Drearspike, that bleak needle of rock which thrust itself up in a forest shunned by most men. A warm fire awaited them in the hidden and guarded covert, together with five more men.

The soldiers were sent outside on watch with others who had come there earlier as bodyguards for those conspirators who had already arrived. The guide was sent to another room to occupy himself with thoughts of his payment, in the company of others who had served a similar function; all were careful to show no curiosity at what might transpire in the main hall. As the light of hearth and candles illuminated the low, smoke-dyed rafters of the place, the gathered men sat and conferred, after introductions were made for those not known to one another.

In addition to the King and the emissary there were these:

Roguespur, son to Fim the Northwatcher, who had escaped the death of his father and nation, being a boy in training in the south during the attack of the druids and wildmen of the Cold Isles. He was light of skin but dark of hair, eye and expression, and there was the gleam of vengeance hunger in his countenance as he sat wrapped in his long scarlet cloak. Around his neck was a chain of thick links and from it a heavy key dangled against his mailed breast. This was the key to the throne hall at his father's castle, and he had dared much to take it from that place when he went alone to scout his foes as they made merry in the stolen castle that should have been his. He was Roguespur, who would never know peace until he had exacted payment for his father's death.

And there was Honuin Granite Oath, Factotum of a large province in the southwest of Coramonde, in former times one of Surehand's closest friends and a renowned warrior and outdoorsman. Though he was now gone fat and much white had crept into his walrus mustache, he was still a man to deal death, as canny as any at warcraft.

Two more sat across from each other at the board, and the most remarkable thing about them was that they were not at death strokes, for these were Angorman, self-proclaimed Saint Commander of the Order of the Axe, and Balagon, Divine Vicar of the Brotherhood of the Bright Lady; they and their respective followers of warrior-priests had been at odds for over fifty years.

For two hundred years the Brotherhood of the Bright Lady had been devoted to deeds of bravery and justice, and had been priests of that noble Celestial Goddess, while at the same time being warriors errant, committed to her to the exclusion of all other women. Their number never stood higher than one hundred, for such was their rule, though they often numbered fewer, it being their habit to seek out the most arduous trials and challenges to exhibit their faith and conviction. To be accepted to the Brotherhood, a man must be a proven fighting man of the first rank and accept religious schooling to earn a priestly vestment; or alternatively, but much less frequently, he might be a priest of the Bright Lady who proved himself at arms on her behalf to the satisfaction of the Divine Vicar. If he had not done so already, he must forswear worldly pleasures, particularly those of the flesh.

Then, nearly fifty-three years before, Balagon rose to Vicarship of that fine and honored Brotherhood although he was but twenty, for his piety was as unquestionable as his moral fibre, and there were none who could stand against him in combat. At that time, from the northernmost isles which even the wildmen did not often visit, there came Angorman, a salty young roughneck who had heard of the deeds of the Brotherhood, seen an image of the Celestial Goddess carved on the bowsprit of a wrecked ship and decided on the spot to join them. He brought with him little but his impudence, his lofty ideals, a sense of destiny and his great axe.

But the roster of the Brotherhood stood at one hundred and he was denied the membership he'd endured so much to achieve. He was put off for a time, made to prove himself, which he did with a martial vigor which impressed even the vaunted fighters of the judging board. But at last he would accept no more forestalling and angrily demanded admittance. This Balagon refused; the Brotherhood might stand at one hundred but no more, and his sense of moral rectitude would never permit Balagon to violate this technicality. Angorman, on the other hand, would not content himself to wait until an opening occurred; thus, hotheaded and heedless to the other brothers' counselings of patience, he set off to found his own circle of warrior-priests, naming himself a Saint. The Order of the Axe swelled with men ready to follow charismatic Angorman for the Celestial Goddess. The years brought hard feelings, and even battle between the two groups, but out of commitment to the Perfect Mistress and a grudging respect for each other, Balagon and Angorman had done their best to abate such friction.

Still, there was no amity between them, and so they sat and eyed each other. Balagon wore his black ringmail, covered with the white robe of his office, and at his side was the broadsword *Ke-Wa-Coe,* which in the Old Tongue means Consecrated of the Goddess. His thin white hair was held back with a simple circlet of leather, and on his finger was the heavy seal ring of his station.

Angorman was dressed all in brown, with his forager's cloak pulled tight against him for the chill. He still wore his hat, for his head was hairless save for the thick, flaring white eyebrows. On that slouch hat, a wide-brimmed and high-crowned trademark, was the brassard of his order, a crescent moon with a great axe superimposed, thick and wrought of silver. Angorman's legendary axe, Red Pilgrim, rested against the back of his chair; it had been agreed that no weapon should be put between any of them met there, and Red Pilgrim was impressive to see—a six-foot handle of ash ending in a flanged double-bit of heroic size.

The last one of them met there was the man who had called them, maybe the only man of sufficient repute to draw them together under one roof, Andre deCourteney. He had come in quickest time, by methods taxing and dangerous—not available to anyone but his sister and a few other adepts.

He was in vestments now, red, stiff-collared robes worked with occult designs, seated in a high-backed chair at the head of the table. When the Seashield and the emissary had made themselves comfortable, he began.

"I welcome you, my lords, and thank you for your attendance on behalf of the true heir to the throne, Prince Springbuck."

The Seashield grunted. "It was gladsome hearing, this word that the Prince lives; I'd gotten rumors to the contrary. There's hope now of getting Strongblade's boot off our necks and ridding ourselves of Yardiff Bey."

Honuin Granite Oath *wuffed* out his mustache and said, "Aye, levies and tithes increase daily and now we have royal proctors peering over our shoulders at every turn so that I look about for them even when I answer nature's calls."

"It isn't the Prince's plan to let this continue unchecked," Andre said.

Roguespur nodded. "But that's not the worst. As our people muster for needless war with Freegate, the wildmen grow stronger in the land of my father. Bey sees to it that they get no interference and the day may soon come when, having spent itself against Reacher, Coramonde will find herself prey to them."

Andre said smoothly, "The Prince is moving his will and arm to curtail this brewing war by denying Strongblade the wherewithal to wage it."

"How?" asked the emissary, doubt in his eyes. Of all there, he least wanted to be drawn into plots and covenants, and so was the most dubious.

The wizard folded hairy hands over his plump paunch and replied, "The Prince has aligned himself

with King Reacher, rallied various loyal units of Coramonde behind him and obtained the help of the Horseblooded. Containing Strongblade at the Keel of Heaven,
he'll send agents to raise the flag of revolt throughout
the suzerainty."

"But," said Honuin Granite Oath, "we've few enough
regular troops left, and the levies are under leaders
loyal to Strongblade."

"Springbuck knows that, and has developed a plan to
use the citizenry of the realm. They will rise to shake
Strongblade from his throne and put out Yardiff Bey."

There were laughs of disbelief and roars of rage then.
Some half rose from their chairs, speaking their opinion
of this speech while the emissary listened silently. But
above all, Honuin could be heard. "Arm the riffraff?
Useless and foolish and worse! It wouldn't stiffen their
spines, it would only put thoughts of banditry and dis-
loyalty in their heads."

"What fighting man will face a battle," queried Roguespur, "when the man who stands next to him is an
untrained woodcutter quaking in his boots and aching
to break and run? Military engagements are decided by
armored, mounted men who know the ways of war. Are
you mad, to put this word before us?" And others sec-
onded his remarks.

At this Andre, brows knitted in anger, raised one
plump-strong hand; from it a blinding light filled the
room and a wind swept through it. They were thrown
back into their chairs, even those servants of the Bright
Lady, cowed by Andre's magic. Hands went to hilt and
haft but the wizard said, "Do not think because I have
invited you here that I will tolerate such effronteries; no
man speaks so to me!"

His uncommon display of wrath silenced them. He
resumed in a more sedate voice. "Some of you have
heard how Bey has sent his first sally against us, the
dragon Chaffinch, and how we have slain him and his
corpse is rotting near Erub. We have help from beyond
this world, albeit mostly aid of council and thought
rather than of force. Yet it is in my mind that they are
the kind of thoughts to turn a country upside down if
they be heeded.

"But mark you this, all my good lords, Springbuck will yet sit on the throne of Coramonde; of that I'm sure. Whether you will or not, you must answer to him in that hour, and if you will attend my rede you will rally to his banner. How say you?"

They frowned in concentration now, weighing decisions. Roguespur was first to reply. "I, who once led a Legion of his own, am only the captain of a small company of mercenaries, now that Strongblade rules. I'm out of favor, yet Strongblade is friend to my father's enemies, and that makes his enemy my friend. For what it may mean, I stand to the Prince."

Honuin Granite Oath said, "They bleed us dry and will eventually replace us in the southlands with their own Court favorites. Better to fight. Take my war vows to Springbuck."

The King of Seaguard was next. "Already have I felt the squeeze of Bey's grasp, and I think it will only grow tighter with time. It will not be long ere that damned spellbinder has the Usurper strangling us with taxes and leeching our trade blood from our coffers into his. I shall stand by the Heir in whatever he requires, yet I hope that we may help him and still appear not to, the better to build our strength for a time yet."

Balagon said, "Those who swear allegiance to the Bright Lady also swear to respect the throne at Earthfast, since the *Ku-Mor-Mai* has ever been our friend. But there appears to be some doubt here as to who has proper claim to that allegiance in these strange days, and so the Brotherhood cannot carry its banner to either camp; we must remain neutral, for the nonce."

Angorman rubbed his jaw and squinted at his old rival, speaking next. "The Order of the Axe will take no side either then, but we will be most attentive to what transpires, and if we think the commands of the Perfect Mistress warrant it, you will hear from us."

But the emissary said in a level voice and with a hint of condescension, "I will not hide this from you: I will take to the Prince Who Sails Forever my recommendation that the Mariners not participate in this strife. As is our custom, we will trade with whomever comes to the quayside and treat with them, but our dwelling place is the bosom of the deeps and we are loath to entangle ourselves and lose Mariner lives in the affrays of landsmen. So will I speak to the Prince of the Waves."

Andre heard them out without comment and absorbed each pronouncement without emotion, making no attempt to sway dissenters. He thanked them for their attendance and suggested they all partake of more meat and drink. The mood lightened, but he took aside each of the three who had declared for the Prince and made plans of communication with them.

Soon, men across the face of the Crescent Lands looked to their weapons, and those who'd seen war before made their peace with their deities.

Sharpen your lances, see to your shields,
Kiss your sweet ladies goodbye;
Grim armies gather to darken the fields,
War-pennants darken the sky.
Call for your horses, make fast your spurs,
Take up your strong panoply;
Fight the Usurper, now, all my brave Sirs,
To throw off his yoke, or to die!

See yonder, Springbuck, son of his sire,
Rightful his claim to the throne.
Hew to his cause, with steel and with fire;
Let our swords make our will known.
High-born and yeoman, all rally 'round him;
Bring forth your edges to hone.
Follow now Springbuck! Our gods have found him
Chosen to rule! He alone!"

"Stand Up, Ye Loyal Men"
(An anonymous mustering song)

Chapter Eighteen

His left hand is under my head, and his right hand doth embrace me.

THE SONG OF SONGS,
Which Is Solomon's

SPRINGBUCK and Reacher were ushered from the camp of the Horseblooded with jubilation on the day after Reacher's victory. Hung over as badly as he was, Springbuck didn't care; the girls had dressed him, taken him out to where someone had already saddled Fireheel and helped him mount. Leading a parade of children, adults and dogs, with the giant wolves pacing them, he and Reacher started off on the long trek back to Freegate.

They drew away from their escort after some time and forged ahead together wordlessly. The wolves stayed at their side for a space, until Reacher raised his hand to dismiss them. At this signal they sped off eastward. As Springbuck watched them disappear, his conscience gnawed at him over his spiteful words to the King. He damned himself doubly, since his remark had probably offended his all-important cobelligerent. He tried to compose some apologetic phrases, but was interrupted.

"I could have used your help last night, ally," said the Wolf-Brother. "I was outnumbered four to one. We might have stood backs together and faced them front to front, if you see my meaning."

Springbuck was astounded by the levity almost as much as by the smile that touched the King's lips.

"I'm . . . afraid I'd have been little help, ally," he returned. "Those daft girls insisted on playing drinking games and singing songs before retiring. I don't know

203

whether we eventually played more serious games or not. I passed out, I think."

"It may be that you were lucky. Men who take many wives are greedy, holding that which they may never fully possess. If any man is capable of pleasing four dancing girls, I acknowledge *him* Champion of the Horse-blooded, aye, and of the Howlebeau and Freegate withal!"

Springbuck threw his head back and laughed, though it smarted. He removed his war mask and hung it from his saddle, shaking his aching head in the wind. He still had a picture band given him by Fahna. It was a beaded ribbon so contrived that, when one spun it around a finger, little figures replaced each other rapidly so as to give the illusion of movement—in this case a galloping horse. Since it was made for a finger on Fahna's little hand, he must spin it around his least finger. He tried it once but it threatened to make him ill to focus on it.

He had been treated to many tales of the Wild Riders who, as it came out, were not nearly as uncivilized as he had been given to think; they merely had a different way of looking at things. Eliatim, his late instructor-at-arms, had spoken little about life on the High Ranges, and the Prince was thankful for this increase in knowledge.

The difference lay in the central concern of the Horse-blooded—mobility. They took their entire culture with them on horseback or in wagons, herding their flocks and other domesticated animals. Therefore they had evolved no ponderous arts, avoiding the superfluous. They had, for example, little in the way of sculpture, since it was impractical to haul statuary around the steppes, so they became their own. They devoted much attention to their clothing, hair, jewelry and other ornamentation, including their treasured horses' trappings. Women were lavish with cosmetics and tattooing was common for both sexes.

Their music was made with easily transportable instruments, but still relied heavily on clapping, stamping, whistling and complex and imaginative blendings of human voices. Because the evening before had been one of revelry, many musicians had become drunk or tired and at last there had been only one man with a drum to provide diversion, an uninspiring situation for the Horse-blooded. The drummer therefore set one beat, which those around him took up by beating on their chests or thighs as they sat cross-legged on carpet and cushion. He then set another, which some women copied by snapping their fingers and beating dagger pommels on drinking gourds; at last he began a third himself. Springbuck had found this to be marvelous fun in comparison with merely watching, and slapped his hands against his chest with a will, rocking in time.

Again, the Horseblooded had few paintings, as such. They incorporated their imagery into their artifacts, such as the picture band. Every tapestry, cushion, scarf, saddle and carpet was illuminated with scenes depicting the life of a people forever moving. All leather was studded or tooled in some decorative fashion. All metal, it seemed, was engraved or wrought to transform functional objects into a portable, enduring art. All wood was carven, painted, or both.

Interestingly enough, women appeared to hold a place equal to men by dint of their responsibility as home-keepers, artists, child-bearers and at times as hunters and fighters. Their voices were of equal weight in councils and they had their own leaders, whose words were carefully heard by the Hetman and the Champion or risk the would-be unthinkable; ignoring them might lead to rifts or dissolution of the tribe. Springbuck had found that entertainers were as likely to be men as women, and a mixed group was the most popular of all.

At the center of life was the horse, symbol of life in this nomadic culture, an animal of religious significance and more. "Horse," in their language, meant literally "hoofed man"—or "woman," according to gender—a member of a species coequal with the human race. If these surprisingly atheological nomads had anything approaching a god, it was the creature who made their existence possible and raised them above the level of the animals they herded and hunted. The rules and etiquette surrounding the care, handling and disposition of their four-footed kinsmen was the single most important body of knowledge the Horseblooded had. It was drilled into the young of both sexes as soon as they were old enough to understand, and carried penalties which were inflexibly enforced. One of their favorite romantic tragedies culminated with the heroine slaying her lover, who'd run their tribe's premier breeding stallion to death to save her life. None of the Wild Riders wore spurs, and quirts were solely ornaments of office. It was, among them, a grave slur to call a man a "foot-plodder," or to say, *"She* is worthy only to *walk."*

They crossed the illimitable High Ranges toward Freegate, and a growing sense of loneliness descended on the Prince, composed of hours spent thinking about his father and anticipating reunion with Gabrielle. The steppes, so pleasant on the outward trip, were becoming oppressive.

Without further major event, they reclaimed Reacher's horse at the outpost and made their way back to the lowlands. But two days' travel from the city, after avoiding the towns and settlements at Reacher's request, they took to the main road again. The King, relaxed and at peace in the wilds, was increasingly tense as they passed through concentrations of people, while the Prince became more at ease.

They were met by a troop of household cavalry whose officer made obeisance to his King. "Your Majesty, how propitious the fate that has us met here when I thought I'd have to scour the High Ranges for you! Yesterday a day saw a large body of Coramondian soldiery move down out of the Keel of Heaven toward the city. At first we girded for fighting, thinking this the first thrust from the west, but the Legion-Marshal who commands them came to parley with Her Radiance, your sister. The Marshal has defected with loyal troops and rallied to the Prince, saying that he is brother to the widow of the slain Duke Hightower."

"Bonesteel!" cried the Prince. "Legion-Marshal Bonesteel! I knew he'd remain true, Reacher. The finest general in the world! Oh, not a lusty brawler himself, but the superlative strategist and tactician, writer of

textbooks, philosopher of battle. We need him sorely.
Not surprising his men should hew to him. Come,
Reacher, I must see him."

Pushing selves and mounts, they were at Freegate's
outskirts the next afternoon and found a vast canton-
ment set up. The sentries were of the Legions of the
southwest and didn't recognize the Prince, but they
summoned their officer, who prostrated himself before
Springbuck. Reacher released his men to return to Katya with word of his arrival, and the two were taken to
Bonesteel's tent.

They found the old veteran bent over a broad table,
maps spread out across it and order-of-battle charts in
his lean hand. Skinny, white-haired and half a head
shorter than Springbuck, he yet had dignity and probity
apparent to anyone who met him. He wore no military
apparel, but rather a simple robe which exposed his
hairless chest. On seeing Springbuck, he dropped his
notes with a glad cry and threw himself—but stiffly—
down on one knee, kissing the Prince's scarred right
fist. Affection welled up in the younger man's heart for
this faithful family friend.

"Your Grace," said Bonesteel, "I have come to place
myself and my men at your disposal, and give what
scant aid I may in reclaiming the throne which is yours
by rights. And every inch the *Ku-Mor-Mai* you look! It
is a year since I last saw you, and I see that you are
older than your years already. I observe that you have
passed through strange places and violence, and there is
in your eye a light which belongs in the gaze of a Protector Suzerain but is new in you. The vocation of arms
has left new marks upon you, and I rejoice that the
blood of Sharplance himself has been refreshed in you."

The Prince cast his war mask aside and raised Bonesteel to his feet. "Most loyal are you, strong right hand
of my father, and rather would I have you with me than
all the assembled knights of Coramonde. When Strongblade is thrown down and Yardiff Bey cast forth, there
will be monuments in plenty to your allegiance."

"Thank you, Your Grace. I have held council with
the Princess Katya—a shrewd lady—and those others

whom she tells me are your adherents. We have discussed tactics and I agree with your plan to work on Strongblade from within. None dared molest me when I broke for the Keel of Heaven in a surprise move, but rumor has Novanwyn in charge of marshaling and executing the invasion of Freegate. He collects his strength slowly, for there are threats of rebellion in the eastern provinces, especially by Bulf Hightower, brother-by-bond to my widowed sister.

"Strongblade draws many men from the northwest, leaving border marches badly undermanned against the wildmen, but they only raid and harry and would not invade without the let of Yardiff Bey. Yet I conjecture that if he had to, he would send them at us. Still, all in all, we shall have to fight a delaying action while the loyalist organization takes root, recruits and tries to bring the impetuous Hightower into line. And those incredible notes left by that MacDonald chap! I would give much to chat with that one; his doctrine will serve us well. But we still want badly for manpower. Hmm, yet there is still much that we may do with a little ingenuity."

Springbuck clapped the bookish Legion-Marshal on the back. "We've just returned from a mission designed to appease that need. Thanks to Reacher here, the Horse-blooded ride with us."

Bonesteel blinked in surprise. "The King? This is His Highness?" He faced Reacher, blushing with embarrassment. "Your Majesty, your pardon please, but I took you for some huntsman or warrior. One seldom sees a King in the trappings of the Howlebeau. Oh, but this news of the Horseblooded is glorious! Why, with light cavalry like them, we have many new avenues open to us."

"Let us repair to my home and discuss them," said the Wolf-Brother.

But Bonesteel answered, "I shall rework the plans I've formulated to take this new factor into account, and have them to you tomorrow when bodies are rested and minds eager." It was agreed to, and the two departed with spirits encouraged.

Reacher went to find his sister when they returned to the palace, but Springbuck, lacking the phenomenal staying power of the monarch of Freegate, wanted only to wash the stench of travel from himself and sleep. He rejected the servants' offer to shave him, having begun a beard, and dozed while they drew his bath, then dismissed them and half-slept as he drifted in the warm, sudsy pool. But seeking his bed, anticipating only a night's sleep, he found it occupied.

Gabrielle waited, lounging on silken sheets, fur covers thrown aside.

"It's thoughtful of you so to come unclothed," said the Prince. "I am thus ensured you are unarmed."

"There is that variety of woman best armed when least attired," she pointed out.

He went to her, noticing a silken sash fastened at the bedstead over her head. It puzzled him, but he didn't take the time to question its portent.

There was no subtlety, no restraint on either part that first time. With the need of a drive long denied, they satisfied themselves in each other with mutual passion, equal abandon. Neither mentioned love, neither had gentle words after their prolonged wait. They tacitly avoided pretense.

Ardor spent, they lay for a time as a cool breeze wafted perspiration from them. She wound her fingers idly in his hair and he looked upward to the silken cord overhead. He jutted his chin toward it. "What thing is that?"

"No ordinary pallet is this. Ensorceled, it's prepared for your return. Observe."

She sat up and began to knot the sash again. Springbuck studied her flawless body, perfect skin, the arresting profile and the mounds of crimson tresses tumbling down the creamy back, and was stirred by new desire. The pleasant drowsiness stealing over him in the wake of their lovemaking retreated. Gabrielle, finishing her complex knotting, blew on the twisted cloth. He found he'd become aroused as fully as he'd been a short time before. He drew her down and once more they entangled, in fervor as intense as the first time.

"Is that the office of the knots?" he asked later, as his fingers traced her spine and her lips rested in the hollow of his neck.

"Yes. Too many repetitions might be injurious, but we're healthy enough to abide some, are we not?" And she would have reached to tie another knot, but he stopped her.

"Stay," he said, "and let us try another mysticism, old and locked into the bodies of men and women at the origins of time." They united again, this time without the rite of knots, and that older magic of which he'd spoken, waiting in all mankind, verified itself.

They both slept late the next day.

But in the weeks which followed he had scant time to spend with her outside councils of war, though he tried to be with her as much as possible. He learned that he must handle himself carefully with her. When he displeased her, carpets had a way of sliding away under him, crockery flew of its own accord and the bathwater was wont to become suddenly and agonizingly cold. The magic with which he was bound to her was stronger than any knotted wisp of silk.

Plans were being considered, altered, revised and often disposed. Agents were enlisted to begin underground activities in Coramonde, several of them from the group of Erubites. Reacher's own espionage corps trained them in skills which would be required of them to build their own units.

A sparsely populated series of dales some way east of the city was cleared and given over to the encampment of the Horseblooded when they began to pour in off the High Ranges. Public announcements quelled the apprehensions of the people of Freegate at the foreign army, the second within their country's borders. Some talk of foreign involvement was heard, but the population in general accepted it that a war of survival was about to be joined.

"We must hold," Reacher advised his people via proclamation, "until the people of Coramonde overthrow the false ruler who misleads them into aggression."

Springbuck became a figure constantly seen at planning sessions and on practice fields. Even the most skeptical troop commanders and governmental leaders allied with him were convinced that this was no layabout Pretender or figurehead. He'd confer deep into the night with Bonesteel, Su-Suru and the others, then rise as early as any soldier for the day's training. He drove himself harder than any of the men he commanded, and usually excelled them unless it was at some martial skill where his shortness of vision interfered. He often went among them, both speaking and listening, the latter even more important than the former. Dressed in Alebowrenian war gear, which had become something of a trademark of his and which he decided to retain, he was easily recognized by the men of the ad hoc army.

Tales sprang up about him, of fairness and openhandedness to his men, of harshness with miscreants and a quick temper like a tropical storm. On one occasion an officer of Bonesteel's Legion, convicted of raping a young woman of Freegate, denounced the Prince and his justice, saying he was no true son of Coramonde to betray one of his own to foreigners. In a rage, the son of Surehand called for the officer to be armed and, with Bar in hand, invited him to impose his own justice and do what he might. They fought, and the officer was as good a swordsman as he'd been accounted, but Springbuck slew him and had his body hung on a hook above the barbican as a caution to all. He gave the girl a generous sum for her dowry by way of compensation in part, the money coming from Bonesteel's laden war chests, and the tale was known to everyone before the evening meal. No such breaches occurred again.

Bonesteel and his most capable under officers instructed the Prince in the handling of steadily larger groups of men, both mounted and afoot, and he took readily to this, and to the set-piece battles they fought on scaled map boards.

The warriors of Freegate and the Horseblooded he concerned himself with little, since the discipline and training of these must be left in the main to their own leaders.

His confidence in his troops and himself grew. He even attempted to become proficient—at close range, at any rate—with the deadly bow of the Horseblooded. This was a composite weapon with a core of flat wooden staving, a layer of split horn glued to one side, a backing of tough, resilient animal sinew glued lengthwise and the whole bound with wrappings of sinew and strung with a cord of twisted hemp with spiral bindings of linen twine. It was a curved bow of remarkable power and, being only four feet long, the best bow a mounted man could want.

But no man complained that he lacked a skill to command, or didn't train as rigorously as they. On the whole, there were surprisingly few incidents of friction between men of such widely varied backgrounds, and part of this may have been due to his strong leadership.

He found his thoughts turning to the future. What of Gil MacDonald? Would he return? It would soon be time to launch the lightning cavalry mission which was to meet the American on his reentry into Coramonde. There were many unknowns involved.

Van Duyn, for his part, feared that the young Pretender and the diminutive King might not be able to hold together the hodgepodge of fugitives, nomads and naturally independent-minded men of Freegate, but the two seemed to doubt their ability not one whit, and time seemed inclined to prove them right in this. That gave the scholar comfort.

As he walked back to the palace with the Snow Leopardess after watching maneuvers, headed for a casual dinner among the roof arbors—which was by way of becoming a custom for them—she said, "D'you know, Edward, up until now—until all this usurpation business—I'd thought to see if someday I couldn't wed the *Ku-Mor-Mai*. What an alliance that would have been! But with everything up in the air, I don't know if the next ruler will be the Prince, Strongblade, Yardiff Bey, you or some other party."

Van Duyn, nowadays an avowed bachelor, was nonplussed; but studying proud Katya, he found himself replying, "If that's to be the prize here, I'll give it my best try."

The Princess, white-gold hair floating around her and flashing in the sun, slipped an arm through his. "I think I should like that," she said. "But since you're not yet a head of state, mayhap a less formal and more private liaison can be established."

Van Duyn felt that happy misery he'd been warning himself against so often in past weeks, harbinger of a new enmeshment.

Somehow, he didn't mind.

PART IV

❧

On Home Ground

Chapter Nineteen

Let the soldier yield to the civilian.
                              MARCUS TULLIUS CICERO

THE silver jet, huge and sleek minister of the technology
that had spawned it and the life to which Gil was returning, skimmed off the runway at Tan Son Nhut, rendering the Delta calm and peaceful under its departure
pattern, a sky-reflective webwork. The plane made one
stop at Yakota Air Force Base in Japan, where Gil
stretched his legs and stood lost in thought, gazing absently into the darkened distance.

The soldier sitting next to him, a big, moody redhead
named O'Riordan, was disinclined to talk, and Gil
didn't much mind. The trip was filled with musings,
snatches of memory from past months thrown up in tur-
bulence to the surface of recall. At last he put them
aside and fell asleep in the wonderful coolness of the
pressurized cabin, high in the chilly air. He awoke periodically to watch as he flew through an accelerated day
and night, jetting eastward as the sun westered.

His delay at Oakland was gratifyingly brief. Landing
at night, he had been outprocessed for separation and
was stepping out of a cab at the airport within six hours.
Men of his type were common enough there, but he
drew glances nevertheless. Lean and drawn in newly issued, ribboned dress uniform, necktie chafing, Gil Mac-
Donald went to the standby counter, uncomfortably
aware of an unusual sensation, the stares of his own
countrymen.

Adolescents, women, children, the elderly—he'd
been apart from them for twelve months and found
himself nervous now that he was plunged back into
their midst in the space of a day.

Midst? No, not exactly. He still wore his uniform,

217

and the bearing that set him at a distance. A young denimed couple clung to one another and showed him hipply outfront distaste. He turned his stare on them like some weapon, ferocity restrained, and an uncommonly intimidating something there made them look quickly away. Waiting for his flight while drinking an unbelievably cold beer, he mulled Edward Van Duyn's words.

"You'll see that soldiers' skills have no market in peace—which is as it should be. Your vocation has you marching to the drum, Gil; you'll find it hard to stroll to the lyre."

He made a stop in Ohio to offer personal condolences to Olivier's widow. A small, pale girl with moist eyes, she resembled her dead husband, the bespectacled machinegunner who'd been torn to shreds by a claymore mine on dismounted scout six weeks before. The visit was awkward for both. He could hear the unspoken question, one she knew was unfair but couldn't repress.

Why are you here and not my husband? Why did you live and not Paul?

He left as soon as he could, saying he had to catch a plane. But he had plenty of time, and used it getting drunk at the airport. On his way to the departure gate, he noticed a newspaper headline: VIOLENCE AT ANTI-WAR RALLY.

He rethought his problems as his plane shot toward Philadelphia. The disorienting effects of his departure from combat were taking hold now. He saw subjectively that he'd left it behind, survived. Did he ever want to leave again? His mind skittered over the incredible events of that twenty-four hours or so in Coramonde.

Undermining doubts of his own sanity began to intrude again. He put them aside; he and Pomorski had discussed the incident many times in private. He had no doubt that it had happened. As far as Gil knew, the others had never mentioned those occurrences to anyone outside the Nine-Mob. Even if they did, who'd believe? No, the facts of the incident were safe from exposure, due simply to human nature.

As time intervened between them and that episode, the other members of *Lobo*'s crew had found it harder and harder to recall. The memory retreated into unreality for them, and then into a sort of forgetfulness, as if it were slowly being eradicated from recollection.

Not to Gil, though. He remembered it all vividly and had the feeling that there was a reason for it, though he didn't know what it might be. He suspected that it was because he was destined to return to that other world, but the unequaled relief of being yanked from war and sent home made him reconsider. He shrugged; he would spend some time not thinking about it, come unwired and get back to it later.

There was time.

Flora MacDonald, née Gilbert, held back her words, but tears welled in her eyes, tears that had nothing to do with the charcoal smoke of the barbecue. Across the picnic table sat her eldest son Gil, home from Vietnam, slightly more recognizable in casual clothes at their backyard party. She'd been amazed at his appearance when he'd walked unannounced into the house a week ago and thrown it into happy bedlam, with unfamiliar creases in his face and the upright saber on his right shoulder. And in days thereafter, more and more changes had become evident.

Even now he sat staring into space, lost in thought, unconsciously taking ice cubes from his finished drink into his mouth and methodically breaking them with his teeth, sucking cool moisture from them. She thought about this automatic use of a source of water against heat and dehydration, and lost control of her tears.

Changes. The second night home he'd rolled from bed with a single terrified scream, "Incoming!" The revelation had kept her awake until dawn.

Then there were his frequent differences of opinion with his younger brother Ralph. Three years separated them, like as many centuries or continents.

She sobbed silently, thinking of the talks that always seemed to devolve into arguments, with Ralph emotional and intense and his older brother quietly expository. Gil's service had put the two irreconcilably in different camps with some unseen barrier between them, their mother and father standing helplessly to one side.

Gil turned his head, musing broken. "What's wrong?" he asked, surprised at the tears.

She shook her head, not trusting to reply. "I'm going to clean up the kitchen," she managed, and retreated from the patio. There were numerous survivors among the afternoon's hot dogs and hamburgers. Ralph had tried a new approach to their old argument, the war, using inductive reasoning. Gil had challenged the chain of logic and the row resulted in Ralph's screeching away on his Honda, taking fury out on the gears.

Gil's father made fresh drinks for himself and his son, Piña Coladas of which he was rather proud, and they sat to watch the sun go down.

"You know what's bothering her of course, don't you?" he said.

"I can't seem to help it; *we* can't seem to. I don't know, it's as if Ralph and I are screaming at each other, and neither of us can hear." He rubbed his eyes with thumb and forefinger. "None of it's the same anymore. I've changed. Don't fit. Ain't tuned in."

"Give it time. Rest as long as you like. Start college, or get yourself organized some other way. You did say you were thinking about school, didn't you?"

Gil took a long pull on his drink. "Once I did. I dunno, maybe I still do. I'm not going back to being assistant something-or-other. It was almost a relief that Sandy got engaged while I was gone; I couldn't talk to her any more than to Ralph."

He was silent for a few minutes. He seldom drank anything but beer, and the liquor was beginning to affect him, bringing on uncharacteristic moodiness. With abrupt decision he said, "I'm thinking of going away again for a while, Pop."

"So soon? It'd break her heart, your mother! Can't you wait? Save some money? You could travel during college vacation, do things in style."

"I don't mean that kind of travel, Pop. It's . . . impossible to explain." He didn't watch his father's face, but lit an insect repellent candle and set it on the arm of his chair, its odor coming to him sharply. At length he spoke, to forestall the pained speech he expected.

"If I go, I'll be gone for a long time. How can I con-

vince you that this isn't just some crazy idea? It's the
only thing I can think of that I want to do, that I *care*
about."

"Well, I don't know how many parents have said it,
but, dammit, if your son is worth his salt there'll come a
time when you've got to say, 'If it's what you want—'
Anything I can do to help? 'Cause I've known you a
long time, kid, and I know what happens when you get
a notion in that head of yours."

Whatever their differences, Gil had to admit that
Ralph had kept his car in first-class shape. The old
Chevy had never idled more smoothly or handled bet-
ter. The day after his conversation with his father, Gil
drove up the New Jersey Turnpike and changed for the
Palisades Parkway. Just after he entered New York
State, he left the Parkway and found the small town in
Rockland County where Van Duyn had told him a man
named Morrows, his former assistant, lived.

Gil located Morrows with a phone directory. It
turned out that the man lived in a rented bungalow. He
answered the door with a cautious look in his eye, a
pale, heavyset individual in his midtwenties, with what
Gil tagged as a false front of condescension.

"I'm here to talk to you about Edward Van Duyn,"
Gil said.

Morrows looked him up and down. "I've already told
Institute Security and the police everything I know," he
replied.

"Never said I was looking for him. He sent me."

Gil was satisfied with the effect. Morrow's eyebrows
shot up and the put-on calm slipped. Regaining composure, he invited Gil in.

The ex-sergeant was sparing with explanations of his
encounter with Van Duyn. He showed the note he'd
brought and requested the two missing components for
the original contiguity machine, the one still at the
Grossen Institute. He asked Morrows' help in using it.

At first Morrows was skeptical, but details of Van
Duyn's instructions, taken in tandem with the handwrit-
ing of the note, convinced him that this newcomer had
indeed spoken with his former research director since

he'd shifted through the interface between universes in his second-generation machine. Morrows went to his desk and returned with sheafs of paper.

"Ever since Dr. Van Duyn left I've been working, trying to interpret his data in full. The equipment works well enough, I suppose, though I haven't activated it since his last experiment. He covered the trail of his research so well that I can't quite ferret out all the details and variables."

"You haven't tried it?"

Morrows laughed nervously, as if some embarrassing secret had come to light. "Tried it myself? Take a chance on a miscalculation that might open a gateway to, say, the heart of a star? Don't be asinine. Oh, once I've collated all my data, and perhaps expanded Van Duyn's findings a bit, and made some preparations and so forth, then I'll use the contiguity." His eyes roamed the shabby little home. Anger etched his voice.

"Do you think I like this? Living on assistantship pay without recognition or a future? It's just that before I jump off into another cosmos, I want to be sure, that's all. Simply a matter of a little more hard information, some more tests."

Then Gil understood. Morrows would never use the contiguity. He'd dither uncertainly, delay one more day or one more week, and in the end he wouldn't go. Gil wondered what it would be like to see the apparatus every day, know you could leave anytime you chose, agonize over dangers and doubts and postpone, forever postpone.

A living hell, he thought.

"If you help me, Morrows, I'll add considerably to your information, maybe clarify some of those variables you've got, nail down some unknowns for you." He knew he could con this man.

Morrows leaned forward in his chair, suspicion and condescension forgotten.

The next day was Sunday. Though he didn't usually work that day, Morrows went to the Grossen Institute. Proceeding according to the researcher's instructions, Gil found an overgrown dirt side road leading to an unused gate in the fence surrounding the Institute grounds. The road had been used to bring in heavy equipment to build a power plant, then ignored and the gate locked. Tall weeds and young saplings had come in since then, effectively hiding Gil's car from the main road. He was thankful for the Chevy's high clearance in negotiating passage.

The fence was unimpressive rusting chain link, more to keep out children and the idly curious than to repel serious invaders. This sleepy town knew little trouble and conditions required only nonchalant watchfulness against nuisances and vandals, not alert defense against determined, forceful intrusion, there being small profit for thieves in the equipment and information available at the Institute. The Grossen dealt exclusively in the abstract.

Gil waited a few minutes at the fence, assuring himself that no one was near, and swarmed over it.

Though the directors of the Grossen Institute were curious about Van Duyn's abandoned apparatus, Morrows' investigations clearly didn't have much priority. He'd been relocated in a converted storage building near the power plant. It had garage-type doors for deliveries, doors that would fit in with Gil's plan.

Morrows was waiting for him and showed him the contiguity apparatus, a square frame of metal perhaps seven feet on a side, held upright by supports. There was surprisingly little ancillary equipment: a monitoring consol and the tuning bank. Morrows warmed the device, studying various indicators with a critical eye. Gil watched and tried to memorize the sequence exactly.

At last the other mated two cables and threw a switch. The framework instantly contained a bright scene, a green field with a warm sun overhead and a tree line in the distance. Gil knew he was looking at Coramonde again.

Morrows threw the switch back and the view faded. He was sweating and his hands were trembling badly.

"Okay," said Gil, "here's the scam."

That evening he returned home, supposedly from visiting Jack McKinny, a former squadmate in the

LURPs. The next day he cashed in his U.S. Savings
Bonds, closed out his bank account and began a painstaking buying spree, starting with the bookstores. Deciding and redeciding what to take, he concentrated
largely on law, political science, philosophy and selec-
tions in mathematics, psychology and education. He
took everything he could lay his hands on about guerrilla warfare; he added them to his own collection, manuals he'd felt the U.S. Army would never miss. Too, he
brought works on medicine and agriculture.

It had been his intention to pick up a quantity of ri-
fles, maybe army surplus or some Belgian FNs, to take
back with him, but the drawbacks stopped him. First
there was the problem of teaching backward peasants to
shoot and not freak out at the noise and blast, something he would have had to do without any other cadremen to help, except possibly Van Duyn. He'd worked
with Vietnamese Civilian Irregular Defense Groups,
and knew how frustrating that could be.

Then there was the snag of maintenance and cleaning, tough to impress on members of a nonmachine
culture. Add the bulky haul of ammunition and
magazines, cleaning kits, spare parts, solvent, oil and repair tools, and the whole idea became untenable, not
counting the cost factor. Too, Van Duyn felt a moral
imperative not to introduce firearms on any large scale
to Coramonde.

In the end he took only those weapons he would use
himself. The only gun he owned was a Mauser pistol, a
ten-round Waffenfabrik commercial model with the
solid-head "new safety" lever. Chambered for nine-mm
cartridges, the pistol had adequate accuracy and hitting
power, though it was a bit old, and would fire the same
standard ammunition as Van Duyn's Browning. Gil located an old canvas military holster to accommodate
the Mauser, along with a braided lanyard and three am-
munitions pouches for extra clips.

He asked with exaggerated casualness if his father
would care to sell his M-1 carbine, trophy of the war in
the Pacific. Mr. MacDonald silently took the carbine
down, fetched clips from a locked drawer and handed
them to his son.

Gil's next acquisition was a Browning Hi-Power, shoulder holster and extra magazines. At the same time, he purchased a good deal of nine-mm and carbine ammunition. He also decided to take his bowie and trench knives.

He spent most of that week around the house. He found everyday life a trifle unfamiliar. Not beyond his ability to adjust, just . . . bland. Nights watching TV didn't interest him except that his parents evidently enjoyed it, and he got to talk to them. He'd never told his mother he was leaving and didn't know that his father had. She appeared to know.

On his final evening at home, a Saturday, he stood at his dresser sorting out his finished plans. He'd packed his cargo into the Chevy. He looked through the things he'd decided to leave behind. Insurance and credit cards, car ownership certificate, Social Security card, proof of membership in this or that organization, address book, dog tags, draft card, voter registration card, army inoculation, Geneva Convention, ration and meal cards; all were fanned out on the dresser.

My life in paper.

He left them, with the single exception of the driver's license. In Coramonde they'd mean nothing. Diplomas, licences, documents and deeds wouldn't be as significant as one bullet. He dropped all his keys, save those for the Chevy, into a drawer.

He lingered over dinner but ate little. For once there was no dispute with Ralph, but all his attempts at humor failed. Finally he rose and kissed his mother. "I'm going. I'll, umm, I'll try to keep in touch."

He shook hands with his brother, both of them ashamed and regretting that anger had driven them apart. With a burst of emotion that surprised him, he hugged his father. Then he drove off into the night, uncertain of the wisdom of it.

He drove slowly at first, savoring the world around him; but coming to the smoky refineries and mazed roadways of northern Jersey, he speeded up. For a moment he had a view of New York City across the Hudson River near the George Washington Bridge. It looked star-lit and infinitely inviting, an enchanted realm to rival Coramonde. He'd been there a number of times, and knew differently.

He hunted up a motel near the Grossen Institute and slept until the next day, waking just before noon.

He called Morrows who, when Gil identified himself, said it was arranged, then hung up. *Good. That means he'll be somewhere else when I break in, and have a cover story.*

He dressed in a khaki shirt, wash-faded denim pants and jacket and his weather-beaten boots, and checked out. He spent the afternoon on his stomach near the unused gate, eating sandwiches and peering through the chain link with binoculars. Once, a jeep made a slow circuit of the building but no one even bothered going in. Under the round glass stare of the binoculars his mouth split into a grin. *Perfect.*

The Jeep made another circuit at about five, just as Morrows had said it would, even as he was preparing to go in. He pulled a pair of heavy-duty bolt cutters out of the car and went to the locked chain securing the gate, then paused for a moment. If he went ahead, he'd not only commit a serious crime or three, but might also exile himself irrevocably. Unexpectedly, his thoughts went to the job his former boss had offered him, to return to the mailroom with a promise of management training.

"To hell with that!" Gil MacDonald realized in that moment that he wouldn't have cared to be president of the company. He much preferred to seek Coramonde and something that might be called adventure. He fumbled the heavy snips into place.

Getting the gate open was difficult, but he persevered. Leaving the car where it was, he ran across the open field to the lab and jimmied the door by main force with a small crowbar. He propped the broken door closed, raised the delivery door and dashed back to his car. He drove into the building without incident, not forgetting to close the gate behind him, and pulled up next to the contiguity framework.

He ran through the preoperative sequence, satisfied that all instruments appeared to be working correctly, though he doubted that he could spot it if they weren't. He connected the heavy cables and was about to activate the interface between universes when a voice behind him said, "The deal was for you to leave this mysterious information of yours behind when you departed."

Morrows, of course. Morrows with a Luger in his hand. Then Gil saw that it wasn't actually one of the German military pistols, but an imitation model, probably a .22 caliber.

"The deal," Gil said calmly to hide his dismay, "was for you to be somewhere else while I ran this stunt."

The researcher laughed nervously. "Should I be? I'd be a fool then, wouldn't I?"

"Gad, has all trust gone out of the world?" asked Gil. He wished bitterly that he had a gun with him instead of having left his in the car.

Morrows ignored the crack. "Now you're through blowing smoke at me. I want answers and I won't wait for them. You'd have a lot of explaining to do to the cops."

Gil stepped closer to him. *Time to shoot craps, man.*

"And if I tell you to shove it? You gonna shoot me with that miserable plinking gun? What's in it, twenty-two shorts? Even if it's hollowpoints, you sure you'll stop *me*? Cause if you don't, your damned head's getting ripped right off, Jack." He hoped he'd read Morrows right.

The other was confused, suddenly seeing clearly that a gun isn't a magic wand—wave it and anyone else must obey. A man with a gun must be ready to use it, and he wasn't. He let his pistol and confidence waver for a moment, and Gil kicked the gun sideways with the inside of his foot, karate fashion, and followed up with a quick hand combination, sending his opponent reeling. Gil hopped once and uncorked a snapping side-kick to the crotch that bent Morrows double in the old, old reflex, and was instantly behind him securing Hadakajime, the forearm choke. The other struggled for a moment, then relaxed as the ferocious hold cut off wind and blood to the brain. Gil maintained it until he was sure that his victim would be out awhile, then gradually loosened it, watching for a ruse.

He hadn't been totally unprepared for this. From his

glove compartment he took a broad roll of surgical tape. He bound the unconscious man tightly but left him ungagged and lugged him to a tree by the road leading to Institute Administration. He judged that Morrows would be safe here and be quickly found when Security came to check out the rumpus he planned to make.

He returned and took two more items from the trunk of his car. From Explosive Ordnance Disposal, demolitions specialists and others he'd met in the service, Gil had picked up a fair knowledge of explosives and even obtained manuals. It was startling to find out how easy it was to produce one's own mercury fulminate for blasting caps, make blasting gelatin, TNT and a dozen or more types of dynamite, not to mention low explosives. With small investment and considerable risk, he'd built two explosive devices. They'd been his primary worry on the way up from Philly, but he'd been fairly confident they'd take the trip safely. Each had a basic alarm clock timer. He set them for one minute, placing one under the control console and the other beneath the programming bank, not bothering to tamp them. He felt a twinge of conscience at the destruction they'd cause, but he had to erase his trail and destroy the prototype machine. He could see the damaged party only as the faceless Institute. With this rationalization, he went on with his work.

He started the Chevy. Leaving the engine running, he threw the switch to activate the apparatus. Again the landscape of Coramonde snapped into view. He started each of the alarm clocks, jumped into his car and gunned it through the interface into Coramonde.

He didn't stop directly beyond the contiguity, but pulled off to one side to avoid flying debris from the impending explosion and halted twenty yards away. He shut off the motor and waited. Thinking to scan for any company in the area, he remembered he'd left the binoculars hanging in their case by the fence at the Institute and made a grossly offensive remark about them. Would there be fingerprints? Hell with 'em; going back was out of the question. He regretted the loss as he waited.

Thirty seconds filed past and the contiguity spewed

forth a ludicrous tongue of flame which seemed, from his angle, to spout from nowhere and end abruptly. Much of the force of the blast had probably been cut off when the machinery was destroyed and the gateway disappeared. In other words, he'd succeeded in sabotaging his only sure way home.

You're a Doomfarer now, son. Whoopee!

He shucked off his jacket, drew the Browning from under the Chevy's front seat and shrugged on the shoulder holster. He spotted what had to be the streambed Van Duyn had described to him, and started the car again. In the distance he saw the village the scholar must have spotted that first evening, but it looked deserted and burned out.

The downgrade to the streambed was steep but he took it in first gear and let the transmission work for him. Wear and tear didn't matter; he'd never use the car again. The stream was a wide, shallow flow with broad, sandy banks. He stopped under a willow and shut the engine off for the last time. Taking his trench knife, a relic of WWI with a foot-long blade and brass knuckles on the grip, he began cutting down shrubbery and branches to conceal the Chevy.

He began to sing:

> "I'm a rambler, I'm a gambler,
> I'm a long ways from home,
> And them as don't like me
> Can leave me alone . . ."

He was sweating hard and had removed his shirt by the time he artfully placed a final branch just so. He'd taken the carbine from the trunk and left it on the front seat, and now he squeezed in past his camouflage and bided his time.

It was dark by the time the sound of hoofbeats came to him. He flicked the carbine's safety off and silently opened the window wider, poking the barrel through the loophole he'd left himself and aligning it directly out before him in practiced night-marksman form. The moon wasn't especially bright, but seconds later he made out a party of riders. They halted at a bend in the stream, difficult to make out at thirty yards and not a promising target. He was unworried; friends or enemies, they'd have no firearms.

He jammed thumb and forefinger into his mouth, gave a piercing whistle. With impressive speed they traced the sound and ranged themselves around the overhanging willow. They were seven, with two extra riderless horses. Six held lances or drawn bows. The seventh, coming forward, said in a warm female voice, "If you are Gil MacDonald, name your metal machine to me, from which Chaffinch was slain. But if you are not, make your peace with your gods."

He laughed. "Hey, hey, cut me some slack Babycakes; its name was *Lobo*. How're long-term parking rates around here?"

The joke was lost on her.

Chapter Twenty

Yet all experience is an arch wherethrough
Gleams the untravelled world.

ALFRED, LORD TENNYSON,
"Ulysses"

They dismounted in haste. Gil slid from his car to meet them. The woman who'd spoken, plainly in command, was dressed in helmet and mail. He could make out little else in the dark except that the top of her helm reached just above his eyes.

"Are you in readiness to accompany us?" she asked formally.

He had a hundred questions but held them. Instead, he said, *"Semper paratus,"* and began to bring out the Chevy's cargo. Much of it they bundled onto one riderless horse, which was fitted with a pack frame. The rest they divvied among them, except for Gil's personal things and weapons. He wondered at the care with which they handled the books, almost a reverence, and began to understand Van Duyn's liking of his Promethean role.

He put on his shirt and jacket and fastened his pistol belt with holstered Mauser around his waist. He loosened the sling of the carbine as much as he could and slipped it over his head and shoulder. The rest of his possessions were in two small packs fastened at either side of the saddle of the other spare horse. He mounted awkwardly.

He bade the old Chevy farewell, but doubted it would.

They started, the girl leading and Gil right behind, and he could tell from the first that the others were holding their pace down to accommodate him. They rode without difficulty in the scarce light and he got the impression they could have ridden full tilt without trouble. His own riding style was more the Sunday-afternoon variety, but he hung in doggedly, rifle slapping his back, and did his best to keep up.

They rode for much of the night with no word except to change point men. He thought of offering to take a turn but decided that it would be as useless as one of these horsemen trying to con *Lobo* for him. They used narrow trails and game tracks, frequently cutting overland with many a backward glance. He knew that they must want to get away from the area of the contiguity. A wise move; the sound of the blast might have attracted attention, and sooner or later the car would be found.

They stopped after long hours without a break and made a primitive bivouac, leg-hobbling their horses—Gil had to be shown how to do it—and throwing themselves down on the ground to catch precious sleep. He thought about introducing himself, or at least engaging the girl in conversation, but they didn't look interested; he let it pass. He, too, was tired and used to roughing it—if not quite in this way—and had no trouble falling asleep.

Awakening was another matter. He'd stiffened up; leg muscles protested their unaccustomed strain and refused to respond. He tried to ignore them after doing a few quick exercises to loosen them. He saw that his horse was already saddled and his companions were almost prepared to leave.

He took the opportunity to scope them out. The men were tough-looking, clad in woolens and scale armor. They carried lances and short bows, straight swords and small shields of leather-covered wood rimmed with iron. He saw that they were equipped for speed and maneuverability rather than heavy fighting.

These were prowler-cavalry, an elite even among Bonesteel's crack Legion. Horsemen nearly as adroit as the Horseblooded themselves, the prowlers were skilled trackers, adept at scouting and deep-penetration patrols. They could live off the land indefinitely, find their way over strange terrain almost instinctively, go undetected in hostile territory and outride pursuit on swift, sure-footed horses. The six here were a quarter of all the prowlers in Bonesteel's command.

The girls was something else again. She was winding her waist-length, honey-streaked hair up to pull on her conical helmet. She fitted it on and he studied the beautiful, deep-gray eyes behind her helm's nasal piece. She was no older than eighteen or so, and wore a mail byrnie and baggy pants tucked into high boots altogether like those of the prowlers; she bore a slender, unadorned sword at her side. He didn't know if she had slept with it close to hand, and it occurred to him that it could be dangerous to find out, especially since the others treated her so respectfully and would be inclined to feel protective.

She considered him frankly for a moment and he found himself uncomfortable. "'I am Duskwind," she said, "and to me has been entrusted the task of bringing you back to Freegate."

"Gil MacDonald. I guess Springbuck and Van Duyn and the others got to whatsisname, Reacher?"

"The Wolf-Brother has rallied many of the steppes tribes to him and some of the forces of Coramonde have defected to our side. Things are more heartening now than formerly."

"The Wolf-Brother?"

"Reacher is known by diverse names in many places. Wolf-Brother is one."

She gestured over her shoulder and their horses were led up. They mounted, and the six prowlers took to their horses. Gil was about to sling his carbine when he noticed an empty quiver at the side of his saddle, fixed there to carry an unstrung bow or short javelins. He found that it held his light weapon satisfactorily, even with the thirty-round banana clip in it.

They set off again, as rapidly as the night before; but this time it was much easier, since they had light. Within moments they passed one of the places remnant of the time antedating the Great Blow, a collection of tall columns of some black stone overgrown with vines sprouting orange orchids. Gil wanted to ask more questions but withheld them. The course was winding, but not as difficult as last night's. He calculated that they were making respectable progress due east. Once, as they rode through a tight dell, a noise to his left drew his glance and he saw a figure duck back out of sight on the ridge line.

"Outlaw, maybe," Duskwind said without being asked or looking around. "Or a peasant hiding from the levies, or possibly just some curious, careful hunter."

They ate in the saddle, quick bites of salted meat and gulps from water skins. By now, Gil had concluded that they were testing him, seeing how well he'd stand up to being led along, waiting for him to give in and start demanding they pause, like some raw recruit. Instead, he kept a sharp eye on their route for ambush and concentrated on improving his riding.

They paused to rest their horses and he took the occasion to stand next to Duskwind. He thought to offer her a Lifesaver—butterscotch, and much the worse for being in his pocket for two days—and she accepted it and was delighted with the taste. He found it difficult to begin a conversation; even with the trail dust on her face she was a very attractive girl.

"Er, are all the squad leaders here good-looking, or are you the exception?"

A weak gambit, but she allowed it a smile, showing deep dimples. "I am no combat leader, indeed. But I've been through this country in the past and I've familiarized myself with the maps at Earthfast, and none of Bonesteel's scouts had been here ere now. What's more, I was growing tired of Freegate. Palace life is boring, and when I tried for a commission in one of the new units, I found my martial skills were insufficient—for the nonce. Still, I can learn."

He found much of the answer obscure, but didn't want to bog down now. "Why would you want to learn? I mean, it's unusual, isn't it?"

"Truly. I've always been impatient with woman's traditional lot. When the Wolf-Brother, my cousin King Reacher I mean, offered the assignment of spying for him at Earthfast, I took it right away. I'd long admired his sister her freedom and activity. But I'd never had the chance to practice the soldier's arts as much as I would have liked. Not for me to sit around a Court cooing, my friend."

He sympathized. It would be awfully rough for a woman to get ahead in a culture where muscles and reflexes settled most of the issues of the day. He supposed he'd better get acquainted with local weapons as soon as he could.

"We must move quickly yet for some time," she said, "even though it's hard on the horses. We shouldn't run into any of Strongblade's troops, since they've mustered at one central Keep, but it's just as well to avoid main roads. We don't want to risk losing your books or you."

"I think that's a terrific attitude," said Gil MacDonald sincerely.

That evening they stopped and made proper camp, unsaddling their horses and rubbing them down. They even lit a tiny fire, since no outlaw or refugee was likely to go against so many well-armed men. The prowlers were inclined to leave Duskwind and Gil alone. He welcomed the situation. He let her fill him in on the background of the war and the Crescent Lands in general, at the same time availing himself of long looks at her. He was rather shy and a bit clumsy at this unfamiliar, agreeable predicament of being thrown together in the wilds with a delectable female. But he persevered, and found it all captivating.

They went with minimal provisions, moving hard and as long as conditions permitted, the limiting factor usually being the horses. Often, a prowler would shoot some small game during the day for the night's meal. Gil was astounded at their proficiency with the bow while ahorse.

He enjoyed Duskwind's company thoroughly, more so as he became used to the constant riding. Though younger than he, she had a self-reliant, confident air appropriate to an older woman. She was an enigma, at times speaking to him of the intricate etiquette and elaborate ceremony of Court and possessed of dainty bearing in jest; at others, joining in the rough joking of the prowlers, who fairly worshiped her. She plainly savored the unpolished life they shared. She often looked tired and he knew that she wasn't used to crude living conditions, but exhausted as she was, she was evidently thriving on it all.

During their talks he learned that war might begin any day now. Bulf, the brother of the late Rolph Hightower, had proclaimed defiance of Strongblade's reign and resolved to have vengeance. Springbuck, Andre deCourteney and their allies were irked by the premature move, but Bulf was a man of conviction, not discretion, and it was generally conceded that a punitive expedition would not be long in coming.

During one campfire dialogue Gil confessed that he was still vague about the origins of the situation in Coramonde. Duskwind, lying on her stomach with chin on hands, came at the subject obliquely.

"What are good and evil in your world?" she queried.

"Uh-uh, Babe. I'm not biting on that one."

"Well, I'll tell you what they are here. They're two classes of forces that have been tottering the world back and forth throughout history.

"Good? Oh, you could say it's a grouping with emphasis on the benign. Peace. Human weal. A constellation of attitudes that, in sum, are beneficent. Evil—and this is handy terminology only, my friend—lusts for dominance, hungers for self-indulgence regardless of others, wallows in violence, revels in pain."

He was lying on his back surveying unfamiliar stars, listening and cracking his knuckles.

"Are you interested in this or not?" she snapped sharply, convinced she was being ignored.

He chuckled. "Go ahead," he said without looking around. "Please excuse my musical joints."

She giggled. "Now, labels sometimes obscure more than they clarify. Good has often masqueraded as evil and vice versa. Not all participants in the struggle are human, either. There's constant warfare between transcendent personalities: demons, elementals, even gods. Humans who participate on those levels are called witches, enchanters, and so forth.

"At any pass, two centuries ago saw a pivotal battle,

when the sorcerers of Shardishku-Salamá tried to liberate the hosts of the Inferno into the real world."

His mind flew to that place. Beads of moisture started at his forehead.

"They were prevented," she continued, "but not before they did grave damage. We'll never know how many heroes rose to heights of glory only to fall in sanguine battle.

"This was the Great Blow and it altered the world. Altered, did I say? Bent, twisted, turned topsy-turvy is better but still understatement. The fabric of reality was rent and many strange things entered the world, and many others left it forever.

"To jump intervening years, Gil MacDonald, Shardishku-Salamá tried its penultimate attack again thirty years ago. This time they were struck down almost at once, and what I've called evil fell back on all fronts.

"In the north, Fim—Lord Roguespur's father— drove the druids out to exile with the island wildmen. In the south, Thom, the Land's Friend and the Sisterhood of Glyffa solicited the help of the men of Veganá to break and raze Death's Hold, a stupendous coastal fortress that threw its shadow across the Outer Sea and harbored foulness. The Prince of the Waves even sent Mariners to help that final assault. Quite unprecedented.

"What happened then we only know now. Yardiff Bey was privy to those who commanded the fight for good, but he was a creature of Shardishku-Salamá—"

"A sleeper," Gil interjected.

"A what?"

"Sleeper. He was huddling with you, but he was playing for them."

"Hmm. I think I see. Bey embarked on this grand scheme of his, using people and spirits, bartering with his own soul and others'. He worked Fim's downfall, and the druids and wildmen hold the north. He had Thom tempted and destroyed. He undermined the throne of Coramonde and set the desert hordes against the Crescent Lands.

"So we're at a crux. Van Duyn tells me that issues of

right and wrong aren't as clear-cut in your world. I envy you and pity you at the same time, but one thing's certain; this war coming at us with such speed could fix the destiny of the world."

Gil rolled over and stared at her across the campfire. "It *is* clear-cut, isn't it?" He lay back, head resting on his arm.

"That's the most jolting thing about this place," he whispered. "Maybe that's what drew me back, but it scares me stiff; a showdown of total opposites. Can anything survive a battle like that? Isn't everyone tainted with at least a little bit of both?"

She watched him drift in thought, and had the fleeting impression that he was mad, or Enlightened.

They crossed the wide, bleak, rocky passage at Barren Ford, taking the moody Blackflood River at its least treacherous point, and swung south to the Western Tangent, eventually passing the giant merestone that Springbuck and the other renegades had left behind them long weeks before.

The small villages and towns he'd seen hadn't prepared him for his first sight of Freegate, and the tall spires on the far side of the forbidding chasm made him gasp. Their escort was dismissed at the barbican after transferring the precious cargo to the metropolitan Guardsmen, and Gil and Duskwind were ushered without delay into a room adjacent to the throne room where yet another consultation of war was under way.

Bewilderingly hurried introductions were made by Van Duyn, who seemed honestly pleased to have him back. Springbuck, sporting the beginnings of a beard, clasped Gil's arm warmly; and Andre pounded him on the back. He discovered that the pudgy wizard was a good deal stronger than he'd thought, just looking at the man. Even Gabrielle vouchsafed him a smile and an inclination of her gorgeous head, sending a shimmer through the swirling scarlet mass of her hair. She was arrayed in a long, close-clinging gown of purest white, which bared her proud shoulders and haughty neck and the green gemstone nestled in the cleft of her scented bosom. Springbuck was proprietary toward her and Gil saw that she'd shifted her favors. Seeing her, he could only pity the scholar.

As he eyeballed the Snow Leopardess and Reacher, Van Duyn took him aside for a hasty conference.

"We rolled snakeyes on the books," Gil said. "I can make out the diagrams and pictures, but I don't seem to be able to read 'em. Every time I try, it's like I've got whadayacallit, word-blindness?"

"Dyslexia," Van Duyn said absently, disappointed. "The translation effect."

"Aw, well, no sense getting bent out of shape about it. I can remember all the important military stuff, I'm sure. You're just going to have to reinvent the rest."

Van Duyn mumbled something. Gil grew indignant. "What're you crying about, Ace? You've got me, haven't you? You know what contour plowing is, and the Bill of Rights. And movable type and Mercator projections."

The other nodded reluctantly.

"I talked to some of those prowlers on the way here," Gil continued. "Want to know a good bet we missed? Something that might've really given us an edge in a long campaign?"

Van Duyn, the problem solver, was curious in spite of himself.

"A couple of crates of antibiotics. Or malaria pills. Seems that during a protracted war around here, there's almost always plenty of disease among the troops. Just as many men get knocked down by dysentery as by arrows. It never occurred to me; when you go into the U.S. Army, they inoculate you for everything but horniness. I was thinking: maybe a few rules for field sanitation would mean as much as an extra regiment. Be careful about food, water, rats and lice and it might make quite a difference, no?"

Van Duyn was already lost in thought along this new avenue. Did communicable diseases function the same way in this cosmos as in his own?

Gil was checking out the royal siblings. "How about them?" he asked the scholar. "The shrimp and the babe in the tough-girl outfit? Can we count on them?"

Van Duyn was suddenly angry. How to tell this insolent punk of the Princess's political expertise? And her fine mind and indomitable spirit? Yes, and her brother's courage and prowess, of course. Let him find out for himself!

"I think you'll find them quite adequate allies," he replied frostily, but Gil didn't miss the look in his eye when it fell on the Snow Leopardess, or her wink when she caught the scholar's gaze. That being the case, the ex-sergeant withdrew his pity.

Chapter Twenty-one

Bring down thunder to the land,
Wrap the lightning in my hand,
Muster, angry, eager madmen at my back;
Have us revel in the din
As the foeman rushes in;
Joyous slaughter, laughing havoc, glad attack.

Help me sever limb and life;
Feed my swordarm, send me strife;
That I pay in full my death-demanding debt.
And when friend and foe lie slain
And I've worked my brother's bane,
Though I don't deserve it, gods! Let me forget!

From "DOOMFARING,"
The Antechamber Ballads

THE next few weeks were devoted nearly exclusively to preparation for battle and defense. Reports from Coramonde grew steadily less auspicious as more levvies were brought from the northwest and southwest, anticipatory of the thrust against the Hightower. While debate raged in the allied councils on whether or not aid should be sent to the ill-omened resistance there, Gil decided to avoid involvement in policy decisions and concentrate on learning to stay alive in this strange style of warfare.

From Freegate's armories he was given a light suit of closely woven metal mesh, wonderfully supple and protective, but he found it inhibitive and heavy on his shoulders in particular, where the bulk of the weight settled. Too, he was issued comfortable cavalryman's boots. Over his armor, he wore a harness to which he fastened the Mauser at his right hip and the Browning under his left armpit, also strapping on his ammo pouches. He kept his trench knife, but presented his bowie to Springbuck, who'd greatly admired it and, forced by the American to accept it, immediately tied its sheath to his right thigh.

Gil also reclaimed the two fragmentation hand grenades—all that had been left aboard *Lobo* after the sortie into the Inferno—from Van Duyn, who'd kept them for him. He was given a medium-weight sword, a hand-and-a-half bastard blade, and found that using it wasn't as easy as it had looked. He got a great deal of help from cadremen and instructors of the allied armies, but his main coach was the Prince-Pretender to the Throne of Coramonde, Springbuck. The American spent the majority of his time at riding and swordsmanship, the former barely sufficient and the latter nonexistent on his arrival at Freegate. He had no particular talent in either area; but by dint of sheer determination and practice, he improved rapidly.

He had good reflexes and excellent hand-eye coordination, but found he had to work hard to build strength and endurance. The fighting men of this violent world took great hardships for granted and considered tremendous exertions part of their everyday life. They'd spent years fighting and exercising in weighty armor with bulky weapons, leading extremely active lives. The result was that the average armsbearer was capable of extraordinary feats of brawn and stamina. The first time he trailed a crew of veterans over a rude obstacle course in armor, it began to dawn on Gil that he had a lot of catching up to do. He worked harder, and they helped him.

His way with a sword was more the cut-and-hew mode than that of the subtle fencer, but his confidence grew. His ability with a bow was nothing this side of atrocious. An archer informed him that it would serve, perhaps, if he could arrange to kill all his opponents from ambush, and them dead drunk. Gil remarked as how that would be difficult to organize in the midst of battle, to which the archer agreed dismally.

The American wasn't much bothered by this, though, since he expected to use guns in combat if he had to. To this end he convinced the prowler-cavalrymen he'd met to teach him to ride as they did in skirmish, reins held in clenched teeth, guiding their horses with their knees, with hands free to use sword or bow, spear and shield. He was assigned the use of a horse of his own, a big chestnut, a seasoned campaigner and well trained to war. Gil immediately dubbed him Jeb Stuart. It was difficult, and he could afford to use little ammunition in practice, but he got some of the knack of managing a horse while fighting, and got Jeb Stuart familiar with the crack of gunfire. Any face he'd lost in early fumblings was forgotten when he used his pistols in a brief, accomplished mounted practice.

In return for Springbuck's tutoring, Gil taught him some of his own tricks. Not forgetting how easily the outlander could disable a man with bare hands and feet, the Prince applied himself to lessons in boxing, karate and other unarmed skills. He also drilled daily with sword and parrying dagger with the best masters-of-arms in Freegate, aware that he might yet have to face mighty Strongblade in single competition.

He and Gil also rode with the various units of the allied armies as they maneuvered and exercised, sometimes watching from the commander's vantage point and at others riding or running in the thick of the clashes. Springbuck often took command, demonstrating growing virtuosity. Gil contributed what he knew of applicable tactics from the history of his own world.

They were soon true cavalrymen. Their reins bore marks and cuts left by their teeth.

The American had only marginal time for activities of the Court in the evening, usually consulting with Legion-Marshal Bonesteel or other major commanders on the relative merits of this or that innovation, or advising on the doings of the growing underground in Coramonde. He saw Duskwind, but was unable to speak to her. She always seemed to be accompanied by this or that male associate, often of what struck Gil as covetous demeanor, and he had no wish to intrude.

The Horseblooded had begun to fill the dales set aside for them near the city, and their massing waxed and grew. Their coming was marked by warm greetings from the people of Freegate with gifts of food, drink and weapons, and toys and sweets for their children. They occupied their time with endless competitions. Primary among these were games on horseback: races, hurdling and other, more dangerous sport. The Wild Riders were fond of jumping saddles with each other at full gallop, changing mounts in midair, of straddling two horses at once and of shooting their bows as they stood in the saddle, or on the back, of a madly racing horse. There was nothing they wouldn't do ahorse on a dare, since the darer was obliged to try it himself.

Gil was enticed into jumping Jeb Stuart through a flaming hoop, finding it easier than he'd expected but no less belly-clenching. There were pony-lifting contests, barrel-lifting contests, wagon-lifting contests and tugs-of-war. Springbuck was hazed into a drinking sport, of which the Horseblooded had many, wherein he and his opponent hopped from foot to foot on a table, draining their flagons while crowing Riders periodically cut at their legs with scimitars. Amazingly, he won. Thereafter his status with the Horseblooded was high.

The two learned the uninhibited jigs and frenzied flings danced by the steppesmen. They also tried their hand at some of the unsuual weapons they saw: the atlatl, boomerang and war quoit—a razor-edged device which, in expert hands, could kill an unarmored man at eighty paces—and smaller throwing disks that reminded Gil of shuriken.

The American felt completely alive. He saw new sights every day; his nostrils were filled with exotic scents and his ears with novel sounds and conversation. He and the Prince tried the noropianics and other intoxicants popular with the Horseblooded. Some brought bizarre dreams and hallucinations, and others simple euphoria.

One Rider in particular they noticed, a tall, bony subchieftain named Dunstan, whose eyes were sunken in dark sockets and made them uneasy. Though his fellows didn't actually shun him, they avoided him, despite the fact that he was an excellent warrior, if melancholy.

It happened that he was at their side when Gil and Springbuck decided to end a day spent in hard rehearsal and, bypassing the usual palace fete, try an evening at a public house that came highly recommended. It struck Gil as impolite to ignore Dunstan, who'd been listening and contributing to their critiques, so he extended an invitation and Dunstan accepted. The American was instantly sorry, for reasons he couldn't clearly identify, that he'd obeyed his impulse.

They went to The Excellent Board where, according to information, "the provender's good and plentiful and the proprietor's not as concerned with rank and apparel as with your wherewithal."

It was an auditorium-sized pavilion in the parkland, not yet filled, since many people were still at their work or some entertainment, of which Freegate offered many. In various corners trained animals, acrobats and mummers performed; musicians, jugglers and prestidigitators circulated among the tables. For the first time the Prince saw a creature called, as Gil told him, a monkey, a sad-faced little beast with a forlornly human look to its whimsical features. It fascinated him.

No one recognized them; Springbuck had left his cock-plumed war mask with his horse. The three spoke slightly, the food deserving their full attention. There were stuffed fowl, venison and mutton, brook trout and snails, all set off by thick ale.

Dunstan became more amiable to the extent that he smiled at one of Gil's dry remarks. Late in the meal, when they were doing more drinking than eating, a boisterous party of twenty or so came in and filled the tables nearest them. The group was composed mostly of young members of the upper classes, slumming with hangers-on mixed in. It wasn't long before a handsome, arrogant boy in gold-trimmed blue silk noticed them.

"Ho, manager," he called out, "perfumes here! Scatter them about that the smell of those vagabonds yonder will not offend the noses of myself and these, my good friends, people of quality." He touched a pomander to his nose theatrically and the girl next to him sniggered. The others traded conspiratorial grins.

"Do you think," another chimed in, "that there are enough scents in all Freegate to expunge their odor?"

"Hopefully," continued the first. "Isn't it enough that

they fill our city with malodorous foreigners without letting them run unwatched through the streets? Damnation, they eat our provisions, skulk through our lands and now they spend our own money crowding us out of our own eating establishments. Is it not infamous? Is it not absurd? We pay to support shiftless ne'er-do-wells for the sake of fugitive sproutling Prince's lust for a Crown."

The manager was bustling in their direction with several husky porters, alerted to trouble by one of the serving girls. Gil knew from experience who, in a row between civilians and off-duty troops, usually wound up on the fuzzy end of the lollipop. Not that he, Springbuck and Dunstan would be ejected; when the Prince's identity was known, there'd doubtless be grudging apologies all around. He didn't feel like letting this presumptuous jerk get off that lightly.

It had been a long day, and he was angry that the evening was ruined. So just as the wit was composing his next gag, the American decided to be undiplomatic and waggled a finger to get his attention.

Securing it, he asked, "Didn't I hear a poem about you in the marketplace today?"

The humorist's brows shot up. As he fumbled, nonplussed, for a response, Gil continued blithely, snapping his fingers in positive recognition. "Sure, I've got it now. Let's see, it went:

'He's the half-blooded son of a seagoing whore
whose mother's feet seldom touched aught
but the shore;
 For while on the deeps, of employ she'd no lack
relieving all hands on the flat of her back.' "

The boy screamed in wrath and the party, now a mob, surged to its feet to punish this impudence, women hollering insults and men clapping hands to sword hilts at this affront to their friend. The humorist's blade, a long rapier, was half drawn when Gil caught his hand, immobilizing it, and drove a hard right up to the solar plexus. Sword forgotten, the other doubled up, giving Gil all the time in the world to step back and measure off a roundhouse kick. The wit went down like a Murphy bed and Springbuck leaped up to face the onrushing crowd as they advanced vengefully toward the American.

The fighting forms the two used confused the gentry and the porters, who'd joined the scuffle in an attempt to throw them out. Springbuck and Gil had no wish to draw swords, but the insults had stung, and if these people wanted to bait strangers and were messed up in the doing, that was their lookout. Hands and feet, elbows and knees, the two had their way of the fight at first. In close quarters the opposition kept crowding and interfering with each other. For a few moments it was satisfying to pay back the unprovoked abuse and dish out a lesson.

But soon they were too hampered to move effectively and were borne backward, crashing down on collapsing tables and held fast by sheer weight of numbers. Through the tangle of limbs and bodies, Gil saw the jokester being helped unsteadily to his feet by the manager; the man pulled a dirk from his sash and handed the manager a bulging purse.

Fear froze the American as he saw that he and his companions were to be murdered right here and now with the purchased complicity of the manager. He redoubled his efforts to escape, without success, and wondered in disgust if he'd made his final miscalculation.

Then Springbuck, in the same predicament, saw that two of his captors had disappeared, followed a moment later by the other two. He squinted up to see Dunstan hurl them, one in either direction, as if they were empty suits of clothes.

Insane light burned in Dunstan's eyes, that thing that made his own people avoid him come to full life now. His face was covered with perspiration and his breath came with extreme rapidity. All the lean muscles of his body stood forth like cables and his lips were flecked with white tendrils of spittle. So completely different was this terrifying apparition from the morose man who'd been drinking with them moments before that the Prince wondered in horror if this weren't some *Doppelgänger*.

The Rider moved with blurring speed, bellowing at the top of his lungs and striking adversaries this way and that with single blows of his fists or swings of his arms. He eluded a sword thrust, seizing the blade and breaking it in his hands. The slashes this left in his palms closed as soon as they'd opened. He ripped away the three men who held Gil, then turned and caught the young wit's knife hand, twisting and breaking the wrist and popping the shoulder ball from its joint in one motion. The youth went to his knees with an ear-piercing shriek, and his female companion, with courage born of sheltered ignorance, struck Dunstan from behind with her reticule. The Berserker didn't even look around but swung a backhanded blow in her direction almost as an afterthought. She was knocked across a bench in a flurry of skirts, her mouth a red ruin.

Dunstan was smashing two more foes together as a muscular porter took the luckless girl's place and broke a stool over his head. The gaunt Rider spun angrily with an openhanded clout that broke the porter's jaw.

Gil and Springbuck had gotten to their feet through a press of flying bodies when the attacking throng drew back in fear and amazement at the savagery of the lanky Rider. Gil could see Dunstan's shoulders heaving as his breathing became more rapid in preparation for another exchange. In an effort to halt the carnage, Gil grabbed the Berserker by the arm.

Dunstan whirled, ready to destroy him, but the dim mist of recognition came to his face. His brows knit as if he strove to recall an elusive memory and his breathing began to slow. Irrationality passed from his face and his rage ebbed. His muscles relaxed and he slumped in Gil's grasp.

Springbuck, meanwhile, had brought forth Bar and his dagger, but might as well have spared the effort. No one in The Excellent Board would have approached them for any reason. Other diners had come to their feet and witnessed the episode, but none attempted to intervene. The Prince, Dunstan and Gil made their way out of the pavilion in silence. When they'd reached their horses, the steppesman disengaged the American's supporting hands. "The weakness is past; now there is only the emptiness and the sorrow."

Gil nodded, and they mounted just as a cry came from behind, a detachment of the city watch. They galloped away low to their horses' necks and didn't look back.

They eventually made their way to a poorer section of the city where the air was strongly redolent of its many middens and soldiers of different units were spending their pay. The inns and taverns were filled, so many sat at the side of the street swigging beer and ale from drinking jars or buckets of wood or leather, taking turns getting them filled at one of the drinking houses or stalls there.

Springbuck purchased a bucket for a copper pellet and waited in a jostling line to have it filled. Again, without his war mask and in such a crowd, he went unnoticed. They sat together, passing the bucket without conversation and taking long pulls at it.

In time, Dunstan said, "You've witnessed the curse of my lineage, the Rage that comes on men of my line. But tonight, too, you've seen an event as never happened before; I didn't strike Gil MacDonald, and the Berserkergang left me. Always before the Rage had to burn itself out. I shall have to think about this."

They drank some more.

"By the way," Gil asked, by way of breaking the silence, "what tribe is that Reacher lived with? Why aren't they here?"

Springbuck explained about the Wolf-Brother's sojourn with the Howlebeau, adding that they had a strict injunction against leaving the High Ranges for any reason, and had accepted a Lowlander among them only out of respect for the King's father.

The American meditatively twirled the Browning around his index finger.

The Prince continued. "There is still a storm of debate about this war and whether we should go to Hightower's aid, but I don't take part in it. Van Duyn and Princess Katya are trying to make sure I'm nothing but a figurehead. Andre and Bonesteel object, but the Snow

Leopardess has the council of Freegate with her and her brother says nothing one way or the other.

"The time to put forth my hand is not yet, but soon, when the day is ripe, I'll make my presence felt." His eyes hardened. "There'll be aid for the Hightower, this I vow."

"Look, is Hightower the name of the fortress, of the guy in charge or what?"

"The Keep is called *the* Hightower, while its ruling Lord, the Duke, is referred to simply as Hightower."

"Oh. Uh, how does Gabrielle feel about all this?"

"Gabrielle!" said the Prince softly, lost for a space in thought. "Yes, she's made me lust after her—or says she has, though I wonder if it doesn't come of me, uninfluenced in truth—so she takes no action and says little, watching all that I do and, I think, finding it all amusing. Sometimes I curse the day I first beheld that spellbinder, that wanting, green-eyed plague, but I wouldn't be without her if I could."

He tipped the bucket, drained it. "Whose turn to service our bucket?" he asked. "Nay, mine again already? I think you two conspire against me. My funds are not without limit, you know."

Gil burped. "It's all found money," he consoled the Prince philosophically. "We left The Excellent Board in such a flap you never settled the tab."

Chapter Twenty-two

He hath brought me into the banqueting house,
and his banner over me was love.

THE SONG OF SONGS,
Which Is Solomon's

THE Lady Duskwind quickly grew bored with life at
Court. Her royal cousin, Reacher, forbade her to go out
into the practice fields to join in military exercises and
she respected his wishes; but it was hard when she saw
that it wasn't unknown for women to ride with the Horseblooded. With the notable exception of the Snow Leopardess, women were seldom given to practicing war
arts in Freegate, though that was slowly changing. She
chafed at this and considered asking to be sent on a
deputation to the gyneocracy of Glyffa, but there was
no need at hand and there were possibilities here in
Freegate.

She related all she could of information accumulated in Earthfast to the eagerly listening intelligence ex-
perts of Reacher's war ministry. She told what she knew
of various Legion-Marshals' abilities or quirks, their
strong suits and weaknesses, what they looked for in a
battle and what they avoided, how they treated their
troops and how they stood in the favor of Strongblade,
Fania and, most important, Yardiff Bey. She checked
maps for discrepancies with those at Earthfast as she
remembered them, described tactics likely to be encountered and the details of Court Life under Strongblade—who his supporters were, what influence and
wealth they had and who might be convinced to plot
against him.

All this she had learned during her masquerade in
Earthfast, through intelligent observation and by drawing it patiently and ingeniously, a scrap at a time, from

251

those she'd met there. To be sure, much of it was duplicated by what Springbuck and Bonesteel knew, but hers
was valuable corroborative data.

Like her cousins, she enjoyed intrigue and statecraft
and relished being close to their seats of power without
envying them. So for a time she partook of the entertainment of Court, but it soon palled without the added
excitement of being an agent in the stronghold of a foreign suzerain.

Still, there were stately dances, crooning minstrels
and musicians who sought to amuse, along with actors,
poets, acrobats, jesters, conjurers and philosophers.
There were ceaseless feasts—the privations of war
might come soon enough, the time to live was now—
with uncountable courses of honeyed fish, glazed fowl,
beef, pork, hotbreads, sweetmeats, mutton, pastries,
iced sherbets, confections, jellied fruits, fine cheeses,
rivers of wine and liquors, a constant flow of beer and
ale, and so on and on.

And there was gossip and scandal. Which knight
wooed the favors of which blushing damsel? Which heroes promised great deeds in the coming war with Coramonde's Usurper *Ku-Mor-Mai*?

Eventually she found all this tedious, and daytime activities were even worse. She was a fair painter and
sculptress, but didn't feel inspired. She was all thumbs
at tapestries, couldn't play the lute, didn't care to teach
birds to speak; she had no wish to weave flower chains
or play the tame, simpering games enjoyed by the more
moderate, fragile ladies who frequented Court. For
reading there were only treatises on war—engrossing,
but few in number and soon consumed—insipid ro-
mances and ponderous religious tracts. She tried to read
the books brought to Freegate by Gil MacDonald, but
they were unintelligible.

She would have spent time with her royal cousins, a
pastime in which she always delighted, but both were
usually occupied with other matters. This was particularly true of the Snow Leopardess, who now devoted
much of her time to Van Duyn. The American, in turn,
was having the time of his life as the intellectual com-
munity of Freegate almost literally fought with each

other for the opportunity to hear his discourses; he was also basking in his station as paramour to Princess Katya.

The Lady Duskwind was frequently pressed for details concerning Gil MacDonald, the outland common-knight who rode at stirrups with King and Prince, and whose opinions were carefully heard and weighed by Bonesteel, the most capable general in modern history. Tales of Chaffinch's demise were being repeated and enlarged upon, and there were those who called the ex-sergeant Dragonslayer.

In truth she'd seen him infrequently since arriving at Freegate, and then usually at a distance, but she was loath to admit it at Court and so contented herself with dropping vague hints and preserving feigned secretiveness. One evening it chanced that he came to Court to fetch Springbuck to hear a courier just in from Boldhaven. Serious and quiet in his green mesh armor, hung about with weapons esoteric and familiar, he waited as the Prince went to change from his festive robes, and his eye roamed to Duskwind and the idler at her side, who was trying to make charming conversation and succeeding only in being boorish. A quick smile came to Gil's lips, then a frown as he spied her chattering companion, and his gaze flicked away self-consciously. Hand on hilt, he pivoted on his heel and left the Court so promptly that he almost trampled a door warder standing behind him.

"Ah, the Prince has left," the carpet knight at her right hand said, "and his foreign liege man with him, yet I think his sorcerous ladylove does not like it overmuch. They tell me the Pretender spends so much time at fencing practice and military drill that she feels slighted."

"Why should he devote so much time to sword practice when he's belike the best bladesman in the armies?" she responded, though she wasn't much curious and her thoughts were instead with Gil.

Her tablemate replied, "Mistress, these affairs have a way of coming down to single combat between principles, and the Prince knows this. His younger brother is said to be a robust foe and a better man with steel than he, and he therefore spends diligent hours each day with the very best masters in the allied armies, to polish and hone his skills. I think he is more than willing for such a contest between him and his stepbrother, would welcome it as alternative to the approaching war."

But she wasn't listening. She was thinking of Gil and felt she understood him now. He'd told her a bit about himself and she sensed his attraction to her, and his hesitation to speak. He was unsure of himself, shy and ill at ease with her, now that she was back in Court. Here was one who'd spent much time at war and forgotten or never learned the technique of flirtation, of subtle seduction. And naturally, this appealed to her.

She made up her mind to remedy the situation and to this end ensured through her cousins that Gil would be at Court the following evening. She arrived in her finest regalia, making sure to be late, on the arm of an enviable escort, a much-admired officer of lancers who'd been soliciting her company for some time. As Reacher had promised, since he went out of his way to keep his capable cousin happy, Gil was seated uneasily at the dining boards next to the two vacancies reserved for herself and her dashing companion. In full, floor-length skirts, laced and bodiced tightly, her bared shoulders and neck scented and her long hair gathered elegantly at her neck, she swept into the room and seated herself next to the American, barely deigning to notice his presence.

He was dressed from throat to heel in close fitting blue-black silk, relieved only by boots, unadorned belt and a small brooch, a silver saber worn point uppermost over his heart. He didn't actually fidget, but he wanted to. The feasting began, and occasionally Duskwind would turn to him with some witty aside or gay remark, sharing the illuminations of her presence with him charitably. He found that his sense of humor had gone into hibernation and could think of little to say. He thought himself miserable, but there was no place he'd rather have been.

The musicians struck a lively dancing air and, by Duskwind's previous arrangement, one of the ladies of the Court inquired if Gil wouldn't join in. He answered lamely that he couldn't, since he didn't know the dances being done there, precisely what Duskwind had been waiting for.

As the courtier left in pretended disappointment, she turned to him with mock severity and said, "Fie, that's poor manners indeed to be nonparticipant in your host's entertainments. Can't dance at all, then?"

He gulped. "Sort of, but nothing like this stuff that you people call dancing." He thought about explaining American dances of the moment and decided he was better off not getting into it.

"Well, then," she said, "all you need is a lesson or two." With that, saying nothing less would serve, she stood up, pardoning herself to her escort, and drew Gil away to a corner of the vast room, behind a huge pillar of stone, to instruct him in the fine points of the dance.

"See what you've gotta go through to be a social lion?" he murmured to himself as she corrected his stance and positioned his arms for him. His collar suddenly felt tight and he wished his hands would stay dry.

The officer of lancers, for his part, was no stranger to Court flirtations and understood with a touch of amusement that he'd been used. Ah, well, another time perhaps. With a shrug he began to cast about for another diversion.

Gil learned quickly. He was not graceful but was well coordinated, and was soon leading her through elaborate whirls, her slim waist cradled in his arm as they glided along. At the finish she pirouetted within his arms. They found themselves standing together, faces only inches apart as the music faded and applause and noise of revelry came from the dance floor.

She waited expectantly and so, of course, he collected all of his courage and kissed her, once rather tentatively and then a second time with more conviction. She responded, but found the kiss a bit rough, his embrace too tight.

"My dear," she gasped, "you must be more delicate or you'll bruise me sure. But come now, let's return to the tables; I'm afraid my companion of the evening will be anxious over my absence."

He trotted happily after her, and when they returned to the bandqueting boards the officer of lancers had taken a seat vacated by a wealthy usurer who'd passed out and been removed by the servitors. He was relieving the tedium of the moneylender's voluptuous wife, who was most receptive. Both Duskwind and Gil thought this terribly funny and roared with laughter, which the dashing officer caught and acknowledged with a nod and a sardonic smile.

The outlander and the Lady talked together of his world and hers, of their pasts and futures. He opened up to her about things he rarely mentioned and, to her surprise, she did the same.

This girl was, he knew, a veteran spy and conspirator at age eighteen or so. She'd killed at need and been his friend's consort. Good sense told him not to become involved; what could come of it but eventual disappointment? But he divined in her a core of honesty and energy, an intelligent mind and a kindred spirit, and told common sense to hang it up.

They drank and tried a dance or two, and if he didn't exactly dazzle the bleacher section with his footwork, at least he didn't trip or stumble.

The gathering began to break up and he offered to see her back to her suite. He leaned against the door frame and they talked in whispers, though there was no one to hear, but were interrupted by a cry that seemed to come from her rooms.

He pulled the Browning from where he'd prudently carried it in his boot and threw the door open, to find the room unoccupied.

The shout had come from the courtyard below and was being repeated and relayed through the palace. Under the window, portglaves of the household ran back and forth with torches and pointed to the sky. The two leaned out to peer upward, and even then he was aware of her closeness and elated by it.

High in the star-specked blackness hung an object of indeterminate shape, trailing long columns of red fire. It circled slowly while they watched and swung away westward.

"It fits Springbuck's description of Yardiff Bey's aircraft," Gil said when they'd withdrawn from the window. "If he's started to reconnoiter, he'll move very soon now. Especially if he's counted the campfires out there and knows how he's got us outnumbered."

He hissed in exasperation. He should have foreseen an aerial recon and planned against it.

"I have to go," he said. "This changes things. We'll be awfully busy before long." His thoughts were already on how they might counteract this disadvantage, make it work for them.

He moved to the door, and she felt a chill breeze that didn't come of night airs. She stopped him with a hand on his shoulder like a timid dove. She didn't want him to go out just now, to order the affairs of battle and let warm possibilities become cool.

She put her forehead against his chest, and he encircled her with his arms. No word passed between them, but she went to the candelabrum and snuffed out the flickering flames with her fingertips, leaving only the fitful light of the small fireplace. She took both his wrists in her hands and led him to her bed.

Deftly, she unfastened the flowing gown and let it rustle down about her ankles, and gracefully she stepped from its folds, snatching the pins from her long hair and shaking its loosened waves around shoulders and down her back.

Gil slowly opened his tunic at its high collar, slipped it off and threw it aside, catching her up in his arms. Her skin was amazingly warm and the scents of her, the perfume at her throat and the exotic, unnameable aroma of her hair, made blood beat at his temples.

He kissed her harshly even as her fingers found the buckle at his waist. But she pulled her head back.

"Softly, my friend," she whispered at his ear. "I'm no rough soldier's woman. The night stretches ahead; shall we squander it in impatience and haste?"

They went to her long, wide bed, and the curves and complexities of their flesh met in embrace. It was, for him, a passage of enlightenment, of increase. Like many men, he knew something of sex but little of tenderness. In war, women had been a commodity bought and sold; there'd been no time or place for love. There was no gentleness; he'd stayed unschooled in affection, ignorant of regard for a woman.

But the Lady Duskwind subtly controlled the night, encouraging or rebuking and guiding his actions, nurturing their lovemaking secretly. He didn't see it overtly at the time; all he knew was that in those hours, underlying the passion for her that superactuated him, there was a great calm and sense of serenity.

Later, a time having come when they spoke quietly of themselves and each other again, she privily questioned her feelings for this foreigner, so stern and fey in some lights, and so vulnerable and unsure in others.

They drifted, heavy-lidded, into sleep. But just before dawn, a challenge was given as the watch was changed in the courtyard below, and she blinked sleep from her eyes to see him sitting bolt upright in bed, the cocked Browning in his hand, alarmed and disoriented.

She pulled him back down. As he slipped the pistol back under his pillow she returned to his arms and, soldier and warrior in her own way, bitterly cursed the Doomfaring.

Chapter Twenty-three

Neccessity knows no law except to conquer.
PUBLIUS SYRUS,
Maxim 553

A SPECIAL parley was called the next morning. Only the highest, chieftains and knights-commander, were even permitted to stand ranged around the room to listen. The leaders of the alliance sat at a large circular pinewood table, since Reacher, a fair man in all things by common testimony, wouldn't sit above or preside over his comrades.

At the table with the Wolf-Brother were his sister, Van Duyn, the deCourteneys, Bonesteel, Su-Suru and his acting war chieftain Ferrian. Springbuck and Gil were to complete the assemblage, and had with them Dustan the Berserker, whom they'd asked to act as a sort of liaison aide.

Ever since the incident at The Excellent Board, Dunstan had followed Gil steadfastly, perhaps because the American had brought him out of Rage, or perhaps because the outlander was more at ease with him than with his own people. Dunstan didn't say, and they didn't ask. As Gil put it, "It's not as if he's whacked out or vicious; maybe all he needs is somebody to keep him straight."

The Prince and his friends waited until the others had been seated for some time before making their way to the meeting room. "I must make an entrance to help make my point," he said.

Gil and Springbuck came forth side by side, Dunstan behind them, through a door held wide by Kisst-Haa, the reptile-man. Nearing the table in step, helmet and war mask clamped in their left arms, they stopped with the American three paces from the table and the son of

259

Surehand a step closer, next to the chair left vacant for him.

Springbuck thrust aside the seat and threw his high-lumed mask on the table. In the silence that greeted him, he asked, "Is there anyone here who does not know the significance of last night's visit? Yardiff Bey has paid us a call to tally our bivouac fires and see what he could of movements between here and Coramonde. This can only mean that he's ready to unleash Novanwyn on Bulf Hightower."

He watched their faces. He had as yet told them nothing new. He'd taken the floor from Reacher, and while the Wolf-Brother was listening with equanimity his sister was obviously piqued. Gil held his breath for the bomb.

"Therefore," the Prince continued, "I shall ride to the aid of the Hightower. Its warders have always rallied to my family at need. Do they deserve less from their liege?"

There were instant objections from the Snow Leopardess, Van Duyn and Su-Suru. Bonesteel was in thought, calculating the military factors and thinking, too, of his sister, Rolph's widow, still at the Hightower.

Gabrielle was contemplating the Prince. War itself drains men, wears them thin, but the relentless exercise of past weeks had built him up, filled him out to something approaching his potential as a man. His friendship with the MacDonald had given him an added self-assurance; even she had had no idea he'd planned this move. Yes, the Pretender had evolved a definite presence, a mind of his own.

Springbuck cut off the confusion of objections by bounding atop the gleaming table and holding up both hands. The voices subsided immediately and most at the table looked at him as if he were under a new, stronger light. Though there were those in the room who thought him mad, Bonesteel was beaming at Springbuck's demonstration.

"I go, too," the Prince resumed, "because this is an excellent chance to give Bey pause while my loyalists established themselves and Freegate braces for prolonged war. We must let Coramonde know that we can lash out over the Keel of Heaven to deter the advances of our enemies."

"And shall we ride with you, then, to be crushed far from our undefended homes?" shouted Katya angrily, her pale face flushed ever so slightly. The sight rather pleased Gabrielle, who sat across from her.

"You speak of following me," he replied, "but I cannot force it, nor would I. You conjecture in terms of defeat. I don't plan on it or fear it." He caught Bonesteel's reassuring nod. "I go, and my Legions with me. If you vote to aid me, so be it and my thanks, but I wouldn't demand it."

Gil exhaled softly. The Prince had the allies over a barrel and they knew it. Without him, there was little hope of delaying the advance of the armies of Coramonde, and the outcome of an unqualified confrontation with the hosts of Strongblade couldn't be doubted. Lacking Springbuck as figurehead, they'd have a much harder time fomenting revolt across the Keel of Heaven; he was their only touchstone of popular support in that country. Their only hope against the vast resources of their enemies was help from an infrastructure in the populace there.

And though the Prince had mentioned it to no one, even Gil, he felt obliged to go to the Hightower because of the death of Rolph Hightower that last night at Earthfast. To him the expedition represented not only a political and strategic maneuver, but an act of contrition as well.

Reacher cleared his throat. He stood up and they all became quiet. "I suggest," he said, "that we take our most mobile elements on this foray. Your light dragoons and members of the Horseblooded, and a contingent of men to leave as reinforcements for the Hightower should that prove desirable."

Katya had slumped her curvy figure back into her chair, legs crossed and heels on the table. She gave her brother a resentful squint and brought her feet to the floor with a clump.

"At least, then, you must let me come along, brother," she grumbled.

But when the strike force had been assembled, Katya was not included in its order of battle. Neither were Van Duyn, Su-Suru and many others who stubbornly demanded a chance to carry the igniting spark of war to the enemy.

Duskwind was particularly miffed; she'd meant to go on the expedition from the moment she'd heard of it. Dissuading her was a nightmare. Gil reasoned and debated with her for as long as he could before losing his temper and telling her to take it up with Springbuck, refusing to intervene and touching off a terrible row. She began to plot in secret, but they didn't permit their romance to suffer for long because of their difference of opinion. They still danced and laughed and drank and sang, exploiting as best they could the short time they had to be together.

And for a while they found themselves a subject of interest in the capricious Court. Frequenters there found fascination in the love affair between the noble-woman and the outlander, with his curious songs, obscure jokes and most of all his conversation with its strange-tasting words and casual references to amazing things from his previous life, things he regarded as mundane.

The two also spent evenings roistering with common soldiers and people of the city, though Gil didn't consider this slumming, but rather moving through more comfortable social strata. He learned local drinking songs and in return taught them his. He followed his new friends through "The Farm-Wife's Jollyboy" or "Tinkers' Caterwaul"; then the musicians would pick up the simple tunes to "Roll Me Over in the Clover" or "The Wild Rover" and they would all bellow away happily.

The interlude didn't last long. With word of the girding for war, Court life became nonexistent as the nobles and their ladies prepared the great houses for danger and austerity.

Gil finally admitted to himself that in those too-few days he'd been avoiding Springbuck, aware that Duskwind had been the Prince's lover before she'd become his. That she might see the whole situation differently didn't occur to him.

One morning he picked up his friend's trail—few failed to note and recognize the plumed Alebowrenian war mask and Fireheel—and caught up with him in the stables of the palace. The Prince was enthusiastically discussing Bar with curious sentries.

"Even if it weren't blessed with unfailing keenness," he said, flexing the weapon through short, glittering arcs, "a fine blade it would be. It's light enough to cut rings around any bulky broadsword, heavy enough to cleave armor, but will match steps with a darting rapier if the man who holds it has a strong enough wrist."

He reluctantly yielded Bar for practice strokes by one of the bolder men-at-arms, then noticed Gil leaning against Fireheel's stall and went over to him.

"We are ready to leave on the morrow," Springbuck said. "Will you be coming with us?" His expression was hard, but when he saw consternation in the American's face he smiled and said, "I think I know what troubles you, but it shouldn't. Duskwind—well, Duskwind I loved once; but she is her own woman and she and I have both grown and changed. You chose commendably, both, and your happiness makes me glad. I don't blame you for taking time from our mustering."

Gil relaxed a bit. "Of course I'm coming," he said, "Got a more important reason for winning now."

"So do we both," the Prince said.

They rode out in the morning sun with Reacher at their side and Bonesteel, Dunstan and a host of men behind. There were banners and flags in abundance: the snarling scarlet tiger of Coramonde, Springbuck's proud stag's head, Bonesteel's token, a nine-pointed green star on a field of white, and Reacher's, a raised fist holding a broken chain, picked out in silver on black. On the breast of Gil MacDonald's armor, the Lady Duskwind had caused to be put a device for him, a saber like that of the shoulder patch he'd worn in the 32d cavalry.

They were a mixed group. Troups of fleet, light dragoons flanked to either side and spaced along the formation, swift security against a sudden attack. Their riding harness creaked and their bits jingled as they paced the column. Imperceivable in the distance, prowler-cavalry scouted their way.

There were squadrons from the forces of Freegate, independent-looking men with gleaming lances, each with an emblem of his choosing limned on his shield and designs on his armor and his mount's furnishings as if he were an approved knight, since they did not hold this prerogative to be limited to a designate few in the Free City.

A brigade of staunch foot was included, with two battalions of pikemen much used in war, who wore ghastly death's heads on their chests and backs, enameled on their byrnies. And the fearsome Kisst-Haa led five of his scaly kin, their fangs and green hides shimmering in the early glow, their eyes like amber lanterns. They'd been frequent visitors to the fields of war and had offered up many enemies on the altars of battle. But although they were loyal to Reacher and went out to fight for the same cause all men there served, the downfall of Yardiff Bey, still men shied away from them, giving wide berth. But they were inured to this, and ignored the unwarranted suspicion.

The Horseblooded rode at the rear of the array, mixing and mingling in the antithesis of rigid military order. But no one doubted their vigor in the use of arms in contention; all had seen them at practice. Their voices were lifted in sweet singing as they came, hair flying behind them, but their scimitars were keen and their spearheads caught the sun and threw it back in fragments. With them was Andre deCourteney, more content to listen to their songs and laughter on the route than to match the discipline of the regular soldiery.

The wearying march across the Keel of Heaven took longer than had the headlong flight out of Erub in the opposite direction. Springbuck, looking at the Wolf-Brother, knew that he must regret that the Kings of Freegate had never fortified their mountain passes. But it had been a matter of pride that the two countries had no wish to put walls, gates and suspicion in the pathway between them.

Just beyond the merestone, after passing once again into Coramonde, they were met by three of the loyalist guerrillas who'd been recruited by the growing underground infrastructure, over which the Prince had, as yet, exerted no direct control. They had a puzzling aspect for him, even as they put themselves at his disposal.

They were common enough, men to turn the soil or fell trees, yet they had the watchful, confident air of frontier sentinels, an aura of new pride. For all that they were tense in the presence of conventional fighting men, Gil knew their look. He wondered if these guerrillas would be willing to lay down their arms and go back to peasant life after the war was over. The Prince planned to use his status as *Ku-Mor-Mai* to solidify his position of authority in Coramonde, to correct injustices and relieve local tyrannies; but still the American doubted if these men would accept any man's absolute authority again.

The expedition pushed on its way harder against the news, recently come, of a great corps wending from Earthfast to the Hightower.

They crossed the Blackflood at Barren Ford, and to Gil's mind came the lines of Walt Whitman:

A line in long array where they wind betwixt green islands
They take a serpentine course, their arms flash in the sun—hark to the musical clank.

They'd borne their guidons to within hours' march of the Hightower when a prowler returned with word that a large armed body was moving toward the Keep and would arrive there at approximately the same time as they.

The Prince stepped up their pace immediately to forced-march speed. Aware that this would be strenuous on his infantry, he still pressed on; arriving late with fresh men would be useless, while coming in time, even if fatigued, might yet save the day.

When the infantry found it difficult to keep up, Springbuck ordered each mounted man to take his turn carrying a footman on the croup of his horse, and it sped their progress well. He dispatched couriers to Freegate with news of this latest turn of events.

They were a short distance from the Hightower when tidings came that the army from Earthfast had settled siege on the Keep. Springbuck left his troops to rest in preparation for the conflict, while he rode forward with Bonesteel, Reacher and Gil to assess the situation.

Skirting the supply and baggage trains in their en-campments, the four came to a hill overlooking the Hightower, a fortress rearing blank walls of lusterless, rust-colored stone and a pylon-like central donjon for which it had been named, a stronghold never breeched. Banners of war flew at the ramparts and men in flashing armor stood in the crenels of the hornwork.

Deployed on the field were units of Strongblade's army. Ominous siege engines, mangonels, catapults, a ram and the framework for a belfrois were off to the rear of the battlefield. Rather than readying for an assault, the besiegers were drawn up for open combat, as if the castle didn't stand between them and their opponents.

Several furtive countryfolk stood near, come to see the peculiar ritual of war and steal what they could from the dead. The four dismounted; no pickets had been stationed at the rear of the field, since the enemy was confined to the Hightower. Gil sneered, thinking what that would cost the invading army.

The peasants, startled by their arrival, shifted around uneasily but didn't leave. "Have there been words exchanged here yet?" asked the Prince.

Scowling, not meeting Springbuck's masked stare, one of them muttered, "Oh, my Lord, it is just some minutes now since a herald and standard-bearer were at the gates of the Hightower, and though we could not make out what it was that they put forth, we know that the Duke has promised to drive them out of his lands, be they as many as the leaves of the trees."

Bonesteel swore, an unusual lapse in him. "This is insane. The might of the Hightowers is their impregnable fortress. Properly garrisoned, it could carry even against this force. But that stupid walrus Bulf is going to try to throw the invaders out by meeting them outside, or so the enemy commander believes by the disposition of his troops. If that happens, he'll vanquish Hightower here and now. What *can* they be thinking of there in the Keep?"

There was no one with an answer. Springbuck gave instructions as to how they'd make their presence felt, even as the long drawbridge slowly lowered over the broad foss. With a prodigious thundering, rank on rank of knights came out to assume formations on the green field. Their metal glittered and their pennons snapped smartly in the breeze.

Caparisoned horses dug impatiently at the ground with shining hooves. The warriors of the Hightower presented a courageous sight but were plainly—fatally—outnumbered. Fewer than one hundred fifty, they were about to go against more than four times their number in horse alone, not counting rows of husky foot, clusters of waiting archers and whatever reserves were held aside.

"Bluff's pride fits him like a noose, set to haul them all high," Springbuck said bitterly.

Chapter Twenty-four

A lost battle is a battle one thinks one has lost.
FERDINAND FOCH,
"Principles de Guerre"

A GUST of trumpetry sounded from the castle, paired with the booming of a herald.

"By mandate of Bulf Hightower, Duke by inheritance of this Commandery, return to us our Lady and be you gone from these and all his lands, you who have come here, or suffer the harsh justice of the Hightower."

There was no counterstatement, only the snorting of the horses and the brush of the restless breeze. A new voice sounded.

"Ye disregard my forewarning," said the man at the lead of the defender's ranks, Bulf himself. "Accept ye must my retribution!"

He gestured to his men. Without trump or drum, they dropped their visors with a single clank, seemed to hang for a moment as on the brink of an abyss, then stepped their horses off at a walk. That sedate step wasn't held long, becoming a trot as they readied long lances and got intervals established, spacing themselves and aligning with the superior force facing them. As Bulf's point came parallel to the ground, those behind dropped in compliance. The entire group broke into a gallop.

Now their foe surged forward, on a course slightly uphill and so to some disadvantage, but in numbers that compensated for this and so at speed.

It was the first time Gil had seen knights of Coramonde in full career. The men from the Hightower resolved themselves into three waves in *V* formation. While the first two charged straight ahead, the third turned aside and began circling around the high wooded mound that broke into the open ground to the southeast.

This Hightower's about to get himself whomped, thought Gil.

"I don't fathom this talk of a Lady," the Prince was saying. "I warrant that's what drew Bulf out, though. Unless I miss my guess, that's a flanking sally that's peeled from his third rank and circled around. Can't see from here, but if that avenue isn't well plugged and waiting, my guessing's for fools."

"A desperate move indeed from Hightower," said Bonesteel.

Gil wondered how anything could stand against these men in iron with their invincible armor, cruel weapons and incredible momentum. Now the enemy launched a second wave, leaving another hundred fifty in reserve. The cavaliers of the Hightower met three times their number with the concussion of an earthquake.

There was clanging and screeching of clashing, tearing metal; lance points met locked shields and horses shrilled. Men and animals fell dead and wounded to sounds of splintering wood. Gil felt as well as heard the terrible collision.

He looked beside him and saw that Bonesteel and Reacher were gone. The time to move had come and nearly gone again.

The ground was littered with men, horses and scraps of armor after the first exchange. Now came the melee, with each man laying about him at his antagonists. Broadswords, maces, axes and martelles-de-fer, the huge war-hammers with their deadly pick heads, all rose and fell and swung in a hurricane of steel. They rained merciless damage on the panoply that had looked so impervious moments before.

Shields were soon battered, uselessly crumpled, and thrown aside so the knights could snatch another weapon to hand in their stead. Helmets crested with badges of the Hightower and other regions were cloven in two or dashed in, their contents destroyed. Whole limbs were severed, still encased in sheared-off armor. More than forty men lay dead or dying from that first impact, many with snapped lances sprouting from their breastplates like lethal flowers.

Through flying dust and whirling steel it was appar-

ent that there was little hope for Bulf, short of relief
from the allies.

The defenders rallied around their Duke, who set to
with sword and axe and did fighting man's work with
good effect. His men formed a ring of death with him at
its leading edge and his standard at its center. He could
be seen to peer about anxiously for his flanking sally.
Gil let his own eyes rove the field.

He caught Springbuck and pointed to the colorful
tent on a rise at the opposite end of the greensward.
There, caftan streaming in the wind, hood thrown back
to reveal the lurid mask, Ibn-al-Yed stood with arms
folded on his chest, watching the extermination of his
master's enemies. Over him flew his scorpion banner,
black on crimson.

Then Bonesteel was back from preparations to turn
the battle.

The Prince gave rapid orders: the bulk of the Horseblooded to go to Bluff's aid with Bonesteel and himself,
the rest of the Wild Riders to assault the entrenchments
and siege machinery, while the Wolf-Brother, with the
men of Freegate and Kisst-Haa's reptile-men, rein-
forced the flanking body, which must have encountered
heavy resistance. The pikemen would keep the enemy
from bringing up reserves and the dragoons were to
harry those reserves or sweep into the foe's camp as
needed.

But before they did, Gil was to take the squad of
prowler-cavalry to capture Ibn-al-Yed before he knew
that events were against him.

Minutes later, Bulf's nephew Sordo, Rolph's son, beleaguered and outnumbered in an ambush to the southeast in hindrance of his flanking sally, was shocked to
see tailed and scaly monsters throw themselves into the
fray on his side, snatching knights from the saddle,
bowling over their horses and chopping men and
mounts in two with titanic broadswords. They also
caused damage with their spiked and flanged caudal armor. In among them darted a small, muscular man impossible to hit, tearing men from their saddle and silenc-
ing them with cestus or clawed glove.

Moments later, grim-faced men in mail fell on the ambushers from the rear and, singing a low, rhythmic chant among themselves, began slaying.

More maneuverable but less protected than the knights, the men of Freegate ran a risk in going against them. Their swords lifted in time with their chant and their eyes were as hungry as those of hunting hawks. They caused death all around, though many of them fell, too. Their wrath wasn't abated or their thirst for battle slaked until they'd driven such of the ambushers as survived from the field.

With them came Andre deCourteney, proving himself as strong a warrior and difficult to face in arms as any man there. It was known then that Andre was a man to reckon with apart from potent wizardry. This was a thing the men of the allied armies could understand and like him for, as was his intention.

Sordo had collected his wits and sent a wedge against the archers firing at him in support of the trap. A four-to-one match that had promised massacre turned to victory before his eyes.

A few of the enemy, finding their swords useless against reptilian savagery and not wishing to face rows of the swords of Freegate, made their way clear by sheer determination and fear and fled, but these weren't many, and Sordo found himself thanking the small man and the plump magician, whom he recognized. Then they all hurried in the direction of the main engagement.

Bulf, too, was astounded at the sudden turn of battle. Horseblooded were abruptly weaving agile horses through the melee, seizing enemy knights with catchpoles and lariats and dragging them from their mounts. The Wild Riders threw knives, axes, maces, short javelins and other weapons of distance with small effect on the men in plate.

They, too, had to take the risk of closing with the ponderous, powerful knights. Still, they were in numbers and no newcomers to battle on horseback; their swords were busy. They also used their bows, firing the arrows they used in war which, by a trick of carving, whistled and screamed eerily as they flew, but to small effect.

The officer in charge of Ibn-al-Yed's reserve elements, seeing all of this, decided not to wait to be ordered into combat. He called for a sounding of the war horn and went to his comrades' assistance, or at least tried to.

The doughty infantry of Bonesteel were forming ranks to prevent that. Kneeling and standing, they established their bristling barrier from one side of the field to the other, and it took both battalions of pikemen to do it.

Ibn-al-Yed's men charged them now, and many foot would have broken at the sight of them in full career, but these wearing death's heads on their byrnies were the hardened core of Bonesteel's own infantry, tempered by many encounters into veterans immovable as fire-blackened tree stumps. Their fifteen-foot pikes wavered not a finger width. This was their profession.

And so it was the knights who broke and drew up short at the points of those waiting polearms, save three foolhardy younger men who plunged to their deaths.

When these were slain, the infantry locked ranks as if they'd never been breached, beginning the risky game of keeping the mounted men at bay with thrusts.

Entrenched engineers and siege artisans, meanwhile, were horrified as a hoard of galloping madmen overran their comfortable positions as wolves fly at the fold.

Waving weapons and voicing ululating war cries, leaping their mounts over obstacles, the Horseblooded took a high redoubt in moments. Here, too, they fired their weird, unnerving arrows, and with several charges put the archers to their heels. The ground was presently littered with bodies stabbed or hacked by their sharp points and edges.

Bulf had recognized the Prince's stag's head emblem, as Springbuck and Bonesteel fought their way toward him through the surging enemy. The son of Surehand wore no armor, but had a shield with his insignia on it. Even among the gaudy Horseblooded, his Alebowrenian plumes stood out. Handling Fireheel with his knees, he engaged two knights, one after the other, and

downed them both. Bar's edge was a cutting plane that
had no trouble negotiating thick plate.

Springbuck turned from his second adversary after
sheering through passegarde, pauldron and shoulder,
just in time to see Bulf go against the commander of the
enemy troops, an accomplished fighter who wore armor
of ancient design that he considered a bringer of good
luck in war.

Blow for blow they hailed on each other, giving no
attention to defense. Over and over they went together
until, by dint of belling sword stroke, Hightower pressed
his opponent hard to stay ahorse. Bulf hammered his
enemy's blade aside and turned his shield with axe
blows, ramming his point home where gorget met helmet.

Blood spurted, and a proud captain became a corpse,
his good-luck piece having failed him for the first and
last time.

But as Bulf made to turn and find a new match,
filled with pride in his victory, another knight came on
him from behind and drove his lance into Bulf's horse
with a will.

Beast and master went down, the charger rolling over
on the helpless man, and the knight struck the Duke
through.

Springbuck spurred forward and rewarded the knight
by sending his head leaping from his body, helmet and
all, with a single sweep; a fitting end for him. In a moment the Prince had unhorsed and, removing his mask,
knelt by Bulf's side. The injured man's breath came in a
rattle, but he somehow recognized the face of the
Prince, whom he hadn't seen in years.

"It's done for me, your Grace," he wheezed. "But
how good to fall on a field of triumph when I'd thought
to lie on one of defeat. Your benediction, if you please,
worthy and well-come son of Surehand, and then please
save my poor sister-in-law from Ibn-al-Yed."

Tears clouded Springbuck's vision; he heard life
leave Bulf Hightower. He felt undeserving of the old
man's respect, but removed the helmet of iron and put
his lips lightly to the still-warm brow, a final salute.

A thought came to him. What had Bulf said? His

sister-in-law! Of course; how else could Ibn-al-Yed have lured Bulf out but to have captured her in some way and used her as leverage? That was why Bulf had joined this unequal fight and sent flankers around, to try to save his brother's widow. Bonesteel, whose sister Rolph's widow was, was standing at the Prince's side, face conformed in anger.

Then they were both running for their horses, gathering men as they went.

With a dozen prowlers at their backs, Gil and Dunstan charged from the trees at the rear of the pavilion of Ibn-al-Yed.

Gil wore a steel cap and held his reins in his teeth as did his companions. With the Mauser in one hand and the Browning in the other, he led the band as they rushed at the unsuspecting bodyguards ringing the sorcerer's tent. Bey's underling seemed to have retreated within.

Since the sentries were giving their whole attention to the battle in front of them, the attack from behind surprised them completely. Most were scattered before they could bring up their halberds.

Their sergeant made to bring the remainder into some order, making them stand fast with the flat of his sword and threats of the wrath of Ibn-al-Yed if they failed.

Gil fired twice into the air over their heads, but still the sergeant made them hold. Gil shot him in the chest and the others broke and fled.

The American jumped from his horse with half his men and Dunstan, leaving the balance to watch the horses.

He hoped that his quarry hadn't escaped, warned by gunfire, but needn't have worried. Racing forward he saw the well-remembered figure in golden mask and billowing caftan step toward him, then heard him cry out in an alien voice, a language known to few.

A weakness of terror fell on them all, even Dunstan the Berserker. They dropped their weapons and collapsed to the ground as the horses went insane. Transfixed as they were, it would have been only moments before they died at the hands of the counterattacking guards, who were summoning courage to return.

But they didn't die. In that desperate instant the blast of a war horn filled their ears, drowning out the intimidating words of Ibn-al-Yed and permitting Gil to shake his head and clear it. Webs of confusion and panic were carried away by the full winding.

He groped at the braided lanyard secured to his harness and clipped to the butt of the Mauser. Bringing the weapon up, he fired as quickly as he ever had, before the startled sorcerer had a chance to resume his litany.

The short range compensated in some part for haste. A bullet crashed into the cantor's leg just below the hip, bursting through bone and changing the incantation to a howl of pain and anger.

Gil climbed shakily to his feet, recovering the Browning and ordering his men to control themselves and their horses. This they did, the prowlers ashamed that they had to be instructed by an outlander and Dunstan with new respect for the American.

Gil turned to find the source of the horn blast and didn't have far to search.

Standing at the entrance of the tent was a handsome woman of middle years, her disheveled hair a gentle brown shot with gray. Her eyes were glazed, as if she saw little of what had happened. Her gown had been partially torn from her, testifying to rough usage. She was plainly a courageous Lady, who'd found some unconquerable core of will in herself; in her trembling hands was a curled horn, its long baldric dragging in the dust at her bare feet.

They all owed her their lives, Gil knew. She's done a deed of uncommon valor, refusing to succumb to the spell of Ibn-al-Yed—an act none of them had been able to emulate.

As gently as he could, he took the horn from her hands and seated her on the ground. Her skin was cold, yet perspiration shone on her face. Gil dashed into the tent to find a robe or blanket; he'd seen shock many times before.

Ignoring food, drink and the military maps strewn on low tables, he strode across the deserted tent to a pile of bedding and cushions, from which he snatched up a fur robe. He didn't miss the confusion of the bedding and the bits of torn cloth that confirmed violation of the woman outside. Has Ibn-al-Yed celebrated victory before the fact of battle? Gil didn't stop to wonder.

He went and saw to his savior's comfort as best he could, judging it better to keep her outside than move her into the tent, where she'd evidently suffered so much. He stationed his men for security and tried to see what was happening on the field of combat.

The day had turned, with the help of the expedition from Freegate.

Holstering his Mauser, Gil drew his sword and stepped over to the staff from which Ibn-al-Yed's standard flew. He severed it as if it were an enemy. The menacing black scorpion wafted gently to earth, never to fly again, for he plunged his sword through it and left it pinned for its initial and final defeat.

Then he turned and saw that, incredibly, the sorcerer had somehow made it to his feet and was attempting to hobble to his tent.

The American bounded after him in a fit of rage and swung him around. With one hand around the swarthy neck Gil ripped off the mask, glad to have someone on whom to vent his anger.

He'd planned to break the man's jaw, punish him for what he'd caused both inside and outside the tent, but instead shrank back.

Ibn-al-Yed was without features: eyeless, mouthless, lacking any characteristic belonging to a human face.

Gil struck the thing before him, hard. He knocked it to the ground with a fury that did nothing to relieve his revulsion.

When the troops of Ibn-al-Yed, having seen their field commander fall, witnessed the humiliation of the scorpion symbol of their supernatural leader, they began to run or fight free of the conflict and fly in the direction of Earthfast.

Gil was joined at that sad pavilion by such of the victors as had survived.

Chapter Twenty-five

It's none of your nobility impelled me on my way.
It's guilt and hate, and love and fear; these roused
* me forth each day.*
Nor had I any righteousness, no heaven-sent
* commission;*
A man's the sum of circumstance, of training, times,
* position.*
The greatest burdens I have known, and conscience
* can't ignore—*
I've bolstered men unto their deaths, I've led them
* into war;*
And am sustained by just one thought: I heard and
* did respond*
And taint myself to drive the shadows out from
* Coramonde.*

"VIRTUE ABANDONED,"
The Antechamber Ballads

BULF had been the only fatality among their leadership.
His nephew Sordo, barely more than a boy, assumed
the Dukedom on hearing of his uncle's death, as was the
custom in their family, although Sordo hadn't been due
to advance until his majority. He was the last of that
high pedigree, save only his recluse grandfather. All addressed Sordo as Hightower, and he did his best to project the dignity his predecessors had.

With him came Springbuck, Sordo's uncle Bonesteel,
Reacher and the rest. The Prince was quiet, appalled by
the sight of so many brave and earnest men put low,
their lives wasted.

When Sordo saw the woman lying in shock on the
ground, he gave a cry. Casting aside his helmet, he
threw himself down at her side and wept. "Oh, Mother!

My father they've slain and his brother, and now this third and worst calamity of all! Surely the foe exacted the bitterest measure of hurt from us!"

Bonesteel, too, wept to see his sister so.

Sordo's grieving subsided as he turned from his mother and spied the writhing thing that had been Ibn-al-Yed, its featureless face and cringing form a study in anonymous fear. It tried to drag itself, leg bleeding badly now, from the fury of the victors. Sordo sprang to his feet and shook a gauntleted fist at the anome.

"You are not the source of all our hurt," he choked, fighting to master the racking sobs. "But much of it issued from you. Would you go now, crawl from your wages? No, don't stir until I make this day dearer yet for you!"

He snatched a short, heavy mace from his belt and rushed to the creature's side, looming over it like an avenging demon. Before anyone could speak, the boy swung the mace over his head and smashed Ibn-al-Yed's unwounded leg at the knee, pulverizing the bone.

An inhuman scream of agony was torn from the innermost depths of the blank head. Such was the pain it felt that the thing pitched forward unconscious. Sordo broke into hysterical laughter and bent over the sprawled body, so wild a look on his countenance that no one could move or speak for fascination of it.

"No swoon will save you from me," he whispered. "I'll kill you by inches."

But Springbuck, nearby, took his armored shoulders in his hands and brought the boy's eyes up to his own. There were only a few years between them, but the Prince looked much the elder, wearier and hardened to mastery of self.

"This one is not for you," he said. "Now go see to your mother. Don't fall to his level by doing his own sort of deed to him. We mustn't become the things we despise; in that lies their surest victory." Sordo stared for a moment, biting his lip, then turned again to his mother.

None of the besieging force could be seen; they'd all been routed when their leaders were thrown down. None, that is, except the dead and wounded who still lay on the bloodied field. Already the injured from the Hightower and the allied expedition were being carried back to the fortress and the dead gathered for their final journey. The victors were preparing to slay their fallen enemies, but Springbuck ordered them to be spared.

"These, too, are my subjects, though they follow false colors," he said. "So let those who are able leave, and tell people the true *Ku-Mor-Mai* is come again to Coramonde. Let those who've been killed be buried with respect and not left to rot. If a man cannot go, put him in the fortress and let him be cared for as we care for our own. When this war is over and my reign is come, there will be enough wounds to bind in Coramonde. I'll open no new one with the killing of more of my subjects than must be; who can make the dead alive once more and placate those who loved them?"

All were taken back by this. It wasn't their experience in war to let live a downed antagonist, who might come after revenge. But Gil nodded in agreement and they knew this was another unusual notion learned by the Prince from the American. When they'd thought it through for a time, most decided it was a good thing.

Then the numb tranquillity of after-battle was snuffed out as a low, chilling laugh filled their ears. The golden mask of Ibn-al-Yed was its origin, though it had been ripped from its owner's head. It rang hollowly and its dark eye sockets appeared to them to hold tiny points of light that brought vivid dread.

"King of fools!" it reverberated. "Princeling of tosspots and strumpets! Do you posture already? No, no, it is too early; you've interfered with the least of my affairs."

Springbuck's hackles rose. He recognized the voice of Yardiff Bey and knew that the sorcerer spoke from afar. The mask of Ibn-al-Yed was obeying its true owner.

"You have my let to kill the mindless thing that wore this false face I forged," it continued, staring upward to a wind-scoured sky. "Ibn-al-Yed became too ambitious. In this way I converted him to a container for my will, another slave for Yardiff Bey.

"Do you think well of yourselves, little warriors? Ah,

stand your ground then; you've only met the vanguard of the first of the armies I'll send against you. Its main body is not far behind. I think it will be more than adequate to deal with this children's outing you call an army. I have the might of all Coramonde to throw at you. It would seem you've abused my calling knock, but that won't discourage my visit. Yes, lock yourselves up in that pitiful stone sty and say farewell to your gods. Your time to fight and fall is now well-nigh."

The mask spoke no more, for Kisst-Haa lunged at it with a hiss and stamped on it with his horn-skinned foot, flattening it under his weight and puncturing it with his murderous claws. The mask could make no other sound after that, even at the behest of its creator.

But news of the approach of another army galvanized the allies into action. They quickly organized evacuation of the wounded and removal of the dead. Springbuck yielded on the disposal of enemy slain insofar as to permit their cremation atop a hasty pyre. As the balefire rose, foot soldiers and others from the Hightower came to aid in gathering up weapons, provender and other useful items from the emptied camp. Stray mounts and deserted picket lines were rounded up.

When Gil and Springbuck saw that all particulars of the mop-up had been established, they rode to the castle, where Sordo had taken his slain uncle and his mother. The Hightower was in an uproar like an ants' nest when its home log is ripped open. But these ants were preparing to fight, not having heard the threat of the mask, and didn't know the new odds they faced. The respite before a renewed siege was to be exploited to the fullest. Foraging parties were sent out to seize any supply or baggage trains left straggling behind, and to exhort the locals either to bring family and flock within the fortress or seek shelter in the deep forest.

Sordo took determined control of his family's liegemen and put them under the direct supervision of his uncle, Legion-Marshal Bonesteel. Then he drew the Prince aside.

"I must go now to my grandsire and tell him that his second and last son is dead," he said. "And while our sorrow is our own, and our loss prideful, I know that he would wish to salute you, however infirm he is."

"Of course I'll come, Hightower. It's your grandfather and the other men of this place who deserve my own tribute."

At this Sordo clapped hand to hilt and bowed. Then he led Springbuck up a broad staircase.

Gil, having seen this and heard it, inquired of Bonesteel what the two had been talking about.

"I thought all Hightowers were dead except Sordo and his mother, no? If there's a grandfather, how's come we haven't seen him before?"

The Legion-Marshal turned from supervising the positioning of a liberated mangonel and looked to one of the castle's lesser towers, pointing at its pinnacle.

"Up there is Hightower the First, builder of this place," the old soldier said. "He was one of the principles of the second coagmentation, a wanderer and a warrior whom any man might admire. He came to Coramonde from sojourns in the far south and made his home here, after swearing allegiance to Springbuck's grandfather. Many battles he fought, and many enemies he slew for Coramonde. He was quick to take anger, but quick, too, to forgive and benevolent to those under him.

"Age never bent his spine. He's the last pureblood of a gifted line of men, blessed with vitality and vigor well beyond the years of us common men. He had entered his sixth decade in power and grace over twenty years ago when gods or demons afflicted him with blindness—no one knows the full story save him, I would guess. He renounced his rule in favor of his eldest son Rolph, who was only eighteen then. Hightower had married late in life. Then he shut himself away in yon tower. His family and some few servants have seen him since then, but no other, I think."

The walls of the stairwell spiraled up the tower and were damp and cold, poorly illuminated by occasional slitted windows. Springbuck scarcely noticed this; it was the usual way in the great castles he'd seen, Earthfast and Freegate being exceptions.

They came to a halt ten steps from where the stairway apparently met the ceiling. Sordo stepped to a fixture on the wall, a fish-head of copper long gone green, mouth agape, looking as if it were swimming toward them out of the very stone. He spoke into the hollow mouth.

"Grandfather? It's Sordo. I must speak with you."

The Prince had heard tales of the eldest Hightower's hermitage and was fully prepared to be told to leave, but to his surprise the ceiling over the stairwell slowly swung away with a grinding of ancient gears. The newest Lord of the Hightower waited a moment, then led the way up the steps into a large, airy chamber.

At the four points of the compass were wide windows fitted with hinged shutters—an indulgence in a frontier fortress, the Prince thought. Though the day wasn't cold, a fire burned in the hearth. The floor was covered with deep furs and all the walls were hung with tapestries. The windlass which had raised the lidlike stone door covered the stairwell was now unattended, and Springbuck couldn't see its operator at first.

"Grandson, come here," said a deep voice. With a start the Prince looked to a high-backed chair drawn up close to the fire.

They crossed to it and stood before Hightower, a man of imposing appearance and a rare warrior. He sat upright, a giant whose frame was utterly unbowed with the eighty and more years weighing on it. Time had been forbidden to steal his strength or slacken his belly, although the hair that grew down past his shoulders and the flowing beard and flaring mustache were purest white.

He wore glittering mail and heavy greaves, carefully maintained through years of disuse; through his belt armored gauntlets were tucked. Across his knees was a plain broadsword in scabbard, of such size that the Prince doubted if many men could handle it at all, much less carry it to war. Springbuck studied this tragic man, the massive architecture of chest and shoulders, the still-strong hands idle in his lap, eyes staring blindly into the fire. Here was a mountain among men bested by a foe he couldn't put down with hand strokes.

Seeing him, Springbuck understood why the old man had, with indomitable pride—some would call it vanity, and be wrong—yielded up his rule and gone into seclusion when he no longer found himself whole.

"I heard the sirens of war in the keep," the giant said, face still turned to the fire. "Then yesterday the distant sounds of preparation for siege, and today the clamor of an army deploying and later the drumming of hooves, the battle horns and the din of the melee, mixed with the screams of the dying. So, I put on this armor I haven't worn since before you were born and waited in the dark to learn what lesson the gods had for us this time. But you have come to me, and another with you, and so I know that the banner of the Hightower still flies over us. Well, that is good; I did not intend to be turned out of my home like a beggar, nor let our enemies kill me easily, but it was hard to wait in the darkness and not know what was to be."

He thought for a moment. "Yes, that was by far the hardest part," he added.

"Grandfather," Sordo began, head high and face set against what he must say, "we've beaten the troops sent by the Usurper Strongblade with the help of the King of Freegate and Prince Springbuck, but your other son fell today and will not rise. Yet he lived to see it a victory, and the other with me is none other than the Prince."

The snowy old head dipped once in acknowledgment. Hightower stood, topping them by a head and taking his sword easily in one hand; he stepped with the sureness of familiarity to a nearby window, breathing deeply in the afternoon air.

"I hope that it isn't too warm for you here my young lords, but my bones ache at times nowadays." He spoke to them as across a wide reach of years or miles. His face worked for long seconds, but what emotions interplayed there they couldn't tell. Without turning to them, he resumed.

"Sordo, son of my son, what will you do? How fares the household? Is your mother well? She always held my heart, a fair little maid forced before it was her time to answer the obligations and duties of housemistress to this pile of masonry."

Sordo swallowed once before lying. "She's well, Grandfather, quite well and safe." He glanced nervously to the Prince, then said, "I'm going to posture the castle against renewed siege, and I think it's best you go back to Freegate along with Mother."

Hightower's control threatened to break. His body shook, yet he didn't allow it to enter his voice. "Now you are Lord of the Hightower. I shall do as you say, but I would rather . . . nay, if things were different I, too, should want an old blind man out from underfoot.

"The two decades I spent here haven't been idle. I have thought much and meditated on the things I have learned. Occasionally, visitors have brought me news of interest. Yet, it won't be difficult to leave, I suppose; darkness is the same everywhere and I carry my imprisonment with me wheresoever I go."

He sniffed the air again. "There is a storm approaching. It will not break this afternoon or tonight, nor even tomorrow. Yet soon, I think, there will be torrents and thunder crashes."

Few in the Hightower knew sleep during the next twelve hours save as a memory.

Chains of men ferried weapons to the walls, bushels of arrows, racks of javelins and spears and other missiles for the repulsion of assaults. Volatile caldrons of vile-smelling, oily fluid were set over channels leading to spouts set in the walls.

The main donjon was readied, its storerooms filled to overflowing with food and its cistern checked against an emergency withdrawal, should the outerworks be taken.

Sordo fitted himself naturally to the task of bracing his garrison; it was the labor he'd been groomed for since boyhood. The third generation was preparing to stiffen the Hightower against one more assault on its dangerous walls.

Chapter Twenty-six

All warfare is based on deception.

SUN TZU WU,
"Art of War"

IT was decided that the garrison would be augmented with infantry brought from Freegate. Springbuck also detached two troops of dragoons to stay behind with those organizing irregular action against the approaching army.

The Prince wanted to stay and command the defense, but had met opposition from his companions, including Reacher. He maintained his stand until, unforeseen, Lady Hightower came to him. "I'm informed that my Lord the *Ku-Mor-Mai* offered to lend his good arm to the protection of our home. Though we thank him, surely he sees that he must remain at liberty and not be detained here? My son will bring us and the Hightower through this trial, as his sire and grandsire have in the past."

Without waiting for a reply she went, ending her confinement to the sickbed she'd occupied since receiving the ministrations of Andre deCourteney, and commenced to help in the affairs of the castle. She'd settled the matter completely. Springbuck couldn't go against the wishes of that great and gallant Lady.

Still, they were left with the quandary of a retreat in a perilous situation. An immense force had been mustered and sent out from Earthfast with the double mission of suppressing outlaw activity and breaking the Hightower.

Now that Yardiff Bey knew of the presence of the allied expedition, it was logical to assume that his commander in the field, Novanwyn, would dispatch a strong element to block and hold the Western Tangent where it entered the Keel of Heaven, to preclude their escape back to Freegate. He could eliminate them and the castle at leisure, since further relief would thus be cut off. The poser was that, though the allies felt that they could cut their way back to the Free City if the odds were fairly well matched, a larger enemy force might be too much for them to deal with. But taking more men along with them against that contingency would both leave the Hightower undermanned and slow them down.

The wrangling was going nowhere when Gil spoke up.

"Suppose we could convince Bey and Novanwyn that we have a bigger army here than we really do? That we're going to stand and that they have a chance to wipe us out, but only if they commit all their muscle?"

Bonesteel thought for a moment, then nodded. "Then Bey would, I think, try to deal us a deathblow. I know old Novanwyn would consider it a fine idea; it fits with his heady notions of audacity and resolve. But how to accomplish this? It may be that Yardiff Bey has seen our strength already through Ibn-al-Yed's dead eyes." The creature that had been Ibn-al-Yed had died the preceding evening, not of its wounds or for any reason they could see other than that it was bereft of the will of its master.

"I've been talking with Andre here," Gil replied, "and I think I can tell you. Now here's Bey, with this aircraft he's so fond of, and he knows that he can use it to scout us, yes? Think about it. Tomorrow, when times and distances are about right—if the reports about his troop movements are true—and our men are active and his are near, I bet he'll make a firsthand decision on how to commit his men. If he has any brains at all, he'll make a flyby and check us out. What I propose here is that we scam our friend Bey."

With the exception of Andre they had all become lost. He elucidated.

"Our boy is clever, right? But he has introduced a new concept in warfare into this world, and I don't think that even he has tumbled onto all the angles. He hasn't twigged that forward air observers can be conned, but, folks, we're going to teach him. Oh, my, yes. I just hope he's never heard of Quaker guns."

"No, no, NO!" Gil MacDonald grated in exasperation. "We can't put mockups out in the open. Look, and get this for once and for all; we've got to make him believe we're trying to *hide* the troops and siege engines, not parade 'em.

"Pay attention! Real siege machinery and so forth inside the walls. Fakes and such down there among the tall trees in that meadow and the soldier simulacra—is that the right word, Andre?—among the trees there, there and all through there. A real trooper every few yards or so later, to scuttle around when the aircraft shows—if it shows—and one string of picketed horses to get spooked and set loose down by the tree line at the rim of the forest. Got all that?"

The officer in charge of the work detail wasn't really sure he did, but nodded and went back to his men. They were still mystified as to why they'd been pulled from siege preparations to do this pointless labor. They were tying bright strips of cloth from torn uniforms around man-high crosses, roughly made from branches and jammed at intervals in the earth near unused cooking fires. Their comrades in the next stand of woods knew no more than they, so they just marked it up as another unexplained whim of Command.

Storm clouds rolled in, hiding the sun, as Andre set himself to cast his glamour. Without Gabrielle to aid him, he found the task desperately taxing, the more so since he must concentrate on precision and at the same time hide his spell from Yardiff Bey. Still, if Bey were both flying his demon ship and assessing the numbers at the Hightower, he'd probably miss the traces of Andre's thaumaturgy.

Alone atop the central donjon, Andre spread his arms and summoned a servant of malignant power. By order of the allied leaders, all men were under shelter and cautioned against interfering or even watching the incantation. Scant enough warning had been required.

The magician reached outward, flexing his arms and

calling in a forbidden language. Moisture ran down his pudgy face and collected on his shaggy chest and pot-belly. His back was soaked and his brow furrowed by the awful effort, as the being began to take shape, a sparkling nimbus of light.

He would have preferred to do this in a proper sanc-tum, but he must be outside to watch his vassal's every move. The being fought his will, its aura flaming an-grily; but he ended its obstinacy with words of enforce-ment and made it agree to do his bidding precisely. With a snarl it sped away, eager to be done with its servitude and back to its own plane.

As it flew, the rude simulacra began to waver and re-form into brightly attired soldiers who stood, squat-ted or lay patiently. And that, in truth, was their only function.

Of all his pleasures, Yardiff Bey most cherished flying his unique sky craft, *Cloud Ruler,* through the high airs. Then he felt master indeed of the wide world unfolded beneath him, removed from the sordid doings and goings of common men. He'd contrived, fought and suffered to achieve its construction, paying a dear price; his hand went to the ocular where his left eye had once been.

Now he leaned forward in his luxurious chair in-board *Cloud Ruler* and uttered a low oath, peering into the ground-glass optical device before him. His mind was only partially occupied with his reconnaissance, since he must keep under his control the fire elemental trapped in the bowels of his ship. He perceived faint traces of magic smelling of the hated Andre deCourte-ney, but so slight were these that he attributed them to minor protective spells and the like. He didn't consider deCourteney a magician of any note.

The demon ship circled lower on red flames while he stared down through his magnifying disk. Bivouacked around the castle were more fighting men than he'd thought possible for his enemies to field altogether. Many more besides were within the walls of the High-tower. Here and there some of them ran for cover, but most were frozen in fear. Good.

He'd have liked to put trees and castle to the torch with his ship, but disliked bringing it low or otherwise endangering the product of his long labors.

Then he was gasping in outrage as a boulder half the size of a horse zipped up from the Hightower. The Keep's biggest stone gun, modified by artisans working under Gil's direction, had barely missed bringing down the Hand of Shardishku-Salamá.

"Chowderheads!" roared the American as the crew reset the long throwing arm of the stone gun. "Don't hit him, dammit! We want to send him on his way, not bring him down. One more now, lower this time so he thinks he's getting above our range. We don't want him to risk another pass."

They needn't have bothered. Yardiff Bey was causing the fire elemental to lift *Cloud Ruler* higher and bring it around on a course for the approaching force from Earthfast. He'd never heard the term beachhead, but he'd long since mastered the concept and didn't intend to see Freegate establish one in Coramonde.

He was disgusted with his commanders' apparent inability to flush out bothersome peasants. Herdsmen who knew every inch of the wilderness and hunters who'd stalked the lion and the deer were tormenting regulars, fleeing for sanctuary to treacherous bog and trackless mountain. Yardiff Bey had contrived through agents to have Lady Hightower kidnapped to force Bulf to fight, and still his field commander had been beaten.

But here, at last, was an open battle to fight. He'd rush up his second great corps and crush these insects as soon as possible.

The return to Freegate began ill.

The bulk of the foot soldiers of Coramonde under Bonesteel were undismayed at the prospect of fortifying the Hightower. Almost every member of the allied leadership volunteered to be part of the garrison; but Springbuck overruled all but one, Bonesteel's second-in-command, a tough old veteran who had experience in siege, useful to Sordo.

Though they were to travel light, Gil made sure they took certain things captured with Ibn-al-Yed's tent:

writing implements, scrolls, seals, maps and order-of-battle listings. To Gil's great unease, he found that a large part of the forces mentioned in the latter couldn't be accounted for. They definitely hadn't been at the battle outside the Hightower. Captives of that engagement were either unwilling or unable to explain this.

With them, too, they took Lord Hightower. "There's much he's seen and heard," Andre said of his old friend. "Much he's pondered that may help us before this struggle is over. More, he'd be of little use here."

Gil, looking at the former Duke, couldn't help but think of the majestic gods of William Blake.

Though they'd planned to take Lady Hightower with them, they didn't. In her own gracious way she forbade it and they couldn't make her leave the Hightower.

Bonesteel gave her and his nephew each a strong hug. He was torn, and would have liked to stay and watch over them, but knew that he'd be needed badly elsewhere.

They left at midnight, taking extremely light rations and leaving most of their supplies. All were mounted, their horses fairly fresh; many had been able to rest briefly in the hours between Yardiff Bey's departure and the call to mount.

They pushed as much as they dared on a journey of such length. Few were their stops; they alternated riding with walking and leading their horses. Hightower had ridden grimly on a mount lead by Andre and, over his protests, was borne on a litter on the shoulders of the strongest when the rest walked. They took main trails to the Tangent. They didn't think that any troops of Earthfast were in the area yet, and the need for haste was great.

For a night, a day and into another night they went. The skies remained threatening, and the Prince was glad he had mighty Fireheel under him. They would stop for food and to rest their horses, make relievements or utter a word of prayer, then go on.

At last Springbuck called a halt, knowing the men must rest before the long trek through the Keel of Heaven. Gil slumped from his saddle, asleep before he hit the ground.

The air was hot and close. Lightning began to flash

intermittently in the east. Men picketed their horses and those lucky enough not to draw guard duty threw themselves down, exhausted.

The Prince was seeing to the arrangement of watches, trying to assure himself of each man's welfare. The seemingly indefatigable Reacher had disappeared hours earlier, loping toward his homeland to reconnoiter. Bonesteel was obviously strained by the ordeal, and Andre was snoring loudly a few paces from the slumbering American.

Of Hightower there was no sign. The night was black, and now thunder swelled in their direction out of the mountains, and spears of levinbolts flew.

Springbuck found the old man on a low, open knoll outside camp, just as rain began in fat droplets. He thought he came up silently, especially in the midst of the growing thunder and racing lightning. But when he was near the other, Hightower asked, fairly bellowing to be heard, "Who draws nigh?"

"Springbuck," he answered, "to see that you come and get some rest now. We have a long road yet to wend."

The hulking old champion didn't move except to raise his head to chaotic skies and open his arms, as if to embrace them.

"Too long has it been since I have stood this close to the earth. Too long between ground and sky in that tower, suffering the wrath of the gods and the wages of mine own folly, content to escape with my life.

"But hearing, smelling, feeling the things of the world again, I remember life, I remember. I must have my whole life again, or none of it."

Springbuck knew Hightower was no longer talking to him, that he was not speaking to any earthly ear. The focus of the storm swept closer.

"Let my penance be done! Take my life and this half-existence, or do with me whatsoever you will. Have I not been punished enough?"

Deafening crashes and blinding lightning swirled around them. The Prince, awed by the fury of the sky, faltered and fell sprawling. Gazing up, he saw Hightower's figure silhouetted not ten yards from him. The man seemed to gather all his substance and, in a voice strained and uncharacteristically shrill, repeated: "*Enough!*" He thrust both gauntleted fists into the air over his head.

A bolt from above struck him, setting forth his shape in blue-white radiance and blasting the Prince into unconsciousness.

He came partially awake, with Andre hovering over him apprehensively. He couldn't hear and blood was running from his nose. Gil was standing and looking over the mage's shoulder. Torches had been brought; in their glare, the Prince made out Hightower. The old man, too, was staring at him; plainly he could see once again. His face held a mien of wonder and fear.

Prince of Coramonde, true Pretender to the Throne of the *Ku-Mor-Mai,* nominal Commander of the joint expedition, fainted dizzily into cordially receptive darkness.

When he awoke again he could hear Gil speaking.

"—not unknown in my own world. The eye's a funny thing, y'know . . ." He sounded very unsure of himself.

Andre answered. "You must stop this distressing habit of yours of trying to explain away the workings of higher powers. Haven't you seen enough since you've been in Coramonde?"

"Yeah, yeah. It's just that I'd rather not see us misconstrue a simple freak of nature for divine intervention."

There was amusement in the wizard's voice. "I've yet to see a *simple* freak of nature, Gil."

The driving rain was loud and steady. Springbuck blinked in the gray predawn, and though his head hurt and he was stiff and bruised, he was generally whole. He was lying beneath a densely leaved tree, sheltered from most of the downpour, the other leaders around him.

Gil noticed he was awake. "Glad you're through sluffing off," he said briskly. "Reacher's back and we've got trouble. Here, take some water; but don't take much."

The Prince gulped greedily from a drinking skin, but

forced himself to stop after a moment. A wave of nausea threatened him. "What trouble do we have?"

"Take your pick," Gil said.

Andre explained. Reacher had scouted and found that the balance of the original force under the late Ibn-al-Yed had been separated and moved, under Legion-Marshal Novanwyn, through the Keel of Heaven to lay siege to Freegate, leaving a holding unit in the mountain pass. The information had come in part from guerrillas in the mountains, which meant that there were two barriers between them and the Free City. The contingent under Novanwyn had swung up and around from the south, combing for guerrillas and so missed the allies by chance as they came down the Western Tangent.

The son of Surehand sighed. Now they were trapped with the only usable pass defended and the second army doubtless in pursuit soon. He cursed the endless manpower of his homeland, not for the last time.

Gil nodded in agreement. "As prevaricating Uncle Gladstone used to admonish me: 'It never hits the fan a little at a time.' Know what I mean?"

Springbuck didn't, nor did he care to be enlightened.

Gil went on cheerfully. "What I figure is, since the holding element's dug in and made themselves a redoubt in the pass at the Keel of Heaven—and isn't all that big—we'll draw them out and hand 'em their ass. Then we'll sucker our way past Novanwyn's main body at Freegate."

The Prince laughed weakly. He supposed the American didn't know how difficult it would be to take high ground from a unit of the Legions.

Gil forged on. "Stand up and walk around a bit, that's right, and I'll show you how we'll do it. Hey, you, send that courier over here!"

Gil had selected from among the remaining light cavalry a former courier. With the captured writing materials and official seals from Ibn-al-Yed's tent, and Bonesteel's help, he concocted a strongly worded, authentic-looking movement orders letter, instructing the officer in charge of the redoubt to come at once with his entire unit to the Hightower, with mention of a general uprising.

The fraudulent messenger had been outfitted with a close, makeshift approximation of a proper uniform. Mud and wear would account for the minor flaws. The plan startled the Prince so much that he forgot his headache.

"Uh-huh. Shocked Bonesteel, too," said Gil. "He said something about revamping the military dispatch system when this is over. It's really all quite simple, buddy; but no one around here ever thought too hard about authenticating messages." He paused and reflected for a moment. "Matter of fact, I got myself in quite a jam that way once."

Springbuck slowly regained his equilibrium. The American elaborated on the details of the plan. Their primary worry was how soon Bey would realize that the force in the Hightower was drastically smaller than he'd thought.

"We have to leave in short order," Gil warned. "Man, if we can just buy ourselves another crummy day or so; if this cloud cover breaks, Bey'll come buzzing around and see what we're doing. The second army's probably at the Hightower already. Hope we'll be able to come up with an idea to take the pressure off Sordo.

"Anyway, it'll be a buster getting to Freegate if the storm is as bad on that side of the mountains. Mud's tail-high on a tall bear."

Chapter Twenty-seven

We will either find a way . . . or make one.

HANNIBAL

THE rain had stopped. The ground was mud, offering untrustworthy footing, but that had made it easier to erase their tracks. They stood in a narrow draw off the Western Tangent, where it threaded the pass through the Keel of Heaven, and waited as they had since noon. The air was chilly and men clamped numb fingers beneath their arms and stamped their feet, since fires were out of the question.

Springbuck, shivering in his cloak, had to give the enemy officer credit. The message had said "all speed," and it was barely a half-half hour after the courier had been sent up to the redoubt when the sound of hoofbeats and marching drums reached their ears. But the commander, in haste to obey orders, had neglected caution. No outriders came to scout the pass ahead of the main body, though if they had, they'd have been silenced and made no difference.

Through the latticework of brush and scrub they'd drawn over the mouth of their hiding place, the Prince and Hightower watched the mounted troops move by smartly. Springbuck glanced nervously over his shoulder to make sure every man in his band was out of sight around a bend in the little ravine. Each had been ordered to stand to his horse to ensure total silence. Since the requirement for armored men was great in this element of their ambuscade, Springbuck had most of the men of Freegate with him, along with some of the Horseblood.

Route drummers were beating quickstep for the infantry moving down the pass. The Prince smiled. The infantry would be in the rear, as hoped, the first to be hit. Excellent!

When the last rank had passed their position, he and his men quickly tore away the camouflage, mounted and hurried to form a column, ready to execute their share of the trap.

A mile farther down, around several turns in the Tangent, Bonesteel, Dunstan and the remainder of the men of Freegate stood patiently behind their abatis and piles of stones. The old Legion-Marshal spoke little to the Berserker. He didn't like this gloomy, unpredictable man and felt ill at ease in his presence. He hoped the fellow would observe some sort of discipline.

From a vantage point on the cliff overlooking the pass, Gil and Reacher saw the engagement shaping up. The American signaled Bonesteel that their enemy was close, then hoped Springbuck and Hightower would have their timing right.

Archers on the cliffs to either side pulled back at his order, lying out of sight and concentrating all their attention on listening for the signal to rise again. Some, jittery, were counting the shafts in their quivers by finger touch or testing their bowcords.

The enemy halted behind their captain when they came around a final turn and saw the barricade barring their way. The captain was confused as to how this emplacement had come to be here in such short time, since the dispatch rider who'd brought Ibn-al-Yed's message to him hadn't seen it—or at least hadn't mentioned it. He assumed that the rider, to whom he'd given word of his immediate compliance and sent on his way, had been taken or killed.

Then he saw the fradulent courier standing with the others behind the abatis, his bright red tunic open now and a makeshift pike in hand. The captain's fury was broken by the sounding of a trumpet by the Wolf-Brother, atop a cliff to his left, blowing with all his extraordinary vim and producing, to Gil's mind, a dooms-day wailing.

Hearing this, Springbuck and his men broke into a

full trot; then seeing the tail of the enemy column, a full charge carried them to the flanks of their foes.

Swords flew and once again the son of Surehand failed to understand how any man could hope to come unscathed through such deadly havoc.

The opposing captain was no fool. Unaware of the attack behind, he ordered a withdrawal until he could assess his predicament. The maneuver turned to confusion and he learned that a battle was being fought at the rear of his column, a little over one hundred yards away, and that he couldn't get to it; his own men were falling back and blocking his way.

Boldly, he determined to carve an escape for his men. Turning back to the abatis, he threw off his ornate cape; drawing his saber, he ordered his trumpeter to sound the charge. As he swept forward with his men to fall upon the barricade, Gil stood and fired a single shot with his carbine.

The tenor of the conflict changed instantly. What had looked to be a close-quarters fight for life became a rain of death against which the captain had scant defense, as archers on cliffs at either side poured a steady, merciless shower into the tightly confined cavalry. Most of the bowmen were Horseblooded, and their moaning arrows sowed fright and turmoil along with injury and death.

To the rear, Springbuck and Hightower were hewing their way through the massed infantry, which had no chance to establish a line, form shield lock or otherwise fight except as individuals—disaster for foot against mounted men.

Gil surveyed the carnage with an expression of stone. Bonesteel attempted to offer terms to the trapped contingent but was refused, and the fighting continued undiminished.

Reacher hurled an occasional rock into the milling men below, but the American didn't lift his carbine. He knew he didn't need to; he'd planned this ruse well and the enemy had small chance of survival.

The enemy captain, assailing the barricade with no success, fell back. A courageous, duty-bound man, he

obeyed orders without question, a valuable officer liked
by his men and known to do the job allotted him. He'd
suffered a wound in his calf from a pike but didn't think
about it as much as about the agonizing certainty that
he'd led his command to its death. Of course, he wouldn't
surrender. He'd been told by Legion-Marshal Novanwyn
that tortures and humiliations were inflicted on prisoners
by animalistic rebels. He reined back viciously and studied the hemming cliffs and faceless walls of the trap.

With a shout, he brought his charger around and got
the attention of his standard-bearer with cuffs, then led
him to a spot along the ridge where a partial landslip
and a slightly easier incline provided what might be
their road to salvation. It was a short way from the
place where Gil and Reacher stood looking down.

The American saw it all and bit off an obscenity.
He'd hoped the slip would be too steep to negotiate—he
knew *he* would never want to try it—but the captain
was a superb horseman and his men were old cam-
paigners. Many of them, taking the path he set them,
fell back. But many swarmed on. If they got to high
ground, Gil knew, they'd sweep it clean, mowing down
the dismounted archers easily, and might turn the tide
of battle.

The Wolf-Brother had sprung to the lip where slope
met cliff top, poised to defend it. Gil impatiently shoved
him aside, took up a stance and waited with his face
stiff and stern.

When the enemy cavalry and their churning mounts
were within yards of the crest he raised the carbine to
his shoulder almost involuntarily. Feeling the cool press
of wood against his stock-welded cheek, he fixed them
in his sight and began firing. Men dropped from their
saddles, only to be replaced by desperate comrades.

The first magazine went quickly, the noise and fire of
the carbine and its devastating effect stabbing panic into
those below. But they were fighting for their lives, willing to face even apparent magic for a chance to live.

The American was sickened. He tried to reconcile
himself; not to have fired would have invited disaster
and death for his side. But that made the cold killing no

less repugnant. He changed magazines and squeezed the trigger as quickly as he could, but more and more men were following their commander up the slope.

Now more archers were concentrating their fire on this sudden advance. Just as the men below began to fall back, their captain, who had miraculously lived through the gunfire, threw a mace he'd carried on his saddle bow.

Gil saw it coming and ducked to one side, but the lip of the crest was eroded and gave way. He fought for a second to get his balance over empty space, then pitched forward an instant before Reacher spotted his dilemma and grabbed for him. He lost his carbine as he went skidding past the enemy captain, who barely missed a cut at him.

Sliding and tumbling, he managed to drop to the floor of the pass with a minimum of damage, but would undoubtedly have lost most of his skin had he not been wearing armor. His steel cap was gone, and he threw back his coif and looked around him.

The place was like a scene out of the Hell he remembered so well. Men and animals were feathered through with arrows. Some of the panic-stricken soldiers were still trying to hack their way through the abatis but most were attempting to retreat back up the pass, pushing at those blocking them and trampling those beneath, adding to the crushing pressure on the infantry facing Springbuck and Hightower.

No one on the floor of the pass had yet noticed Gil. He picked himself up groggily and pulled out his pistols, weighing his chances of either fighting his way to the barricade or scrambling back up the slope. Having witnessed one such battle already, he knew that his chances in such a riot were damned poor in spite of his firearms. He glanced back to size up the slope, but saw that the captain was bearing down on him, fell and fey, saber raised, thoughts of escape submerged by the lust for vengeance.

The Browning clutched to his chest, Gil raised the Mauser and trained careful aim on the plunging, charging officer. When the man was within a few yards he fired. The pistol report startled the horse and picked his target out of the saddle. There was a neat black hole in the captain's corselet and surprise on his face.

All the archers on both cliffs had concentrated on the group attempting the slope and eliminated the threat of a *coup de main*. But it was still no safe place to be, Gil knew. Even if he managed to get to the top—a doubtful venture in armor—he'd likely be arrowed by a careless bowman from his own side.

The enemy had taken advantage of the redirected archer fire to charge the barricade again, hacking at it with swords and sending arrows, javelins and toss darts through and over it.

Gil blasphemed. He had a choice between downright stupidity and suicide. His one shot had been noticed and several troopers turned toward him, closing with their swords high for the butcher blow.

He skipped backward to the cliff face, bracing his back against it, and began to use his pistols judiciously. He knew he'd never get a chance to reload.

Springbuck and his men pushed hard. They did well, although their opposition was trapped and fighting for life.

But in the van of the attack was Lord Hightower.

His sight returned, his nerve and confidence restored and whatever demon of depression that occupied him gone, he was venting all the cyclopean energy so long and unwillingly curbed. He swung his greatsword without pause or check. His iron-rimmed shield, covered with many plies of tough hide, turned aside any blow or missile and buffeted many men from their feet.

Soon all who would have been in his way and with whom he'd have closed shied away and turned in another direction in the melee. He threshed deeper into their ranks and at length was alone, a solitary reaper harvesting foemen. Though the Prince and his men did their best to follow, Springbuck began to think that Hightower would carry the day all by himself. With the return of his sight had come a renewal of his strength in combat. Last of his puissant, long-lived line, he made this his hour and there was no man who could stand before his arm or overbear him.

Those who saw him coming could only fall back in dismay and fear that some harsh, frost-haired deity of the distant north had contracted to ride with the Prince of Coramonde.

Gil crouched, nerves taut, by the foot of the cliff and watched the riders circling in front of him. He'd driven them away once, but now the Browning's slide was locked back, magazine empty. He dared not turn his attention to reload it for worry that a stray arrow or aimed spear would come in his direction; he'd already dodged two javelins.

Somehow the men sensed that he hesitated to shoot. Though his weapons were frightening, they knew now that this man was no wizard. They meant to kill him before they themselves were killed.

He didn't take his eyes from them as he let fall the Browning, switched the Mauser to his left hand and drew his sword. He condemned his luck at not being able to grab a stray horse, but they wouldn't let him near with the smell of gunpowder on him. One man rode in on him, fast and low, a long iron throwing dart in his hand and his shield protecting him. Without a clear shot Gil was forced to pick the horse out from under him.

It took the last round in the Mauser.

He tucked the pistol into his belt rather than let it hang by its lanyard or take the time to fumble it back into its holster, and dropped into an uneasy guard.

The man whose horse he'd shot sprang to his feet, sword out, and rushed him. Gil found that his own blade, a replacement for the one he'd left pinning the scorpion banner to the ground and one he'd considered rather heavy and awkward, was now weightless. A small part of him knew it for adrenalin.

His antagonist had a shield still on his arm, but was shaken from his fall, despite his quick recovery. Gil snatched the big trench knife from his belt to use as a parrying blade, as he'd seen Springbuck do.

They began their duel.

He'd expected to be on the defensive but found himself as much the aggressor as his opponent, with a dexterity he hadn't known he possessed. Their swords cut and parried and diligent drill was repaid with survival. Unlike his foe, he didn't shout or mock and insult. A half-dozen times he blocked cuts that promised to lift his head from his body or sever him at the chest. The trench knife wasn't adequate to stop full strokes of the other's blade, but its threat helped even the match.

The blades became a blur and he fought by reflex. Then he found himself thinking a move or two ahead and used compound movements with unconscious smoothness. Time and again he let learned responses parry ferocious cuts in prime and tierce.

His slash was shield-blocked by his foe and he managed to take the return stroke on the knife; if it hadn't had brass knuckles on its grip he'd have lost fingers. He avoided a knee to the groin in an incredibly violent corps-à-corps. It was only by chance that he bobbed to the left as the man gathered a mouthful of saliva and spat it at him, or he'd have been momentarily blinded and permanently killed.

But in spitting, his antagonist had cocked his head forward, and the exposed throat triggered another kind of reflex in the American, who tried to chop at it with his left hand. Though the blow was clumsy—his hand still held the knife—it staggered the other and gave Gil a split second to drive the knife blade into the soft area just in front of his foe's right ear, below the rim of his helmet. It took maximum effort, a stroke that only a strong man might use effectively, but it succeeded and the cavalryman was dead even as he sank to the ground.

So much for the niceties of combat; chivalry be damned. Gil thought it interesting that he'd lived through his first sword fight and very, very gratifying.

During the match, the elements under Springbuck and the whelming Hightower had broken through. The old hero's booming voice called for surrender and was met in moments by a pass littered with weapons. Gil picked up his Browning and examined it. Doubtless it and the carbine were clogged with dirt and sand. Cleaning them would be a bitch.

He didn't see a dismounted man near him turn, cock his arm and aim a spear at him, but someone else did.

The man was slain before he could release his weapon by a stone hurled with bulletlike speed and accuracy. Gil heard the impact and saw the man slump, skull shattered. He glanced up to see the Wolf-Brother gazing down calmly. Reacher hadn't even bothered to pick up a backup rock.

Overconfident shrimp, huffed Gil MacDonald.

Chapter Twenty-eight

And I saw askant the armies,
I saw as in noiseless dreams hundreds of battle-flags
borne through the smoke of the battles and pierced
*   with missiles, I saw them.*
>   WALT WHITMAN,
>   *"When Lilacs Last in the Dooryard*
>   Bloom'd"*

"BECAUSE," Gil said wearily, "even if we *do* fight our way through the army surrounding Freegate, there's another right on our heels, and it'll seal us in again but good. We'd be stuck, trapped, static. On the other hand, if we stay outside and organize the people in the countryside, we might be able to do something useful. Maybe we could regarrison the pass redoubt before it's too late or enlist more of the tribes of the High Ranges and liberate Freegate from outside."

Reacher was unconvinced, unconvincible. He meant to go back to his city and lead its defense; he wouldn't listen to logic or pleas. His dreams had instructed him to do so he said, adamant.

"Reacher, my friend," Springbuck said. "You understand what our scouts tell us? There is a large unit outside your gates and an enormous one following us hard. We've many wounded and scarce time. We're liable to be decimated between two foes. I doubt seriously if we could hold our own against the first corps alone, if it has all Freegate at bay."

The Wolf-Brother remained solemn, indifferent. "Do not come then. I must go back."

"And I'll go with you!" rumbled Hightower, and he clapped Reacher on the back, staggering him. "The debt I owe you won't be paid until I've done you a service. Besides, I don't like all this talk of skulking and

304

hiding and consorting with peasants and masterless men. You came when you were needed and aided my kin. Now let's bash our way into Freegate and I'll show you how Hightower can brace for siege. And when they've dented their skulls and worn themselves out on your white walls, we'll break 'em and send 'em yelping on their way with a boot to their cracks."

Gil muttered under his breath and wondered why he'd left Philly. Too late to second-guess now, but the next time anyone tried to tap him for interuniversal service . . .

Springbuck knew that Hightower's remark had been a rebuke of sorts to him. He said to Reacher, "If this is your wish, ally, then I bow to you; you have been staunch at my side. Perhaps it is for the best. Many of our men need care." He was also thinking that a leader mustn't be too proud or stubborn to see another's viewpoint. Too, he sensed that the Wolf-Brother would never yield. To chivy him on it would risk an end of their coalition.

Besides, Gabrielle was still in Freegate.

"Okay, all right," Gil conceded. "We'll do it your way. But we don't just have to romp in and slug it out. We must do this fast and sneaky, and maybe there's a way. Pray Yardiff Bey hasn't figured out how we played games with his generals' communications or had time to warn his other field commanders about it."

They'd taken up positions and made preparations by moonrise, two hours after dusk of the day after the battle in the pass. They'd managed to rest and had avoided contact with enemy patrols with the exception of one, shortly before sundown. That one they had destroyed to the last man.

Gil's plan was uncomplicated but dangerous. The main body of the expedition formed up and moved slowly through the woodlands to the southeast of the city barbican, tracing the rim of the chasm. They made their cautious way toward the bridgeway with Reacher and the prowlers afoot, eliminating the occasional sentry without commotion. Since the plateau on which the city stood featured only one connection to the surrounding lands, the enemy had massed all his forces in that area, sure that the decisive action would take place there.

To the northeast, on the opposite side of the encampment from the barbican, Gil, Springbuck, Hightower and a small group of selected dragoons were poised just beyond the outermost ring of guards, hidden from sight. Gil was thinking that if everything didn't come off fairly simultaneously they could all pack it in. Springbuck decided it was time to move and said so. Gil gnawed a thumbnail and turned to the cavalrymen, four of whom were buglers.

"Remember: when we're through the first cordon of sentries, start blowing *To arms,* but keep with us. When I give you the word, switch to *Rally here,* and don't fall behind! I just hope those boys bagging *Zs* in the tents can't tell you from their regular tooters and follow procedure."

Speed would be their only chance. There were fewer than twenty of them.

The American looked toward Springbuck, difficult to discern in the darkness. The Prince raised his arm, so Gil clamped his reins in his teeth and drew his pistols, his heart banging in his chest. If he hadn't drifted away from his religion, he would have prayed in that moment.

Springbuck's arm dropped. They were off with a rush, brandishing weapons and guiding their horses with knees and teeth-held reins. Swooping through dimness they rode down the first line of sentries, who barely had time to cry out in alarm. Gil opened up with both guns, yelling through clenched teeth. The others were yanking torches from the ground, riding past tents and slashing ropes, spreading fire as they went.

Gil waved both arms over his head and the buglers blared their notes. Men were jolted from sleep by fearsome explosions and urgent bugles: *To arms!* As trained, they groped and stumbled to prepare for battle in the midst of what they'd believed to be a secure camp. Officers were as bewildered as enlisted men, and none more so than the camp commander, Midwis. The bugled message changed shortly: *Rally here!* Stand to your banners and rally to us! Still fuzzy with sleep, soldiers moved to do what was required of them.

The officer in charge of the watch force maintaining guard on the barbican dispatched a rider to find out what was going on, then belabored his men to do their job, keep their eyes on Freegate and stop trying to peer at the excitement behind them.

At the onset of the action, Reacher and the main force of the allied expedition moved ahead as quickly as possible. Rolling along the entrenched army's right flank, sending their foes reeling and convoying their wounded along as fast as they dared, they battled time and distance as well as the spears of their enemies.

Some calls for aid went out now to the camp commander, but most of his men were already responding to the false bugles and were beyond recall for the moment, charging to the—to them—alien sound of gunfire and praying that they weren't going to be ordered to join battle with supernatural beings.

Leaving a wake of burning, collapsing tents and mowing down disorganized defenders, the small band of attackers at the far side of camp had beaten their way to approximately the center of the bivouac. It was hard to see clearly, though the blazes behind helped a bit, and Gil was careful not to shoot without making sure it wasn't a comrade in his sights. They broke into a parade area and began to rampage around its periphery. Gil paused to fumble new ammunition into his pistols with frantic haste, no easy task when mounted, especially with the Mauser.

A score or so enemy cavalry came onto the parade ground from the opposite side; deducing correctly that these men in uniforms similar to theirs were nevertheless enemies, they charged. It took all the rounds in both the Mauser and the Browning to break that charge.

Springbuck was laying about him with Bar and thrusting a torch at whatever looked flammable. Hightower chopped his way through adversaries, thick armor taking dents and nicks, but the man within apparently indestructible. He threw down his ruined shield and pulled from his side a mace with a heavy ball and long, wicked spikes.

Gil drew his horse up next to a platform of logs, a reviewing stand of some sort. He vaulted onto it, tied his reins to the rail and pulled his carbine from its saddle scabbard. Taking stance, he knew the peculiar calm that often came to him at such times. He began to fire rapidly at the milling riders whose faces he couldn't see. He felt something brush his leg and looked down to see an arrow quivering in the wood near his boot. Archers were casting their shafts at him from the left. He threw himself prone and continued to fire, dropping several bowmen and dispersing the rest.

The platform trembled and he looked around. From nowhere, a fully armored knight in plate had ridden up to the platform; unable to reach Gil from the saddle, he had somehow managed to dismount and clamber over the rail. Though ungainly when not on his charger, the knight lumbered on, sword raised.

Gil brought his carbine around and pulled the trigger; but its breech was open, the magazine spent, and the American knew with heart-stopping surety he was to die.

And he would have died, except that the knight, as was the style in his own circles, wore sollerets with long, articulated, pointed toes. As he stepped nearer to kill the outlander, his metal footwear—well suited to stirrups but impractical under these circumstances—tripped him. He tottered for a second in his heavy plate, then fell to one knee.

Gil bounced to his feet, shifted his grip on the carbine and drove its butt under the open visor, and again, shaking with fear reaction. The knight toppled with a resonant clang and didn't move.

Now defense was becoming organized and members of the raiding party were falling back around Gil, hemmed in on all sides. Swords flashed in the night like fish in some deep pool. Gil slung his carbine and plucked from his belt the two fragmentation hand grenades he'd saved against desperate resort. As if at range practice, he tore the GI tape from the bodies of the grenades, pulled the pins, let the spoons fly free and hurled them as far as he could in the direction in which the party must soon make its way.

The dull metal egg-shapes arched through the air, timers marking the seconds. They landed in dense clusters of troops, unnoticed for a moment until the detonations sent bits of metal through flesh, riddling horse and man. Opposition fell back at the twin reports, and raiders could see that their way through the smoke was cleared for the time being.

Gil, reloading his pistols for the final run, dropped the empty Browning magazine and spent Mauser clip—irreplaceable, but no time to fiddle with them now—and called for the others to follow him. He launched himself off the platform onto Jeb Stuart, returning the carbine to its sheath.

Springbuck, shaken by the grenade concussions, waved his torch and cried, "No, I shall lead. Buglers, sound the call as I have told you!"

The buglers, hearing him, blew four last, baleful notes. They didn't sound the battle flourish of the *Ku-Mor-Mai,* but rather "The Crown's Retribution," notes to mark state executions and other occasions of high vengeance. Those who heard were astounded and afraid. It seemed as if a death sentence had been passed on them by a phantom monarch come with flame, thunder and sword irresistible.

With Springbuck at their head, the small party began its reckless dash for Freegate.

With mass and ferocity, the great Kisst-Haa and his kin—who'd had no chance to participate in the fight at the pass and were thus more avid for combat—parted the way for the main force of the allied army as they fought their way along the chasm's edge toward the barbican. Once they'd driven the enemy back temporarily from their objective, Bonesteel arranged his men in an arch to dig their heels in and hold, while wagons of wounded were trundled across the stone bridgeway, the vehicles scavenged from the abandoned redoubt after its former defenders had been disarmed and released.

Foremost of those who fought the action there was

Dunstan who, though he held his place, met every man who came to him in combat with glad killing-fever.

The bridgeway was blackened and burned in places; the defenders had been compelled to use liquid fire against sallies on their gates. Andre, driving the lead wagon of casualties, stopped at the gatehouse. Holding a torch close by his face, he called up to the amazed sentries in the bartizan to open for him.

The officer of the guard, already confused by the distant sound of gunfire and battle, dithered over whether or not to comply. He was saved by the arrival of the Snow Leopardess in answer to his previous summons. She stood to the wall and, recognizing Andre, commanded that the gates be opened.

As the wagons were being hurried in, Katya got a rapid explanation from the plump magician. Just then Lady Duskwind, again in armor and wearing a sword, arrived at the head of a complement of household cavalry. She'd heard the distant noise of battle and had seen what would be demanded. The tall Princess's eyes smoldered with the lust for combat and she called for a horse and quickly ordered them to ride forth and support those holding at the barbican. The officer of household cavalry objected and received a short, scathing rebuke, after which he loosened his sword in its sheath and waited unhappily.

With borrowed sword and buckler, Katya turned to her troops.

"Sabers, gentlemen," she said evenly, as if it were some minor military acknowledgment she asked. Their swords swept out in avid unison.

Then she galloped for the gate. It was her way; rather than order them to follow, she challenged them with bold example.

When it had first arrived, the host from Earthfast had bested the men of Freegate and the remaining Horse-blooded in the open beyond the city, and driven them into confinement. Su-Suru had fallen in that battle, and several of the reptile-men had been among the many others slain. It had been the Snow Leopardess' first major engagement and she seethed for repayment.

But her arrival didn't change matters on the far side

of the bridgeway very much. The besieging army was coordinating its actions and driving the allies back to the barbican. She steered herself into a gap in the ranks with a feline howl; agile and competent as any Wild Rider, she traded strokes with an amazed soldier and downed him. Her brother was there, but couldn't pause to talk to her. He swung two appropriated swords in a whirlwind around himself, and those whom he touched died.

Over the tumult they heard the grenades' detonations. The King, knowing the others were now making their last break, began to slash furiously to prepare way for them. Kisst-Haa crowded next to him and swung his colossal blade with cold, elliptical precision.

Shot heralded the arrival of the Prince and his companions. Counting Springbuck, Gil and Hightower, there were seven left. They were, in this segment of the conflict, effectively at the enemy's rear. They barely slowed as they fell on the men of Earthfast and cut their way ahead, finding it relatively easy to do so. Few wanted to ride against the terrifying guns of the American or the gory broadsword of the aged titan beside him.

The first Springbuck knew that he'd broken through was when he was nearly pared from his saddle by a screaming warrior-goddess with long, white-blonde hair and red-stained saber. He parried with his bowie knife and called Katya by name. She checked her return stroke and laughed for joy.

Now it became a matter of slowly falling back through the barbican and across the bridgeway. One by one, all the regular troops were sent dashing back to Freegate, galloping for their lives, while Reacher and Katya, Springbuck, Hightower and Gil held shoulder to shoulder along with Dunston and Bonesteel, who stoutly refused to leave. Even Kisst-Haa and his fellows were commanded to go; they were mighty fighters but would slow the final retreat too much. The Lady Duskwind was told to go by Gil, with an emphatic bellow; but after hanging back for a minute, she chose to stay near until the American came with her.

Bonsteel was met by a far younger man and could no

longer find energy to match him. He was thrown down with a death wound, but lived long enough to see Dunstan, suddenly come to sanity at this tragedy, slay the man who'd dealt him his last injury. And when the Berserker tenderly took up the old general to bear him back to the city, Bonesteel, beyond pain, had just enough time left in his life to wonder why he'd so mistrusted this man, had never taken time to make him a friend, and to be sorry for it.

The Princess' horse whinnied in terror and agony as an arrow found it. She managed to jump free as it fell, but wasn't on her feet long. Hightower leaned over; hooking one hand around the back of her knife belt, he hauled her across his saddle. He spurred toward Freegate, hot on the heels of Dunstan, with the Snow Leopardess objecting in the loudest of voices.

Gil, guns empty, unleashed a cut. He was trying frantically to defend himself and look after Duskwind. He turned to tell her again that she must go back, and saw her features twisted in agony; a toss-dart had sped from the opposing ranks and was lodged in her side. She began to slump in her saddle.

He screamed in shock and grief. Catching her as she fell, he held her to him and raced for the gate.

When Hightower, Katya, Gil and Duskwind were nearly at the entrance to Freegate, Springbuck called for Reacher to come and disengaged himself from the press. The King told him to be off, that he would follow, and the Prince went.

As he raced back to the city, Springbuck heard gunfire from the gatehouse; Van Duyn, come too late to ride out but contributing his share. Something bright caught the Prince's attention; with a rush of panic he spied Yardiff Bey's aircraft hovering off to the right on streamers of red demon-fire.

Reacher held the bridgeway alone now, giving the others precious seconds to withdraw. His two swords were impossible to see, licking out and swinging back and forth to lay open or thrust through any who came close. He danced back and forth, but never retreated or yielded an inch of the entranceway to his home. The soldiers wavered irresolutely; he'd already slain several of their champions and many other accomplished warriors besides.

At last there was none to go against him and the bright imperatives of his blades. He stood waiting silently. For an incredible moment in time the King held the bridge, facing down a numberless host as much by bravado as skill at arms, a deed to be told and retold long afterward.

He brought his swords to his sides, still for the first time, and yet there was none to challenge him. Then Reacher threw the bloodied blades down scornfully, and no man dared meet his gaze squarely; the monarch of Freegate was master of them all as if they were a pack of hounds at his feet.

He turned to go. From the massed men Desenge, the feared and deadly aide-de-camp to Legion-Marshal Novanwyn made his way through with blows and curses and charged the Wolf-Brother with his long, heavy spear Finder at ready. It had been said Desenge could never miss with Finder, and to prove it true he threw the weapon with a lunge. It flashed at the King's chest with speed that none could follow.

None, that is, except Reacher. He bent and crouched, avoiding the spear and catching it in his right hand. Straightening, he took Finder in both hands and contemptuously snapped it in two with a single surge of arms and chest. Then he flung the pieces from him and they arced out to either side, over the low walls of the bridgeway and into the chasm below, and it was the end of a weapon that had many evil deeds to its name. When they saw this, the troops were more loathe than ever to attack the King.

Desenge frothed with rage. Unsheathing his sword, he ran at Reacher with death in his eye. The Wolf-Brother knocked the blade aside in anger, catching Desenge by the throat and belt, and heaved the big man over his head, holding him there despite his frantic efforts to escape. Van Duyn, watching from the turrets of Freegate, was reminded of Hercules choking life from the giant Antaeus. The King grimaced with effort; he closed his fist and his opponent's widepipe was crushed.

Flinging the body of Desenge out over the chasm,

Reacher turned to run. But now two more adversaries leaped to meet him. These were Kanatar and Deotar, twin sons of Midwis, who was camp commander and second-in-command to Novanwyn.

They were fair-haired and held in fondness by their father and their men, strong at war and loyal to Strongblade because their father was. Deotar's armor was black, with silver trim, and Kanatar's was silver with trimming of black; Deotar rode a black horse and Kanatar a white.

They'd broken through after much trying to face this King who was so feared. He'd faced about and fled, so they laughed and mocked him as they pursued.

Reacher hadn't run from them, but from what he'd seen above and behind them. For, having learned how his armies had been outfought, tricked and frustrated, Yardiff Bey had vowed at least to have the life of the King, and to this end swooped down on trails of fire. He didn't want to bring *Cloud Ruler* too close to the well-defended city, but his manic rage had the better part of him and he swept in, disregarding the hazard to himself and his own army.

Reacher ran for his life as the twins galloped after and the sorcerer bore down, intent on incinerating him. Horses the Wolf-Brother could outdistance, and did. But the airship overtook the twins and Kanatar and Deotar died, burned alive in molten armor, victims of Yardiff Bey's single-minded intent. Their father Midwis gave a wretched cry and buried his face in his hands.

The race narrowed to the king and the sorcerer, who leaned over the looking lens. Reacher's feet barely touched the ground. He ran as he'd never run before, having acquired some of the fire fear of his lupine foster brothers, and he was as close to hysteria as he'd ever been. Nonetheless, his running was disciplined, arms and legs pumping and head bobbing up and down in regular rhythm with his controlled breathing.

The King caught up with the others at the gate, but the defenders in Freegate hadn't been idle. An engine hurled a metal-shod stone at Yardiff Bey's predator ship.

Like a fireless meteor it flew, narrowly missing the

craft and falling into the jungle in the chasm below. Bey's high regard for *Cloud Ruler* suddenly quenched his desire for immediate revenge. He ordered it to sheer off and make altitude.

But by that time the would-be victim and the others were safely inside the gate.

That night, when he'd had reports from pale, shame-faced subordinates on the events of the last several days, Yardiff Bey brooded in his tower sanctum at Earthfast. He considered asking the guidance of his masters in Shardishku-Salamá, but knew this would be interpreted as a sign of weakness and inadequacy.

He weighed recent news. Word had been leaked to the Mariners of the store of ship-fighting engines; boarding pikes and grappling hooks were being prepared in Boldhaven. Now they came to trade in fleets, with hands seldom far from cutlass hilts, and it was rumored that they'd laid down two-score keels for craft of war.

Roguespur, that hotblooded cub of cursed Fim, had, by sudden march in the night and deceit, taken a key border fortress and manned it with his own mercenaries and rebels mustered from the wilderness of the north.

And only this evening Honuin Granite Oath had sent a solicitous message, bathed in crocodile tears, that eleven of Strongblade's ministers in his area were being systematically and mysteriously assassinated.

A new shape of things was forming in the sorcerer's mind, incorporating the new ideas filling the heads of the rabble, the disconcerting, clever innovations against him and the perplexing weapons his foes were using. He remembered the humiliating occasion in the Inferno sharply, but was sure that the machine wagon had been dismissed from this cosmos.

It wasn't, he was certain, the work of Van Duyn. That one was all theory, all discussion and generalization. No, this was the crafty influence of another, and Bey was sure he knew who that other was; it must be the one he had seen through the eyes of his mask-slave Ibn-al-Yed at the Hightower. It was the younger alien, the one called Gil MacDonald; he seemed to be the causative factor of anomalies in the plans of the Hand of Shardishku-Salamá.

A precarious situation had come to be. Though the sorcerer hated to tear his attentions from other phases of his grand scheme, he decided that he must remove the unpredictable, unlooked-for cipher that was Mac-Donald. He already knew from cursory investigation that the man had no presence whatsoever on spiritual levels. He was in no sense a magician, and therefore had scant defense or resistance against supernatural manipulation. Unlike Springbuck, deCourteney and the rest, he wouldn't have been provided with incantations to protect his soul.

The sorcerer stood up, crossed the enormous pentacle on his sanctum floor and considered possible configurations for appropriate magical procedure. It might be complicated, take time and require great effort, but he had confirmed his decision to do it.

MacDonald must be eliminated.

Chapter Twenty-nine

Defense is the stronger form with the negative object, and attack the weaker form with the positive object.

KARL VON CLAUSEWITZ,
"On War" (prefatory note)

LIFE in the beleaguered city, Springbuck found on the day after their spectacular return, wasn't as despondent as he'd feared.

True, rationing was in effect, but allotments were adequate. There were enormous stores of food, and cultivated ground on the plateau to provide more, plus forage for herds and flocks. The job of maintaining a watch at the gatehouse was uneventful, as the encircling army was looking to its wounded and repairing its bivouac.

Though Gabrielle demanded he remain with her for the day, he rose late in the morning; donning fresh attire, he belted on his sword and went out to see what could be seen. When he arrived at the bailey, he found the men there grimly surveying the countryside, pointing and clutching their weapons in anger. At first he thought an assault was being prepared against them, but following the pointed finger of the guard officer he saw what had so aroused them. To the northwest, by squinting somewhat, he could discern the smoke of many fires climbing through the sky. He instantly knew this as the burning of outlying farms, garths and villages.

An unintelligible growl went up from the gathered soldiers. At the rim of the chasm on the Western Tangent, a large horde was leaving the forest, on its way to join the besieging army.

Despair was on the watchers' faces as they witnessed long files of sturdy, glittering knights winding their way to the camp. Behind the chivalry came closely ranked

infantry, many with some bundle or bag of plunder tied
to belt or back. They carried kite-shaped shields and
long, black-varnished pikes. They looked hardened.
There were many companies of them, many war banners riding the wind. Then came baggage wagons
flanked by lancers and bearing archers as escorts.

More squadrons of cavalry divided the baggage wagons from those containing food and provisions. After
these came more infantry, men of the west of Coramonde in Teebra, who wore the skins of wild animals
over their hauberks, and necklaces made from the claws
and fangs of hunting beasts. They wore bonnets of eagle
feathers and didn't carry guidons, but had before them
animal totems mounted on poles.

There were strings of extra mounts next, fresh and
high-stepping, then additional archers, the sharp-eyed
men of Rugor, whose sport was shooting chestnuts from
high branches with their arrows. Last came more dragoons.

"This is only part of their second army," the watch
commander said to the Prince. "Off there, where the
fires are, there must be many more. These are here too
early to have set them."

That sounded logical to Springbuck. Send part of
your force ahead to bolster those confining your enemy
and use the rest to raze any outposts, burn out resistance and make a thorough forage, scouring the land so
food and shelter would be denied any guerrillas who escaped.

One of the men at the wall began to scream oaths
and threats at the unheeding foemen, clashing his sword
against his shield.

"His home," explained the officer, "is there, where
the smoke billows thickest. It was a farmhold this morning."

The Prince wanted to make some sympathetic remark, but found none that wouldn't sound hollow in his
own ears.

Instead, he set off back to the palace.

When he arrived, he found that the leaders of the
alliance had been called to council in Reacher's belvedere. They were already assembled, looking much as the

men on the baily, except for the undemonstrative Wolf-Brother and Gil MacDonald.

The American had just come from the deathbed of the Lady Duskwind. His face was frozen, as vacant of emotion as Ibn-al-Yed's had been. Hearing this news, Springbuck tried to offer condolences, and knew a grief of his own. Gil waved them away. He'd lost many friends to war, known that special bereavement many times. But this was a sorrow beyond even that.

She had lost conciousness just at the gate of the city and never awakened. He'd been at her side through the night, futilely, as massive internal bleeding took her from him by inches. She'd crossed the threshold of death almost imperceptibly. He had refused to believe, would not leave her.

He'd sat with her and cried for hours, speaking aimlessly without knowing that he did, trying to sort out emotions he couldn't even name and coping with pain so great that he knew no word for it. In the end, he did the only thing he could think of; he went out to pick up the parts of his life left to him.

The rest of them avoided eye contact with him and withheld their words of consolation, seeing that he didn't want them.

The Prince addressed the group.

"It seems Yardiff Bey will divert every fighting man in Coramonde to destroy us."

Hightower grunted. "Let them come! They'll never take this city. *Pah!* I've inspected it myself, and damn if it isn't the finest fortification I've ever seen! They'll spend themselves on us by day, and by night we'll harry them. The men still in the hills will poison their wells and ambush their outriders. Perchance more help will come from other tribes of the High Ranges and Freegate's upland tributaries.

"With no way to get food, our enemies outside will be desperate before they're three months camped at our door. When their bellies force them to slaughter their own horses we'll sally and that will be that."

The rest considered this; the Prince said quietly, "No."

They turned to him. "My Lords—and Lady—this

will be unlike any siege you here have ever seen. You're
used to fairly small armies fighting fairly autonomous
wars and battles, but this bids to be a new kind of conflict. With unlimited manpower, the army outside the
barbican will be able to keep itself supplied, even if it
must stretch its lines back to Earthfast. We haven't sufficient numbers outside the city to harry them.

"You're thinking that their size may shrink after a
few months; but with proper planning and supply, they
can carry this effort through the winter and wait us out.
Yardiff Bey can even afford to rotate the men here so
their morale will not flag. He has no dearth of coin with
which to pay them, with the coffers of Earthfast at his
beck and call.

"Too, he's shown he can come up with new tactics,
and ideas like that demon ship. He could very well have
some way of bridging that grand foss out there or cracking our walls, or bringing Freegate down around us.
How long could we last if he sent plague against us?"

Now Katya was on her feet, hands gripping her
knives, perfect face contorted with hatred. "No one
asked you to come to us. If you are caitiff, go then.
Mayhap it's not too late to throw in your lot with your
stepbrother."

He shook his head. "I never said we have no hope, or
that there's no chance for us to hold fast. But we cannot
think in the terms we've been used to. We cannot wait
them out and assume they won't be able to come at us
in some unforeseen fashion."

Reacher pursed his lips. "Where, then, does that
leave us?"

Springbuck ran a hand over his sparse beard and
chose his words carefully. "We have some things which
hold good promise. Our enemies *are* a long way from
home, and as yet regard the bridgeway as the only entrance to and egress from Freegate. Van Duyn and Gil
MacDonald might have an idea of a way to alter matters in our favor. And, we have the deCourteneys, who
may prove to be the most important asset of all." Gabrielle smiled at this; Andre watched without comment.

"Lastly, most of the drive of Earthfast rests in one
man right now, Yardiff Bey. It is to nourish his hungers

and glorify his masters that battle has been joined. If we can conceive of a way of striking at him, we will have a chance to cut the head from the monster."

The meeting turned to further haggling and hypothesizing, but they were all on a more productive track now. The Prince was satified that he'd brought their thinking closer to the demands of reality without robbing them of hope. As the council began to break up, he made to speak again to Gil, but stopped when he saw that the outlander had grown pale and was sweating, his breathing labored.

"You must rest," Springbuck said. "You accomplish nothing with this."

Gil smiled wanly, and a droll reply was on his lips when he winced, as a wave of dizziness overcame him. It was Hightower who caught him as he slumped to the floor, and Katya who bawled for the house physician.

He was taken to a guest chamber nearby and examined. The doctor, finishing his probings and scrutinies, shook his head.

"I can find nothing wrong," he confessed; then he amended, "or rather, I can't find the cause of whatever strange malady this young man suffers from."

By this time Gil was drifting into and out of conciousness and hallucinating. Andre came to his bedside and leaned his ear close, listening to the fevered ramblings. He said, "My sister and I would like to be alone with this man; I think this is no natural affliction, or any illness conceived in this world. It is work for us."

The rest left and the wizard and his sister took up stations on either side of the bed. They made mystic passes with their hands, chanting, and soon an evil entity crackled there, contained by their wills but impervious to them otherwise.

"A working of Yardiff Bey, no doubt of it," Andre said when they'd rejoined their comrades. Gabrielle nodded silently to Springbuck.

"He's drawing Gil's essence, his soul, from his body. We could only catch a few particulars on the periphery of the spell, but I think that the leeching will be fulfilled at the passing of midnight. Bey is in some high place, bending all his concentration to the task. He evidently considers Gil of importance and finds him more vulnerable to sorcerous attack than any of us who belong here on this plane. Gil's soul is estranged from its home world to begin with, and that makes things much easier for Bey. And, too, there is this profound depression, blighting Gil's resistances."

"Well, the lad's been a great help," Hightower sighed. "But if that spell-cooker thinks this will quail us, he's wrong. Ah, it's a shame the boy must die with no chance. Is there nothing we can do?"

Andre shrugged. "Of that, what shall I say? We've had no time to study matters. Yet Yardiff Bey has turned every power at his command to this labor. He's locked in a pull so mighty on Gil's soul that I doubt if I can counteract it, even if Gabrielle and I join our fullest efforts."

Springbuck was thinking furiously, suppressing a violent urge to strike out with his hands, to channel his emotion into blows. This was nothing that could be met with a frontal onslaught, he chided himself. The way of the Kareteka wasn't for this situation. What did that leave? The Gentle Way, perhaps. Take advantage of your opponent's strength somehow.

If you're pushed, give way. If you're pulled . . .

Inspiration burst into his head and he let out a shout. The others stared at him and he tried to explain to them, ordering details in his mind as he went along.

"If Yardiff Bey's exerting force on Gil, pulling him as it were, can we not use this? Suppose Andre and Gabrielle, instead of trying to counter Bey or resist him, add their power to his? We already know they can move people and objects between places. What if they used Bey as a terminus? We could break the incantation and maybe even slay him."

Their mouths opened in surprise, all but that of Gabrielle, who was thinking this through calmly. "It might mean the end of the war in a single blow," she said. "Yes, I'm sure it can be done. I've never experienced so intense a line of energy as this one from Bey to Gil. Andre and I can metamorph it, add to it until it becomes like the bridgeway outside the city."

Her brother snorted. "It will be nearly as easy as saddling an avalanche, but not so safe by half."

But his sister was serene. "We will do it, dear brother, because we must for the sake of a friend, mustn't we? Now, don't be so downcast; when has my power failed us?" She seemed a very rampart of reassurance to overtop them all, granting them confidence from her own ample stores.

The Snow Leopardess was smiling, but her eyes were slitted and there was death glee in them. "How many of us can you take?" she purred.

Andre was clucking his tongue in thought. "I don't know. Bey must be in his sanctum at Earthfast, the high place in which we saw him. Springbuck, how big is that outsized pentacle of his there?"

"Earthfast! But that's it then; Strongblade and Bey together and unready at Court. We could slay both at a single turn! I only saw the pentacle once, with my father, so far back that I can scarce remember. But at the time it seemed big enough for a game of chase-ball."

Andre was calculating more rapidly than he liked, a careful and methodical practitioner by nature. But he dismissed caution now; it must be all or nothing at a single cast.

"To allow for some error, let us say a dozen, including myself, and the gods help us if the pentacle prove too small!"

If any of them doubted Springbuck's abilities as a commander, they had their misgivings assuaged by his quick decisiveness in the next minutes and hours. He organized the proposed raid without falter.

Andre and Gabrielle were deeply engrossed in their own private conversation, bustling away to consult charts and tomes of their own. The main problem was in excluding unneeded volunteers and putting together an optimal group.

The Prince would lead, and of course Gil must come. Van Duyn, with rifle and pistol, would be of great value, as would Reacher. Andre, rather than his sister, was the obvious one to accompany the spell, as he put it.

Springbuck hedged very little. He knew that a direct staircase connected Bey's sanctum to the throne room, the only entrance to it aside from the main portals.

His two major worries were the archers at the sides of the throne room and the giant ogre guards on the royal dais. With these in mind he included Kisst-Haa and bade Dunstan find him the four best archers in Freegate. Hightower must come, too, if for no other reason than that he was one of their best fighters, but also because he'd earned the right to help avenge his son's death in the halls of his enemies. They'd take Ferrian, acting Champion of the Horseblooded, too, and Dunstan.

He reviewed the list in his mind: twelve. To give himself a margin of safety, if that word could conceivably be used, he decided to take only three bowmen rather than four, since Kisst-Haa occupied the space of at least two men.

They assembled in a large room into which Gil had been brought on a litter. His sword and knife had been strapped to him, his carbine put at his side. The Prince noted that Dunstan had selected the archers diplomatically. One was a prowler, one a Wild Rider and one a member of Reacher's own guard.

Ferrian was quiet, but Reacher took him aside for a moment and spoke to him briefly. Then the two clasped each other's forearm in a fierce grip, the grip, Springbuck thought, of friendship reborn.

Andre and Gabrielle had drawn a huge pentacle, circumscribing it with obscure and powerful runes, many of them the runes of Shardishku-Salamá and of Yardiff Bey.

They crowded into the center of it, ranged around Gil's litter. Van Duyn shifted his ammunition belt, noticed that his hands trembled, and smiled encouragingly to the only onlooker, Katya. Kisst-Haa, who'd had the situation carefully explained to him, endeavored to keep statue-still so as not to jostle anyone inadvertently.

As the deCourteneys began to chant the spell to interdict that of Yardiff Bey and warp it to their own purposes, Springbuck had a moment of surprise that the Snow Leopardess hadn't raised any objection at being excluded, on her brother's insistence, from the raiding party.

As the chanting grew louder, though, he saw her countenance fill with that hunting light, and as Andre moved to his place within the pentacle for the final segment of the cantrip, the Prince felt his grasp on reality slipping. Katya, with a triumphant yell, bounded into the defined area of the pentacle and crowded at her brother's side.

She mussed his hair playfully. "Didst think you could keep your big sister from this? Am I not a Doomfarer, too?"

Springbuck dimly heard the King reply, "I wish that you had not come, but the choice is made. Look to your knives now, and 'ware the foeman."

Chapter Thirty

Victory is a thing of the will.

FERDINAND FOCH

ALONE in his aerie, the Hand of Shardishku-Salamá perspired and concentrated on completing the incantation he'd implemented to ensnare Gil MacDonald's soul and fetch it to him. There were many agencies to call upon, many oaths to invoke and yield, the utmost care and attention to be exercised. None of these were beyond his competencies, though; wasn't he the greatest thaumaturge in the world, aside from his masters?

As the spell reached fruition, Yardiff Bey felt interference, and his supernatural servants complained of a counterspell of great efficacy being laid against them. He attempted to ken what had generated the opposing magic, or whom, but couldn't; he was unable to divert his concentration from completion of his risky work. Yet even as he spoke its concluding words, he was aware of terrible wrongness. The lamentations of his demonic slave brought him to the jarring knowledge that, for the first time in his memory, his magics had been subverted.

A suffused glow of blue appeared in the center of his pentacle. Before he could cast a negation, a sulfurous cloud roiled and vanished. There stood in its place an armed company, among them his worst enemies, poised and ready to slay.

He didn't gawk or try to repair the irreparable. His thought was of escape, saving redress for this insulting intrusion for another time. But the raiders were between him and the door leading to the roof and *Cloud Ruler*. With a hand motion he caused the opening of the door behind him, leading to the lower stairwell, then turned and plunged down the steps.

326

Reacher was first to react, for Yardiff Bey had signaled the door to shut after he'd gotten through it. The King sprang to intervene between door and frame, to strain and arrest the closure, but only succeeded in slowing it. In a moment Hightower was with him, and together they stopped the door, managing to keep it open a few hands' width. But this was gap enough for Kisst-Haa, stumping up after them, to wedge clawed hands in and pull the portal irresistibly wider, opening it again.

Gil knew that same feeling that comes with healthy awakening from a fever dream. Now that the energies seeking to drain him had been abated, life swelled in him. One side of his mind was coming out of the all-encompassing sorrow of Duskwind's death, braving to deal with it subjectively. His brain had known it, but somehow now, in this bizarre turn of events, his skin and heart and loins learned.

He'd held her hand at the last, feeling the remarkable warmth of her ebb slowly until the brown-gold fingers were cold. It came back now, that feeling, an emphatic declaration of her departure. He accepted it with a species of welcome; it was some excruciating sacrament that passed him, vengeful, into a state of unholy grace. He took up his carbine and a grim smile touched his lips.

Springbuck leaped through the reopened door, Bar in one hand and his knife in the other. "We must move apace," he called, and with that was in hot pursuit of the vanished magician.

Though they'd lost mere seconds, the Prince did not overtake the sorcerer. At the bottom of the stairs the arras covering the lower portal had been ripped away. As Springbuck charged into the brightly lit room, the general furor was eloquent word that Bey had passed this way and given the alarm.

The atmosphere of the Court hit them like a storm front, compounded of the heat of revelry and its exertions, the smells of the drinking, the seductions and the sweaty laughter of the evening's merrymaking. They were stopped for an instant by its tropical intensity, as tipsy surprise changed the faces of the guests there.

The Prince was shoved aside from behind by

Reacher as an arrow hissed down past him to splinter on the hard flooring stones. Court archers were warned, and marshaling to carry out their duty, while terrified courtiers flooded toward the main doors. The three ogre-guards had closed ranks around Strongblade, who stood in white-faced fury on his dais. The Usurper's lips were drawn back, his hatred of the true Heir plain. His hand clutched Flarecore's hilt at his side.

Gil and Van Duyn were through into the throne room, adding to the uproar with the sound of gunfire, concentrating on the bowmen along the walls. Kisst-Haa had unslung a wide shield from his scaly back; using it to cover himself and Dunstan along with one of the raider archers, the prowler-cavalryman, he barged his way to the main doors, scattering the mob to either side with brutal ease. Even in former times, the Court had known its affluent and idle, and under Strongblade this had become the common type, no challenge to Kisst-Haa.

The raider archers were sending arrows of their own winging at their opposite numbers along the walls as trumpet calls came from the outer halls, the guards reacting to the unprecedented invasion. The two Americans were firing hastily, thankful that the wall archers were in plain view rather than hidden behind iron or stone.

The Prince could see no sign of Fania, and took no time to seek her. Some of the nobles had mustered themselves and were counterattacking at the behest of the screaming Strongblade. An Earl in golden finery, known to Springbuck, came at him in a frenzied flèche; but the Prince sidestepped, locked hilts with him and delivered a thrust through his ribs with the knife. He searched for Yardiff Bey but couldn't see him.

A knot of courtiers had gathered at the foot of the dais. These were rugged men, brutes and bullies who'd been set at Strongblade's feet by hunger for power and privilege. They saw their precious, newfound rank at hazard and were determined to make sure it wasn't ended by the premature death of their false *Ku-Mor-Mai*. Springbuck moved toward them, even as Ferrian and Hightower crowded past the two Americans to help. There began the deadly carillon of swords.

Reacher had sprung to the near ledge before the archers there were well aware of his plan; he killed one with a single ripping blow of his clawed glove, and began moving on the rest, using the corpse as a shield.

Kisst-Haa had made the main doors by means of fangs, armored tail, shield and outsized broadsword. He caught two advancing soldiers' polearms on his shield and bulldozed them into those behind, sweeping the household troops from the room with one push and driving them back into the corridor. He jumped back as the prowler with him fired two arrows through the still-open doors. Kisst-Haa swung the portals shut, threw the thick bar and left Dunstan and the archer to keep it from being reopened; then he turned and lumbered back toward the dais.

The sharp smell of gunpowder was in the air. Two men at the foot of the dais were down with the Snow Leopardess' knives in them, and the remainder wavered before the onset of Ferrian, Hightower and Springbuck. Andre was close by, trying to locate Yardiff Bey without success.

So quickly and willfully had the raiders begun that they'd done amazingly well. The archers who hadn't been shot or knocked from the ledges by bullets, arrows or the Wolf-Brother had jumped for their lives, and the majority of the courtiers still hadn't presented much of an obstacle. The two remaining raider archers at the dais end of the throne room—the Horseblooded and the man of Freegate—moved to join the third to hold the main doors.

But swords and other weapons were appearing among the crowd. Even the dissipaters maintained by Strongblade and Fania would do damage when forced to fight for their lives. Several seized a bench for a rush at the doors. Katya, seeing this, yelped, grabbed a fallen sword and ran to stop them; Reacher jumped to help her. There was bloody fighting at closest quarters.

Archog, leader of the ogre-guards, grunted to his fellows and those two advanced down the steps of the dais roughly pushing aside those who were in their way and moving into the mayhem. The first fell into an exchange with Hightower, who was hard put, even with his renowned might, to meet those strokes. Yet somehow he did, but had to fall back step by step and could effect no attack of his own.

Not so Kisst-Haa, who'd flung aside his shield and locked in combat with the other ogre. Of the two, the reptile-man was a trifle larger and his weapon heavier. Yet it was a close thing, and the throne room resounded to the contestants' bellows even above the tumult. Their enormous blades moved like darting tongues of light, and men fighting near them could only do their best to stay out of the behemoths' way.

Gil, a new magazine in his carbine, was the only one to spy Hightower's predicament as the old hero was forced toward a wall by the machine-like advance of the ogre he fought. The American brought his weapon up and fired, but such was the creature's weight of armor that the bullet went *spanng!* and ricocheted to the far side of the room.

The monster loomed over its human adversary, preparing to deal a final flurry of blows, when Gil ran up behind it, jammed the carbine muzzle into the opening between the rear lip of its helmet and the armored neck, and squeezed the trigger as rapidly as he could. Two shots crashed upward through thick bone into the ogre's brain before a spasm snapped its neck backward and the whole body went rigid. The tilting helmet rim bent the end of the carbine barrel, but Gil couldn't stop the reflex that triggered the third shot and resulted in a small explosion. The American was knocked down as a shard of metal plowed a groove in his forehead, and other shards plucked at the mesh covering his chest and arms. His cheek was scorched by the fireball effect, hit by grains of powder that would normally have been consumed in the gun barrel.

Springbuck, who with Ferrian had been trying to carve a path to Strongblade and who'd planned to make his way through the opening at the foot of the dais left by the ogres, was frustrated when the gap closed too quickly. He and Ferrian launched themselves at the

men, fighting for a chance to down Strongblade before
the inevitable arrival of reinforcements. Van Duyn's
shots at the Usurper were useless as the heavily plated
Archog protected Yardiff Bey's bastard son from bullet
and arrow.

Two more came at the Prince, a rash noble with an
ambitious rapier and an officer of mounted infantry
with a long sword, but in doing so they both threw their
lives away; he was beyond the reach of common men
and cut them down one and two, cleanly and with
hardly a pause.

Then fear caught at his heart. He heard the dull
booming of a ram and knew the household troops were
battering at the doors.

Events had developed into two separate actions. The
three archers, Dunstan, Reacher and Katya—the latter
two having taken up swords—were holding the doors;
Springbuck, Ferrian, Hightower and Kisst-Haa were
trying to get to Strongblade. To one side Andre helped
Van Duyn pull Gil's leg from under the corpse of the
ogre he'd killed as Gil swore uselessly.

Kisst-Haa dealt his ogre-foe a final blow, driving his
greatsword completely through the sturdily armored
torso. Withdrawing the blade, he took in the scene at
the throne and moved with decision. Since the Prince
couldn't get at his enemy through the press of men, the
reptile-man seized him from behind and prepared to
carry him, literally wading through a wave of steel. But
he stopped as he saw Ferrian kill a last antagonist and
penetrate the defense there while Hightower guarded his
back. Archog's temper parted and he drew his own
greatsword and charged this human upstart.

Kisst-Haa shifted his grip on Springbuck; taking advantage of this new opening, he carefully tossed the
Prince over the heads of the remaining opposition onto
the dais. Strongblade saw him coming and jumped back
as Springbuck landed awkwardly. The Usurper, who'd
pulled on a pair of gauntlets, brought Flarecore out with
a threatening sweep. Then Strongblade put a hand up to
steady the unadorned circlet of gold that was the Crown
of Coramonde, as if to assure himself it was still his.

None of the men at the foot of the dais had time to

turn and help their liege; Gil was free and had drawn
his sword, helping Andre, Van Duyn and Hightower
keep them busy. He used his trench knife and all the
skill he'd acquired in recent weeks, and needed them.
Van Duyn's M-1 jammed, and he drew back and jacked
the operating rod handle to clear it, swearing.

Ferrian was doing poorly with the ogre Archog, and
Kisst-Haa was circling them, tail lashing, seeking a
chance to join the fight. At the rear of the room a crack
had appeared in the doors; as the rest of the raiders at
that end formed a perimeter of deadly swordplay
around them. Reacher and Dunstan the Berserker
braced their backs against it.

Springbuck and Strongblade confronted each other
for the first time in months. Seeing his "brother" again,
the Prince knew a twinge of doubt. Here was Strongblade, who had ever been his master with a sword.
Springbuck thought he could win, but was he overesti-
mating himself?

Then, with a rush, determination came. He'd returned with the mightiest warriors in the world at his
back, graduate of battle and rightful *Ku-Mor-Mai*.

He addressed himself to Strongblade. As they came
en guarde to decide the fate of the suzerainty, he sent
the heavy knife singing into the ornate wood of the
throne.

"As it was written before our births," Springbuck
said, "let us measure swords, one weapon apiece, and
the winner wear the crown."

Strongblade was still as capable a swordsman as
Springbuck had ever met, but he also had to move
Flarecore, a heavier sword, and the Prince felt that this
gave him an advantage. For a moment he experienced
the fear he'd always felt of Strongblade, of his primal
ferocity and cruel strength, then dismissed it resolutely.
Carefully preserved memories of his antagonist's favorite attacks and advances rose before him like an invisible chart of the duel's possibilities. He tried not to become preoccupied with them.

The match filled the entire field of his senses, hypno-
tizing him so that he forgot the fierce contest around

him and coolly worked with a sword as he never had in his life. And if his ancient blade didn't blaze angrily against its rival, that was the impression it gave those who saw it then.

Strongblade was surprised by Springbuck's new virtuosity but not distressed by it, as they fought back and forth before the throne, neither gaining nor giving up more than a pace or two. Strongblade made a semicircular parry, moving from a high to a low line of engagement, and Springbuck threw all his sinew into a bind that drove his foe to the very edge of the dais. When he had the Usurper at the brink, the Prince stopped and stepped back, sweat running from his face, and permitted Strongblade to return to the center of the platform.

"I'll end your reign here, so there's no uncertainty about it," he said.

The other, outraged beyond anger, intoned in a' low voice, moving Flarecore in slow passes. The Prince's eyes went wide as the sword's blade grew bright, passing through red to white, and ran with coursing flame.

Flarecore burned! Strongblade had been given its activating spell. Gritting his teeth, Springbuck began the duel anew.

At their first tentative touch, black sparks jumped from the blades. The Usurper's gauntlets protected his hands. The Prince was thankful that he wore the leathers that covered him from knuckle to elbow, and for Bar's belled hilt. The conversation of blades was a shower of dark fire-specks and they were both burned, though Springbuck, with chest and upper arms bare, fared worse.

His opponent's swordsmanship was, as ever, excellent, barren of any frivolity or excesses. It seemed, as it always had to the Prince, a stern sermon in motion and steel against others' overindulgence in flourish or bravado.

Meanwhile, Ferrian could no longer hold against the advance of Archog and made to back away. But the creature blocked his sword and reached out for him with its free hand; in a moment both lost their balance and rolled on the floor. Ferrian, having lost his sword,

snatched a long knife from his boot top and pushed up
the visor on the ogre's helmet as the creature gathered
him in a terrifying hug.

The man's knife was coated with the poison that his
people used, so deadly that it would have killed even
the ogre quickly. But Archog released its hug and seized
each of Ferrian's wrists in one of its own hard hands.
With a ferocious caricature of a laugh, it lunged forward and clamped its wide, fanged mouth over his right
arm, biting through flesh and bone and severing the
limb that held the knife. Then it flung the man from it
and howled in maniacal glee.

His right arm gone from midbicep down, Ferrian
groped in some half-mad attempt to continue the struggle. But Van Duyn was at his side and stopped him,
then used his belt as a tourniquet. He thought the
wound too terrible for Ferrian to live, as the Horseblooded collapsed. Andre came to help, laying down his
sword.

Kisst-Haa, who'd seen all this but hadn't been able to
strike for fear of hitting Ferrian, gave a bellow of sheer
animal rage at this ruthless display and threw himself at
the ogre. They tumbled together on the paving stones,
tearing chunks of flesh from each other and snapping
savagely. The reptile-man grabbed the ogre's wrists, just
as Archog had done to Ferrian and, powerful as it was,
the ogre was no match for infuriated Kisst-Haa, who
thrust his great muzzle against the open visor of the other's helmet. With a merciless bite, he took away most of
the exposed face.

Leaping up and standing astride the ogre's convulsing
body, Kisst-Haa shrilled a steam whistle of victory, then
wheeled to help Reacher and Katya hold the endan-
gered doors. One of the archers had fallen and another
was wounded.

Gil and Hightower had broken the sword wall at the
foot of the dais and the fighting in general subsided as
they all turned to watch the duel that would decide their
fates.

Springbuck couldn't afford to meet the strokes of
Flarecore squarely on, less so now that it burned with

occult flame; step by slow step he was being driven to the edge of the dais behind him without even the hope of the mocking courtesy he had extended his opponent.

Think, think, he exhorted himself. *You can't stand against this sword; it's probably only Bar's enchantment that keeps it from being severed or melted to slag. You can't beat the sword; beat the man!*

Then it came to him. He backed carefully until he was nearly off the dais, but not quite. He was, however, off the embroidered carpet on which they'd stood and fought. As he parried in quinte a stroke which would have opened him from crown to crotch, he knelt and grabbed the end of the carpet with his free hand and yanked it.

But the trick wasn't successful. Though Strongblade went down on one knee, he kept his balance and retained Flarecore. Springbuck desperately looped the end of the carpet over Strongblade's sword and right arm. The material immediately burst into searing flame and the Usurper fell backward with a cry of woe, trying to extricate himself but only managing to drag the carpet around and with him, entangling himself in it still more as he fell down the steps of the dais wrapped in a sheet of crackling death. His clothes were alight; and as the Prince watched in horror, Strongblade died with his lungs filled with the were-fire of Flarecore.

Even as Springbuck called for those standing near to extinguish the flames, the light in the sword was no more and the fire was gone. They knew that Strongblade's short, violent life was over.

Gil laid down his sword and went to see if he could help Andre and Van Duyn with Ferrian. Reacher and Dunstan stood away from the door they'd been warding and the King of Freegate put aside the bar. When an officer of the guard entered at the front of his squad, the Wolf-Brother said in a loud voice that all might hear: "The true *Ku-Mor-Mai* is back and the false one dead. Bow your heads and ask his amnesty, that you ever conspired with traitors."

The officer, not slow of wit, took in the scene quickly and, seeing which way events were moving, did just that, bending his knee. So did his men. Instantly all the courtiers and nobles still able to do so followed suit, paying homage to their new ruler.

Dunstan, who had some of the Berserkergang in him yet, was roving the crowd with his eye. Suddenly he cried, *"There!"* He sprang forward, charging in pursuit of Yardiff Bey, who'd slipped from the genuflecting throng at the side of the room, Fania beside him. The sorcerer was moving toward the staircase which would take him back to his sanctum. Van Duyn moved to block his way, raising his Garand, but the magician pulled the Queen from behind him and a bullet meant for the heart of the sorcerer found Fania's white breast moments after her son had died.

Yardiff Bey brushed the appalled Van Duyn out of his way and dashed up the staircase, but Dunstan was right behind like a coursing hunting dog.

"Don't let him get to the roof!" Gil shouted, snatching up Andre's sword in the heat of the moment and coming after. He was winded by the time he came to the sanctum, but the sight that greeted him in that chamber made him forget his condition.

Yardiff Bey had drawn Dirge and was fighting madly with Dunstan. Their blades licked at each other and Dunstan, the better swordsman, pressed the sorcerer hard.

Then Dunstan disarmed Bey with a quick twist of blades. Bey held his empty right hand out toward Dunstan, and from his voluminous sleeve came a spurt of yellowish smoke or fine powder. Dunstan fell to his knees, choking.

As Gil rushed forward to help, Yardiff Bey stepped back and made a Sign with his hand. Hellish flame leaped up in a ring, for Dunstan was in the center of the pentacle. Trapped in the circle, Dunstan leaped up to hurtle through it to his enemy, but something bounced him back. He tried to cut through it, but though his sword passed it freely, he himself could not.

Gil tried to pull him out by means of the blade, cutting his hands in the doing, but couldn't. Then the American realized that he had Andre's sword with him.

He tore at the pommel knob and pulled out Calundronius.

He tossed the negator at the invisible wall and gave Dunstan's sword another tug. Bitter cold and searing heat seemed to travel down the blade and enter him, and stars exploded in his brain. Both he and Dunstan tumbled headlong, the Berserker free of the pentacle.

Gil sat on the floor, dazed, but Dunstan raced after Yardiff Bey again. The American staggered to the door and saw them both wrestling out on the broad flat terrace there, near *Cloud Ruler*. Though Dunstan still appeared to be in Rage, Bey held his own somehow. The sorcerer contrived to take the Horseblooded in an odd, choking hold. Then he struck him on the side of the head, knocking Dunstan senseless.

Gil pushed himself through the door, but before he could get to them, Yardiff Bey had taken Dunstan over his shoulder and disappeared into a hatch.

The blast of *Cloud Ruler* departing knocked Gil sprawling again, and the accumulated punishment he'd taken blacked him out.

Chapter Thirty-one

And all should cry Beware! Beware!
His flashing eyes, his floating hair!
Weave a circle round him thrice,
And close your eyes with holy dread,
For he on honey-dew hath fed,
And drunk the milk of Paradise.
                    SAMUEL TAYLOR COLERIDGE,
                    "Kubla Khan"

"IT's difficult to tell just what happened," Andre said a few moments later, when several others joined Gil in the tower. The American had just recovered consciousness.

"But Bey is gone," Andre continued, "and Dunstan with him. He obviously couldn't use any sorcery on you; he didn't have time, because Calundronius was near. It's our bad luck that you didn't get closer to his demon ship with it."

The wizard tugged his lip in thought as Hightower growled, "Is there no way we can stop him, that treacherous he-witch?"

"There is a possibility. Somewhere here is stored an artifact, a crystal which imprisons a supernatural being of great might. One could exact a service for releasing it; it might intercept Bey for us. I shall have to contain Calundronius before we search it out."

Reacher interrupted. "No, there is something else that we must demand of this entity if we find it. I want to be taken back to Freegate as quickly as possible to carry word of our victory and end the siege."

"Then it will have to be that instrumentality," Andre said, "for my sister and I are both exhausted."

Yardiff Bey sat within his ship, the least part of his power used to control it.

There was no sign of it in his features, but he, who had long since mastered pain and exterminated any gentler emotion in himself, was in agony.

His supreme Design shattered beyond recovery! Decades-long efforts brought to nothing! The completion of Shardishku-Salamá's most intricate plan had been torn from his fingers. His minions and allies would founder, rudderless, in his absence.

As *Cloud Ruler* sped from Earthfast, a new thought pierced the darkness that threatened his mind: where to go? Mercy was unknown to his masters. He shuddered as he thought what forms their retribution could take. He saw with an awful clarity that there could be for him nothing but unending exile and the bitter sustenance of ruined aspirations.

Then he thought of Dunstan, whom he'd taken prisoner on the spur of the moment, thinking that a hostage might be useful; the man seemed a close companion of the hated Gil MacDonald. Might that fact hold some promise, or was he deluding himself?

He sighed and hung his head, almost torpidly, and tried to decide if he wished to continue to live.

In the throne room, Springbuck had taken the Crown from his adversary's brow and, wiping it carefully on the dead man's cloak, placed it on his own head. The raiders stood silently while household troops, nobles and the rest of the courtiers knelt.

When he'd given them leave to stand, the *Ku-Mor-Mai* looked out at them, squinting a bit at indistinct features in the middle distance and beyond.

"It's been the subject of some humor in Court beforetimes," he said, his voice firm and full, "that my eyesight is not all it might be. Know, then, that today I see well enough to reckon who is here and who is not, and who stood beside my brother and who didn't. You in this room and the others who conspired with Strongblade are well known to me."

At this many in the chamber went sickly and pale. At least one pair of knees gave way, those of an aging merchant who had to be steadied by his trembling wife.

"But you have a hope. I want no more strife and partisanship in Coramonde. Therefore, let any who wish to gain royal clemency throw themselves with a will to ensuring justice in the realm, and healing the hurts of war. A time will come soon when I will personally look into the affairs of each and every one of you; let none be slack or miserly. Now go, leave me. Spread the tidings: Springbuck has taken the throne and a new day is come in Coramonde."

The besieging army at Freegate was mounting a major assault. A great sow had been built, a ramming gyn covered with sturdy wood structured by iron and protected against fire with layers of clay. They were pushing it onto the bridgeway in front of them as the sun peered over the horizon.

Then a dark figure passed across the sky and fear went through them, as a bat-winged shape, manlike but larger than any man, alighted on the bridgeway before them. The demon's pinions swirled for a moment as it deposited its burden, carried these many miles from Earthfast, and was away with a victorious scream, free at last of indenturement to mortals.

Legion-Marshal Novanwyn, directing the advance, recognized Reacher, King of the free city, standing in their path with a long bundle over his shoulder.

"Strongblade is dead," the Wolf-Brother said in a voice extraordinary, in him, for its weariness. "And Springbuck is *Ku-Mor-Mai*."

So saying, he flung his bundle out and unrolled it. There was the charred body of Strongblade, burned ghastly but recognizable in death. Word spread like sheet lightning through the ranks. Novanwyn said nothing.

"You are commanded to give up this siege and return to Earthfast," Reacher continued, "and to lift, too, the siege at the Hightower."

The Legion-Marshal had no intention of returning to answer for his conduct to a new sovereign. "What illusionist's foolishness is this? Whatever trick has brought you here has mystified our eyes and caused us to imagine the body of the rightful Suzerain. But I say we'll never abide by your word. Freegate will fall to us, fall to us this very day, and you'll answer up to our questioning when my inquisitors have their way with you."

He was about to say on when he went rigid and his eyes widened in surprise. He pitched to the ground and from his back there stood the hilt of a long dagger. Behind him was Midwis, his second-in-command, Midwis whose sons Kanatar and Deotar had been incinerated on this same bridgeway by Yardiff Bey and who wanted nothing more to do with the sorcerer's affairs.

Midwis turned to the deputy commanders. "Pull back the sow. Form the hosts for march; we are for the Hightower and Earthfast as soon as we are able."

In his new quarters—formerly his father's and briefly Strongblade's—Springbuck toyed with the bowie knife he nowadays wore under the bothersome robes of Court. His Alebowrenian gear stowed in a chest, he still felt uncomfortable in fine raiments.

Across from him sat Gil MacDonald, nursing a tankard of thick beer, his face still carrying a puckered, healing scar from the explosion of his carbine, and his cheek was tattooed from the powder burn. He was meditative, often his habit these days, searching down inside himself and examining feelings and thoughts.

On a small study desk were quills, inks, paper and items of reference with which the new Protector Suzerain was—partially at Gil's instigation—working on journals and poetry tentatively called *The Antechamber Ballads.*

Part of his latest poem ran through Gil's mind:

> Now hurting others never was my pleasure,
> Nor causing wanton cruelty my aim;
> But if what's worth preserving has a measure,
> It's our willingness to see it through the flame.

Gil rather thought it showed promise. It was a prejudice of his that introspective writings be required of anyone in authority.

But just now Springbuck was pacing the floor.

"So," he was saying, "I have decided to send Flarecore back to Veganá. There's more than one war being fought, and Flarecore may well spell victory or defeat away in the south, at the tip of the Crescent Lands."

His gaze suddenly went far distant. "We barely know what's happening there. What battles are being fought that might bring safety or peril to Coramonde? It's a formidable mission, going well beyond our better maps. It may be the linchpin of any further war with Shardishku-Salamá. Andre and Gabrielle agree it's the thing to do."

Gil cleared his throat delicately. "Speaking of Gabrielle . . ."

"Say it. She's hardly tolerant at the best of times. What with all my time taken reordering the realm she is the most difficult problem that I have now. Do they speak of it at Court?" He chuckled with little humor. "I can control a suzerainty, but how may I command her heart? Or mine? Sometimes we say that we cannot stay with each other, and then of course we do. I don't know what will come of it all. Shallow as it may sound, I think we both content ourselves with the moment."

Gil nodded. He didn't think that attitude shallow in the least. He knocked back some more beer. "And Van Duyn? Still determined about your abdication, is he?"

"*Hah*! His idea of representative government included himself at its head—for the interim! No, we arrived at an arbitration. I gave him stewardship of a collection of city-states in the north. Several of them have council governments already, and he found that acceptable—as an empirical testing situation. I surrounded him with spies, of course, and Katya is with him, at least for the nonce, so I doubt he'll get into much mischief. Besides, he and she may come up with something I can use in reconciling all the tyrants, councils, divine leaders, plutocrats and other political wretches with whom I have to deal."

Gil snorted. "More than likely your agents'll wind up having to save his hide from his new flock."

"Well, I wish him all luck. Had it not been for him I suppose I'd be dead, or at best an exile for life."

Gil reflected where he and the Nine-Mob would be

had it not been for Van Duyn's intervention and Andre's spells. "How about Hightower?" he asked.

"He didn't want to resume his title as Duke; he says his grandson's doing well and doesn't see any reason to jostle Sordo's elbow. Too, he and Andre have been doing a good deal of conferring and investigating. Hightower has found his own new tracks to walk. Oh, and Andre says that Ferrian is healing nicely; a kind of miracle that he lived at all."

Springbuck's face became more disturbed. "None of us thinks the troubles with Shardishku-Salamá are done. Their vitiations have spread across the face of the world, through its skies and its roots. I fear me that great contests are yet to come."

"Wouldn't be surprised. Man, we were losing the last one until that eleventh-hour raid. Maybe you should think in terms of taking the war to them?"

Springbuck shook his head. "There are too many things to do here for the time being. Perhaps later on. For example, what shall I do with all the troops who fought against me? I could disband the levies and Legions, but what about the officers and leaders who were willing to fight Freegate and me? Too, that would leave Coramonde badly underdefended, what with new sorties by the wildmen of the north. On the other hand, I can't just return those units en masse to their garrisons."

"You'll think of something."

"And the peasants and yeomanry who were in the underground are yet restive. It'll take a thousand reforms to satisfy them; I'm not sure it can be done."

"I rode through Kee-Amaine today. The people looked content, prosperous. And the refugees are moving back to their homes."

"Oh, yes! Many of my . . . former nonsupporters have goodly amounts of money and influence. They've been persuaded to commit both on a long-term, no-interest basis to reconstruction and improvement projects. Much of their savings went, too, but I've left them their working capital, and their heads."

"Gad, tough-and-direct, eh? Just don't kill the goose who lays the eggs."

"Most assuredly." There was a silence then, and different events echoed in each man's mind. Springbuck built himself up for a question of his own.

"What of you, Gil? Will you stay or will you go? You're plainly restive, but I don't know what you want."

Gil got up and went to the balcony and looked out at Coramonde, its exotic sounds coming up on the light breeze and drenching sunlight. At his side hung the sword of Dunstan the Berserker, to which he somehow felt attached.

He watched Springbuck's stag's head banner flutter and crack high over Earthfast, under the snarling crimson tiger of Coramonde. After a time he said, "I've been talking to Andre and Hightower. I've made up my mind to try to find Dunstan. And kill Yardiff Bey. Andre gave me a lead."

"If that is what you wish," Springbuck said quietly. "Do you know how unlikely it is?"

"Maybe, maybe not. I've just got this gut feeling that Dunstan's alive." He slammed his fist on the balcony's railing. "What do you want of me? Should I sit around forever and mourn her? You can't do that; I learned that with the first friend I lost in combat. Dunstan I might be able to help, but Duskwind I can't."

"We all mourn her, Gil. Go, find Dunstan if you can. You can have men, money, anything you'll need of Coramonde."

Gil MacDonald, ex-sergeant late of the 32d Cavalry, Doomfarer, nodded to himself. His mind was already working on the practical details of the endeavor. He hoisted his stein to the wide world.

Adventure!